A
MADAM
of
ESPIONAGE
MYSTERY

INDIA BLACK
AND THE SHADOWS OF ANARCHY

AVAILABLE FROM CAROL K. CARR AND TITAN BOOKS

India Black
India Black and the Widow of Windsor
India Black and the Rajah's Ruby (eNovella)
India Black and the Shadows of Anarchy
India Black in the City of Light (eNovella, July 2014)
India Black and the Gentleman Thief (August 2014)

INDIA BLACK

AND THE SHADOWS OF ANARCHY

A MADAM of ESPIONAGE MYSTERY

CAROL K. CARR

Titan BOOKS

INDIA BLACK AND THE SHADOWS OF ANARCHY
Print edition ISBN: 9781783292349
E-book edition ISBN: 9781783292356

Published by Titan Books
A division of Titan Publishing Group Ltd
144 Southwark Street, London SE1 0UP

First edition: June 2014
1 2 3 4 5 6 7 8 9 10

A CIP catalogue record for this title is available from the British Library.

Printed and bound in Great Britain by CPI Group Ltd.

Did you enjoy this book? We love to hear from our readers.
Please email us at readerfeedback@titanemail.com or write to us at
Reader Feedback at the above address.

To receive advance information, news, competitions, and exclusive offers
online, please sign up for the Titan newsletter on our website:
www.titanbooks.com

INDIA BLACK
AND THE SHADOWS OF ANARCHY

PROLOGUE

"It's a damned shame," proclaimed Lord Wickard, Earl of Ebbechester, and a power in the land, "when a feller can't feel safe in his own country." He glared at his companions, who, having just finished an eight-course dinner by Francois, the Frog chef at the Albion Club, were now meditating upon the mellowness of the port and the age of the Stilton provided by the same establishment. The earl drew vigorously on a Romeo y Julieta and breathed smoke on his fellows.

"A damned shame," he reiterated, more forcefully this time for the sake of old General Woodcliff, who was deaf as a post. "What the devil is the government doing letting in all these bloody foreigners? They're a menace."

The men round the fire stirred themselves to mutter pensively.

General Woodcliff stroked his magnificent moustache and said, "Venice? Venice? Lovely town and all that, what with those deuced odd boats and those grenadiers with the funny hats, poling them along."

"You mean gondoliers," corrected one of the diners.

"Impractical design, of course," added the general. "Hate to attempt a landing under fire in those tubs."

"Anarchists!" boomed the earl. "Every one of them anarchists. Tell me why Scotland Yard hasn't packed up the lot of them and marched them down to the cliffs of Dover and kicked them over the edge?"

A diffident voice was heard to murmur that this activity would surely constitute murder, and not even a Tory government could countenance such behavior on the part of the police.

The earl plunged on, bitterly. "I wouldn't scruple at murder. After all, that's what these fellers are doing. They cut down poor Carrington the other day when he was out for a ride. Killed the horse, too. Damned shame, that. Had all the makings of a good stud."

This aroused much indignation among the group. One fellow had to summon the waiter for more port.

"They've made threats, you know, to wipe out the entire aristocratic class of England," the earl continued.

The general had by now deciphered the conversation. "Balls!" he said. "Thing to do is send in the Scarlet Lancers. Mow 'em down, like we did the Sikhs at Goojerat in '49."

"Not quite as simple as it sounds," contributed one of the diners, a minor government official and cool fellow known as Carsty. "Apparently these chaps—"

"And women," interjected the earl. "Some of these chaps are women."

"And women," added Carsty. "The point is that the government has allowed in so many Macaronis and Frogs and Russkis that you can't tell friend from foe."

"Send 'em all back," said the earl. "Why should we allow a pack of Russians to settle down in the East End?"

Carsty cracked a walnut. "There is some concern that if

they were returned to Russia, they'd be murdered. You know, because they're Jews, or revolutionaries who want to assassinate the tsar. Sometimes"—Carsty pried the sweetmeat from the shell—"they're both."

"Proves my point," said the earl. "If the Russians don't want these troublemakers, I don't see why we should be forced to put up with 'em."

"Hear, hear," said the general, waving his glass. "Ought to put 'em down like we did the blasted Indians who mutinied in '57. Catch a few of the crafty bastards and tie 'em to the barrel of an artillery piece. Makes a hell of an example for the others, when the bugger's fired."

There was universal approbation among the group. The general might be edging toward senility, but he still had his wits about him when it came to crushing rebellions.

"I suppose," said Carsty, "that we'll all have to keep a sharp eye out for threats. These anarchists do seem fixed on the idea of destroying our finest families."

"What have we ever done to them?" asked young Arbuthnot.

The others looked at him pityingly. A good chap, but not a first-class intellect. A deuced fine shot, though, and always useful at making up the numbers for a game of polo.

The earl deigned to enlighten him. "They're lunatics, Arbuthnot. They seem to think that every man is fit to rule himself, and governments aren't needed. They want to kill off the old guard and the monarchs and let the common man and the workers have a go at running things." He paused. "Or not running things. For the life of me, I don't know how they expect things to happen unless someone's around to make sure they do. Do they really think a coal miner could manage British foreign policy? Confusing business." He shook his head briskly. "Anyway, what they believe is of no importance because it's all balderdash."

"Balderdash for which they're willing to commit murder," said Carsty.

"Put 'em on the firing line," the general urged. "We'll see if they're willing to die for that balderdash. Most of these rebel types are cowards at heart. Most of 'em not fit to polish your boots."

The group concurred with this assessment, and then conversation turned to more important matters, such as whether Romeo y Julietas or Partagás gave the finer smoke, and would the impending war between the Russians and the Turks mean a disruption in the supply of caviar from the Caspian Sea?

Shortly after midnight, the earl rose and took his leave.

"Wash out for anarchists," Arbuthnot called gaily after him. Arbuthnot was very, very drunk.

The earl looked fierce. "Just let them try me. They'll soon find they've meddled with the wrong man."

"That's the spirit," said the general.

A yawning cloakroom attendant bundled the earl into his coat and muffler and handed him his hat. The earl dropped a coin into the man's hand. Word had already been delivered to the mews that the Earl of Ebbechester desired his carriage to be sent round.

The driver touched his whip to his brim as the earl came down the steps. A footman opened the door, and the earl stepped up into his carriage, subsiding gratefully into the rich leather seats. The footman draped a woolen blanket over the earl's knees, shut the door and rapped on the carriage. The horses stepped out and the earl sighed contentedly. A fine dinner, amiable conversation, excellent port. The simple pleasures of life. And now home to bed, to crawl between freshly ironed sheets while his valet placed two hot water bottles at his feet.

The door of the carriage was jerked open and a rough voice said, "Here, guv." Something round and heavy and metallic rolled across the carriage floor, crashing into the earl's feet. The earl smelled a familiar smell, which took him back to delightful days on the moor, with the pheasants whirring into the air as the beaters drove them along. Gunpowder. The carriage rolled a few feet forward, and exploded.

1

Ah, springtime in England. Fleecy lambs frolic on the green hills, their white wool sparkling in the sunlight. Apple blossoms float like snowflakes across the fields. Crocuses and daffodils dot the landscape. Warm zephyrs caress the pastures, and the pale blue sky gleams with promise.

But not in bloody London. Not this year. This spring, the citizens of the Big Smoke were being treated to daily deluges from the heavens. Thick clouds roiled overhead, and the crack of thunder punctuated every conversation. You might think that London could do with a bath and sheets of rain are just the thing to accomplish that task, but you'd be forgetting the voluminous coils of smoke that issue from every hearth and home and the reeking fumes from the factories. When the rain comes down in this city, it comes down as brown sludge, ruining bonnets and cloaks and covering the houses with a layer of silt. The streets had become rushing torrents as the drainage system filled to overflowing. A stroll to the pub meant wading through clumps of straw, fruit peels, and bits and bobs of human waste. The stench was overpowering; the whole city smelled fetid and sour, like a vast sewer.

It had rained so much and so often that any day now I expected to hear a stentorian voice issue from the sky: "Here, Noah! Get moving, you lazy bugger! I want fleas, a pair of 'em. And make sure it's male and female this time. That last lot you brought in was both ladies, and we won't be getting any baby fleas from those two. What's that? Rats? Of course I want rats. Two of every kind you've got. And don't forget the lice. They're thick on the ground over in the East End." Lightning flashed and thunder rolled. "Eh? Couldn't hear you, Noah. Sorry about that, only time's wasting and if I'm going to get this flood under way, I've got to keep the weather on schedule. Tarts? You want to know if you should bring some tarts? I'm beginning to think I should have entrusted this job to someone else, Noah. Hell, no, we don't want any tarts on board. They'll contaminate the whole ark with their wanton ways. Besides, it's their kind we're trying to eliminate with this exercise. So get back to work and find me some parasites. Politicians? I said parasites, didn't I? Of course politicians qualify."

Well, I had to amuse myself somehow, even if I was in danger of provoking the Ancient Bearded Bloke in the process. The blasted squalls were keeping customers from the door, and my bints were growing sullen from lack of trade. I suppose I should take half a mo and introduce myself. I'm India Black, proprietress of Lotus House brothel and occasionally, when the mood suits me and the prime minister asks me politely, a secret agent in service to the British government. I don't care if you don't believe it; it doesn't make it any less true. But just so you'll understand, I'll explain how I found myself chasing Russian spies and saving Vicky from a Scottish assassin.

Until a few months ago, I'd been minding my own business and running Lotus House. I have a head for business, if I do say so myself, and the bordello was raking in cash from the military officers, government clerks and secretaries, and the minor aristocracy who compose my clientele. I run a refined establishment, with clean whores, Cuban cigars and good liquor. The girls are well fed, and I'm mostly successful at keeping them away from the gin, and as a result they're plump, rosy and inviting. It costs a bit more to take care of the sluts, especially when, if left to their own devices, they'd be lying in the gutter with their lips glued to a bottle, but I don't stint when it comes to expenses. On the other hand, I don't hesitate to charge a stiff price for the services on offer at Lotus House. Why shouldn't I, if the gents are willing to pay?

So things were rolling along merrily, until one Sunday afternoon a pudgy cove named Latham slipped his cable at Lotus House and departed this life. I could have dealt easily enough with the fellow's death, but for the fact that he turned out to be a clerk in the War Office carrying around a secret memo discussing the state of Britain's military (dire, I suppose, would best describe it). I was unaware of this, of course, and thought I had only to worry about disposing of the body, when a poncy bastard named French entered the picture. He was a special agent for the prime minister, that dear old queen Disraeli, and wanted to get his mitts on Latham's memo. I would have obliged him, but the confounded document had disappeared. It seems the Russians (treacherous Slavs) also wanted to lay hands on the memo, as they had a mind to invade the Ottoman Empire if they thought they could get away with it, and the strength of the British Army was just the kind of information they needed to know. Latham's document ended up at the Russian embassy, and I found myself roped into retrieving it. French affects to be a gentleman, but there was nothing nice about the way he blackmailed me into recovering the War Office memo. It was a wild ride, I tell you, with me ending up as a prisoner of the Russians not once, but twice, and a fair amount of swordplay and gunplay and bumps and bruises. We made a good fist of it, but in the end the memo disappeared into the sea off Calais, along with the wily and wolfish Russian agent, Major Ivanov.

Whenever French is around, I complain loudly about the experience, but the truth is that I found the whole scenario a good bit more thrilling than umpiring spats between whores and paying the butcher. I've always had a taste for adventure (who'd run a brothel if they didn't?), and careering around England, trailing Russian spies and shooting Cossack guards turns out to be my cup of tea. And there's the added bonus of consorting with the most powerful men of the land, who are prepared to grovel charmingly when they ask for my help. What more could a woman want?

Consequently, when French came calling again, asking for my help in protecting the Queen from a group of Scottish nationalists, I was only too pleased to assist. We caught the leader of that crowd of assassins, but not before blood was spilled (oh, not Vicky's of course, or we'd still be hearing about it) and yours truly stared death in the face. I still shiver when I think of looking down the barrel of that revolver and seeing the bloody murder in the eyes behind it. I admit that after that adventure I'd been content to put up my feet for a bit and drink tea while my tarts did the heavy lifting. But inactivity palls, and between the lack of espionage missions, the blasted weather and the venomous atmosphere of a cathouse with too many pussies and not enough mice to play with, I was getting bored.

French, you see, had disappeared. I hadn't seen him for weeks. The last I'd heard of him was a note I received the day after our return from Scotland. Two words, scribbled in pencil on a piece of grubby notepaper: "Called away." There was no mention of where he'd gone or why, or how long he'd be away. I can tell you, I was chapped.

Aside from the fact that he is often brutally oblivious to his need for my help, there could be only two reasons why French would bolt and not take me along. First and foremost, he has an exaggerated notion of my feminine vulnerability. If his current mission was a dangerous one, he might have felt compelled to go it alone. I found that a bit hard. I mean, the bloke's exposed me to the clutches of the *Russians*, for God's sake, who don't hesitate to apply the whip to their own poor serfs in the name of national security and surely wouldn't baulk at doing the same to the odd British agent who'd landed in their midst. Not to mention the fact that it was me who had saved French from being cut down by a Cossack guard wielding a bloody great sword. I'd felled the man with one shot from my .442 Webley British Bulldog. In short, I could take care of myself *and* French, and had proved it. If French thought he was protecting me by heading off to do a bit of spying without me, there'd be an unpleasant surprise waiting for him when he returned.

But there was a second reason I thought French had vanished without seeing me. He knew I was waiting for the first opportunity to tackle him about his family. I'm only surmising that he has one, of course, as he's never said a word about them. I have only the prime minister's casual slip when he sent us off to Balmoral, enquiring about French's "fa—," causing French to change the subject faster than an Irishman can down a pint of Guinness. To be fair (and this is likely the last time I will be, so take note), I hadn't disclosed much of my own past to French, but that's because I don't know much about the old pedigree. Given French's guilty outburst when Dizzy spilled the beans (you may recall from that previous adventure that French interjected the word "father" to put me off the scent), I'd wager that somewhere in a London suburb is a rosy-cheeked blonde with a litter of rosy-cheeked moppets, all waiting for dear Papa to return to his family's bosom. Of course, it's French's prerogative to have as many little sprats as he wants, and if he wants an insipid little wife, jolly good for him. He should, however, let his fellow agents know in the event, for example, that the fellow agent fails to save him from a Cossack guard with a bloody great sword and has to deliver the distressing news to his poor spouse.

Between French's disappearance and his avoiding any explanation of his clan and the blasted weather and the annoying tarts mooching around Lotus House, cleaning out the pantry and not earning a shilling, I was in a sullen frame of mind. I'd been brooding for weeks, and I fear my looks were beginning to suffer. A little of the gloss had gone from my raven black locks, and my blue eyes were now a little dull, having nothing to spark a flame of excitement in them. Worst of all, I'd grown a little pinched about the eyes and mouth, from frowning at the thought of the high old time French must be having, dodging bullets and matching wits with sinister foreign types with thick moustaches and heavy accents while I rotted away in St. James, riding herd on a bevy of unruly sluts.

So it was that I was moping by the fire one April afternoon in 1877, while the wind blew the shingles loose on the roof, the rain bucketed down and the whores lounged about stuffing their faces with Mrs. Drinkwater's comestibles, though how they managed to bolt down a hunk of gingerbread that weighed as much as a cannonball, I do not know. It's no excuse to say that Mrs. Drinkwater was drunk when she baked it, for she's always drunk. I've no idea if her cooking would improve if she were sober. I have wondered whether, if she weren't drunk most of the time, she'd have the initiative to find a position that did not require her to consort with half-naked bints and elegant wastrels. I stabbed my piece of gingerbread with the tines of my fork and was not surprised to see that they left no impression. I sipped the watery tea Mrs. Drinkwater had provided and grimaced. Thinking of my cook inspired me to rise and rummage through my drinks cabinet. I located a bottle of brandy and poured a generous dose into my cup, returning to the fire and the French novel I'd been paging through idly. I could hear Mrs. Drinkwater humming tunelessly as she rootled around the hall, bringing fresh tea and muffins to the tarts while they giggled and gossiped in the parlor. Rain fell in sheets against the window, and the coal fire hissed at my feet.

Someone hammered at the front door so violently that it shook. In the hallway, Mrs. Drinkwater staggered against the wall and dropped her tray, which clanged like a fire bell as it skittered over the marble tiles. The whores shrieked and spilled their tea, and I stormed into the foyer to bring some order to the house. Mrs. Drinkwater was collecting muffins and bemoaning the fact that "they won't be eatable now, having fallen on the floor." As they hadn't been edible to begin with, I felt certain the loss would be minimal. Indeed, the customer at the door had probably saved the girls massive indigestion, it being difficult for the human body to process lumps of iron. The girls had abandoned their tea and raced upstairs, elbowing each other and claiming first dibs on the fellow at the door. Bless their wee hearts; it had been so long since a chap had braved the elements that the bints had all forgotten who was next up to the wicket.

No worries, though, as I remembered (being a madam requires that you excel at that sort of thing) that it was the turn of Clara Swansdown (or Bridget Brodie, as she was known when she was at home in Ballykelly), although it might be a regular out there in the rain who already had a favorite in mind.

Mrs. Drinkwater was on her hands and knees on the floor chasing down an errant muffin, so I went to the door myself. I flung it open, smiling broadly and ignoring the rain in my face, for I truly was glad for a bit of custom. Only there'd be no shilling earned at Lotus House from this fellow. I took in his stiff posture, sober black suit and immobile countenance and knew at a glance he was not here to be jollied into smiling by a winsome tart with gooseberries for brains.

"Miss Black?" He didn't wait for my confirmation of this fact. "I've a message for you from Lord Beaconsfield."

"From Dizzy?"

The officious bloke frowned faintly. "The prime minister, yes. He wishes you to accompany me at once to his rooms at the Langham."

"Now?"

"It is a matter of some urgency. I have a carriage waiting."

Well, when the prime minister of this sceptred isle deigned to summon one, what could one do but go? Besides, something interesting might be afoot.

"One moment, please, while I fetch my cloak."

I left the dour bloke in the foyer with the water puddling around his feet and found Mrs. Drinkwater in the kitchen, where she was consoling herself over the ruined muffins with a generous tumbler of sherry. I informed her that I would be out for dinner, but to make up some sandwiches for me before she had anything more to drink. She sniffed a bit, no doubt thinking me brusque, but I knew that if she waited much later she'd be pickled to the gills and asleep under the table when I got home. I collected a hooded cloak and an umbrella from the stand in the hall and was ushered into the waiting carriage by the somber messenger.

He didn't look the type for idle conversation, nor, indeed, for divulging even so much as his name, so I sat back and contented myself with pondering why the British prime minister had sent directly for his sporadically willing servant, India Black. My previous meetings with Dizzy had always been arranged by French. Well, that was not quite an accurate statement. Usually French scheduled the meeting and dragged me along to it, just to be sure that I'd fall at the feet of the old charmer and agree to steal into the Russian embassy or masquerade as a maid at Balmoral.

My first thought, of course, was that French had cocked up his latest mission and needed my help to straighten out the affair. I felt the urge to fluff my feathers and preen a bit, to be followed by some well-deserved indulgence in the pride of sin (one can always ask forgiveness later), when a dreadful thought struck me like a blow. What if French had been injured, or worse, had gotten himself scragged? I could see it, I really could, given the poncy bastard's ridiculous commitment to the standards of conduct he'd learned at Eton or Winchester or wherever he'd spent his youth. It would be just like the man to offer his opponent the chance to get off the floor and recover his knife before the fight continued. My stomach clenched and I felt a faint palpitation near what I assumed to be the location of my heart. Damn Mrs. Drinkwater's wretched food; I must find a proper cook someday.

I cast a glance at my traveling companion, to see if the news of French's fate might be discerned from his expression, but deuced if it wasn't like staring at the Sphinx's profile. There was nothing to do but watch the rain drench the few pedestrians on the sidewalks, and drum my fingers on my knee until the Egyptian statue cast me a sidelong glance and I dispensed with that diversion. It wasn't far to the Langham, but it felt like we had journeyed to Edinburgh by the time we arrived. I piled out of the carriage, ignoring Dizzy's messenger, and made for the door.

I set a sharpish pace to the prime minister's suite, and my chum just managed to maneuver around me to knock on the door and announce our presence before I burst into the room like a schoolmaster smelling smoke in the dormitory.

2

Benjamin Disraeli, prime minister of Great Britain and her colonies, was lounging before the fire, wrapped in a paisley shawl and paging slowly through a thick sheaf of papers. He looked the very picture of an aging libertine from the Levant, with his hooked nose and olive skin, reclining on the sofa in a canary yellow dressing gown of velvet with a sable collar and a bottle green silk fez covering his thinning black curls. All that was missing was a hookah and the ladies from the seraglio.

"Miss Black is here," said his minion, quite unnecessarily as Dizzy had looked up from his papers and bestowed a charming smile on me.

"Thank you, Barnard. Please wait until we are finished, and then you may escort Miss Black home." The fellow bowed himself out, and I was alone with the prime minister.

He started to rise, but I hurried forward and gave him my hand. He bent over it with a kindly expression. "I'm so pleased to see you, my dear. Sit next to me if you will. We have much to discuss, but I would be remiss if I didn't offer you some refreshment before we begin. I believe you are fond of whisky?"

While I waited for a glass, Dizzy made small talk about the weather and the Russians (he's a great one for discussing the Russians, and at the moment they were kicking up a fuss in the Ottoman Empire again and Dizzy was having a spot of trouble with the rascals). I nodded sympathetically while he railed about Ivan, but I was studying him carefully. He hadn't been at all well while we were up at Balmoral, and the place is not exactly a health spa, what with the winds whistling down into the valley off the snow-covered Cairngorms and the Queen refusing to allow fires in any of the rooms. The prime minister was pale (a difficult feat to achieve with that swarthy complexion), and now and then a dry cough interrupted the flow of his conversation, but it would take more than a cold to stop Dizzy once he's got the bit between his teeth, and so I listened to a lengthy diatribe about the perfidious Russkis. I had to force myself to sit quietly and hear him out, though I was champing at my own bit to find out what had happened to French. I was as nervous as a curate accused of sodomy, but I nodded and smiled and made appropriate noises while Dizzy blathered away. I derived some small consolation from the thought that if things had indeed gone wrong for French, Dizzy would have gone straight to the point. Then I remembered that Dizzy was a politician and constitutionally incapable of direct speech.

The old boy finally ran out of steam. He pushed back a ringlet of hair from his forehead and grinned wryly. "Forgive me, my dear, for rattling on about my present concerns. You must be wondering why I've asked you here."

"Yes," I replied. Sometimes I marvel at my sangfroid.

There was a light rap at the door and Barnard pushed it open. "Superintendent Stoke has arrived."

"Ah," said Dizzy. "Be so kind, Barnard, as to show him in."
He turned to me. "Superintendent Stoke is with Scotland Yard.
He has some information about the matter we'll be discussing."

I really don't enjoy meeting Yard men. Sooner or later one of
them is bound to remember me from a previous encounter, and I
can assure you that any such meeting would not redound to the
benefit of India Black.

Stoke shuffled in, removing his hat and bowing to the prime
minister, and I breathed a sigh of relief. I'd never met the man.
He was of the elderly statesman type, with a high, bald forehead,
a gaunt face and a moist yellow moustache badly in need of a
trim. He nodded at me and at Dizzy's invitation, seated himself
near the fire. I sipped my whisky and waited, for Dizzy's lengthy
peroration on the subject of the Eastern Question had obviously
been a means of passing the time until Stoke appeared.

A manservant provided the superintendent with a brandy and
refilled my glass with some fine Scotch whisky. I do so enjoy good
spirits, especially when they are free. And how many people can
say they've imbibed with the prime minister in his dressing gown?
However, it occurred to me that I'd likely find myself paying for
the whisky in some fashion before the night was over, and it
would be best to keep my wits about me. I took a demure sip.

"And now, Miss Black, we'll get down to brass tacks." The
prime minister rearranged his fez. "Have you been reading
about these dreadful anarchists in the newspapers?"

"I have. They seem to be popping up everywhere."

"Like bloody weeds," growled Stoke. "Shut down one cell
and another appears overnight."

"That is the issue we'd like to discuss with you, Miss Black.
The government is concerned at the number of terrorist incidents
perpetrated by these cowardly devils."

"The assassinations?" I asked, for unless you were blind and deaf, you couldn't have missed the uproar caused by the murder of several of Britain's leading luminaries. (Or so the newspaper johnnies called them, but I was willing to bet that more than half of them were just the sort of inbred aristocratic bloodsuckers the country could do without. Naturally, I did not share this view with Lord Beaconsfield and Superintendent Stoke.)

"Indeed," said Dizzy. "Lord Carrington was murdered on his daily ride by a bomb planted in a rhododendron bush. Sir William Tetford's greenhouse was blown up and Sir William and his wife were killed. Last night, the Earl of Ebbechester was cut down when someone threw a bomb into his carriage. These are just the atrocities perpetrated in Superintendent Stoke's area of authority. There have been others, all over England."

"And you have no idea who is behind these acts?" I asked.

Stoke sucked his moustache and squinted at me. "Foreigners for the most part. Ashamed to say a few misguided English men and women seem to have joined these bands of ruffians. Heard of the Paris Commune?"

I had not, but resigned myself to doing so. Fortunately, Stoke proved to be excellent at brief summaries.

"Name they use for the radical government formed in Paris in 1871, just after the Frenchies got pummeled by the Prussians. Supposed to be a movement of the people, the working man in particular. Real French government feeling a bit battered and let the people try their hand at running the place for a bit. Proceeded to make a hash of things, passing daft laws that abolished interest on debts and night shifts for the bakery workers. Took over all the property of the Catholic Church. Ended badly, of course. These things often do. French officials finally pulled themselves together and threw out the extremists. Bloody business, that.

Lots of the ne'er-do-wells chucked out of Paris ended up here, still burning to put down the ancien régime, only now they've got their eyes on our aristocrats and our government."

"You mean that gaggle of foreigners they call the Communards?" I said. "Those poor folk in Seven Dials?"

If you're not familiar with the Seven Dials area of London, let me acquaint you with its principal features: filth, sewage, cramped rooms, diseased beggars, loathsome shops, ragged urchins and fallen women of the lowest type. I don't detest my sisters who live and ply their trade in that slum, but I'm jolly well glad I don't.

Stoke nodded grimly. "After the Commune disintegrated, wasn't safe for the radicals to stay in France. Moved here in droves and congregated in Seven Dials. Joined now by their compatriots from Italy, Germany, Poland, Russia. Every bloody anarchist who's had to hare it out of his own country has found a home in London."

"Any reason we shouldn't send them back?"

"Requires careful handling," said Stoke, savoring the taste of his moustache. He glanced at Dizzy. "Political issues and what have you. Mr. Gladstone—"

Dizzy growled. You had only to mention the name of William Gladstone, former prime minister, leading light of the Liberal Party and Dizzy's greatest and most detested political enemy, for Dizzy to lay back his ears and show his teeth.

"That self-righteous prig. He's marching about the country, pontificating on our duty to protect the rights of men to speak freely and engage in political discourse without being shot for their efforts. He says we can't possibly force these people back to their own countries where the authorities will imprison them or torture them or kill them."

"Would happen, of course," said Stoke.

"Of course," echoed Dizzy. "But the pious old fool seems to forget that in offering a safe harbor for these radicals, he's created a nest of vipers. These zealots did not give up their ideals when they came to London. They still want to destroy aristocrats and monarchs and bring down governments, and they're not particular about which country they destabilize. While they enjoy our English hospitality, they're planning to demolish our nation. The newspapers are clamoring for the arrest and prosecution of the killers of Carrington and Ebbechester and the rest. Every editor in this city has challenged the government to do something. Our citizens are afraid to walk the streets for fear they'll be caught up in an assassination attempt. The situation has become untenable, and we must do something about it."

Dizzy quirked an eyebrow in my direction, and I took a hasty draught of my whisky to fortify myself for what was to come.

"That is the reason I have called you here tonight, Miss Black. Superintendent Stoke and I would be most grateful for your assistance."

"What is it that you wish me to do?" I already had an inkling, knowing as I did how the pretty young French girls supported themselves and their families in the Communard community. The authorities have so little imagination. If there's a prostitute in the mix, well, let's call in our own resident slut to deal with the matter. It was likely that Dizzy and Stoke wanted me to strike up an acquaintance with some of these girls to learn what they knew of anarchist plans brewing in the Seven Dials. I'd hear what the two men had to say, but I wasn't about to go slumming in the vague hope of picking up gossip.

"Need counterintelligence operatives," Stoke said wetly through his moustache. "Not enough fellows on the force to spare the men myself. Prime minister's fellows all engaged on other matters."

So presumably French had gone away on a mission for Dizzy.

The prime minister spoke. "We were most favorably impressed by your performances during the affair of the War Office memo and the resolution of the matter at Balmoral." His voice was smooth as treacle and his smile saintly. I girded my loins and waited to see what he proposed.

"We'd like you to infiltrate one of these anarchist groups and report to us on their activities." The saintly smile grew grim. "It will be dangerous."

"Will I be the only agent on this mission?" I asked with what I thought was a remarkable display of coolness, considering that the idea of penetrating a group of nihilists who played with gunpowder and dynamite without French by my side was, shall we say, daunting.

Dizzy nodded. "You have always worked with Mr. French in the past. Unfortunately, I have assigned him to another matter and he is unavailable at the moment. You would act alone, but of course Superintendent Stoke and I will be available for advice and counsel."

A fat lot of good that would do when the bullets were flying or the dynamite was exploding, but I refrained from giving expression to the thought. The prime minister and Stoke were eyeing me steadily, their faces deliberately blank. If I said no, would I ever get another opportunity to strike out on my own? Or would I be consigned to the part of French's lieutenant, forever destined to play a subordinate role in these affairs of state? If I failed, I could wave goodbye to any future other than madam of Lotus House, but if I succeeded, well, who knows what vistas might open up to India Black? I entertained a brief image of an audience with the Queen and French looking on admiringly as I collected a gaudy medal from the old trout. I do believe it was that vision of French humbly applauding my achievement that decided me.

"I'll do it," I said.

Stoke expelled a breath, and Dizzy nodded gravely. "I felt sure that you would. Now, the superintendent will inform you of what you need to know."

There was a pause while Stoke extracted the ends of his moustache from his mouth. "Rumors all over the city," he said. "New group formed. Call themselves the Dark Legion. Silly name, of course, but these anarchist groups go in for such drivel. Black Banner, Black Flag and similar rot. Dark Legion is new, formed by chaps who were active in the Paris Commune. Implicated in bombings and assassinations in Europe. Got a bit hot for them there, and they've moved operations to England. Been operating north in Manchester and out in Liverpool. Now they've come to London. Word on the street is that the leader is one of the most influential men in the anarchist community. Chap named "Grigori." Find him and we cut the head off the snake."

He paused to slurp his moustache. "Need the leader," he repeated. "Here's what we want you to do. Join the Dark Legion. Find out who's behind them. Description, address, anything. My men take it from there." He looked lugubriously at me. "Got to be careful. Anarchists infiltrated routinely by intelligence agencies and police. Paranoid lot. Kill you quick if they think you're a government agent."

Bugger. This would be tricky. I'd be spying on a group of people who suspected everyone of being a spy. I was beginning to wish my first individual assignment had been trailing some Turkish diplomat to the opera and seducing him afterward. I find Turkish men remarkably attractive. There was a fellow once, reminded me a bit of French, actually—

Superintendent Stoke interrupted my reverie. "Informant tells me there's a French prostitute named Martine. Supposed to be affiliated with the Dark Legion. Maybe a member, maybe not."

"Here is where your special skills will be useful, my dear," said Dizzy, as if I hadn't already figured that out on my own.

"Martine works for old Mother Edding. Know her?"

"I've heard of her," I said. "Runs a brothel in the rookery at St. Giles, near Seven Dials. Squalid place." Curse it, I thought. I've only been around Stoke for half an hour, and already I'd forgotten how to speak in complete sentences.

"Want you to hire Martine, take her to your place," said Stoke.

That brought me up short. "I'm not sure about that. Mother Edding runs a very different establishment from mine. My customers are used to an immaculate house and first-rate toffers, not dirty baggage. I'll have to see this Martine first, to see if she can pass muster. I can't ruin my business by bringing in some unwashed bint who's used to servicing common sailors and such."

"Bathe her," said Stoke. It did not appear to be a suggestion. "Pretty girl. Jump at the chance to get out of Mother Edding's. Suit your customers just fine."

I dismissed the disturbing thought that Stoke might know what my customers liked. There were more important issues at hand.

"I'll look at her," I said. "If I don't think she'll work, I shall have to find another way into the Dark Legion. I have to earn a living, you know. I can't put my business at risk."

Stoke's face darkened. "Thought you said she was your agent, Prime Minister."

"Yes, yes," said Dizzy smoothly. "I'm sure Miss Black will find a way to accommodate your suggestions, Superintendent, while retaining her own, er, professional integrity." A meaningless piece of twaddle, that, but Stoke seemed soothed, and I'd worked with Dizzy before, so I knew not to put much stock into what he said. I felt confident I'd find a way to wriggle into the Dark Legion if this Martine girl couldn't cut the mustard. They were men, after all, and if I do say so myself, there are very few of Adam's sons who can resist India Black.

Stoke had brought a case with him, and now he unloaded a stack of papers and handed them to me. "Background material. Read it tonight. See Martine tomorrow."

I tried to disguise the irritation I felt at his peremptory tone. No doubt I failed; I'm not much good at standing to attention just because some bloke has barked an order.

"How am I to reach you, Superintendent?"

"Address is on the papers. Send a messenger. Someone you trust."

"Then it will be a young fellow named Vincent."

Dizzy nodded approvingly. "A good lad. Not, er, the most dapper in appearance, but very useful."

"You'll have to instruct your men to watch for him. He's a street Arab, so they'll probably toss him out on his ear if he tries to approach you."

"Tell him to say that he comes from India Black. Be sure to reach me, then." Stoke extracted his hunter from his pocket. "Must run. Any questions?"

"No. I'll be in touch," I said. I stood, prepared to also take my leave of Dizzy.

He put out a hand. "If you can remain with me a minute longer, Miss Black, I've something to say to you."

My heart contracted. Had I been wrong? Had Dizzy been

saving the news that French had been abducted by Russian agents and found in the Thames?

Stoke bowed himself out, and Dizzy waited until the door had closed behind him. The old man looked at me searchingly. "Are you ready, my dear?"

"Ready?"

"To venture out on your own? I certainly think you are, as does Mr. French. But it is entirely up to you."

"You consulted French?"

"Briefly. Communications are difficult, but I did manage to get word to him. He seemed to think you capable."

Damned faint praise, that, but I admit to feeling a ridiculously warm glow at the confirmation of my skills from his nibs.

"You needn't worry, sir. I'm ready." God help me, I sounded positively eager.

I returned to Lotus House to find Mrs. Drinkwater retired to her room (for the remainder of the night, if the volume of snores and the empty bottle in the hall outside her door were any indication). She had in fact prepared a plate of sandwiches and left them on the deal table in the kitchen. I carried them into the study and, once I had pared off the hardened crusts and the curling edges of the roast beef, settled down to this unsatisfactory repast while I scanned the documents Superintendent Stoke had sent home with me. For the most part, these consisted of reports written in the impenetrable lingo that civil servants love, be they government ministers or police constables. I resigned myself to wading through it and spent two hours perusing the papers. At the end of this session, I was not much wiser than I had been after Stoke's seminar in the prime minister's room. The

Dark Legion was a shadowy organization, rumored to include among its members an expert in the construction of explosive devices (referred to as "infernal machines" in the reports) and various brands of foreigners, all of whom had been deported from or fled their native countries due to their avowed pledge to overthrow the governments of said countries. The French girl, Martine, was thought by police informants to be the daughter of a prominent Communard who had died when the French government had attacked the forces of the Paris Commune, ending that particular utopian idyll. Like many other young girls in the expatriate community, she had found herself required to earn a crust as a whore, but this had apparently only fired her enthusiasm for anarchist causes.

The connection between her and the Dark Legion was vague. Stoke's men had heard talk on the street that Martine had a relationship of some sort with one of the men who had formed the cabal. The man might be a friend of her dead father, or her lover. Some of the memos made for interesting reading, as some lucky detective had been given the task of appearing at Mother Edding's establishment and requesting a quarter of an hour with Martine on numerous occasions. Unsurprisingly, the detective had been unable to pry any information out of the girl. I snorted when I read that, for I reckon Martine had sussed out immediately that the bloke was a copper. That skill is one of the first you learn in this business, or you don't last long. I expect Martine had gleefully passed along the information that the Dark Legion was under investigation to her friends in that organization, which made my assignment all the more difficult, as the members would really be on guard now.

I put away the papers and spent a bit of time ruminating about how to approach Martine. I fancied I'd do a better job than the plod who had enjoyed Martine's charms, but I'd have to provide the girl with a plausible story to avoid arousing suspicion myself. After all, it wasn't every day that a madam of one of the best (well, nearly one of the best) brothels in London condescended to visit the rookery of St. Giles to hire a prostitute. Then there was the issue of Mother Edding. I had never met the woman and didn't consider her a rival, but I knew how I'd feel if some other abbess came prowling around, enticing my girls to up stakes and move. Running a brothel is just like any other business: you've got to protect your assets. Mother Edding might prove troublesome.

I spared a moment to savor the situation. This very morning I had been lounging about, bored as a regiment between battles, and here I was now, ready to take on a rival madam and a collection of dangerous radicals. It should prove interesting, I thought. In retrospect, that is not the word I would have chosen.

3

The next morning I sent for Vincent. While I waited for the young cub to appear, I attended to some household matters, paying the outstanding accounts, prying Mrs. Drinkwater out of bed, and dragging her to the kitchen to feed the girls. Then I unlocked the top right-hand drawer of my desk and took out my Bulldog revolver. I swabbed the barrel, rotated and cleaned the cylinder, and loaded the weapon. I wrapped a handful of extra cartridges in a handkerchief to add to my purse. In my line of work, it pays to have a bit of protection. Dreadful times we live in, when a lady has to carry a weapon when she ventures into certain parishes of the city. I intended to have the Bulldog on my person when I made my foray in search of Martine. Seven Dials was no place for a woman of quality traveling alone, but I didn't hesitate to venture there with the revolver in hand. Anyone who trifled with me would end up with powder burns on his bollocks.

I went into the kitchen to wash my hands and found Mrs. Drinkwater slumbering at the table with her chin propped in her hand. I prodded her chair with my foot as I went past and enjoyed the satisfaction of seeing her head flop forward and her eyes spring open. She looked wildly about the room.

"It's only me, Mrs. Drinkwater. Please have lunch ready at one o'clock. I'll eat in my study."

I took her surly growl as acquiescence and retired to my study. There I sat down at the desk and drew forth a sheet of plain cream stock, with my name embossed upon it in ebony ink. I unscrewed the cap of my sterling silver pen (a present from an admirer; I do so love admirers) and flipped open the lid of the inkwell. Preparations complete, I sat and stared at the paper. In truth, I'm not a great one for writing letters. Oh, I write the odd note to the greengrocer or the wine merchant, but one can hardly call that correspondence. There are no maiden aunts in my life, nor kindly vicars who've taken an interest in my education (at least, not in the generally accepted sense of that phrase). I admit that my skill in the art of drafting missives is nonexistent. I don't mind making such an admission, as there are dozens of other skills at which I excel. I disclose the foregoing, of course, to explain why it took such a long time for me to set pen to paper.

I'd another consideration weighing on my mind, and that was the recipient of the letter. I have mentioned the Balmoral affair previously, and if you've read my account of the threat against the Queen's life, then you'll remember a withered narcoleptic with a taste for snuff and tales of deceit and treachery by the female of the species. I refer, of course, to the Dowager Marchioness of Tullibardine, in whose employ I masqueraded as a lady's maid at Balmoral. I can't say I enjoyed the experience, having to launder the old lady each time she snorted a quantity of snuff and then expectorated it by way of an explosive sneeze. Nor did I appreciate her preference for sleeping during the day and remaining as alert as a fox vixen during the hours of the night.

As I had never met the woman before our visit to Balmoral, and had no expectations whatsoever that I would ever set eyes on the dilapidated wreck again, it came as quite a shock to me when she acknowledged knowing my mother. Worse, the old bag had shouted out this revelation as her train pulled out of the station at Perth, leaving me agog on the platform. I was disconcerted, as you can imagine. I vowed then and there to track down the marchioness and pry from her whatever information she might possess. But it was a long way to Scotland, and I wasn't keen about making the trip before ascertaining that Her Ladyship had something of value to tell me, which explains why I was chewing on the top of my pen at my desk and staring out the window at the rain this spring morning.

After a quarter hour or so, I issued a stern injunction to myself to stop dithering and get on with it, for Christ's sake, and so I applied myself laboriously to my task.

"Forever in your debt—"

No, strike that. God knows how the marchioness would interpret such a phrase. She'd probably expect me to move to Tullibardine and live out my days reading her to sleep at night.

"Urgent that I know—"

What was I thinking? That sounded desperate, and India Black was never desperate. I chewed the pen and muttered and tried half a dozen sentences, wasting a ream of paper (and the cursed stuff was expensive) and splattering ink all over the desk, until I finally settled on the following:

The Dowager Marchioness of Tullibardine
Aberkill House
Tullibardine, Scotland

Dear Lady Aberkill,

I trust this letter finds you well and in good health. I understood from your last comments to me on the station platform at Perth that you knew something of my mother. I would be much obliged to you if you could provide further specifics, as I have little information about her.

Yours sincerely,
India Black

It was short and to the point, which, I recalled, the marchioness was herself in her communications, though this one was undoubtedly more polite than anything I'd ever heard the marchioness utter. I sealed it up, relieved that the chore was done, and consigned it to the hall table, to be delivered to the post office by Mrs. Drinkwater. I returned to my study to find Vincent seated by the fire. The brat had deliberately chosen one of my prized Queen Anne chairs, upholstered in a watered silk of china blue.

"How the devil did you get in here? And move out of that chair immediately. You know you're not allowed on the cushions."

"I came in the back door. Mrs. Drinkwater's asleep in the kitchen. Put your 'air back on, India. I'm movin'." He gave me a little smirk, to let me know he could stay in the Queen Anne if he chose to but for reasons of his own, he was relocating. Vincent is like that, you see. He's a veteran of the London streets, more used to taunting authority than complying with it. I judged Vincent's chronological age at between ten and fourteen, but he could be thirty for all I knew. He had a cracked voice that could shatter glass, the cunning mind of a Russian arms dealer, the morals of a Bedouin raider and the personal hygiene of a cave dweller. Save for the cleanliness issue, he was the perfect ally in the London underworld. I trusted him implicitly, except with my bolsters, and as long as he stayed upwind.

"'Eard from French?" he enquired.

"Not directly," I said, wincing as I caught a whiff of *eau de filth*, "but the prime minister passed on a message to me."

"Ole Dizzy? When did ya see 'im?"

"Last night."

Vincent sat up eagerly, eyes sparkling like those of a mongoose who'd sighted a cobra. "We got spies to catch? Or is the Queen up to her knickers in hassassins again?"

I hesitated. I needed Vincent's help, but I knew the bugger would want to be in the very heart of things. All I needed was a messenger at the moment, but knowing Vincent, I feared he'd figure out a way to apprentice himself to a bomb maker in some anarchist cell and blow up half of London.

"I've been asked to hire a bint who is associated with an anarchist group. I'm to try to get information from her and pass it along to Superintendent Stoke at Scotland Yard." Well, that was half my assignment. I'd let Vincent know about the spying half when I deemed it necessary.

"Is that all?" Vincent was disappointed. "We could do a lot more than that. We could join one of them groups and find out who they're gonna bomb next. That would be better than sneakin' around after some tart."

"At the moment, all I need is a messenger. Are you willing to help me?"

"'Course I am," said Vincent. "I just wish we could 'ave some fun while we're at hit."

"You never know what will develop. Just look at what happened in Scotland."

The thought that we might encounter fanatics who would wish to kill us cheered Vincent enormously. I cracked a window, and we spent a pleasant half hour discussing my meeting with Dizzy and the superintendent and whether I'd encounter any difficulties in prizing away Martine from Mother Edding. Vincent had a few suggestions for getting the girl out of the Seven Dials brothel, but as all of them involved violence in some form or another, I dismissed them.

"Really, Vincent, the girl would be stupid not to recognize that Lotus House is a superior situation. I'll make it worth her while to come here. She won't turn me down. Certainly Mother Edding won't have any difficulty in replacing her. There are dozens of girls in the Communard community who would jump at the chance to earn a few pence."

"Wot makes you think this Martine is one of them anarchists?"

I shrugged. "I've only Superintendent Stoke's opinion that she is. He has informants in the Communard community. I hope the information is accurate. Otherwise, I'll find myself with a French tart I know nothing about."

"Does she speak English?"

That brought me up short. I hadn't even thought of that. It wouldn't matter to the customers if the girl couldn't *parlez-vous anglais* as long as she was pretty, but it would be difficult to explain the financial arrangements of the house to her. Damn. How did I get myself into these situations? Well, I'd cross that bridge when I came to it. I made arrangements with Vincent to stop by Lotus House at several appointed hours during the day to see if there was a message for delivery to Superintendent Stoke, assured Vincent that if we had the opportunity to kill any spies I would not do so without him, and agreed on a sum for his services (greedy little bastard—I'd have to get some money from Dizzy or I'd be out of pocket myself).

The next morning after breakfast, I selected an ensemble for my visit to the Seven Dials area. Considering my destination, a pair of sturdy boots that would withstand a river of sewage and an old dress that could be discarded and burned after use might seem the safest bet, but I had a whore to catch and I wanted to dazzle the girl with the opportunities awaiting her at Lotus House. Consequently, I selected one of my most fetching outfits, a tie-back underskirt in scarlet silk and a long draped overskirt of pinstriped navy wool with a matching jacket bodice that fitted so tightly my natural assets were displayed to their fullest. Thank goodness the fashion of bustles was disappearing; it would have been a job of work to navigate the foul, stinking streets of Seven Dials with yards of cloth hanging off the rear of one's skirt. I chose a pair of black boots of sensible, not fine, leather (a girl has to make some concession to the weather) but with an arched instep and thin high heel that made me sway voluptuously before the mirror. How I'd look when I had to stagger down the uneven bricks of the streets of Seven Dials was another matter entirely, but I didn't dwell on that thought. A high-crowned hat with a rolled brim in navy blue completed my attire. As the rain was bucketing down I added an umbrella to my kit. I looked rather fetching, I thought. Most men wouldn't have turned me down, and I doubted whether an impoverished French girl could resist the prospect of one day emulating the madam of Lotus House. I went to the study and took the Webley and the handkerchief of extra cartridges from the drawer. Their weight was reassuring.

Mrs. Drinkwater had braved the elements to summon a cab for

me, and I climbed in carefully, smoothing my skirts and calling out my destination to the driver. The carriage shifted as he climbed down. A pale face, slick with rain, appeared in the window.

"Beggin' your pardon, miss, but that area is... is—"

"Unsafe?" I suggested. "Dangerous? Disgusting? Yes, it is. Nevertheless, I intend to go there. Should you like the fare, or must I find another cab?"

The driver scratched his head, causing his hat to tip precariously to one side. A sheet of water cascaded from the brim.

"But—"

"I absolve you of all responsibility."

"But—"

"Oh, for heaven's sake. I'll pay you double the fare. Now, may we go?"

"Paid up front?" the driver asked.

I fished some money from my purse with ill grace and dangled it in front of him. "Here is half now, and I'll pay you the other half upon our return."

The sight of the coins was persuasive. I do believe a shilling is better than whisky at generating courage.

We drove north with the rain thrumming on the roof of the cab, dodging drays and carriages and splashing pedestrians as we rolled through the water running in the gutters. What a delightful day for an excursion, I thought gloomily. Our destination did not warrant any enthusiasm either. I brooded as we drove northeast, passing Leicester Square and turning onto St. Martin's Lane. In a matter of minutes we had reached the confluence of roads known as Seven Dials. It's a bit of a mystery as to how the place got its name. Only six roads converged there originally, and a pillar with six sundials on it was erected there, so you'd think it would be Six Dials. But another road was built and the pillar was torn down and now it's known as Seven Dials. Typical of London, as it defies logic. However, it doesn't matter what they call the place, as a more apt name for it would be Hell.

We hadn't come far from Lotus House, but by God, this was another world entirely. I'd grown up in London and seen a fair bit of dirt, poverty and disease, but even I was overwhelmed in this part of the city. A crowd of filthy creatures surged around the cab: diseased whores, gin-addled beggars and half-naked children with matted hair and wild eyes. There were lunatics and cripples, the starved and the sick, the maimed and the hopeless. A crowd formed at the sight of the cab and converged on us, hands outstretched. The driver cursed and lashed at them with his whip, and the horse pawed the ground and whinnied in fear.

I thumped on the roof with my umbrella. "Drive on. We don't want a riot."

The driver left off using the whip on the swarming throng and laid into the horse. The poor nag surged forward, scattering barefoot children and gaunt men and women in rags, and we were clear, for the moment.

In his stack of memos, Superintendent Stoke had provided me a description of Martine, which sounded promising, and the address of Mother Edding's brothel. It was located on Endell Street, a gloomy byway of scum and squalor. Sagging doors and rotting window frames adorned the houses, and the groundfloor shops did a listless business in bruised fruit, old clothes and broken furniture. The brothel itself was no better than the rest of the neighborhood, housed in a decrepit building of smokefouled brick. Two men were sheltering in the doorway from the rain. One, who still possessed a collar, had it turned up against the cold and wet. The other poor chap wore only a thin shirt against the chill. I ordered the driver to stop before the house and beckoned to the fellow in the shirt. I suppose the finely gloved hand waving from a cab was enough to entice him, for he sprinted into the rain and skidded to a halt at the window. His eyes widened when he saw me.

"Is this the address of Mother Edding?" I asked.

The poor brute shivered and nodded.

"Will you deliver a message for me? I'll give you a bob."

"Aye, I will."

"Listen carefully, now. Tell Mother Edding that a young lady wants to speak to her at the corner of Bloomsbury and New Oxford Street. If she comes in a quarter of an hour, she'll hear something to her advantage and earn a crown for herself."

I made him repeat the message, then handed him a shilling and sent him on his way. He tucked the coin in his pocket and bounded up the stairs. I waited just long enough to see the door of Mother Edding's establishment open to his knock, and then instructed the driver to move along. We drove a short distance and then circled back to Endell Street, stopping within view of the brothel.

We had been there less than five minutes when the front door of the house opened and a bulky figure, bundled in a thick woolen shawl, trundled down the steps and set off. I couldn't have been sure that Mother Edding would rise to the bait, but in this neighborhood it would take an abbess of indescribable stupidity to ignore a message that promised some advantage to her. The two fellows who had been skulking in her doorway set off at a rapid pace behind her. It appears everyone in the Seven Dials has his eye on the main chance. I suppose the two thought they might pick up some crumbs of information or provide some of their own to the obliging young lady in the hansom cab.

The driver deposited me in front of the steps, and I dashed through the downpour to the door. I hadn't much time; I'd had to choose a meeting place close enough to entice Mother Edding to venture out in this weather. I knocked and then tried the handle. It opened easily, which is not surprising. What shopkeeper would lock his shop to keep out the customers? As I suspected, the place was disgusting. To my right was a fusty parlor, reeking of stale smoke and gin, the furniture scuffed and the cushions limp. A steep staircase climbed the wall before me. The wallpaper had bubbled and cracked and now dangled limply in thin strips. From the rear of the house I heard the clank of pots. The smell of boiling cabbage permeated the air. The place seemed deserted. The gloom was Stygian.

Verifying that the parlor was empty, I gathered my skirts in one hand and dashed lightly up the bare boards of the stairs, making as much noise as a herd of camels let loose in the halls of the British Museum. I expected to see a few heads popping out of rooms, but no one stirred. Damnation. I'd wasted a perfectly good dodge on Mother Edding, only to learn that all the whores were out drinking last night's takings. Well, now that I was here, I'd do a thorough search. If I couldn't find Martine, perhaps I'd stumble across a bint who could tell me where to find her.

I cracked open the first door to reveal a naked woman sprawled on the bed, snoring prodigiously. Superintendent Stoke's informant had described Martine as dark, slim and boyish, with brown hair and eyes. The bint on the bed had a mop of dirty blond curls, thick ankles and the complexion of pastry dough. I closed the door and moved on.

I struck lucky at the very next door. I pushed it open, expecting to find another tart having a snooze, but found instead a young lady sitting in a chair by the window, staring wistfully out the window at the falling rain. This had to be Martine, for she was lithe and slender, with olive skin and a thick mass of mahogany hair that tumbled down her back. Beyond presentable, and thank the Lord, she was reasonably clean.

She looked up calmly, but I could see the curiosity in her eyes.

"If you're looking for Mother Edding, she went out a few minutes ago. I don't know when she'll return."

She spoke English, albeit with a charming lisp and a pronounced French accent. The customers would go wild for that voice, that figure and that air of virginal naïveté.

"Are you Martine?"

"I am Martine. Who are you?"

I extended a hand. Martine hesitated briefly, then put out her own.

"India Black," I said. "You may have heard of me?"

The girl shook her head.

"No matter," I said. "I have heard of you."

"Oh? From whom?" Innocent as a kitten, this one.

"One of my customers."

"What is his name?"

"It makes no difference. Someone who has seen you and believes your talents would find better use at my brothel. I've come to make my own assessment of you."

She lifted her chin, and there was a hint of a challenge in her eyes. I had pricked her with my words. I admire a bit of fight in a girl, so long as she doesn't work for me. This Martine might not prove to be such a submissive miss after all.

"I should think you would find me an excellent addition to your establishment. However, I know nothing of you. What kind of services do you provide?"

I smiled reassuringly. "The usual services. My girls are

topdrawer, as are my customers. Only military officers are permitted at Lotus House; the ranks are strictly forbidden. Lots of aristocrats visit, as do several members of Parliament. And I've a number of clients who like the theater. I don't suppose you'd object to donning a costume now and then?"

She glanced unconsciously at the threadbare shift she was wearing.

"I provide your dresses, food and lodging. You won't walk out with anyone without my permission. You will submit yourself monthly to a medical exam, at my expense. You will not chew, take snuff or smoke on the premises. You may partake of alcoholic beverages, but if you do so to excess, you will have to find work elsewhere. You will bathe regularly. I run a clean establishment, and my customers are gentlemen." I smiled. "I mean that only in the sense that they can afford to pay more for the services, of course, for when it comes to sex, I have yet to find a true gentleman. Now then, are you prepared to consider a change from your present circumstances?"

I had meant to overwhelm the girl with the description of the luxuries she could expect at Lotus House. Mother Edding could clearly not compete in the same arena with India Black, and it was best to get it all out on the table, especially as any minute now the aforementioned abbess might storm back to the house, livid at being made a fool of by a strange woman in a hansom cab. I needed to work quickly if I was going to carry this *poule* out of the henhouse.

"Come, my girl," I said briskly. "This may seem like a dream to you, but you must decide quickly whether you will come with me or stay here." I gestured at the room. "I can promise you a proper coverlet, instead of a thin blanket. You'll have a choice of dresses and a place to bathe. There will be three square meals on the table. And I'll pay you far more than Mother Edding can."

"How much?"

I knew I'd got her then. "How much does Mother Edding pay you?"

She named a sum and I appeared shocked. "Is that all? My word, that's cheap."

"What will you pay?"

I was sorely tempted to double the amount and be done with it, but as the figure would still be substantially less than what I paid my tarts, I'd have a mutiny on my hands if Martine or any of my other employees found out. Whores are great ones for ganging together when they feel one of their sisters has been mistreated.

I named my price.

Martine gasped. "I don't understand why you—"

I broke in. "I've told you. I've a client who likes your looks. As he's an excellent customer, I hate to disappoint him. Now I need your answer, for I fancy that old Mother Edding will be back soon."

"I'll do it," she said. You'd think the bloody girl would be grateful, but just for a moment I caught a glimpse of resentment in her eyes. Well, I wouldn't begrudge her some bitterness at being handled so abruptly. If I hadn't been under some time constraints, I might have used more charm and not bludgeoned the girl with the benefits of Lotus House. Needs must, however, and my present need was to vacate the premises before the abbess of this august establishment returned to find me pilfering her whore. I gave Martine the address of Lotus House and instructed her to call there the next morning at ten, cautioning her not to let Mother Edding know where she had gone, as I was concerned for Martine's safety if the madam took umbrage. I did not mention that neither was I keen on the idea of a run-in with the stocky figure I'd seen stamping down the street.

I was feeling most pleased as I traveled back to Lotus House at having plucked Martine from the clutches of Mother Edding without an ugly encounter or the spilling of any blood. Of course, the girl had yet to show her face at my door, but I had little doubt that she would be there tomorrow. She didn't seem at all stupid, and only the densest of bints would stay in the horror of Seven Dials when she had the option to hie off to my establishment where there was food on the table and the customers had washed within the last decade. For the first time since that fateful visit to Scotland, I felt a rush of excitement at the prospect of tomorrow and what it might bring.

4

I really must learn to subdue my exuberant nature, for tomorrow brought not a smidgen of espionage, but a mutiny among my whores. Promptly at ten o'clock Martine had knocked at the door of Lotus House, bearing her earthly belongings in a stained and battered traveling bag of ancient vintage. The rebellion commenced within a quarter hour. Mrs. Drinkwater had shown Martine to her room with instructions to fill a bath and stand by as the girl washed away any companions who might have accompanied her from her previous abode. I was having a think in my study, musing on how I would subvert Martine and worm my way into the Dark Legion, when a gaggle of howling whores burst into the room, still in their dressing gowns and slippers, and scenting competition.

The mob of tarts advanced to my desk. What was that piece of continental fluff doing here, when there wasn't enough custom for decent, honest British girls? What if one of their regulars preferred Martine's Gallic attributes to their own buxom charm? Was a French whore entitled to more money? Who got the yellow dress tonight, they wanted to know, having agreed that yellow was definitely Martine's colour, with that tawny skin and those warm brown eyes, but that wouldn't be fair, as it was Ethel's turn for the yellow, and how could I expect them to work when I turned things upside down by bringing in a Frog slut who probably didn't speak the King's English? I felt like the Widow Capet before the Revolutionary Tribunal.

I daresay I had a better grasp of how to handle rebellious subjects than Marie Antoinette, for I just sat with my head cocked to one side, exuding dignity, and let them chunter on until they'd run out of steam. I've learned that if you let the bints maunder on for a bit, it relieves their feelings on the subject and leaves them with the erroneous impression that they've scored a victory of sorts. I waited patiently until the last expostulation had evaporated in the air, and then fixed them all with a gimlet eye. You can't run a brothel if you quail at the sight of a few dissatisfied employees. Over the years I've developed a stare that could drive nails, and I used it now to good effect. It wasn't long before every whore in the room was searching the floor for hairpins that had gone missing.

"You surprise me," I said reproachfully. "Don't I look out for you? Don't I keep you supplied with the latest fashions and give you meat twice a day? Don't I see to it that every one of you gets enough custom to make a decent living? Show me another abbess who takes such care of her girls." Inducing guilt in one's employees, I have found, is a useful technique in controlling unruly strumpets.

It proved so today. The girls blushed and mumbled and traced patterns on the carpet with the toes of their slippers. Like most mobs, they lost their spunk when their quarry didn't take to her heels and flee.

Clara Swansdown wrung her hands and had the grace to look

ashamed. "Sure, and you know how it is. We're on edge, all of us, what with the rain and the wind and being stuck inside and the fact that not enough chaps are showing up to keep even one of us busy. We know you take care of us, we do and that's a fact. But if we don't get some trade soon, our old mothers and children will go hungry."

"I understand, Clara," I said, and I did, for most of the bints sent a few coins to their parents or young brothers and sisters, or in some cases, had their own children to support, farmed out to women who employed themselves taking care of the youngsters of wayward women. "Spruce yourselves up tonight and look lively, for you'll have your choice of prospects. Now then, go and have some tea and make Martine welcome. Will you do that?"

They went out, meek as sheep, and I mulled over the options for bringing in enough gentlemen this evening to make good on my promise. Now don't think that I've become a soft touch, for I haven't. It was in my own best interests to keep the bints occupied so that Martine's introduction to the brothel would go smoothly. It was going to cost me some money to accomplish this, but I knew what had to be done. Accordingly, I sat down and penned a note to Major Rawlins of the Royal Horse Guards, inviting him and a few of his fellows to join me tonight at Lotus House, where they could enjoy a bevy of alluring females and unlimited whisky at a ten percent discount. I'll tell you, it hurt to write that last part, but I bit my lip and steadied my hand and signed my name.

I also took the opportunity to pen a note to Superintendent Stoke to let him know that I had succeeded in luring Martine to Lotus House, and I scribbled a detailed message to Sir Ashton Birkett-Jones, inviting him to visit me at his convenience, and, as I needed his assistance in a small matter, to enjoy an evening of love, gratis (not with me, of course). That pained me almost as much as marking down the whisky for our brave lads in uniform, but I resigned myself to sacrificing in the name of queen and country, and set myself to figuring a way to claim the loss of income as expenses payable to Her Majesty's agent.

Vincent was due within the hour for one of his regularly appointed stops at Lotus House, so I set the messages aside for him and found Mrs. Drinkwater in the kitchen, idly stirring a pot of stewed chicken while she polished off the contents of a bottle of cloudy gin.

"Please prepare some bread and butter for Vincent, and give him the leg off that chicken you're boiling into mush. And don't light any matches in here, or the whole house will go." Poor Mrs. Drinkwater. She doesn't even pretend to be insulted anymore. She bobbed her head shakily, and I repaired to my study.

It's said that patience is a virtue and if that is so, then I am pleased to add it to the long list of moral qualities in which I am deficient. Personally, I have never discerned the slightest value in waiting. If something is worth having, it is worth having now, and if something needs doing, then why put it off? Unless of course, it involves emptying your purse, which, in my view, can be delayed indefinitely. I am not a rigorous thinker when it comes to ethics. You will have detected from the foregoing statements, however, that I was anxious to proceed with some aspect, nay, *any* aspect, of my assignment. I planned to have a little talk with Martine after she had made herself presentable, and no doubt Vincent would want to know all the details of Martine's recruitment when he arrived, but until then I had little to occupy my time.

What I needed was a session on the piste. Before you excite

yourself unnecessarily, I am referring, of course, to that great killing art: fencing. French had introduced me to the sport, and while I proved an unwilling pupil when we commenced our sessions, I must say that I soon found myself enthralled with this athletic diversion. It proved remarkably effective at improving my figure, which needed little in the way of enhancement, or so I am told, but nevertheless, I found I needn't lace my corsets quite as tightly after only a few sessions with the rapier. Rather to my surprise, I also discovered the thrill of clashing blades, headlong rushes and the shriek of the blade as it whips past its target. Bloody exciting, it is, to dance out of danger only to rush forward on attack and plant the point of your sword against your opponent's (namely, French's) chest.

With French gone, I'd had no one with whom to bout, and my fencing skills were growing rusty. Oh, I did my best, improvising a dummy of burlap, stuffed with straw and balancing precariously on an iron stand, which I poked halfheartedly now and then. If I ever faced an immobile, thick-witted villain, I'd emerge triumphant, but if the fellow was portable in the least, I'd have my work cut out for me. I did entice Vincent into a bit of practice one day. He'd been itching to get his hands on the rapier French had given me as a present, so all I had to do was offer to let him use it if I could practice on him. Things turned out badly, for Vincent had even less regard for the conventions of fencing than I did, and spent the entire session jumping off furniture and swinging the blade around like a blasted pirate, not to mention sweating like a bloody sailor becalmed in the Doldrums and emitting a rancid odour that nearly blinded me. I called a halt when he stabbed a hole through my curtains. The study smelled liked the baboon cage at the London Zoo, and it was days before the foul stench left the room.

With no sparring partner, I whiled away the hour until Vincent's arrival by glancing through the morning papers. The anarchists were at it again, printing up broadsides and plastering them all over London, calling for the rise of the working man and the fall of the government, and urging the poor to claim what was rightfully theirs by scribbling the nearest nob. The toffs were reported to be all aflutter, with wives and children being moved to country houses to avoid becoming targets. The reporters were lathered up about the nasty foreigners in our midst, and the editors were calling on Scotland Yard to round up anyone with an accent and send them packing. London, indeed all of England, was on edge. The news made me even more anxious to get on with things.

Vincent arrived and I fed him tea and bread and butter at the kitchen table. Mrs. Drinkwater had produced the chicken leg, and Vincent tore into it like a starving fox while I recounted my adventures at Mother Edding's. As these involved no knives, bullets or blood, Vincent was not particularly interested.

"So all you know 'bout this 'ere Martine is that Superintendent Stoke thinks she's one of them anarchists."

"Or associates with them."

"Ain't much to go on. Wot if you've 'ired a dud?"

The same thought had crossed my mind. I could only hope Stoke's information was accurate, or I might indeed be saddled with a useless trollop. It was imperative that I insinuate my way into her confidence as quickly as possible, not only to discharge my duty to Dizzy but also to ensure I'd not taken on an extra mouth to feed.

"You might make some enquiries around Seven Dials, Vincent. I wager you'll have a better chance at finding out Martine's relationship with the anarchists than Stoke's informants."

Vincent acknowledged his superiority to the police in this regard, finished his repast and left to deliver my various messages.

The afternoon was waning, and I sent Mrs. Drinkwater to summon Martine to my study for a little chat before the evening's festivities began. The girl hesitated in the doorway, and I summoned her into the room with a wave of my hand. The bath had wrought a miraculous change; the girl's hair was soft and lustrous and her skin luminous. I'd chosen an exquisite silk dress for her, in a delicate shade of rose pink that made her tawny skin glow. Ethel would have no reason to complain, as she would have the yellow dress tonight.

"An improvement from Mother Edding's, is it not?" I enquired. I pointed to a chair, and she sat down obediently.

"Yes, mademoiselle."

"Mrs. Drinkwater has informed you of meal times and such?"

"Yes, mademoiselle."

"And the other bints? Civil, are they?"

"Yes, mademoiselle." She hadn't lifted her eyes from the floor during this conversation.

"Come now. You mustn't play the docile damsel with me, or indeed with my clients. They come here for a bit of fun. So pinch your cheeks and put on a smile. The gentleman callers like a frolic. They don't want to spend the evening with a miserable cow. They can do that at home."

She straightened her back and flashed me a dark look. There was a current beneath that placid surface.

"That's better," I said. "We'll be having a group of military chaps in tonight, from the Horse Guards. They're a lively bunch, and as soon as they see a fresh haunch in the larder, they'll be all over you. Just remember that these fellows are not the louts you've been servicing at Mother Edding's. You'll be expected to flirt and flutter your eyelashes and amuse the customers. However, tonight you'll be providing your service to someone rather special. Play your cards right and you may end up with a few baubles in your pocket. Whatever you're given is yours to keep."

She looked astonished at my largesse. Well, I've found that if a strumpet has an attractive place to work where she rakes in the money, and she's allowed to keep the tortoiseshell combs and cheap necklaces that are thrown her way, she's apt to prove a steady and reliable hand. Of course, this philosophy of management has served me poorly on one or two occasions, when a girl has gotten too big for her bloomers and waltzed off to set up her own shop, but I usually have the satisfaction of seeing her at my door in a few months, begging for another chance. It's amazing how few people are truly blessed with an entrepreneurial frame of mind.

"One last thing about the chaps who visit Lotus House," I said. "They're important fellows, you know. Military officers and junior ministers and such. Of course, beneath that public school veneer, they're just men. But you must behave yourself with them, or they'll cause you and me no end of trouble." I let a little wrinkle of disgust disfigure my brow. "It isn't right, naturally, but there it is. They're toffs and we're not and it's always best to remember that. Someday," I added, sighing dramatically, "we'll get our due, but until then, treat them with caution."

Martine looked at me quizzically. Damn. I would have to be more direct, but then one usually does when dealing with bints. They're a literal bunch.

"We may not like bowing and scraping to the swells, but for now that's how we earn our shillings. The day will come, though, when they'll get what's coming to them. You wait and see."

I was thankful that Mrs. Drinkwater chose that moment to announce that Mr. Birkett-Jones had arrived, sparing me from further elaboration on the eminent demise of the aristocracy. I certainly didn't want to overplay my hand with Martine, but I was anxious to plant the idea that while India Black catered to patricians, she wasn't overly fond of the class.

Birkett-Jones was a roly-poly Tory MP with a predilection for dusky sylphs with doe eyes. He took one look at Martine and emitted a low whistle of admiration. He darted forward and grasped both her hands.

"'Pon my soul, India! Didn't I tell you that she was magnificent! What a creature!"

I have to hand it to Martine. She managed a winsome smile at the old coot, though I could see her impulse was to bolt like a frightened horse.

"Mr. Birkett-Jones is the gentleman of whom I spoke when I met you at Mother Edding's. He is the one who induced me to approach you."

Birkett-Jones wrung her hands heartily. "Indeed I did. One day, quite by chance you understand, I happened to see you at Covent Garden. Well, I was struck dumb by your beauty. I made enquiries at once, and when I found that you were reduced to working for that awful woman, I immediately thought of Lotus House and what an addition you'd be here."

"You were correct, sir. Martine is a charming girl, and we are pleased to have her here."

"Come, my dear," Birkett-Jones said. "Let us have a glass of wine."

I gave her an encouraging smile and as she was towed past me, I whispered in her ear, "He's a nice bloke and he pays handsomely. Now go bewitch the old devil."

I must remember to commend Birkett-Jones on his performance as the Enamored Gentleman. I thought it perfectly calculated to dispel any suspicions Martine might harbor regarding the reason for my recruiting her to Lotus House. I knew I could count on the bloke to pull off the role with ease, as he was one of the best orators in the Commons, with a silver tongue and a passion for amateur theatricals. He'd been more than happy to impersonate my "valued customer," especially as he'd been rewarded with a bit of rumpo (on the house) for his pains.

The contingent from the Royal Horse Guards appeared shortly after Birkett-Jones and Martine had disappeared upstairs, and I spent half an hour jollying along the major and smiling coquettishly at the stalwart fellows he'd brought along. I've never seen such magnificent moustaches and perfect posture. I stayed just long enough to be sure that the guardsmen had paired off with the girls and there were to be no quarrels, and then I repaired to my study. It had been a long day, quelling the trollops' riot and spoon-feeding Martine with my radical views and arranging Birkett-Jones's appearance and the revels for the major and his comrades in arms. I was feeling rather done in, so I removed my shoes and stretched out on the sofa before the fire with a glass of whisky in my hand while I reviewed the day's affairs. It was a relief to have the preliminaries out of the way, to have Martine in hand and the introduction to Lotus House over, but I could not dismiss the nagging doubt gnawing at my mind. In short order I'd have to convince Martine that I was an abbess with a social conscience, ready to throw in my lot with an anarchist group of which Martine, according to Superintendent Stoke, might know nothing, or might have heard rumours, or might belong. It had also occurred to me that Martine had wasted little time at taking me up on my offer of employment. I remembered Superintendent Stoke's observation that the anarchists were a paranoid bunch, often infiltrated by government agents and wary of outsiders. Those anarchist chappies might already be on to Stoke and his men and his latest recruit, yours truly. Martine might have her own agenda in moving to Lotus House. This would be a dicey business. I consoled myself with another whisky and the thought that I'd been running bluffs all my life and had been rather successful at it, and would undoubtedly pull off this bit of entertainment on behalf of Her Majesty's government.

I heard a hullabaloo from the foyer, with the front door swinging open to crash into the wall, startled exclamations from the army boys and a bass voice (presumably the major's, as it was loud enough to be heard over cannon fire) barking commands. I had half-risen from the sofa to inform the major and his compadres to remember that I ran a respectable establishment and I'd be grateful if he'd gag his lads, when Mrs. Drinkwater reeled into the room, swaying like an ancient cart horse on the way to the soap factory.

"Ish thash Eddinsh woman," she mumbled. "I tried to shtop her."

Blast. The chap who'd delivered my note to Mother Edding must have described me to her, no doubt for a small fee. Still, with thousands of whores in London, what were the odds that Mother Edding would have recognized India Black? I paused a moment to consider the fact that I had obviously become a known figure among the other madams of London, my fame reaching (apparently) even into the bowels of Seven Dials. I had only a second to enjoy this revelation, for Mother Edding charged through my study door like a Jersey cow whose calf I had taken for weaning. She was a stout old bawd, with a Falstaffian girth and a coarse grey moustache fit for a sergeant major.

"I've come for me girl," she said. The bass voice in the hall had belonged to her. This was not reassuring.

"I've no idea what you are talking about," I said. Well, I'll admit it's always a bit of a stretch for me to act innocent, but it was worth a shot in this situation. One can always resort to force if necessary.

"Don't pretend you don't know wot I'm talkin' about. Conjure 'er up speedy like, or you'll need a bucket to collect your teeth."

So much for innocence. A harder line would be required.

"You don't own the girl. Martine is free to work at Lotus House if that's what she wants."

"Wot you want with that dirty bit of muslin, anyway?" Mother Edding asked. She waved a hand, which I noticed was the size of the average stoker's. "You got a fine house 'ere. I'll bet you can get any girl you like to work 'ere. Martine's me best earner. I need 'er. Don't be a greedy sow."

"She won't be coming back with you," I said. "I've hired her and that's the end of it."

Mother Edding drew herself up to her full height, which was almost as tall as her full width. "Oh, yes? We'll see about that. Martine!"

The chandelier quivered, and my bone china vibrated on the shelf. The hum from the drawing room, where the guardsmen and the bints had resumed their flirtations, ceased abruptly.

"Martine!" the old abbess shouted again, rattling the panes in the window.

Well, that fired me, it did. It had been some time since the collection plate at Lotus House had been full, and I wasn't about to let this brawny madam ruin the evening's festivities.

"You will leave my house immediately or risk the

consequences," I said, stalking toward her. I hoped to intimidate the old stump into leaving peacefully, for in truth, I wasn't entirely sure how to make good on my threat.

Mother Edding cackled. "You'll 'ave to 'eave me out on me ear, India. But I'll 'ave Martine wif me when I go."

Bloody hell. The wretched woman was proving confoundedly difficult. My temper was not improved by the sight of half a dozen bints and as many guardsmen gathered outside my study door, collectively holding their breath. The bints looked worried; the blokes, titillated. It is times like these that make me wonder what the Revered Bewhiskered Fellow was thinking when he created the male sex.

Major Rawlins pushed his way through the crowd. "May I be of assistance, Miss Black?"

Yes, I thought, you bleeding well could. Except if I rely on a customer to toss out my interloper, it will be all over London before the night is through that India Black is incapable of protecting her brothel and her whores. Every madam in my neighborhood would be swanning into Lotus House, tempting the sluts with promises of greener grass once they jumped the fence, and quicker than you can say "Snip, snap, dragon," I'd be back where I started. I wasn't going there.

"Thank you, Major, but I can manage. I would like you to escort the young ladies and your men back into the drawing room. Please enjoy the refreshments and pay no mind to any sounds you may hear from the study."

He looked a bit shocked but nodded stiffly and herded the tarts and the soldier boys from my door. I closed it behind them and turned to Mother Edding.

"Now, look here. I've no intention of letting Martine leave with you. However, I'm an abbess too, and I know what a blow it is to lose a good employee. Let me pay you something in compensation. Say, the equivalent of two weeks of Martine's earnings. That should give you enough time to find another girl to take her place without losing any income. That's a fair deal, I think." If there's one thing I know, it's brothels. Mother Edding had probably already found another desperate soul to fill Martine's place and was paying her half what she'd paid Martine. The old girl hadn't come here expecting to get Martine back; she just wanted to make the point that I shouldn't waltz in and snatch her trollops out from under her nose, at least not without some recompense.

It pains me to admit when I am wrong, but in this case, I was mistaken. Badly mistaken. Instead of accepting my generous offer, Mother Edding reached into the folds of her clothing and produced a pigsticker.

I admit to feeling some consternation at the sight. My rapier was in its case on the mantel; my Webley Bulldog revolver in the drawer of my desk. I conned the room rapidly for a weapon within arm's reach. The closest object that fit the purpose was a crystal vase of slender proportions or a Georgian silver candlestick on the chest by the wall. I chose the latter.

Mother Edding smiled grimly beneath her moustache. "So that's 'ow it's goin' to be, is it? Well, come on, then. Let's get this over wif. The sooner I slice your pretty face, the sooner I leave 'ere with Martine."

I did not react to these sinister words; I daren't give the stocky figure the least impression that she had frightened me. I took three swift steps to the chest and picked up the candlestick.

"Hah!" crowed my opponent. "You takin' me on wif that?"

"Why not?" I said. "You're old and slow. It wouldn't be a fair fight if I had a knife."

She let out a blood-curdling scream and lunged at me. I'd have thought the old girl was about as a spry as a Clydesdale, but she moved with surprising speed. My fencing lessons stood me in good stead, though, for just as she came barreling in with the knife outstretched, I swiveled my hips and dodged the blade. She might be fast, but stout as she was she had trouble halting once she had a head of steam. She sailed past me, the knife waving in the air, trying to locate my heart. I brought the candlestick down on her arm as she swept by me. She stumbled and cried out, and I thought I'd had the best of her, but the blasted creature floundered upright, the knife still in her hand, and turned a venomous glare upon me.

"Oi, you've done it now, you little slag. You'll be in 'ell before the night is over."

"Be reasonable, Mother Edding," I said soothingly. "You know quite well that we can play this game for some time, and I'll win every round. Your heart will go while you're trying to chase me down. Why don't you just accept the money I've offered? We'll shake hands and call it square, and we can both get back to running our businesses."

She answered with a snarl, a switch of the knife to her other hand and another galumphing charge in my direction. I feinted right and went left and by the time she'd pulled up, I was on the other side of room, taking my Bulldog from my desk drawer. I leveled it at her as she turned.

"That's quite enough of this. Drop the knife."

She did so but with ill grace. Then she spat on my Turkey carpet.

Blimey. The bitch had no idea what that carpet had cost.

"Sod you," I said. "I was going to give you the money I offered and send you on your way, but now that you've done that, you can just take yourself out of here before I do something rash."

"Sod yourself," she said, sneering.

"What a riposte. Now get out."

She walked heavily through the study door, casting murderous glances at me over her shoulder, and I followed her down the hall to see that she exited the front door.

She paused on the step and looked back at me. She was shaking with rage. "You'll regret this."

"I don't, and I won't," I said, locking the door in her face.

I knew I'd made an enemy. So had she.

5

It's all well and good for Dizzy and Superintendent Stoke to sit in their offices, creating elaborate schemes to achieve their objectives, and moving agents and chief inspectors and ministers and other such creatures about like so many pawns on a chessboard. I reckon it amuses them to imagine themselves in control of the board. It would do them both a world of good to come to Lotus House sometime and see how difficult it is to actually execute their plans. All this is by way of saying that over the preceding weeks, Martine had developed the characteristics of a brick wall. The girl had stymied me at every turn when I tried to ingratiate myself with her. Oh, she was pleasant enough; she was clean and sober and good with the customers. In any other circumstances, I would jolly well have been thrilled to have her on the staff. But since my brief was to use her as an introduction to the Dark Legion, I needed more than just a model slut.

I was also hamstrung by the fact that within my own establishment and on the street, I had a reputation for cultivating a certain class of customer: politicians on the rise, sons of peers who would someday succeed their fathers and grace Lotus

House with their titles, military officers who garnered attention in dispatches from the far-flung posts of Britain's empire. Having worked hard to establish this clientele, I'd appear dashed odd if I began to advocate killing the very same fellows I'd been at pains to lure to my brothel. My whores would be confused, and my competitors would swarm like a school of piranhas, picking off the choicest customers with tales of my radical views.

Between my inability to penetrate Martine's air of polite reserve and my reluctance to become a frothing revolutionary overnight, I was making little headway with my assignment. Oh, I certainly tried, dropping barbed comments into conversations with Martine about the shameful exploitation of us poor whores by the propertied few and indicating my general desire to see the class system abolished in Britain, but she just looked at me solemnly with those soft brown eyes and nodded thoughtfully, never offering so much as a hint of her own political views. I questioned her about her background and made noises about the bravery of the Communards in establishing their own government in Paris and wasn't it a damned shame they had been turfed out and were now being hunted down all over Europe? This at least generated a spark in her eyes, but she still didn't rise to the bait. Without some cooperation on her part, I was beginning to feel a bit desperate. I even worried that I was laying it on a bit thick, and I needed to scale back my attempts to portray myself as a friend of the working class or I was bound to rouse her suspicions.

You'd think Superintendent Stoke would understand that establishing relations with Martine without ruining my business would take a bit of time and ingenuity, but barely a week had passed since Martine had arrived when the bloody man started sending me messages, demanding to know my progress at prying information from the girl about the Dark Legion. I dithered and stalled and sent brief notes that indicated I was proceeding slowly and would have information for him soon, but after three weeks of that the officious clot sent a rather blistering missive indicating that he needed leads and he needed them now.

I gave the matter some thought, and then summoned Vincent.

Two days later I met Martine in the hall. I nodded cordially to her and started past her, then checked my progress abruptly as though I'd just experienced a revelation.

"I say, Martine. Have you a minute to spare?"

"Of course," she said demurely.

"Come down to the study with me."

She followed me obediently and when we arrived, I shut the door and locked it behind her. She looked startled for a moment, but I gave her a reassuring smile and went to my desk. I made a great show of unlocking the top drawer and fishing out a few sheets of foolscap and casting dubious glances at her all the while, as though I was debating whether to show them to her or put them back in the drawer for safekeeping. She watched me silently, though I thought I detected curiosity in her gaze.

I shuffled the papers and pursed my lips, giving a great impression of someone having a dreadful time making a decision. Then I took a deep breath and expelled it loudly, looking directly at Martine.

"Can I trust you, Martine?"

"Certainly, mademoiselle. You have treated me very well."

"Excellent. Your demeanor and behavior have impressed me since the day I hired you. Consequently, I have decided to ask your assistance in dealing with a small matter."

"But of course. I shall do anything for you."

I hesitated momentarily (I might consider a second career on the stage) and then reluctantly handed over the papers to the girl.

"What is this?" she asked.

"These documents came into my possession a few days ago."

"But how—"

I interrupted her. "It is not necessary that you know how I came to possess them. I want only to know if you can make use of them."

"Make use of them? But what are these papers?"

"It appears to be a confidential memorandum from some bloke at Scotland Yard to his superiors, discussing his plans for the penetration of various anarchist cells."

She lifted her eyes to meet mine, chewed the inside of her lower lip and then thrust the papers back at me. "I don't understand why you are showing me these papers. I know nothing of any anarchist, what do you call them, cells."

I ignored the outstretched papers. "Look here, Martine. I know you've been living amongst those Communards in Seven Dials. I read the newspapers. I know the entire area is overrun with radicals. I'll be hanged if you don't know a few of those chaps."

She looked at me warily. I didn't blame her for not trusting me. Why should she? This girl had learned the hard lessons well. I'd have to be patient with her, which was bloody inconvenient. Especially with Superintendent Stoke breathing down my neck.

I took the document from her outstretched hand and placed it on my desk. "I'd have thought," I said slowly, "that among your acquaintances there might be someone who would like to know about the Yard's plans."

"Why should you want to give these plans to people who want to bring down your government?"

I feigned surprise. "My dear girl, this government is not mine. It belongs to the rich and the powerful. To the aristocracy and to the men who visit this brothel. Do they care what you or I think or want or need? Do they spare a thought for the starving children while they enjoy their champagne? Certainly not. We're invisible to them. I'll take their money, but don't think I like the buggers. Why, I don't give a tinker's damn for the whole pack of them. If a few brave men and women are willing to eradicate some of these useless predators, then I'd be pleased to offer them what assistance I can. Right now, that assistance takes the form of this document."

I'd worked myself up over the inequities of this world, and I was afraid I might have been a touch histrionic, but Martine proved susceptible to a bit of passion, as the French are prone to be. She held out her hand. I placed the papers into it.

"I have a friend who may be interested," she said. "I shall take the memorandum to him."

I nodded, looking very dignified and grave, as though we'd sealed a bargain of some sort, which, in a way, I suppose we had.

"If I leave now, I should be back in time for the customers this evening."

"See to it," I said, reverting to the role of madam and business owner. Well, it wouldn't do for Martine to think she could take liberties just because we had become co-conspirators.

A few minutes later I heard the front door close and stepped to my window. Drawing back the curtain, I watched Martine stride purposefully away through a thin drizzle that coated the pavement with a nasty glaze. A moment passed, and then a disreputable youngster padded after her, dodging among the pedestrians who recoiled in horror at the smell as he passed, which is quite an accomplishment considering that this is London. Vincent was on the case.

Of course it wasn't a real memorandum I had given to Martine. I'd drafted it up one night in my study, firing my imagination with a tumbler of brandy and a review of the background material Superintendent Stoke had provided me about the Dark Legion. You can be sure I did not disclose any plans to infiltrate anarchist cells by hiring young bints and masquerading as a radical madam. I included some rather anodyne prescriptions for chatting up mysterious foreigners in pubs known to be frequented by revolutionaries, following newly arrived immigrants from Russia, Germany and Italy, and attending public meetings of antigovernment organizations. Useless drivel, of course, but it wasn't intended to be an accurate representation of Superintendent Stoke's plans regarding counterintelligence in the anarchist community. All I needed was a plausible-sounding report to convince some paranoid types that Old Bill was paying close attention to their activities. Vincent had twigged immediately to my plan, and unsurprisingly had a chum who could make flash notes so pukka you couldn't tell them from real bank notes. Faking a memorandum from Scotland Yard would be easy compared to that, especially when I supplied a specimen of the real thing from the pile of paper Superintendent Stoke had provided to me. The price seemed reasonable (although I was sure Vincent was pocketing a percentage), and I reckoned I could fiddle the account of expenses I'd deliver to the prime minister so that no one would be the wiser. I did not trouble myself about the number of falsified documents that would probably flood the city, allegedly issued by Superintendent Stoke. They'd probably run the gamut from orders to discharge a rum cove from gaol to warrants for the seizure of vast quantities of gin. I hoped

Vincent made a fair sum from such proceedings, as it is unlikely he'll ever turn his hand to gainful employment.

I'll say this about Martine: for a whore, she was jolly dependable. She returned to Lotus House just at teatime and put her head around the door of my study.

"My friends were pleased to receive the document you sent," she said.

I looked up nonchalantly from my French novel, which I'd picked up as soon as I'd heard the front door open. "Were they? I'm so glad. I hope they find it useful."

"I'm sure they will." And damned if Martine didn't give me a genuine smile, the first I'd seen from her since she'd taken up residence in my brothel.

"Perhaps we may provide your friends additional information from time to time," I said. "The gentlemen who frequent Lotus House are often careless and indiscreet. Now then, you'd best prepare for tonight's customers."

Martine nodded and closed the study door, and I heard her brisk footsteps on the stairs. A moment later the door opened and Vincent strolled in looking enormously pleased with himself.

"'Allo, India."

"Crack the window and take a pew," I said. "I'll have Mrs. Drinkwater bring us some tea."

"Hexcellent news. I'm near dead from 'unger."

Well, you'd have to be, wouldn't you, to eat Mrs. Drinkwater's cooking?

I rang the bell and waited until the aforementioned lady tottered into the room with a plate of cakes and the tea things rattling ominously on a tray, then bade Vincent tuck in. In between prodigious amounts of stewed tea and Mrs. Drinkwater's rock cakes (need I say that in her case they are aptly named?) he described Martine's visit to Seven Dials. Vincent does like to embellish a bit, so I had to put up with a fair amount of twaddle about Martine being suspicious and looking over her shoulder a lot and Vincent having to dart in and out of doorways, worried all the time that some foreign cutthroat might slit his gullet, but I finally wrestled the bare facts from the lad. Martine had marched straight to the Bag O' Nails, a filthy den of iniquity on New Compton Street that served copious amounts of gin to a clientele consisting of costermongers, criminals and fallen women. Naturally, Vincent felt right at home.

"She went right up to the landlord and hasked 'im a question, and 'e nodded 'is 'ead at some coves in the corner, like, and she went up to 'em and one of 'em seen 'er comin' and got up and met 'er and 'e put 'is arm around 'er and kissed 'er and they went outside together and I followed 'em down the street 'til they spied an alley and they went into hit and I tiptoed after 'em and found a snug hole to crawl into be'ind some crates and I couldn't 'ear wot all they said, but I seen 'er 'and the bloke the papers and 'e looked 'em over and put 'em in 'is pocket. Then 'e went back to the pub and she come back 'ere."

Mind you, Vincent provided this succinct description of events through a mouth full of cake and it required a strong stomach to keep my eyes on the lad.

"What did the fellow look like?" I asked.

"Ooh, 'e's a 'andsome bugger alright. Got a 'eadful of shiny brown curls and a curly brown beard to match. Martine was moonin' over 'im like a lovesick cow."

"Have you ever seen him before?"

Vincent shook his head. "Not on my patch, I 'aven't. 'E looks like a Frog to me, which I reckon would explain 'ow Martine knows 'im. You want me to find out who 'e is?"

"Yes, I think you'd better visit the Bag O' Nails again and see what you can turn up. But don't be obvious about it."

Vincent gave me the scornful look this comment deserved.

"It's not that I doubt your skill, Vincent. But Superintendent Stoke did say these anarchists are a suspicious bunch. I don't want you to get your skull bashed in nosing around the Bag O' Nails."

"Ain't you sweet," said Vincent.

"I am not sweet. I just don't want your death on my conscience." Well, I wasn't about to allow Vincent to go all soft and sticky on me. Next thing you know, he'd be labouring under the misapprehension that I cared about him.

The pup gave me a cheeky grin. "Don't you worry about me. I ain't about to let a bunch of garlic eaters get the best o' me."

"Just remember that neither the bluebottles nor the do-gooders think dynamite is a solution to the world's problems. These radicals do. They won't be throwing you into the clink or a home for wayward youths if they catch you. Be careful, Vincent."

"Aye, aye, admiral." He sketched a mock salute and finished his tea. He stuffed the remaining rock cakes in his pockets. "I'm off to the pub. Wot're you goin' to be doin' while I'm 'avin' a glass of ale and spyin' on this French feller?"

"I'm glad you asked. Before you start drinking gin with the garlic eaters, could you make a detour by Dizzy's office? I need a favor from the old boy."

After dispatching Vincent, I attended to the afternoon post. There wasn't much of it; as I've explained earlier, my list of correspondents is not extensive. It is, in fact, nonexistent. So it was that the marchioness's letter stood out a country mile, being the only one that had arrived. I stared at it for a moment, like a novice snake charmer about to open the cobra basket for the first time. I wandered around the room, tapping the letter on my open palm, staring at the elegant copperplate script on the envelope (surely not the marchioness's handwriting, who was ninety if she was a day and couldn't write a legible hand if her life depended on it) and the snuff stains around the edges (which clearly belonged to the old bag). I poured a glass of whisky, sat down at my desk and drew a deep breath.

"Oh, curse it," I muttered, and stabbed the bloody thing with my letter opener. A small square of paper floated out of the envelope and onto my blotter. I fortified myself with a drink and unfolded it gingerly.

Dear Miss Black,

I have read your letter with, frankly, a degree of astonishment. I do not recall mentioning your mother's name in the course of our many conversations. Perhaps you are mistaken? In any event, I regret that I can be of no assistance to you.

P.S. I trust you are keeping well, reading the Good Book, and have finally learned how to do hair.

Yours sincerely,
Lady Margaret Aberkill
Dowager Marchioness of Tullibardine

I read the letter again, just to be sure that the wicked biddy had signed her name to such a blatant lie. "God rot her," I said when I had finished. I'll admit that at the time my nerves were a bit frayed from catering to the marchioness's capricious demands and narrowly escaping death at the hands of a mad Scottish assassin, but I could clearly recall the marchioness's words to me on the railway platform at Perth: "Ye are yer mother's daughter," she had screeched out the window of the carriage as the train pulled away. "Ye remind me of her. She was a brave girl, too." Fair enough, the wicked woman had not actually mentioned my mother's name. But hang it all, it was evident she knew my mother. No amount of mental exhaustion or brushes with death could have caused me to misinterpret those words. The marchioness was lying. She was a cagy old harridan, but having once admitted an acquaintance with my mother, why should she now disclaim any knowledge of her? I whipped out the writing paper and pen and ink and jotted down my reply.

Dear Lady Aberkill,

Don't play the addled crone with me. You explicitly said that I reminded you of my mother, which is a difficult comparison to make unless you had known her at some time. After reading to you each night until the break of dawn, washing you down every time you sneezed and seeing that you didn't embarrass yourself in front of the Queen (at a significant cost to my own health), the least I deserve from you is an explanation of what you said at the station. Kindly reply forthwith, or I shall be on your doorstep.

Yours sincerely,
India Black

You may think that I lack tact. You would be correct. I've about as much use for tact as I have for patience, which is to say, none at all. Besides, the marchioness herself was about as tactful as a wasp. She wouldn't be lulled by sweet words into telling me what she knew. Nor, if I'm completely honest, would she be coerced by my threat to visit her in Scotland. As it was, I reckoned the only effect of the letter would be to send her into gales of derisive laughter. I had thought that we'd parted on pleasant terms and thus found her reluctance to share any information puzzling. I was not disposed, therefore, to be polite.

I was stamping around my study and muttering curses on the old pussy's head when the first customer of the evening arrived. Mrs. Drinkwater was still sober enough to open the door and escort the chap into the study.

"Mr. Brown," she announced, and lurched back down the hallway to the kitchen.

I had never seen Mr. Brown before. He was a comely young fellow with pale blue eyes, a cloud of blond curls and an amiable, if somewhat vacant, expression. He removed his hat and bowed his head. "Miss Black?"

"Mr. Brown."

"The prime minister sent me."

He looked a tad young to be Dizzy's man and did not appear to be the sharpest blade in the scabbard. However, presumably the prime minister knew what he was about, and it wasn't for me to question his choice of this young colt to perform the task I'd suggested in my message to Dizzy.

"Indeed," I said with a trace of the skepticism I felt. "Then you know what to do. I'll introduce you to the girls, and you can choose any one of them you want, so long as it's Martine. You'll recognize her immediately; she's the dark one with the French accent." I gave him a sharp glance. "Have you ever done anything like this before?"

He smiled, and I noticed a glint of mischief behind the mask of

80

affability. "What are you asking, Miss Black? Have I been with a prostitute before? Or am I skilled at the art of disinformation?"

"Both would be useful talents in this instance."

"Then put your mind at ease. My performance shall be flawless."

"What have you and Dizzy planned?" I remembered that I did possess some manners. "Please sit down. May I get you a drink? Whisky? Brandy?"

He chose whisky and soda and sipped it appreciatively.

I poured myself a glass and joined him on the sofa. "Now, then. Tell me the yarn you'll be spinning for Martine."

He swirled the liquid in his glass. "I shall be an agreeable young fop named Brown, who, by virtue of his uncle's patronage, has found a place in the Foreign Office. I don't really give a damn about politics, and I jolly well hate meeting all those strange exotic types. Dreadful manners, most of them, and smelly to boot. Why, just this week, on Wednesday, I must spend hours with the Russian legation at Moreland House, trying to hammer out some sort of arrangement about what bits of the Ottoman Empire they want when that bloody thing falls apart. I hope those anarchist chappies don't find out about the meeting. It would be like shooting fish in a barrel. They could wipe out lots of Ivan's top politicos and generals in one go, not to mention embarrassing the hell out of Her Majesty's government and putting a nasty spike in Russo-British relations."

"Very neat," I said. "But bear in mind that Martine is a bright girl and if she is involved with the radicals, she'll be on the qui vive when it comes to a fellow dropping a story like this in her lap. Just because you made an excellent Hamlet for the dramatic society doesn't mean you'll persuade her."

He gave me a reproachful look. "Come, now. The standards of my service are slightly higher than that, as I'm sure you know. Rest assured, Martine will have a great deal to report to her comrades tomorrow, and she'll be utterly convinced that she has winkled it out of a brainless young nincompoop who couldn't hold his liquor." He drained his whisky and stood up. "I suppose you'd better introduce me to the girls and start plying me with alcohol."

I escorted him to the drawing room, where I introduced Brown to the tarts. He proved an immediate hit, with his blond curls and congenial manner. I let him chunter on a bit, then while he was engaged in an exchange of ribald pleasantries with Clara Swansdown, I snagged Martine and took her to the window.

"What do you think of our guest?" I asked her.

She gave me a slantindicular look. "He seems a pleasant fellow."

"Yes, he appears to be a nice young man. Not a lot of brains rattling around in that head of his, I should say, but he does have other attributes that recommend him."

"Oh?"

I had Martine's full attention now. "What sort of attributes?" she asked.

"During my chat with him, he mentioned that he is employed at the Foreign Office. He seems a very foolish chap who likes the sound of his own voice. He might prove to be imprudent. You might learn something of interest from him. It's Agatha's turn next, but if you think you'd like to spend time with Mr. Brown, I'll work something out with her."

Martine flashed dark eyes in Brown's direction. "If you don't think Agatha will mind?"

"I'm the abbess here. If I tell Agatha not to mind, she won't." In truth, I'd have to pay Agatha what she would have earned. I totted up the expenses I was incurring and moodily followed Martine back to the circle of tarts and Dizzy's man Brown.

From a bint's perspective, he seemed a good-natured fellow whose experience encompassed the missionary position and nothing else. He was putting away the liquor at pace, growing ever more tipsy and giggling like a schoolgirl at the witty repartee of my employees. Either Brown had a hollow leg, or there was one aspidistra that would be dead from alcohol poisoning by the end of the evening. He was proving himself quite a favourite with the girls, as most of them had probably come to the conclusion that the evening's work would consist of helping the fellow stagger to a room, where he'd pass out and sleep for several hours while the bint hurried downstairs and found another gentleman in the queue. Eventually I thought that Brown had established himself, and encouraged him to choose one of the young ladies. After much dithering and flattery of all the females in the room, he finally selected Martine, with enough pretty reluctance that she left the room with a little smile of triumph on her face at landing the easiest catch of the night. I had to hand it to him, Brown was a dab hand at his job.

6

On Wednesday evening I was polishing my rapier with a glass of whisky at hand, listening to the patter of raindrops against the windows, when a newsboy went by in full cry. I leapt to my feet, flung open the door and chased him down the block. A crowd had gathered around him at the end of the street, and papers and coins were changing hands at astonishing speed.

I skidded to a halt next to the local butcher. "What's happened, Mr. Bradley? What's the newsboy going on about?" I tried unsuccessfully to wrestle the paper from the butcher's grip. He held firm, though. Confound it, I'd have to fight my way through the crowd to get my own copy.

"It's those damned anarchists again," Mr. Bradley said, breathing heavily through his whiskers. "Some bally jokers calling themselves the Dark Legion have blown up Moreland House."

"Bloody hell!" I was genuinely astonished. I had hoped Mr. Brown's story would inspire some act by Martine's group of friends, but I hadn't expected them to take on the project of demolishing one of England's most notable government buildings.

I shouldered my way through the crowd, stepping on toes and

shoving aside blokes who turned to snarl at me until they saw my face and figure and then they couldn't make way fast enough. Being a looker is a tremendous advantage in life, and it would be foolish not to use one's natural endowments at every opportunity.

I took the paper the boy thrust out at me, looked appealingly around for a gentleman willing to lend me a bit of the ready (in my excitement, I had of course exited Lotus House without a farthing to my name) and smiled graciously at the three blokes who shoved coins into my hands. I thanked the lucky winner who'd paid for my paper and scurried back to Lotus House. I didn't even stop to dry my hair but plonked down in my chair and avidly scanned the headline.

"Blow me down," I whispered and swallowed the whisky in my glass.

ANARCHIST OUTRAGE IN LONDON— EXPLOSION AT MORELAND HOUSE

Several explosions rocked Moreland House this afternoon at approximately three o'clock this afternoon, throwing Pall Mall into a state of excitement such as your correspondent has never before witnessed. There were three separate detonations, each of which sounded, according to bystanders, like a thunderous blast from a cannon. The explosions destroyed the frontage of the building facing the Mall and leveled the guardhouse at the entrance. It is fortunate that the police constable who might otherwise have occupied the guardhouse was in fact not on duty at the time. However, two carriages that were standing at the curb in front of the building were destroyed, with shards of wood and fragments of iron from them being found several blocks from the scene of the blast. A number of pedestrians in the area and occupants of adjacent properties received minor injuries from flying glass and debris. In all, fourteen persons were affected and received treatment for their injuries. Fortunately for the bystanders, the area directly in front of Moreland House had been closed to pedestrian traffic for the reasons hereinafter described.

The toll could certainly have been much larger, as members of Her Majesty's government were scheduled to meet with a legation from the Russian embassy at Moreland House today to discuss the settlement of certain outstanding issues related to the situation in the Ottoman Empire. However, several members of the Russian legation had succumbed to influenza in the last few days and it was deemed necessary to postpone the meeting until their recovery. Had the meeting taken place, several luminaries of the Foreign Office and the War Office would have been in attendance, as would have Count Peter Shuvalov, the tsar's ambassador to the Court of St. James, and several prominent officers of the Russian military forces.

Superintendent Stoke of Scotland Yard was immediately on the scene and informed your correspondent that the Yard had received a message moments after the explosions from a heretofore unknown group of anarchists. Superintendent Stoke reported that the message was brief, consisting only of the words "Death to all tyrants," and signed "The Dark Legion" in an unknown hand. Readers will recall that previous acts of violence against certain peers of the realm have been attributed to other radical groups, such as the Black Flag, but the destruction of Moreland House is the first evidence of the existence of the Dark Legion. Superintendent Stoke vowed to apprehend and punish the members of this group for their perpetration of this cowardly act. This paper encourages the police to act swiftly, as the failure to capture these dastardly anarchists can only increase public concern and trepidation. When innocent men and women must walk the streets of London in fear, the Home Office and Scotland Yard must spare no effort or expense to halt this series of alarming events. The failure to eradicate these craven creatures who callously attack our people and our institutions is an ominous sign. Perhaps it is time to consider a change of leadership at the highest levels of the institutions in which we have hitherto entrusted our lives and safety.

I had barely had time to digest the story when a messenger arrived with a rather peremptory note from Superintendent Stoke, summoning me to a meeting at Dizzy's suite, posthaste. I trundled over in leisurely fashion and found the prime minister engrossed in the evening papers and the man from the Yard pacing the carpet.

Dizzy peered over the top of his paper at me. "Well, well, India. I must give you credit for drawing the Dark Legion out into the light of day."

Superintendent Stoke did not join in this faint praise. He sucked the ends of his moustache and looked sour. To give the chap his due, some esteemed members of the press had suggested, in their usual subtle fashion, that the job of hunting down anarchists might be too much for the old boy and he should retire to a seaside bungalow. I suppose my feathers would have been ruffled too, had I been in his shoes.

He blew the tips of his moustache from his mouth. "Oh, yes, the Dark Legion has emerged from the shadows. Unclear to me, however, that the demolition of Moreland House was necessary to confirm what we already know: Martine connected to the organization, and the Dark Legion is bloody dangerous. Cost of the operation was exorbitant. Home Secretary none too pleased with the whole affair." He cleared his throat and glanced at the prime minister. "Questioned the wisdom of the plan and the efficacy of your agent." He cut his eyes at me, just to be sure that I knew to whom he was referring.

As you might expect, I did not allow a little sarcasm to dent my confidence. I might have hatched the plan to plant information about a spurious meeting between the Russians and the British with Martine, but of course I'd had the assistance of Dizzy in providing "Mr. Brown from the Foreign Office," and that of the superintendent himself in securing the perimeter of Moreland

House. His function had been to ensure that no one (least of all an anarchist with not one, but three, bombs) penetrated the area around the building. It was difficult to envision how someone with enough dynamite to demolish half the structure had slipped past the contingent of plainclothes officers guarding the place. I pointed out this fact to Superintendent Stoke.

His moustache fluttered wetly. "Had the place surrounded. Don't know how those bloody foreigners got through. Damned elusive fellows."

Dizzy sought to pour oil on troubled waters. "Your men had successfully cleared the area and Moreland House was empty, Superintendent. Let us be glad that only property was damaged, and that there were no fatalities. And the fourteen people who were hurt? Have they recovered from their wounds?"

"Weren't any wounds," said the Superintendent. "Fabricated that for the benefit of those impudent fellows in the press. Let the Dark Legion think they accomplished something with their bombs."

"Very clever of you to provide some sham injuries, Superintendent," I said. "Perhaps that will distract the Dark Legion from noticing that the guardhouse was empty, the street closed to pedestrians and the meeting with the Russians cancelled. The whole project practically screams 'We knew you were coming' to any anarchist blessed with even a farthing's worth of intelligence. I fear that in your zeal to ensure that Moreland House was deserted and the area safe, you may have compromised my position. Martine and her cohorts may suspect that with my connivance, Martine has delivered tainted intelligence to the group and that the members narrowly avoided being entrapped by the police. You may have placed me in some considerable danger."

The only sounds in the room were the faint rustle of Dizzy's collar as his head revolved in search of an escape route, and a moist, sucking sound from the superintendent as he nibbled his moustache. After a lengthy chew and a think, he spat out the ends of his soup strainer.

"Can't very well kill a dozen Londoners just to make your story square."

"I agree that would have been an extravagance. But perhaps you could have planted a few dead bodies around the area. Surely you had some spare corpses in the morgues you could have pressed into service. In fact, you needn't have gone to even that much trouble. Why not just create a poor widowed policeman, a year from retirement, with seven children, whose bad luck it was to draw guard duty today?"

The superintendent sniffed audibly. "Can't let these anarchists appear too successful. Cause a panic, it would. Then where would we be?"

Dizzy was growing restless, no doubt because he'd been excluded from the exchange between the superintendent and me. "It is a delicate balance we must strike," he murmured, staring at us over steepled fingers. "Any intelligence the anarchists glean through Miss Black must be considered by them to be both accurate and credible. Concurrently, Superintendent Stoke and I must consider the public welfare and avoid endangering innocent people."

"And how do we accomplish those two mutually exclusive goals?" I asked.

"If Mr. French were here," mused Superintendent Stoke, "he'd undoubtedly formulate a plan that would achieve our objectives."

I gave that notion the attention it deserved, which is to say, none at all.

"As he's not here, you shall have to rely upon me," I said,

with a serene smile at the superintendent.

"May we count on you, Miss Black?" The old duffer must be taking fire from the press and his superiors at the Home Office; his tone was a trifle plaintive.

"Of course." I stood briskly and put on my gloves. "No more messing about with fake documents or fake Foreign Office chaps. It is time for me to join the Dark Legion."

Upon my return to Lotus House I wasted no time in summoning Martine to my study. She entered with her usual gravity and poise, but there was a flush on her olive cheeks, and her brown eyes blazed. I didn't think it was gin that had given her such a celebratory air.

"You asked to see me?"

I picked up the newspaper I had purchased that afternoon. "Have you heard the news? About the destruction of Moreland House?"

"I have. Such a tragedy," she said, but her words were belied by the twitch of her lips.

"The tragedy," I said, "is that the whole affair was a shambles. Not a single politician or general killed."

Martine stiffened.

"I assume that the information about the meeting between the government and the Russians came from Mr. Brown?"

She nodded briefly.

"And that you passed along this news to your friends?"

She bit her lip. "Yes."

"And that this"—I waved the paper at her—"is their handiwork?"

"It is." She was on the defensive now.

"What a waste of bloody intelligence," I said.

"The Dark Legion struck," Martine said coldly. "But for

some unfortunate circumstances, many would have died."

"But they didn't, did they? A perfect opportunity, gone to waste. The Dark Legion, eh? Is that what you call yourselves?"

"It is the name we have chosen."

I regarded her coolly. "Do you know why I hired you, Martine?"

"Mr. Birkett-Jones—"

"Birkett-Jones be damned," I said. "I'll accommodate a customer from time to time, but only if it's in my interest to do so. *I* decided to take you on because I thought you might prove useful to me. You know my feelings about the buffoons who run this country. I brought you to Lotus House because I thought you might have some contacts among the radicals who could make good use of the morsels of information that fall into my lap from time to time."

She squared her shoulders. Her eyes were luminous with passion. "And we have done so. We have acted upon the knowledge I gained from Mr. Brown."

"Well, you've made a hash of the whole business."

"It wasn't our fault the meeting was postponed. It's almost as if—"

"It was bloody bad luck," I cut her off. I didn't want Martine to devote much time to speculating about the reason Moreland House had been deserted when the bombs exploded.

"Tell me something, Martine. Do you trust your comrades in the, what is it, the Dark League?"

"The Dark Legion," she corrected me. "Yes, I do. They are all committed to the cause. And despite our failure at Moreland House, we will continue our work until the rich and powerful are cut down."

"Your enthusiasm is splendid, my dear. But zeal is not enough.

You must be effective. If the Dark Legion cannot deliver the goods, I don't see why I should continue to hand you the scraps of intelligence I gather here at Lotus House. You would agree, wouldn't you, that your employment here has been of benefit to your anarchist friends?"

"Certainly," said Martine.

"Well, perhaps I'm being too harsh," I said, tilting my head and giving her a forgiving smile.

She let out a breath and smiled tentatively back at me.

"After all, your brothers in arms clearly know how to construct a bomb. Three of them, in fact."

"We have an excellent bomb maker," she said as if she were recommending the family dressmaker.

"I should like to meet him," I said.

Martine's hand flew to her mouth. "Oh, no. I do not think that would be possible."

"Why not? It seems to me that if you are to rely upon me to supply information to your friends, and I am relying upon them to use it wisely, then we all have to trust each other. To put it bluntly, I wish to meet your companions so that I may evaluate whether the Dark Legion is suited to carry out the kinds of activities I have in mind, utilizing the information I provide."

She gnawed her lip and then one of her fingernails. "There might be difficulties," she said eventually. "Our members are cautious."

"As am I. It's difficult enough to keep the police out of my business. I certainly don't need to get involved with amateur anarchists who might lead the Yard directly to my door."

We stared at one another for a time, with her mulling over my suggestion and me wishing she'd make up her mind so that I could attend my first meeting of the Dark Legion.

She gave a Gallic shrug. "Your concern is valid. I will arrange a meeting."

"I shall look forward to it. You may return to your duties now."

She paused at the door and looked back at me. "I would not take this risk for just anyone, you understand. You have been a good friend to me."

Gad, I hoped she wasn't becoming sentimental. That could make things deuced awkward when I handed her over to the police.

The anarchist brigade didn't muck about. The next afternoon, I followed Martine through the door of the Bag O' Nails, that same drinking establishment visited by Martine and Vincent a few days ago. I entered with some reluctance, not because I was afraid of radical foreigners but because the place could have used a good cleaning. I could see why Vincent had been comfortable here; the level of filth met even his exacting standards. My boots made sucking sounds as Martine and I crossed the floor. I judged that the tables had last been wiped about the time our present queen had ascended to the throne. The scent was invigorating: equal parts stale beer, stale vomit and stale sweat, with just a hint of herring. I walked gingerly, tucking in my skirts to avoid touching anything.

Martine made directly for a table in one of the far corners, where a couple of coves were arguing vociferously. One sported a head of wavy dark curls and a beard to match—obviously the bloke Vincent had observed with Martine. The other fellow was a short, fidgety chap with restless eyes and tangled black hair. He was yammering relentlessly in the bearded one's ear. I didn't imagine the expression of relief on the latter's face when he caught sight of Martine. He put a restraining hand on his companion's arm, who looked annoyed at the interruption of his sermon and looked round for the reason. Spying Martine, he jumped to his feet and rushed to meet us. He caught Martine's hands in his and leaned forward for a kiss, but she executed a deft maneuver that left him staring after her with his lips still pursed.

"Julian," she gushed at the bearded fellow, looking up at him with adoration. I can't say that I blamed her for doing so.

Vincent had said the man with the beard was handsome, but he'd neglected to describe him as the veritable Adonis that he was. On closer inspection, his hair and beard were a deep, rich chestnut, which shone brightly even in the sulphurous gloom of the Bag O' Nails. He had a manly jaw, a resolute chin and sapphire eyes. He would have looked at home on the parade ground in an officer's uniform, save for the slightly undomesticated look about the eyes, which in my opinion merely added to his allure, having as I do a fondness for men who are not entirely civilized. He was indubitably the fairest fellow I'd seen in some time, and it took all my strength to stop staring at his features long enough to attend to Martine's introduction.

"Miss India Black," she said, and then, glowing with pride, she indicated the handsome fellow. "This is Monsieur Julian Bonnaire."

I uttered something infantile while Bonnaire bent over my hand.

"Charmed," he purred, and held my hand for a moment longer than necessary, gazing into my eyes.

He was remarkably clean for an anarchist, and his manners were impeccable. I reminded myself sternly that it was my cardinal rule never to mix business with pleasure, but I confess I contemplated briefly the consequences of disregarding said rule. Since I'd devised the rule in the first place, I considered it mine to amend as circumstances change. It wouldn't do to share my thoughts with Martine, however, for it was clear she'd marked Bonnaire as her own.

"And this," said Martine with a trace of disgust in her voice, "is Flerko."

I looked down at him. The poor blighter wasn't much taller than Vincent. Flerko's beak was prominent, his lips thin and blue. He seethed with suppressed energy.

Flerko quivered to attention. "I am Russian," he announced.

"Delightful for you," I murmured.

"I sell fish." That accounted, at least in part, for the aroma of herring I had detected in the Bag O' Nails.

"I have been persecuted in my homeland."

I seemed destined to hear the History of Flerko in staccato bursts, but Bonnaire intervened.

"Please sit down, Miss Black. Would you like a drink?"

I considered the options. The ale in Flerko's glass was murky. I fancied the whisky had been brewed last night and the gin would be the infamous "blue ruin," which was useful if you were stripping wallpaper but should be avoided otherwise.

"Nothing for me, thank you, Mr. Bonnaire."

"I was driven from Russia," Flerko hissed.

Bonnaire and Martine ignored this assertion. As this seemed to be the prevailing custom, I followed suit.

"Thank you for agreeing to meet with me, Mr. Bonnaire."

"It is my pleasure. Martine speaks well of you, and I am assured by her that you share our views."

"Indeed, I do. Otherwise, I should not have employed Martine and provided her with such scraps of information as I have been able to acquire."

"You seem uniquely situated to continue to do so."

"I am."

Bonnaire drew a thin cheroot from his pocket. "We are

always interested in the affairs of our esteemed leaders."

Flerko produced a match and scraped it across the table with such vigor that it snapped. "Esteemed leaders! Pah! Tell us where to find the bastards and we'll kill them like dogs in the street."

Clearly, Flerko was an enthusiast. I don't much care for enthusiasts, as they tend to drag you into the barrel just as it's going over the falls. Steer clear of this one, India, I thought to myself.

Flerko, however, had other ideas. He lit a foul-smelling pipe and scooted his chair closer to mine. "In London, I sell fish. In Russia, I am an intellectual, a poet and a novelist of no small repute."

I edged away from him, which incidentally placed me closer to Bonnaire. Martine took note and her lips tightened. The Frenchman paid her no heed but inclined his head in my direction, with an indulgent glance at Flerko.

"You mustn't mind our friend here," said Bonnaire. "He's been treated roughly by the Third Section."

Stoke's briefing had been thorough; I recognized the name of the tsar's secret police.

"My ideas were too progressive for Russia," Flerko said sadly. "I advocated democratic elections and confiscation of land from the aristocracy to be distributed to the peasants."

"Those ideas are too progressive for England," I said.

Flerko's eyes blazed. "So I have learned. I came to London so that I might express myself freely, and I find the nobility here just as reactionary as in Russia. For many years I deceived myself, believing that the privileged classes could be persuaded to share their wealth with the workers who had created it for them."

It's a deuced good thing Flerko had passion, as he was clearly deficient in the common sense department.

"I have realized that we must take drastic measures to affect such a change." A bubble of froth flecked the corner of Flerko's mouth. "We must remove those who claim the right to rule their fellow men. We must slay the rich and destroy the government."

Martine glanced nervously around the room. "Careful, Flerko. There are ears everywhere."

Flerko wiped away the spit from his mouth with the back of his hand and glared ferociously at her. "Let the police try to take me. I will kill them all."

Enthusiasts are not only dangerous, they're tedious. I hadn't come here to listen to a deranged poet advocate wholesale slaughter. I had to check the urge to ask the time and send Bonnaire to find a cab. The Frenchman must have sensed my total disinterest in Flerko's fulminations, for he smiled gently and patted Flerko's arm.

"You must understand the trials our comrade has endured. He suffered much at the hands of the tsar's agents. He is a man of culture and taste, yet he is forced to degrade himself by flogging fish just to earn a place in a doss house each night. His anger fuels a great commitment to our cause."

"I can see that," I said. "He must have been very disappointed to learn that the meeting at Moreland House had been canceled."

A frown creased Bonnaire's face. "We had hoped to eliminate many important men. It is unfortunate that the meeting did not take place."

I kept a close eye on the bugger to see if that "unfortunate" coincidence had aroused any suspicion, but he merely took a moody sip of gin and contemplated the pitted surface of the table.

It might be useful to remind Bonnaire that Martine's intelligence had been valuable to the group. "It is regrettable that the Russian delegation was struck down by influenza," I said, "but quite encouraging that the general information Mr. Brown shared with Martine was accurate. The newspaper reports confirm the meeting had been scheduled. Perhaps we should concentrate on cultivating the loquacious Mr. Brown. He should have other news to share, and he seemed quite satisfied with Martine."

Martine shot me a warning glance. I could see she wasn't best pleased that I'd reminded Bonnaire of just how Martine had come by the information about the meeting at Moreland House.

Bonnaire raked a hand through his chestnut curls. "Indeed. I would be most interested in anything Mr. Brown has to tell us. He seems a singularly garrulous young man."

"There are quite a few of his type in the government. And as long as the primary qualification for obtaining a ministerial position is whether you attended the right school, there always will be. I fancy that I have become an expert at ingratiating myself with the Mr. Browns of this world."

Bonnaire settled in his chair and lifted his glass, studying me over the rim. "So Martine has told us. She also advises that you are prepared, indeed, have been seeking a means by which to provide the fruits of your labours to people who are willing to act upon the information you obtain from these Mr. Browns."

"I trust Martine has also told you that if I am to continue to supply reports to such people, I should like to meet them to assure myself that they are, shall we say, capable people."

There was a glint of displeasure in Bonnaire's eye, and I could see I'd annoyed him. That was the point, naturally. Most people are easily played. Infer that they're not good enough for you for whatever purpose, and they'll bend over backward to convince you that they are. I was pleased to see that anarchists are just like other people, really, except for that nihilistic death wish so many of them seem to have.

True to form, Bonnaire assumed the expression of a brush

salesman and leaned forward with his elbows on the table.

"I can assure you, the members of my organization are more than capable, Miss Black. As you mentioned the newspapers, you will no doubt acknowledge that our bombs caused significant damage to the building. Had anyone been inside, they would surely have perished. We are professionals, Miss Black. Provided we have precise intelligence about our target, we can eliminate it."

I favored him with one of my most winning smiles. "Forgive me if I appear to doubt you, Mr. Bonnaire. Before I purchase a wine for Lotus House, I taste it. If I buy a bolt of silk, I examine it. It's a habit I've acquired over the years. In the cases I just described, I was concerned only with saving my money, but in providing information to you and your organization, I run the risk of becoming involved with the police. Surprisingly, they are more tolerant of trollops than of anarchists."

Bonnaire chuckled. "That is true of most policemen, whether in Paris or Moscow or here in London."

"You understand, then, why I wish to meet everyone."

He cocked his head. "Oh, yes. However, I am not entirely certain why you want to help us at all."

It was time for my best imitation of a closet radical. That meant manufacturing a fiery gleam in my eye and a quivering intensity in my voice. I launched into the story of my life upon the streets, with a lot of sob-inducing tales that would have reduced the average Christian to tears. I described the swells who preyed on young girls, and the degradations I'd endured just to earn the cost of a bun, and my growing realization that I was a victim of a tyrannical system dominated by the rich and powerful. My yarn was convincing for I was telling the truth, but at that point I had to diverge from the factual and fabricate a chapter or two about my growing sympathies for my fellow human beings and my desire to create a Utopia with these hapless creatures, where we'd all work together and share the proceeds of our labours (which made me sound a bit like that old crank, Sir Thomas More, and look what happened to him). This last bit was hard going, and I nearly choked as I said it, for of course my natural inclination is to shove my fellow man overboard in order to grab the last place in the lifeboat. Luckily, Bonnaire, Flerko and Martine seemed to think I had been overcome with the passion of my convictions rather than gagging at the thought of sharing my hard-earned cash with the ragged chaps here at the Bag O' Nails.

I finished off this load of codswallop with some well-aimed darts at the bloody toffs who ran our society like their private fiefdoms and expressed the view that as Darwin's theory of natural selection had failed to make much headway among the aristocracy, it was time someone stepped in and helped out Mother Nature. At this point Flerko seized my hand and began spouting some Russian nonsense and covering my poor paw in kisses. I managed to extricate it from the Russian's grasp (not without difficultly, for though Flerko was a weedy chap, he was strong). The odour of herrings wafted up to my nostrils, and I reckoned the neighborhood cats would be trailing me back to Lotus House.

Bonnaire looked amused at Flerko's antics, but then his smiled faded and his expression became grave. "Your history is a sad one, Miss Black, but I am pleased that you have overcome the misfortune of your youth and are now willing to join in our struggle."

Gad, I hoped he wasn't going to ask for money. I hadn't considered that in anarchist eyes, a successful madam might be good for a few crowns.

"I will do my best to obtain confidential information for you from my clients," I hastened to say. "That should enable your group to eliminate some of the oppressors of the people." I was seized with a fit of coughing. I was going to have to practice spewing such rubbish until it sounded natural.

Flerko lunged for my hand again with a fervid exclamation, but I'd seen him coming out of the corner of my eye and managed to get my mitts in my lap before the fellow could lay hands on me.

"Comrade Flerko seems convinced of your commitment," said Bonnaire, stroking his beard. I held my breath, waiting for his verdict. Martine stared at him anxiously. After a long moment, those bright blue orbs of his settled on my face and he smiled. It was a smile of acceptance. I exhaled slowly.

"Tonight at midnight," Bonnaire said, rising. "Meet me here and I will you show you the way."

7

If there was one thing worse than entering Seven Dials during the daylight hours, it was venturing into that vile den as the city's clocks were striking midnight. The driver of the cab I'd hired was as nervous as a bitch whelping her first litter. I didn't blame the man; I sat with my hand in my purse, clutching the Bulldog and wondering if I'd make it to the Bag O' Nails in the pristine condition in which I'd left Lotus House. The rain that had blanketed the city for days had ceased, but one of the city's mucilaginous fogs had descended on the streets, covering every surface with oily drops of water and obliterating the already inadequate light from the gas lamps. It was as dark as the inside of a coffin tonight, but the streets throbbed with noise. Most of the inhabitants of the area appeared to have foregone the domestic comforts of hearth and home (likely because such things were nonexistent here) and were roaming the streets in various stages of drunkenness. A low roar issued from every public house we passed, and the street rang with the raucous cries of street vendors, ladies of the evening and their customers. Ragged children roamed in gangs, eyes glazed from the gin they'd been tippling, swarming around the hapless drunks who crossed their paths and plundering the pitiful sods' pockets with abandon. Even the poor nag pulling our cab was apprehensive, his ears pricked and his head swiveling at every shriek and wail. All the noise was playing hell with my nerves as well, and I nearly screamed when a dirty face appeared in the window of the cab bawling incomprehensible gibberish at me. I yanked the Bulldog from my purse and thrust the barrel into the man's nostril. He disappeared from view.

The cab drew up with a jerk, and I peered out the window.

"Where are we?" I asked the driver.

"Bag O'Nails," he replied, and pointed into the viscid fog with his whip.

Dimly I perceived a faint amber light through the swirling brume and detected the drone of well-lubricated voices.

"Are you sure this is the place?" asked the driver. The door crashed open and a cone of light split the fog briefly; the drone increased to a low rumble.

"As much as it pains me to admit it, I believe we have arrived," I said. I handed the driver some coins and made a reluctant exit from the relative safety of the cab. He didn't bother counting the money but shoved it into the pocket of his coat, slapped the reins against the horse's rump and cried, "Hi, get up there, Bill." Bill stepped out with alacrity, and in a moment I was alone.

Then the wolf pack moved in. I saw a half dozen lean faces, eyes glistening with a predatory gleam as shadowy figures closed around me in a circle. A dirty claw reached out and plucked at my cloak.

"Oi, look at that. That'll fetch a good price."

"Forget the cloak, you stupid clot. Look at 'er!"

I'm not usually one to forego compliments, but I thought

it likely there might be complications if I accepted this one without demurring. I extracted the Bulldog from my purse and cocked the hammer. The noise was uncommonly loud in that thick atmosphere, and the feral lads who had been advancing checked their movements.

"Now, chaps, who'd like to be the first to get a bullet in the chest? Come on, don't be shy."

"She's got a barker," said the chap nearest me.

"Well, take hit away from 'er," one helpful fellow suggested. "Wot are you worried about? She'll prob'bly cry if she pulls the trigger."

"Wot if she shoots me?"

"Ah, go on. She ain't gonna shoot you." There's one in every crowd, always standing at the back, mind you.

I've mentioned before that I lack patience. I had a meeting to attend and an anarchist plot to uncover and I couldn't stand around here all night palavering with the Seven Dials Debating Society. I pointed the Bulldog skyward and pulled the trigger. The revolver roared.

I surveyed the results and was gratified.

The coves who had encircled me had disappeared into the gloom. The Bag O' Nails had gone as quiet as a Carthusian charterhouse. I replaced the Bulldog in my purse, lifted my skirts to avoid the worst of the mud and walked inside.

My entrance attracted roughly the same amount of attention that a bucket of chum would have provoked from a school of piranhas. I suppose there are women who would have been gratified at the shouts, whistles and graphic gestures that met my arrival, but I just fixed the pub's patrons with that gimlet glare of mine and stalked across the room to the table in the corner, where Flerko and Bonnaire were enjoying a convivial glass together. I wasn't sure my welcome would be at all warm, for I could hardly have done more to draw attention to myself short of spontaneously combusting, but Flerko bounded up like an untrained gun dog to greet me, and Bonnaire bestowed an utterly ravishing smile upon me. I petted Flerko briskly (actually, I shook his hand) and let Bonnaire plant a moist and lingering kiss on my knuckles. 'Twas a pity the bloke's political views were so dicey; I would have enjoyed a dalliance with this handsome Frog dandy.

"I heard a shot," said Flerko anxiously.

"Yes," I murmured. "I heard it, too."

"It sounded very close. Did you see anything?"

"I could hardly find my way from the cab to the door," I said. "The fog is terrible tonight." I saw no need to inform my companions that I had fired the shot, nor indeed even that I was armed. Bringing a revolver to one's first meeting with a group of paranoid radicals would hardly make a good first impression.

"A London particular," said Bonnaire. "What a quaint name for fog. I do not think of the English as being a quaint people."

"We English are pragmatic, but underneath, I am sorry to say, there is a streak of whimsy."

"There is no whimsy in Russia," said Flerko. "Only sorrow. So long as the tsar rules, there will be only suffering and pain for my people."

He looked so downcast that I tried to cheer up the little fellow. "Well, we shall just have to strike a blow for liberty in London."

Flerko nodded and knuckled away a tear.

Bonnaire looked at me and shrugged. "He is often like this. He is homesick for Russia."

Flerko pulled out a thin gray wisp of linen and blew his nose vigorously. "Do not mind me. I am better now."

Bonnaire reached into his vest and extracted a cheaply made watch. "We should be going."

Flerko brightened, presumably at the thought of planning the death of some aristocrats. Bonnaire took my arm and guided me through the crowd, with the Russian bringing up the rear. I endured another round of suggestions and comments that would have sent our dear Queen Vicky into an apoplectic fit but which fazed me not one whit, having heard them all (or worse) before. We escaped from the fug of the bar into the street (which, to tell the truth, didn't smell any better), and Bonnaire steered me along with his hand under my elbow. I was grateful for the guidance, for I'd have been lost immediately. Bonnaire seemed quite at home in these squalid streets and completely unfazed by the thick fog, traveling at a rapid pace that left me clutching his arm and struggling to stay abreast. Flerko trailed along behind us, stepping on my skirt and muttering in Russian, while he kept an anxious eye to the rear to be sure we were not being followed.

Until that moment I confess that my assignment had seemed a bit of a lark, really. I'd matched wits with Martine and persuaded Bonnaire and Flerko of my bona fides without a great deal of effort. True, there had been that sordid brawl with Mother Edding, the nagging notes from Superintendent Stoke and the visits to the insalubrious environs of Seven Dials, but on the whole the entire affair had not been unpleasant. Martine seemed a nice girl, save for a streak of the revolutionary in her. Bonnaire was a charming fellow. Flerko was a comic character; it was hard work imagining the fizzy little chap handling a bomb without it exploding in his hand. But that trip through the dismal streets and disgusting alleyways of this wretched part of London marked the moment I began to realize that this was not a pleasant diversion from the drudgery of running Lotus House.

It was Flerko who first set me on edge. His nervous energy had increased tenfold since we had left the Bag O' Nails. He was right on my heels, breathing raggedly and darting glances into every alley and doorway we passed. The heels of his boots beat an anxious tattoo on the cobblestones. His trepidation communicated itself to Bonnaire, for as we walked he tightened his grip on my arm and increased his pace until my toes were barely touching the ground.

"Not far now," the Frenchman said in a low voice. "Flerko?"

Flerko melted into the churning mist. Bonnaire pushed me gently to the right, and we made an abrupt turn into a narrow passage, flanked on both sides by tall tenements of bricks blackened by decades of soot and smoke. Feeble light filtered through smudged windows, making the fine mist glow wanly. Bonnaire halted, loosening the grip on my arm.

"We'll wait here for Flerko," he said. I noticed that his other hand was secreted in his pocket, where, I had no doubt, there was a weapon of some kind.

"Let's move out of the light." Bonnaire drew me into a foul-smelling doorway. The affable appearance he'd displayed previously had disappeared. He was wary now, his body taut with tension. He conned the passage slowly, first in one direction, then in the other. My skin prickled, and I found it difficult to catch my breath, a condition due, no doubt, to Bonnaire dragging me along at such a swift pace.

"Is there really a chance we've been followed?" I whispered.

"One can never be too careful," Bonnaire said, pleasantly close to my ear. "The security services of many countries are active in London. And the English police have become very busy lately, trying to find and disrupt our meetings."

Did I imagine that his fingers momentarily tightened around my arm? I took a deep breath and admonished myself to remain calm. All this bobbing and weaving might be nothing more than a shot across the bow, to see how I'd take to a life of clandestine meetings and dangerous associations. It would take more than furtive theatrics to frighten India Black.

I discharged my own cannonball in Bonnaire's direction. "I hope your friends can be trusted. I'd hate to think I'm fraternizing with informants."

Bonnaire leaned closer, his lips nearly grazing my ear. "So would I."

Flerko materialized from out of the fog.

To Bonnaire's raised eyebrow, the little Russian shook his head. "There is no one. It is safe."

Without a word, Bonnaire seized my arm once more and we traversed a narrow passage, emerging into a dingy street and hence into a dank, rat-infested alley. I could hear their squeaks of alarm, and once my boot made contact with a cat-sized body. I shuddered. I can cope with anarchists, but vermin are another matter entirely. Bonnaire ignored the scrabbling feet, and Flerko flapped his hands in a futile attempt to scatter the disgusting creatures.

We arrived at our destination then, and not a moment too soon in my opinion. An evening spent trundling through foul streets, dodging rodents and police spies, can provide only so much entertainment. Bonnaire had pulled up short at a warped door leading into what had once been a tobacco shop but was now a vacant storefront. While Flerko acted as sentry, Bonnaire inserted a key into the door and pushed it open. It had been recently oiled, for it swung open without a sound. The Frenchman led the way inside and gestured for me to follow him. Flerko made a final check of the street and then scuttled nervously through the door, closing it behind him.

"We are going downstairs, Miss Black. Kindly place your hand on my shoulder and follow me down the steps."

I fumbled in the dark, succeeding in entangling my fingers in Bonnaire's beard and poking him in the eye before finally managing to find his shoulder and grasp it firmly. He lurched into movement, his shoulder dropping precipitously.

"The first step," he said, unnecessarily.

We floundered down the staircase, which is to say that I did, Bonnaire moving as gracefully as a man could with a woman tethered to him. It was as black as pitch, and the air smelled of mold and rot. Flerko was right on my heels, pressing against me in what I hope was merely nervous tension at the upcoming meeting and not the precursor to an unpleasant experience for India Black. For a moment, as often occurs to even the most highly trained operative, I wondered how I had gotten myself into this situation.

We reached the bottom of the stairs. Bonnaire removed my hand from his shoulder and tucked it through the crook of his arm. "It is only a few steps now," he said.

He was as good as his word, for we walked only a few paces before he halted and addressed the Russian. "Flerko?"

A match scraped shoe leather and burst into flame, revealing a foul corridor with paint peeling from the walls and water stains on the ceiling, and a battered door that had once boasted a coat of varnish. Bonnaire turned the handle and the door, like the one into the shop, opened soundlessly. Flerko, shielding the match with a cupped hand, strode into the inky blackness. In a moment two candles were burning and Bonnaire had shut the door behind us.

I looked around with interest, as I had never been in an anarchists' den and was curious as to what I'd find there. It was a shabby place, the walls streaked with damp and a distinct odour of mildew, which, I thought with some irritation, would likely penetrate my clothing before the night was out. Anarchists did not appear concerned with creating a cozy environment in which to plan assassinations. A warped and battered deal table of inferior wood and a half dozen mismatched chairs occupied the center of the room. The table bore a lantern, which Flerko now lit. I was idly glancing about, wondering why radicals couldn't spring for something a bit more congenial, when I spotted something I hadn't noticed until the lantern had produced its feeble light: a second table, covered with alarm clocks, a stack of packets wrapped in paraffinned paper, coils of copper wire, an assortment of cheap vest-pocket pistols, detonators and springs, and screws and nails of various sizes. In short, all the makings of what the press had taken to calling "infernal machines" and the rest of us called "bombs." I had Superintendent Stoke to thank for my ability to recognize these nefarious tools, as he had provided me a detailed description in my briefing papers. I hadn't realized until that moment that I might actually encounter these items. I was regarding them with a mixture of horror and fascination when Bonnaire wandered over.

"Our factory," he said.

"Impressive," I murmured. I noticed that the packets were printed with the words "Atlas Powder A," and felt the hairs on my neck rise. Well, I don't know how the rest of you would react when you came face-to-face with lignin dynamite for the first time, but I have to say I found it a bit unsettling.

"Our bomb maker is quite experienced. He has spent some time on the Continent, and also in Ireland. You will meet him tonight."

"Does he have all his fingers?"

Bonnaire laughed. "You are an amusing woman, but I should warn you that my comrades are serious people. Most of them have spent time with the security agencies of their countries, and that experience has removed any inclination to see the humourous aspects of life."

"I'm sure it would. I'll bear that in mind." I appreciated the warning; I didn't want to get off on the wrong foot with my anarchist pals, and if I had to forego my usual lighthearted approach to life for a few meetings, I would.

"What about you, Monsieur Bonnaire? Have you been the guest of the Sûreté?"

Bonnaire's smile was grim. "I have. But the French police are more civilized than their Russian or German counterparts. I was merely questioned, not tortured. Still, it was an unpleasant experience and one I wouldn't care to repeat."

"I've had my own encounters with the local plod. They can be quite nasty if they like. And the whole city is in an uproar over these assassinations. I expect the police might forego their usual courteous habits if they caught a foreigner with a bomb in his pocket."

Flerko had disappeared, presumably to keep watch, but he bustled in suddenly with a brutish fellow in tow.

"Ah," said Bonnaire, advancing to meet the new arrival. "Thick Ed. How are you?"

Thick Ed? Well, if it wasn't polite it was at least accurate. The fellow was built like a bull terrier, short, wide and stout. He'd cropped his dark hair until it was nearly as short as the heavy beard that swathed the lower half of his face. His features were coarse, and wiry black hair sprouted from his nostrils. The enforcer of the group, no doubt. My first impression was that Thick Ed had not been recruited for his intellectual prowess.

Bonnaire introduced us, and my hand was crushed by a meaty paw. Thick Ed mumbled something in what might have been English.

"Thick Ed is our engineer," said Bonnaire. "He designs and constructs the bombs we use."

With those thick fingers? I made plans to be elsewhere when Thick Ed was at work.

Thick Ed produced an incomprehensible noise that might have been an acknowledgment of Bonnaire's comment, or a belch, and wandered over to his worktable. Bugger. Would it be rude to leave now?

I cast a sidelong and wistful glance at the door and found that my escape route had been blocked by a slim fellow with a ruddy face and a cold eye.

Bonnaire followed my gaze. "Ah, Harkov."

Harkov advanced slowly into the room. He nodded at Thick Ed, who had his face buried in the interior of a clock and therefore ignored him, and at Flerko, who sprang up and kissed his hand with delight.

"My comrade," Flerko gushed. "I am so glad you have returned safely. We have been very busy in your absence. You must hear of the attack on Moreland House. There was great destruction and—"

Harkov held up a hand. "In good time, my friend. All in good time. First, I must greet our new associate. Bonnaire, you will introduce us."

Bonnaire nodded obediently. "Miss India Black," he said, "Pyotr Alexeyevich Harkov."

Harkov gave me a firm handshake and a quick appraisal. I can't say I took to the man. I'm not fond of Russians generally, having been imprisoned in the Russian embassy at one time and carried off across the Channel by the tsar's agents.

To date I hadn't been much impressed with this anarchist lot. Bonnaire seemed a bit cavalier and not overly bloodthirsty. Flerko had passion in spades, but the thought of his twitchy fingers on a detonator was not comforting, and Thick Ed seemed, well, thick. Harkov, however, could have been the model for any theatrical poster featuring Slavic villains. Dark eyes glittered like chips of obsidian above slanted cheekbones. His cheeks were sunken, with two deep lines like sabre slashes on either side of a thin, tight smile. He wore his hair sleeked back, exposing a sharp widow's peak that plummeted precipitously down his forehead. I could smell the hair pomade from where I was standing.

There was an air of authority about Harkov that I found puzzling, as my impression of anarchists was that they were all individualists who would rather die than submit to another man's authority. I hadn't imagined it, though, for Flerko had danced attendance on Harkov since his arrival and even Bonnaire seemed cautiously deferential. I wondered if Harkov could be the leader of this charming pack and the man Superintendent Stoke wanted, but in the string of names Bonnaire had rattled off during his introductions, he hadn't mentioned "Grigori."

Harkov gestured at the chairs around the table. "Please be seated, Miss Black."

Flerko and Bonnaire joined us. Thick Ed remained at the workbench, his attention riveted on a length of wire. I chose a seat with a view toward the bomb maker. If he started fiddling with one of those packets of dynamite, I might need to ask for directions to the lavvy.

Harkov settled himself comfortably. "I must thank you for the information you have provided to us, Miss Black. It has been of stellar quality."

"I'm glad to be of service to the cause," I said with just a hint of fervor, not wanting to overegg the batter at this point.

"I am sorry that I was not here to see the results, but I was on the Continent attending a conference."

A conference of anarchists? Superintendent Stoke would want to know about that.

Harkov produced a monocle and a clean handkerchief and began to polish the eyepiece. "Martine has vouched for you, and Bonnaire here believes you would be a useful addition to our group." He finished cleaning the monocle, screwed it into his eye and scrutinized me through the lens. "However, I should like to hear myself about your interest in our enterprise."

The bloke made it sound like I was proposing to buy railway shares from him. There's nothing like politics to warp the brain and cause people to start speaking in euphemisms. Why can't they just say what they mean? Nevertheless, I didn't show my irritation at the uncanny resemblance between this Russian radical and the Tory politicians I'd encountered in my own country, but launched into my soliloquy. I won't bore you with the details, as you've heard it before in this account, but suffice it to say that I threw in all the appropriate phrases at critical points of the narrative, chuntering on about my hatred of the nobs and the desire to strike a blow for freedom and all the rest of the twaddle you might expect from an initiate at a meeting of a secret society when she's trying to impress the gang. I reeled it off easily; lying is second nature to a whore, or it should be if she means to be a successful whore. You've got to learn the knack of telling a portly gent with gout that he's as strong as Hercules without giggling, or your bank account will be empty.

I finished my spiel with a resolution to assist the group in any way that Harkov and the others might determine. Harkov thought it over for a minute, those thin lips creased into a straight line, his dark eyes nearly closed. Flerko looked anxious and jiggled his leg under the table, while Bonnaire observed Harkov with a neutral visage. I plastered a pleasant expression across my face, though I was feeling far from comfortable. What would happen if Harkov decided my bona fides weren't bona? Would he march me out into the alley and put a bullet in my head? Strangle me with some of that copper wire Thick Ed was fondling and toss my body into the Thames? I was berating myself for having failed to reload after firing off that shot outside the Bag O' Nails and wondering if I'd be able to get the Bulldog out of my purse in time, when Harkov removed the monocle and placed it in his pocket.

"You can continue to provide us accurate intelligence about the movement and location of government ministers and peers?"

"Yes."

"And you are prepared to provide financial support for our efforts?"

Curse Martine and Bonnaire. They hadn't said a word about money. I had no idea what dynamite cost, but I reckoned I was about to find out. I hoped Harkov was just probing, trying to gauge just how committed I was to the cause. I'd be hanged if I'd fork over any of my hard-earned guineas to this lot; Dizzy and Superintendent Stoke would just have to come up with the cash, if necessary.

"Of course," I said.

Money talks, even among those who affect to despise it. Harkov beamed, directing a satanic smile at me that made my blood run cold. Flerko sighed in relief, and Bonnaire relaxed.

"What is the topic of discussion tonight?" asked Flerko.

"We must wait for Schmidt," said Harkov. "In the meantime, I

116

have brought whisky and we shall have a drink to pass the time."

A capital idea, I thought, for by this time my nerves were as frayed as a fishwife's shawl. So we had a drink and Flerko and Harkov talked anarchist theory (deadly stuff, that; I nearly fell asleep during Flerko's tirade) while Bonnaire smoked a cigarette, Thick Ed hummed a music hall tune as he tinkered with one of the alarm clocks, and I did my bit to lower the level of the whisky. It was all very cozy, but I hoped this Schmidt chap would arrive soon and we could move the evening along. My tolerance for anarchists was growing fainter by the moment and I was bloody tired.

My prayers were answered sooner rather than later (a clear indication of celestial favor if there ever was one) when Thick Ed lifted his head and announced, "I hear footsteps. Schmidt is here." The bomb maker frowned. "And someone is with him."

"Ah," Harkov said smoothly. "So he has brought him tonight. Schmidt also has found a new recruit for our cell."

A draft of wind whistled through the room as the door opened, and a professorial type with a shining bald head, gold-rimmed glasses and the beard of an Old Testament prophet bustled in. He looked like a kindly soul, with plump, red cheeks and a dimpled smile, but I spared him only a glance, for the new recruit that accompanied him was French.

8

Our eyes met and French inclined his head politely, just as any gentleman would when entering a room with a single female in the crowd. I acknowledged his courteous gesture with a graceful nod, and then he turned his attention to the men in the room. I would like to have given him the reaction his appearance at the meeting deserved, namely a poke in the ribs and a furious tongue-lashing, for the poncy bastard had surely known I'd be found among the Dark Legion. After all, he'd approved Dizzy's plan for me to infiltrate this gang. But I restrained my natural instincts, as any agent worth her salt would do under the circumstances. The tongue-lashing and a bit of physical violence could wait, and they'd feel all the sweeter for the delay.

Schmidt introduced him first to Harkov, who mustered a parsimonious smile and a reserved handshake. Flerko pumped French's hand but did not hide his curiosity, and Bonnaire was his usual suave self, extending languid fingers and murmuring *"Bonsoir, monsieur."* Thick Ed contributed a grunt from the workbench.

Then it was time for my introduction to French. His cool

fingers enveloped mine, and he bowed over my hand prettily, but his grey eyes were distant, betraying nothing. I matched his demeanor with only a hint of the inquisitiveness I thought any normal anarchist might exhibit. We separated and I slipped away to stand by Bonnaire's side, a fact that escaped neither Bonnaire nor, I was absurdly pleased to see, French.

Harkov took charge and motioned us peremptorily to take our seats. I found it deuced odd that everyone deferred to him; this meeting was hardly the democratic exercise I'd expected, but as I was not au fait with the finer points of anarchist etiquette, I reckoned I'd just have to get Flerko alone and find out why Harkov had assumed such an air of authority. I was eager to hear what French had to say for himself, but before Harkov could give him the third degree about his radical views and the size of his purse, Schmidt plumped down opposite me and subjected me to the exacting scrutiny of a small boy examining an adder.

"I have looked forward to meeting you, Miss Black. The facts you have shared with us have been most interesting." If the name hadn't been a giveaway, the accent was. Schmidt was a German.

"Quite useful, too," added Bonnaire.

"But for the damned influenza," Flerko said, "we'd have struck a mighty blow at Moreland House."

"Indeed," said Schmidt. There was a twinkle in his eyes, but I thought it might be a glint of steel. "And now you have decided to join our merry band."

"There is much to be done," I said. "I'll continue to provide information, but I'd like to do more for the cause." I sounded like a right pillock, but Flerko was beaming at me and Bonnaire smiled and fingered his beard. Harkov stared at me, his dark eyes thoughtful. I didn't dare look at French.

"Why?" asked Schmidt.

So I went through the whole song and dance one more time, though I did abbreviate the saga as by then I was heartily sick of the story and I reckoned Bonnaire, Flerko and Harkov were as well. I allowed myself to get a little hot at the notion of all those toffs paying for the privilege of rogering the fallen women of Lotus House, but I didn't overdo things. Harkov's unwavering gaze and sardonic expression were unnerving, and for some unaccountable reason, French's presence had made me as edgy as a vicar giving his first sermon.

I finished reeling off my tale and waited for Schmidt's interrogation to begin, but Harkov surprised me by abruptly addressing French.

"And what about you, sir?" he enquired. "Schmidt has of course told us of your experiences together in Manchester and Liverpool. You've provided a great deal of financial support to our cause, and now I understand that you wish to be more actively involved in our affairs as well. Is that correct?"

"Indeed it is, sir," said French.

"Yet Schmidt tells me that you are a member of the very class we intend to destroy. Your family owns mines, I believe he said. What was it?" Harkov turned to Schmidt. "Coal? Tin?"

"Both," said French. "Coal mines in County Durham. Tin mines in Cornwall. My family has also expanded into manufacturing in the north of England, principally ironworks."

"Then why should you seek to demolish the fruits of your family's labours?"

"Our wealth is not the fruit of our labours. It was built on the backs of poor men and women," French said bitterly, his face flushed. That was a nice touch, I thought, and vowed to make French tell me how he'd done that.

"You ask why I have turned against my family. If you could

see the conditions in which our workers slave so that we might dine off silver and drink champagne, you would understand. We have exploited our workers so that we might live a life of decadence. We are parasites, living off the sweat and tears of others, without a thought for their health or happiness. In short, sir, I am ashamed of my family and what we have done. I intend to do the honourable thing and fight for the rights of the weak and the poor." French had caught just the right look, equal parts humility and righteous anger.

Schmidt had been fiddling about with a large pipe, cleaning and filling it with tobacco. Now he lit the bloody thing and a noxious cloud enveloped the table. "Mr. French has been financing a series of newsletters and pamphlets for the workers, explaining their rights and urging them to down tools until their managers see fit to pay them a decent wage. Now he has decided that words alone will not accomplish the great task before us."

Schmidt's pipe belched black smoke. "You are not the first of your class to turn your back upon your relations in search of a better world. Our own leader, Grigori, comes from one of Russia's greatest noble families. He too has rejected their ideals and has vowed to annihilate all those who stand in the way of progress."

I'd been half-listening to French's performance and pondering a change of the wallpaper in the drawing room at Lotus House, but the mention of Grigori snapped me to attention. Harkov was not the man we were after (though it would be no great loss to society if he ended up sent back to the Russians with instructions to deliver him to Siberia). At the mention of Grigori, Harkov's eyes flashed and his hand moved involuntarily as though to silence Schmidt.

Schmidt forged on. "When Tsar Alexander II freed the serfs

in 1861, Grigori was sure that Russia was finally on the path to freedom and dignity for all its people. But liberating the serfs has done little to improve their lot. They are still uneducated, still clinging to myth and superstition. The nobles were forced to turn over land to the serfs, but they chose the most barren fields to give to the peasants, and the poor creatures are required to pay for this land. Some of them must pay for fifty years or more. Grigori has tried to persuade his fellow noblemen to treat the serfs fairly, but they refuse to change. Like you, Mr. French, Grigori has decided that change can only be effected by drastic means."

I wondered why, if Grigori felt so strongly about the wretched former serfs, he wasn't back in Russia trying to assassinate the tsar, but running a brothel has taught me some useful diplomatic skills. "I take it Grigori has been exiled?"

Flerko snorted. "He fled Russia, just before his arrest. I was not so lucky. The Third Section—"

"Yes, Flerko, we know what you have endured," Bonnaire said soothingly.

I had been puzzling over the conversation and now I spoke up. No doubt the manual for government agents recommends keeping your mouth shut and your ears open when you're infiltrating a group of international criminals, but I've yet to read the manual and probably never will.

"Forgive me, Mr. Harkov, but there's something I'd like to ask you. My review of anarchist literature"—I was stretching the truth a bit, as I hadn't read any of that nonsense either, save for the information provided by Superintendent Stoke—"indicates that every man, and woman, of course, is considered capable of governing himself or herself, and thus no man has the right to govern another."

French was giving me the eye, willing me to be silent, which is the surest way I know of encouraging me to talk."

"Yes?"

"Well, if that is the case, then why do you refer to Grigori as your leader?"

Harkov's smile was laced with condescension. "You must explore the theory in more depth, Miss Black."

I looked suitably chastened.

"But to answer your question, a group of men and women may freely choose to appoint one of their own as a leader. The critical point is that the decision is made *by* them and not *for* them. We have recognized that Grigori has certain attributes that will permit our group to function more effectively."

Bonnaire laughed. "Money."

"And education and contacts and many other things that make our task easier," said Harkov primly.

"I see," I said. "Thank you for explaining."

Schmidt knocked his pipe against the chair leg. "We should administer the oath, Harkov."

The oath? Anarchists took an oath? That seemed a bit structured for a group whose aim was to bring about the end of society as we knew it.

"Do you choose to join us?" asked Harkov. "You are free to refuse. Only an oath freely given binds a man to his brothers."

Naturally we said yes, having been sent to do that very thing by the prime minister and Superintendent Stoke. I had visions of knives and the mingling of blood while we chanted something ancient and mystical, but the oath taking turned out to be a tame affair. Harkov asked French and me to stand, and we both did so, rather self-consciously. At Harkov's direction, we placed our hands over our hearts. I screwed my face into a solemn mask and prayed I wouldn't guffaw at an inappropriate moment.

"Repeat after me," said Harkov. "I believe in the innate equality of all men, and I vow to respect my brother's liberty."

French and I spoke out loudly, parroting Harkov, though I felt the urge to ask why our sisters didn't get some consideration as well.

"I vow never to use violence or usury to take my brothers' property."

French was word perfect, but I put "usury" before "violence" and thus spoiled the effect.

Harkov glared at me. "I vow," he continued, "to speak honestly to my brothers and never to deceive them in any way."

I concentrated and made it through without error, and I can assure you that I didn't hesitate at all when I lied about not lying.

Then everyone gathered round and clasped hands. Flerko's sweaty palm enclosed mine, and Bonnaire grasped my other hand.

Harkov looked solemn, like a priest about to deliver the wafer.

"You have become a member of the society of free men, and, er, women," he added, catching my eye. "We are bound together now in the noble enterprise of liberating all men, and, er, women, from the authority of the state and the oppression of the aristocracy." He lifted his hands, raising French's and Schmidt's, and the rest of us hoisted ours.

"Brothers!" said Harkov.

"Brothers!" we all exclaimed. "And sisters!"

"Sisters!" we echoed.

Harkov startled me by enveloping me in a bear hug, and then all the chaps lined up to embrace me and to clutch French in their arms. I was a trifle fretted by this, as Superintendent Stoke's briefing materials had mentioned that some anarchists believed in the concept of free love, a notion obviously dreamed up by some bloke because even a radical female of average intelligence ought to know that free love was nothing but another name for prostitution, without the exchange of money. Some women might fall for the charm of unkempt beards and fervid talk about equality, but India Black wasn't about to dispense her favors to any of the men of the Dark Legion (though under other circumstances, I might have fancied the handsome Bonnaire). But as a madam I've had quite a lot of experience in separating business from pleasure, and I wasn't going to combine the two pursuits while I was weaseling my way into a cell of flaming zealots.

After all the cuddling and clinching, Harkov poured whisky and everyone gathered around the table, including Thick Ed, who reluctantly left off testing a spring and joined us. I reckoned we'd finally get down to business now, planning our next attack, but damned if the meeting didn't degenerate into a philosophical discussion about the usual anarchist shibboleths: greedy parasites who exploited the working class, reactionary policies of the present European governments, and the torture techniques employed by the various security agencies (this last, predictably, resulted in an outburst from Flerko about Russia's Third Section that took some time to quell). Vincent would have lapped this up, but I found it tedious, as indeed it was. Nevertheless, I had to make a show of appearing interested, and so I stuck a few verbal daggers into the aristocracy and the politicos and made enthusiastic noises about striking them down and otherwise burnished my laurels as a champion of the people.

Then Schmidt briefed us on the contents of a pamphlet he and French intended to publish, addressed to the costermongers of the East End, informing them of their rights as free men and merchants of the city, which inspired Flerko to yet another eruption, this one over the brutal treatment meted out to the costers by the police, who were known to upset their barrows and empty their wares into the street out of sheer malice. Bonnaire reported on the state of the group's finances. French spoke sparingly, adding a comment here and there and appearing the earnest inductee. Harkov nattered on at length about the meeting he'd just attended in Lyme Regis, in which he and a few other ardent compatriots had talked about a concerted plan to set England ablaze with synchronized bombings, at which point Thick Ed actually uttered a few words about the practical difficulties involved in such a scheme until Harkov irritably cut him off.

Everyone was getting snappish by then for it was quite late. Indeed, it must have been the wee hours of the morning before everyone got tired of debating abstract principles of anarchism and Harkov announced that we would meet in three days' time, at the same hour and place. We should be prepared, he said, to discuss our next operation at that meeting. I felt a surge of excitement, for I'd finally have something to report to Superintendent Stoke.

Bonnaire cupped a hand under my elbow. "I'll escort you to New Oxford Street. You should be able to find a cab there, even at this hour."

It was kind of him, but what I really wanted to do was cut French from the herd and pump his nibs about his recent activities. At the moment, he and Schmidt had their heads together and French had his back to me.

"Shall we go?" asked Bonnaire. Flerko had materialized at his side, like a nervous shadow.

Bugger. I resigned myself to seeing French in three days. By then I would have concocted a plan to get him to myself. It occurred to me that I hadn't the slightest idea where he lived, although it was unlikely he was residing in his own home while playing at being a radical sympathizer. He certainly wouldn't be staying anywhere in the filth of Seven Dials, being as fastidious as a cat when it came to his appearance.

Our trio was almost out the door when Schmidt halted us with a word. "If you are walking to New Oxford Street, Bonnaire, then perhaps Mr. French should accompany you." He cuffed French gently on the shoulder. "We know our way around these streets, but it is not wise for strangers to travel alone. You will be safer with Bonnaire and Flerko."

My Bulldog would be far more useful in warning off footpads and fingersmiths than Flerko's twitching, but as I did not want to draw attention to the fact that I was armed, I said nothing.

We trekked out into the fog. Schmidt lifted his hat and disappeared into the murk, followed by Harkov and Thick Ed moving off in different directions.

"This way," said Bonnaire, grasping my elbow. The others fell in behind us, and Flerko began to chatter away to French about the inhumane conditions at Third Section headquarters.

Damn and blast. My heart had lifted when French joined us for the walk, but with Bonnaire attached to my side like a bloody leech and Flerko monopolizing French, I wouldn't be able to have a private word with the man. Perhaps when we reached our destination I'd have the opportunity to sidle alongside French and arrange a rendezvous.

But that ambition was thwarted as well. After slithering through refuse and stepping over sleeping drunks, we arrived at the cabstand where a few yawning drivers were gathered around a brazier drinking tea. They looked up drowsily. We must have made an odd tableau looming out of the dripping mist: an English gentleman, a beautiful, well-dressed but obviously experienced woman, and two foreigners, one of whom conveyed a distinct piscine odour.

French spoke up. "Good evening, gentlemen. We shall require two cabs."

An old fellow with a crushed bowler and a pipe between his teeth stirred. "Where to?"

French looked enquiringly at me, and I gave the address of Lotus House.

"Not far," said the old gent. "I'll take you."

"And I wish to go to Fleet Street."

I flung a quick glance at French, for his objective lay in the opposite direction from Lotus House. He hadn't paid me a jot of attention tonight, and I wouldn't put it past the fellow to have chosen his destination deliberately to avoid sharing a cab. He evaded my eyes but tipped the brim of his hat in my direction. Bonnaire handed me into an ancient hansom with sprung seats and the smell of mildew, and the last I saw of French, he was haggling with a wall-eyed driver over the cost of conveyance.

The drive to Lotus House seemed to last an eternity, and I fumed the entire way. My head ached, I was drained from the effort of playing the revolutionary hellion and I was furious that French had made no effort to arrange any sort of meeting before the next assembly of anarchists. For God's sake, we were both agents of the Crown and you'd think the fellow would want to share some information and formulate a plan for getting our hands on Grigori, but French had ignored me for most of the evening. I considered the notion that he was just being cautious; for all I knew I might even now have Harkov or Thick Ed or any one of the others on my tail, and so might French. He was a wise bird, was French, and even I, who was prone to check the depth of the water by plunging in, could see the sense in being wary. That did not, however, mean that I wasn't desirous of getting

French in a headlock and forcing him to divulge all his secrets, professional and personal.

I blame French for what happened next. If I had not been seething over his behavior, I would certainly not have exited the cab without bothering to check the street. I flung a few coins at the driver and mounted the steps of Lotus House, fishing in my purse for the house key. I was rummaging through the contents with my head bent in concentration, when I heard the scrape of shoe leather on the stone step and I looked around just in time to see a cosh whipping through the gloom toward my head.

I got a hand up, which helped to ward off the blow, but pain juddered through my forearm as my attacker struck again and I staggered, half-falling against the door. I tried to raise my fist to hammer on the door, but my arm hung, nerveless and inert, at my side. Then I felt a mighty blow on the crown of my head, and the last thing I remember is the dim yellow glow of the gas lamps fading, first to starry white pinpricks of light and then to velvet black.

A grimy thumb pried open my eyelid and a bolt of lightning pierced my brain.

"Bloody hell," I said, and rolled over to burrow my face in the pillow. This action was not sufficient, however, to cloak the noxious stench that had pervaded my room.

"Open the window, you stunted little sod," I said in a muffled voice.

Vincent probed cautiously at the back of my head, and I let out a howl that would have done credit to a countess birthing triplets.

"Get your bally hands off me," I shouted.

"Should I get some brandy?" Mrs. Drinkwater sounded anxious.

"Only if it's for me, you bloody woman."

"It ain't cracked," said Vincent, running a finger along the base of my skull. The thought of where that finger had been was enough to make Lazarus leap off his cot, and I rolled over and glared at my ragged nurse.

"Kindly remove your hands from my person." I did my best to sound severe, but the act of turning over and inhaling an unadulterated dose of pure Vincent made my stomach heave.

Vincent whipped a basin under my nose, and I retched like a drunken sailor. Mrs. Drinkwater vanished, her hand fluttering to her breast in dismay. After I'd finished emptying the contents of my stomach, I sank back onto the pillows, exhausted, the beat of my pulse pounding in my temple like a piston. Vincent set aside the basin and kindly dabbed my mouth with his handkerchief. If I didn't die from the blow to my head, I'd surely be felled in short order by some loathsome disease.

"What are you doing here?"

"Ole Drinkwater sent one of the 'ores for me at the crack o' dawn. She couldn't sleep last night and she was cleanin' in the kitchen. She 'eard a shindy outside the door and run out and saw a man with a cosh standin' over you. She said she screamed and he run away and there you was on the ground, out cold and wif the blood runnin' out your nose."

Mrs. Drinkwater cleaning in the middle of the night? More likely she was creeping about, filching my liquor. Still, it would be churlish to be ungrateful. Not everyone would have ventured outside to interrupt a cosh-wielding assailant.

"She could have sent for the doctor," I muttered, struggling to sit upright. Ooh. A mistake, that. I refrained from further movement.

"Aye, she could 'ave," agreed Vincent, though he looked offended that I preferred the ministrations of a qualified medico to his own well-intentioned assistance.

"Wot 'appened to you? Did one of them anarchist buggers bash you over the 'ead?"

"I don't know who it was. I couldn't see. It was dark and the fog was thick." I pressed a hand to my forehead. "But it wouldn't make sense for one of them to follow me all the way back to Lotus House and attack me here. I was with them for hours. They had plenty of opportunities to whack me."

"Well, you've chapped somebody good and proper, to get a wallop like that."

The light began to dawn. "Mother Edding," I said gloomily. "The old bitch."

"An ole woman done that to you?" Vincent asked skeptically. "It's a 'ell of a drubbin'."

"Of course not," I snapped. "She's hired someone. Mrs. Drinkwater said my attacker was a man. Mind you," I added, "she could have done it herself. She's as stout as a Berkshire sow and twice as mean."

"Wot you gonna do about it?"

"I'll sic the Bulldog on her if she tries it again."

"You ain't gonna give 'er some of 'er own medicine?"

"I haven't time for that. I'm in the midst of playing spies, and Mother Edding will just have to wait until I can give her my full attention. Maybe I'll ship Martine back to her when this affair is over with a note apologizing for the inconvenience. Which Mother Edding won't be able to read."

I could see the lad was disappointed, but whether it was due to my reluctance to take on the stout, elderly madam or because I'd been felled by a thug for hire and not an anarchist, I wasn't sure.

Vincent sat down on the mattress at my feet.

"Not the bed," I cried. "A chair, for God's sake. Take a chair."

Vincent shrugged and dragged a spindle-backed chair to my bedside.

"Tell me about the meetin'," he demanded. "Are you gonna scrag someone? Who's gonna get hit next?"

Mrs. Drinkwater lurched into the room, bearing a glass of brandy. She staggered to the bed and handed it to me. By the length of time she'd been gone and the alcoholic haze following her like a cloud of perfume, I presume she'd had a medicinal jolt herself. I swallowed a mouthful of the brandy and waited until the top of my head condescended to join the rest of my skull.

"I'll bring you some broth," said the cook, and disappeared to make a perfectly good beef bone and a pot of water into a disgusting sludge.

"Well? Wot 'appened last night?"

He wanted every detail, so I recounted it all, struggling a bit to remember some of the hazier moments (that humbug about the rights of man, for example). When I reached the part where French had walked in the door, Vincent clapped his hands in excitement and sprang out of the chair.

"'E's back? Where the devil 'as 'e been?"

"I've no idea. He hardly spoke at the meeting, and he didn't say a word to me directly."

Vincent nodded thoughtfully. "'E's a sly dog, alright. Trust 'im not to let on that 'e knew you." Naturally, my own artfully concealed acquaintance with French drew no praise.

The brandy was working its magic and my head had begun to clear, though a steady drumbeat throbbed in my veins. "I need to get in touch with him before the next meeting of the anarchists. Do you think you can find him?"

I hadn't meant to cast aspersions on Vincent's professional skills, but I'd obviously touched a nerve.

"Wot do you mean, can I find 'im? If 'e's in Lunnon, I'll run 'im to ground before noon."

His easy assurance irritated me. I had no idea where French might be found. I did not know his address or the name of his club (the poncy bastard surely belonged to several of those). I didn't even know his Christian name, a fact that annoyed me no end. It nettled me so much that I persisted in dreaming up improbable names for the chap, which in turn chafed him. I'd had a great deal of sport out of French with that little game, but at the moment I would have foregone the pleasure of vexing the man if I'd only known how to reach him.

"Tell him I want to see him, but don't you dare say anything to him about Mother Edding." I wasn't keen that French should know I'd been careless enough to be ambushed by a portly bawd's hired hand. He might draw the conclusion that I wasn't up to the task of taking down a few dynamite-toting foreigners.

Speaking of foreigners, I remembered that I'd tasked Vincent with checking the background of my newest slut and her acquaintances in the anarchist community.

"What have you learned about Martine?"

"Nuffink to worry you. When she ain't 'ere, she's 'angin' around Bonnaire. She's sweet on 'im. When she ain't taggin' along after Bonnaire, she's visitin' her mates."

"Does Bonnaire feel the same about her?"

"Nah, I don't fink so. 'E's nice enough to 'er when they're togevver, but 'e don't appear all that interested in 'er. She's useful to 'im. 'E sends 'er off wif messages, and she pays for his baccy at the smoke shop."

"And her mates? What are they like?"

Vincent shrugged. "Most of 'em earn their bread on their backs, but one sells apples and another one sells matches. Nice girls, I reckon, though they all speak Frog when they're togevver. I been close to 'em and I can't make out wot they say."

"And Bonnaire?"

"'E showed up a year ago, best as anyone can remember. 'E's a quiet bloke, but a devil with the ladies. Got one on every corner, 'e does. Keeps 'imself to 'imself most of the time, but folk say 'e 'angs out with a crowd of political types."

"So he is what he purports to be," I mused.

Vincent shrugged. "Wotever that means."

The lad was set to dash off in search of his hero, but I had another assignment for him. While he waited, pacing the room, I scribbled a quick note to Superintendent Stoke to inform him that I had successfully penetrated the Dark Legion. I said nothing of French, for I'd no idea whether Dizzy had informed the Scotland Yard man that another of the prime minister's agents had also infiltrated the group. One lesson I'd learned from that ballyhoo at Balmoral was that the government was a great one for not letting the left hand know what the right was up to. I informed the superintendent that the elusive ringleader of the anarchists was a chap named Grigori, and I'd try to find out more about him at the next meeting. I signed my name with an assertive flourish and asked Vincent to deliver it before starting his search for French.

"And, Vincent? I'll need you back here on the day of the anarchists' meeting. I want you to follow me there and when the meeting is over, I'll want you to dog Harkov. Find out where he goes after the meeting. Perhaps he'll lead you to Grigori."

The prospect of action pleased Vincent enormously, and he was over the moon at the news that French had returned. The little chap scurried out with a cheerful grin on his face. I lay back on the pillows and contemplated putting the Bulldog to my head. That should surely cure my headache.

9

I dozed, and woke to the sound of Mrs. Drinkwater staggering into the room with a tray in her hands. She plonked it down on my lap, and I beheld a bowl of gelid brown slurry.

"Has the wind shifted? I can smell the abattoirs at Smithfield."

"You eat that up," said Mrs. Drinkwater. "You'll be fighting fit in no time."

I contemplated the bowl. She meant well, but even Vincent, who had a cast-iron stomach, would have baulked at the sight.

"And here's a letter for you."

The envelope was addressed to me in a spidery hand and flecked with dozens of miniscule brown spots. Snuff. No prizes for guessing my correspondent. I tore open the flap and smoothed out the letter.

Dear Miss Black,

It's no use playing on my sympathy, and I'm damned surprised that you tried. I wouldn't have expected that of you. And there's no point in coming up here, as I have nothing to say to you.

Yours sincerely,
Lady Margaret Aberkill
Dowager Marchioness of Tullibardine

I crumpled the letter in my hand and hurled it at the wall. "Bloody woman! If I didn't have a brothel to run and an anarchist plot to foil, I'd catch the first train to Scotland and strangle the wretched old hag."

"Don't you upset yourself over a letter," said Mrs. Drinkwater. "You have some of that nourishing broth I've brought you. That'll settle your nerves."

Possibly it would. My stomach, however, would be another matter.

"Fetch me my clothes, Mrs. Drinkwater. I'm going out."

"What? In your condition? You've just had a thump on the head. You'd best lie down until you feel better."

I flung back the bedclothes and tottered to my feet. I listed dangerously to port, and Mrs. Drinkwater steadied me, muttering under her breath about stubborn fools and the virtues of beef stock. She held me upright while I struggled into my clothes. I drained the last of the brandy, winced as the alcohol hit my gullet, and staggered to the door. Mrs. Drinkwater clucked and flapped in my wake as I descended the stairs.

"Summon a cab for me, Mrs. Drinkwater."

She uttered a protest, but one look at my face convinced her that I was not to be deterred.

Nothing but the marchioness's letter could have induced me to leave the house. My head throbbed and my forehead was clammy. My stomach churned. I struggled weakly into the cab and as the horse sprang forward, I fell back against the seat.

Paying a call was the last thing I should be doing at the moment, but the letter had spurred me to action. If the marchioness refused to discuss my mother with me, then I would talk to someone who would.

It was only a short distance from Lotus House to the area around Haymarket, and had I been feeling my usual self, I'd have walked despite the pelting rain. The streets were thronged with carriages, hansoms and omnibuses. Pedestrians dodged in and out of the traffic, and street vendors bawled the virtues of their wares. Newsboys thrust papers through the open window of the cab, shouting the headlines at me. It was utter bloody chaos and the cacophony made my ears ring, but the roar died to a muted hum as we turned into Oxenden Street. It never ceases to amaze me that all you have to do to escape the din of a London thoroughfare is to walk down a side street, where you'll find a silence as profound as that of a country village. Not that I've spent much time in country villages. And not that I like country villages, but some people do. There's just no accounting for taste.

The driver hauled on the reins and the wheels creaked to a stop in front of a pleasant house boasting a fresh coat of glossy blue paint on the shutters and a gleaming brass knocker on the door. My pulse fluttered in my throat, and there was a regimental drummer pounding a cadence in my head. For one moment I considered crawling back into the cab and nipping back to Lotus House, but I gave myself a stern talking to and told myself to buck up, and before I could change my mind, I sailed up to the door and lifted that gaudy brass latch.

A meek young miss in a gray uniform, white apron and a lawn cap opened the door.

"Yes, ma'am?"

"I should like to see your mistress," I said. "Tell her India Black is here."

"I don't think she's at home to anyone at the moment," said the maid.

"She'll see me." My expression brooked no argument, for the shy creature moved aside and I stepped into the house.

"I'll just run upstairs and let her know you're here." Her feet pattered up the carpeted stairs at dizzying speed. I leaned against the newel and wished that the silly goose had directed me to a drawing room or a parlor or anyplace with a chair. I'd bet the accommodations were first-rate. The hall was immaculate, with a gilded mirror polished to icy perfection on one wall, a spotless floor of black-veined marble, and vivid carmine wallpaper patterned with roses. A vase of hothouse lilies stood on a polished rosewood table. All very nice and proper, even if the scarlet paper did imply that the house's owner might have been, in a former life, a trifle louche.

I heard a low-voiced conversation in the hall above me, and then the maid flew breathlessly down the stairs past me, frightened eyes darting in my direction. That pleased me, for it meant that my presence hadn't pleased her mistress. I might even enjoy this encounter.

"India Black."

I've yet to hear Edina Watkins say my name with any inflection other than the faint condescension I heard now. That throaty voice brought back a flood of memories, none of them pleasant. I raised my eyes to the top of the stairs where the tall figure of my mother's last employer had appeared. Edina had always loved an entrance, and too late I realized that I had played into her hands by mooching around the bottom of the stairs like some supplicant at the court of the empress. I should have waltzed into her best room and made myself at home. Ordered coffee, even, from the timid rabbit who'd answered the door. It was too late to correct the situation now, so I determined to make the best of it.

"Hello, Edina. It seems retirement agrees with you; you've put on a stone. Or is two?"

Edina had been a stunner in her day, a wasp-waisted beauty with flaxen hair and hazel eyes, and a low husky laugh that enchanted customers and froze the blood of anyone who crossed her, like yours truly. It was true she'd gained weight. Her tiny waist had ballooned, and her breasts would have done credit to a wet nurse. She wore a silk dressing gown of sea green silk and a pair of leather slippers in a muted dove grey. She was still a handsome woman, in a blowsy sort of way, but the bloom was definitely gone from the rose, which pleased me no end. Amazing what a bit of schadenfreude will do for one's spirits. I felt almost cheerful.

Her gown rustled as she advanced down the stairs. Her mouth was tight with anger.

"Why are you here?"

Too late I remembered the reason I had come. Dash it all, one of these days I was going to have to make an effort to stop charging into battle before war was declared. I needed this woman's help, for as most of you will have concluded by now, I was here to ask Edina a few questions about my mater.

No doubt you're pondering why, if I knew where Edina Watkins lived, I had not dropped round for a chat before now. The truth is that I hated the viper. Just the sound of that low voice, dripping with disdain when she uttered my name, was enough to induce a murderous rage in me. Until now, I'd refused to see the woman for fear I'd run a blade through her or draw out my Bulldog and put a bullet into that cold heart of hers. I was only here now because the bloody Marchioness of Tullibardine had roused a curiosity in me that I had long suppressed. Despite the marchioness's protestations, I was sure she knew something of my mother's life before London. The only other person I knew who could tell me about my mother was standing before me now, her face flushed with fury.

I'd spilled the milk already, so there was no point in trying to play up to the venomous bitch.

"I've come to ask you some questions," I said. "About my mother."

A smirk tugged at the corner of Edina's mouth. "And why would you want to know anything about that useless cow?"

You can see why I despise the woman. The only reason I kept my temper in check was because I refused to give Edina the satisfaction of knowing she'd pricked me.

"She may turn out not to have been so useless after all," I said mildly, though I itched to plug the woman with my .442. "I've found out something about her. It may be worth some money."

Edina can no more resist money than a horse can resist a lump of sugar. I'd been counting on her greed and I was glad to see that I hadn't underestimated her. She kept that frozen, lofty look on her face, but there was a flicker of interest in her eyes.

"Money?"

I shrugged, leaving it to Edina's imagination to supply the details.

"I'll need to know more about her if I'm to benefit. Look here," I said, very bluff and confidential, "we may not like each other, but there's no reason we couldn't do each other a good turn."

She snorted. I had to admit that given the icy freeze that had existed between us all these years, it was more likely I'd slit my own throat than do Edina a favor.

"Not interested?" I said, very nonchalantly, and making as if to leave.

She was torn, I could see, between wanting to see the back of me and adding a few shillings to her pile.

Avarice won. People are so predictable. All you have to do is waggle a few bank notes under their nose and they start to pant.

"What do you want to know?"

"A few details." I was dismissive.

"Such as?"

"Her life before she came to you."

Edina nodded, lips pursed. "Nothing in life is free," she mused.

"I learned that lesson at your feet, Edina."

She looked at me sharpish, but I kept a neutral expression on my face.

"I'll take half."

"Half?"

"Of whatever you get."

"Ten percent."

"Ten!" she squawked. "I'll not tell you anything for less than forty."

"Twelve."

A stranger might have given in at this point, concerned lest he have a case of nervous collapse on his hands, but I hadn't spent all those years at Edina's knee without learning how the game is played. We haggled for some time, with Edina getting more and more agitated until she finally realized that I wasn't going to give in and so she grudgingly accepted twenty-five percent.

"But I'll need twenty pounds now," she said, when we'd concluded our negotiations.

"Three," I said, and we started all over again.

By the time Edina had agreed to seven pounds and I'd coughed it up to the blond snake, my head was vibrating with pain. I had yet to get the information I'd come for, and I had my doubts whether I'd be able to palaver with Edina for much longer. Luckily, the prospect of mammon had thawed Edina's manner somewhat, and she now produced a decanter of gin and two glasses. We shared a toast, though I had to pronounce my part through gritted teeth as the gin hit the top of my head like a sledgehammer.

"You've got a quarter of an hour," said Edina, drawing her dressing gown around her and pouring another tot of gin for herself.

"An hour," I said automatically.

We settled on thirty minutes, which was probably more time than I needed, but you can't let your opponent get the better of you.

I had vague memories of the early days at Edina's brothel, when my mother and I had first arrived at Edina's door, and the experience of my mother's last illness was seared into my heart, but I remembered little of what had gone before, and it was that sort of information I needed from Edina. Not, of course, that she would be inclined to tell me much, and what she would tell me might be half lies. The only hold I had over Edina was money, and I'd have to be prepared to part with a goodly sum.

"Do you know where my mother and I had been living before we came to your academy?"

Edina smiled at the word. "Such a nice name for a brothel," she said, "if a bit pretentious."

"Edina?"

"Right. Well, I seem to remember that she'd been living

somewhere grand, with some flower of society. She always acted so superior, your mother. A lot of the toffs liked her. They said she had class." Edina sniffed. "As if I didn't," she muttered, revealing the root of her dislike for my mother, and for me (though eventually I'd given her plenty of reason to hate me, too).

"Did she tell you anything about this man? His name? Where he lived?"

Edina nursed her gin and ruminated for a minute. "I believe the house was in Kensington." She frowned. "Or was it Belgravia? Somewhere like that. I remember she talked about the garden, and the library. He was a great one for books, this gent, and your mother said she could read all she wanted. I expect that's where you learned to read. Waste of time, that. No need for a tart to read books. Look what an education did for your mum."

I hastily swallowed the last of my drink and reminded myself that it was too soon to thump Edina. I needed to know more.

"You had a few books when you came here. Always had your nose stuck in one of them. When the laundry needed doing, we'd find you up in the garret, lost in a book. I had to take the birch to you to get any work out of you."

Ah, happy days. I wondered how much longer I could resist the urge to snatch up the poker from the fireplace and apply it to Edina's skull.

"What happened to the man? Did he die? Is that why we came to you?"

Edina rocked back with laughter, dribbling gin into her lap. She dabbed at the dressing gown, still snuffling merrily. "My, that's a romantic picture, India. True love. Poor fellow dies young. Your mother turned out of the house by the man's family." The smile vanished from her face, replaced by triumph. "Rot. Your mother got sick and lost her looks. She was no good to him then. He wanted a beautiful wench on his arm, not a walking skeleton. He sent her away, and you with her."

"If she was wasting away, why did you take her in?"

"Someone had to, didn't they? I felt sorry for her."

That was a bloody lie. Edina had as much sympathy as a scorpion.

"You mean she was still good enough for your customers," I said. I had gripped the glass in my hand so tightly I was sure it would break, which meant I'd soon have a shard of glass to plunge into Edina's wicked heart.

"Don't you say a word about my customers. They were fine gentlemen. Mostly. Anyway, they were good enough for the likes of your mother. No one else would have her, especially not with a brat in tow. You were just another mouth to feed, you know. You should be grateful for what I did. I could have turned you out into the street, but I didn't."

That was true. After my mother's death, Edina could have tossed me out with the clothes on my back and left me to fend for myself. She had saved me from that fate by keeping me around as slave labor, forcing me to scrub floors and clean up after her whores, beating me when I disobeyed (which was bloody often) and feeding me with the scraps from the table, which, I can tell you, did not amount to three squares a day. And when I turned twelve, she brought a bloke to my room and informed me that it was time to earn my keep. She left us alone, which was a mistake on her part, for I fought like a hellion and succeeded in planting a toe into my visitor's tools that left him gasping for air on the floor of my room, whilst I gathered my meager belongings and hightailed it out the window, never to return to the kindly embrace of Edina Watkins. I might have ended up in the life she'd planned for me, but it had been on my own terms and on my own account. If I owed Edina anything, it was a thrashing. Someday, I'd give it to her. But not today.

"Did my mother ever tell you the name of the man?"

Edina gave me a cat's knowing smile. "If I give it a think, I can probably remember it."

She stared at the ceiling, humming a little tune under her breath, and when I hadn't appeared to cotton on, she looked at me from the corner of her eye and sighed. "Worth more than seven pounds, don't you think? That name."

I knew she'd hold out for more. For the fourth time I negotiated with the old crocodile. I found the additional three pounds in my purse and put it in her outstretched hand. I was feeling deuced odd by then. My head was playing up, throbbing like blazes, and Edina seemed to be drifting in and out of focus.

She was counting the coins when I produced the Bulldog. Her hands froze, and a vein twitched in her eyelid.

"Is this the way you do business, India? We have a deal. You've paid me, and I'm going to give you the name."

"I just want to be sure that you tell me the correct name. If you do, I won't be back here. If you lie to me, expecting me to pay you more money, I'll come back and we'll have a conversation you won't enjoy."

"I'm not enjoying this one," she said. Edina might be a callous witch, but she had spirit.

"The name," I said.

It might have been the Bulldog or the feverish gleam in my eye that prompted her, but she opened her mouth. "Charles Goodwood."

The name meant nothing to me. I looked at her sternly, just to let her know I'd be back if she had misled me, and tucked my Bulldog back into my purse.

As you can imagine, the conversation was over at that point. Edina didn't even have the courtesy to show me to the door. I let myself out and breathed in the moist, fetid odor of London with relief. In comparison to the atmosphere in Edina's parlor, the air outside smelled fresh. I trotted away from the house at a fair clip, though my knees felt weak and my hands were trembling. I needed a bath and a whisky, and then some more whisky. The encounter with Edina had left me shaken. I'd rather consort with anarchists than spend another minute in that woman's company. Then there was the matter of my petty cash, which was now short ten pounds. But I'm not one to agonize over life's little difficulties. I had a name. And if Edina knew what was good for her, it would be the right name.

Vincent was waiting for me at Lotus House, sprawled in a chair with his feet on the fender of the fireplace and having a dram of my Martell brandy.

"You oughter lock up the liquor," he said. "Ole Drinkwater's passed out again."

I noted the level of brandy in the bottle and decided Vincent had made an excellent suggestion. "You should be thankful. Otherwise, you'd be waiting outside the kitchen door."

He gave me the eye roll this observation deserved, then examined me more closely. "Wot's the matter wif you? And wot are you doin' out of bed, anyways?"

"I had an errand that couldn't wait. Did you see Superintendent Stoke?"

"I 'ad to dodge a few blue-bottles, but I put the message in 'is 'and."

I frowned. "He was supposed to let his men know that you'd

be bringing messages to him."

"I reckon they'd 'ave let me in if I'd tole 'em who I was, but I thought I'd 'ave a romp and see 'ow easy it'd be to get into Stoke's office wifout anyone seein' me."

My headache made me irritable. "Next time, do as I say. You'll end up in the clink, and I'll have to waste time getting you out of there."

Vincent stiffened. This was one dig too many. "Damned if you would. I can take care of myself. Hit's alright for you, consortin' with them dynamiters and 'avin' all the fun, whilst I'm runnin' pieces of paper about like some kind o' messenger boy."

He had a point. I don't like to be left out of the action myself.

I retreated gracefully. "You're quite right, Vincent. What did Stoke say?"

"He read wot you wrote and then 'e said, 'Hit's about time.' "

"Ungrateful bastard." I collapsed in a chair. "Pour me a drink, will you?"

Vincent obliged, and took the opportunity to fill his glass. Oh, well. What's a little Martell between friends?

"That's all he said?"

"'E thanked me for bringin' hit to 'im and gave me a farthin'." Vincent produced the offending coin from his pocket and held it up for me to see. "Wot'll that buy you, eh?"

"Did you find French?" I asked casually.

Vincent was truly irked at this question. "Did I find 'im? O' course I did. Wot do you take me for? Han hamateur?"

"I didn't mean to insult you, Vincent." I was half-irritated myself at the apparent ease with which Vincent had located French.

"'E wants us to meet 'im tonight at ten o'clock, in St. Paul's churchyard."

We? All I had wanted Vincent to do was deliver a message, but I should have guessed that he'd worm his way into the *affaire des anarchistes*.

10

After Vincent had taken his leave, I staggered upstairs to my room and collapsed on the bed. I didn't even bother to remove my boots; just pulled a blanket over me and dropped immediately into sleep. I had a good long nap, for it was growing dark when I awoke and I could hear the girls bustling about, talking and giggling as they prepared for the night's work. A quick glance at the sky confirmed that the rain had evidently tired of the city and gone elsewhere for the evening. Not only did that signify an increase in customers, it also meant I wouldn't get a thorough soaking on the way to my rendezvous with French and Vincent.

I shed the clothes I'd worn to Edina's and considered burning them, as they seemed to reek of sulfur, but I put that down to my imagination and threw them into a hamper for Mrs. Drinkwater to sort out. I flung on a dressing gown and proceeded to stalk the halls, poking my head into various rooms and barking orders at the sluts. It's best to keep them on their toes, you know. Otherwise, they'll be helping themselves to your cosmetics and pawing through your dresses. I left Clara Swansdown in charge for the evening, with strict instructions to the girls to mind her, and strict instructions to Clara to collect what was owed without dispensing any favors or I'd put her on the first boat back to Ballykelly.

As Mrs. Drinkwater was still snoring happily at the table, I treated myself to a chop at a nearby restaurant and toward ten o'clock began making my way to the church. I was anxious to see French, as the chap owed me an explanation of his appearance at the anarchists' meeting, but I was mindful that the radicals were a paranoid lot and since they feared infiltration by government agents, they might just have set someone to watch my movements. I had also not forgotten that some hireling of Mother Edding had cracked me over the head last night and might attempt a second attack. Consequently, I took care to confirm that I was traveling alone to the rendezvous, stopping now and then to dart down an alley and doubling back on my own track from time to time.

French had chosen a dandy location for a meeting. Contrary to what you might think, I was not headed to St. Paul's Cathedral but to the parish church of Covent Garden of the same name. It's a quiet place, for though its classic portico faces one of the most raucous squares in London, the churchyard in the rear of the building is as isolated as a village chapel at night. Given the area's history, a lone gentleman and a lady conducting an assignation in the dark churchyard at a late hour would not arouse curiosity. Neither would Vincent's presence, as a passerby would assume the boy was loitering with intent and make haste to the nearest lighted thoroughfare. Our conversation should be a private one.

I let myself in by the lych-gate, which screeched like a banshee on its hinges. That put paid to arriving without announcing myself.

"India?" The voice belonged to French.

"Yes. Where are you?"

"We're under the beech tree."

I joined Vincent and French under the outstretched branches of an ancient tree. I could just make out their figures in the dim light emanating from the windows of the nearby houses.

French brushed past me to stare down the street up which I had walked. "Were you followed?"

"And good evening to you," I said. "Of course I wasn't followed."

"You're certain?" he asked, still conning the street.

"Absolutely certain. I was careful. Were you?" Men can be so condescending; it's good to give them a little taste of their own medicine. Especially when, in this instance, I had spent my youth dodging predators through the streets of London and French had spent his sitting in some drab schoolroom with other little poncy bastards, conjugating Latin verbs.

"Schmidt and the rest spend most of their time trying to ferret out informers. They trust no one, and it would be normal procedure for them to send someone to shadow you."

"That thought had occurred to me," I said drily. "Which is why I am sure that no one followed me here. I was discreet."

"I'll slip out and take a look," Vincent volunteered, and before French or I could say a word, he'd slipped off into the darkness, as silent as a wraith.

One can be annoyed that one's ability to arrive at a rendezvous without a tail is being doubted, or one can overlook that fact and interrogate the secret agent chap who has dropped from sight and reappeared like a magician's assistant. Possessing an equanimous temperament, I chose the latter. I'd have to work bloody fast, though, as Vincent would not be gone long, so I dispensed with the usual courtesies.

"I trust you enjoyed yourself up north," I said, sending out a flanking attack to open the skirmish.

"I've not been away on holiday, India. The prime minister sent me to Manchester on a mission of the utmost urgency. I scarcely had time to send you a note." He looked at me sharply. "You did receive my note?"

"I vaguely remember a dirty scrap of paper with a word or two on it."

"I didn't have time to explain further. Nor, I might add, permission to do so."

"Permission?"

"Don't ruffle your tail feathers. There are some matters the prime minister believes should be known only to a very small group, most of whom are other ministers. You needn't feel you weren't trusted enough to be included in this affair, at least initially. Apparently the prime minister has now felt it necessary to ask for your assistance."

"Did you keep him informed of your movements? Did he know you were going to be at that meeting last night?"

"I don't provide him with details, and nor, presumably, do you. If what you really want to ask is whether I knew you'd be there, the answer is no, I did not. Lord Beaconsfield said that you were trying to penetrate the group, but he was not aware that you had succeeded and would be at the meeting."

"Does Superintendent Stoke know Dizzy sent you after these chaps?"

"The prime minister may have told him, although I doubt it. Dizzy prefers to use his own agents on political matters, and he considers anarchist plots to be more of a political issue than a criminal one. I expect that Stoke approached him to ask for more resources to find the Dark Legion and destroy it. The prime minister suggested you as an undercover agent, knowing that we would likely cross paths soon, as we were both attempting to find the man behind the cell, namely this Grigori that Schmidt described at our meeting."

"Did you meet Schmidt in Manchester?"

"Yes. He was a member of a local cell there. I spent several weeks establishing my cover as a liberal intellectual who had denounced his family's exploitation of the workers but who had retained enough of the ill-gotten gains to fund publication of various anti-government tracts."

"How tedious, especially if you had to write the drivel yourself."

"It wasn't difficult. In fact, it was rather enjoyable. Did you know that I can now call a banker a profiteering bloodsucker twenty-seven different ways?"

"A useful skill," I observed, "but only in certain circles. Tell me, why did Schmidt come to London? And why are you here?"

"Schmidt told me that the anarchists' leader, Grigori, has come to London to establish a unit of anarchists. Schmidt was sent to recruit new members here. I've been biding my time in Manchester waiting for Schmidt to return. When he came back last week, I volunteered to come here with him. I told him that the police had come round to my lodgings, asking questions about my political activities, and that I needed to go elsewhere for a time. I also told him that I wanted to do more than write polemics against the aristocracy and the government. I was ready to act. He invited me to come with him and to meet the local cell. Which, I was surprised to learn, included you. And that is what I have been up to since I last saw you. Your turn now. Tell me what you've been doing."

I told him about Dizzy and Superintendent Stoke, and how I'd recruited Martine and given her false information about the meeting at Moreland House, which, incidentally, was never going to be held, as you no doubt have ascertained.

"Do you think the members of the cell have accepted you?" asked French.

"I think I've passed muster. Harkov seemed to trust Bonnaire's judgment. And Flerko would accept anyone willing to assassinate an aristocrat. I have to say, though, that I wouldn't want to spend much time with any of those chaps. Naturally, I would like to meet Grigori. I hope he'll be at the next meeting and we can nab him then."

"I doubt that he'll put in an appearance. I went to scores of meetings in Manchester and he never came once. I didn't even know his name until last night. He's an elusive fellow."

"Poor Superintendent Stoke won't like that. He's under considerable pressure to stop the assassination attempts on England's peers."

"It can't be helped. All he has to do is sit in his office and stew. We're the ones on the ground. I expect that you and I shall have to demonstrate our own commitment to the cause before we're introduced to Grigori."

"That could prove difficult. What if they ask us to prove our loyalty by shooting a peer of the realm?"

French stroked his chin. "I rather think that would depend on which peer they had in mind." Had French just made a joke? He quirked a brow at me. It *had* been a joke. I believe the old boy is beginning to loosen up a bit.

"I think we should expect that we'll have to participate in their schemes," he said. "We'll have to find a way to circumvent their plans without giving ourselves away."

"Oh, right. That should be simple, considering the whole nest of them is obsessed with informants and turncoats."

It was no use arguing with French or pressing him to formulate a plan for dealing with this awkward contingency. He's a great one for dealing with things on the fly, is French. I'd be wasting my breath trying to convince him that we should think through our moves in advance. Besides, Vincent would return at any moment and I had other things to discuss with French.

"Did your family miss you while you were away?"

"My family?" He sounded puzzled.

"Yes, you know. Endearing little woman, flock of cherubs, faithful retainers, aged spaniel? That sort of thing?"

French's jaw clenched; I could see it in the dim light. "I don't have an aged spaniel."

"All clear," Vincent announced, appearing abruptly, and silently, at my elbow.

I suppressed a scream. "Bloody hell, Vincent. I wish you wouldn't creep about like that."

"'Ow else do you sneak up on someone?" asked Vincent.

"Well, you're not meant to sneak up on me."

French cut into this exchange. "I have to leave here in a few minutes. I have an appointment and I mustn't be late."

I was dying to ask, but of course his nibs wouldn't condescend to tell me anything about said appointment. He'd been downright chilly about the spaniel.

"Vincent, I'd like you to tag along after India when she meets Bonnaire and Flerko and follow them to the meeting. I want you on Harkov's tail when he leaves us."

"I've already instructed Vincent to do that," I said. "I am capable of managing this investigation without your assistance."

I suppose my interest in his family had irritated the chap, for he ignored my comment and spoke to Vincent. "Be careful, my lad. These fellows are rough."

This sort of solicitude from me would have spurred Vincent to sputtering indignation, but coming from his hero, this warning merited an uncharacteristically meek response: "Righto, guv. Wot do you want me to do after I tail that Russian bloke?"

"We meet here again on the night after the anarchist meeting, at the same time," I said, before French had a chance to utter any more instructions. "And, French? Do be careful that you're not followed."

My parting shot had rendered French incapable of more than a strangled oath, and he stalked off into the warren of streets around St. Paul's without bothering to take his leave. I said goodbye to Vincent and waited until he had scuttled off, and then let myself out the lych-gate and set off in the direction French had taken. I thought it would be a kind gesture on my part, to see that he arrived safely for his appointment.

I had to gallop to catch up with him, but I'd paid careful attention to the route he'd followed. I dodged down an alley in pursuit, running on my toes to avoid the clatter of my boot heels on the cobbles. The thick night air muffled my footsteps. The alley terminated at its junction with a narrow street, lined with small shops and offices. Gas lamps cast a sickly yellow glow and illuminated a shadowy figure striding stiffly away down Southampton Street toward the Strand. I smiled. I could tell by the set of his shoulders that French was still annoyed. I trotted after him, being careful to scout out hiding places as I went: a shadowed doorway here, the gloomy entrance to a shuttered shop there.

We covered the short distance to the Strand in this fashion, and I have to say that French didn't bother to turn round once to see if he was being dogged. Unfortunately, I would not be able to point out this egregious professional error to French, as I would then have to admit to tailing him. Life is unjust in so many ways. Still, I would tuck this memory away and bring it out in the future, at an opportune moment.

French reached the bright lights of the Strand. Despite the hour, there was a good crowd about, streaming out of the restaurants and pubs, all very jolly and boisterous. French ducked into the throng, and I darted forward, trying to keep the crown of his hat in view. As you can imagine, a woman of my appearance soon attracted unwanted attention. Every bloke who'd had a pint fancied himself a wit, and there was a steady stream of ribald comments and suggestions hurled in my direction, along with the odd whistle. I saw French's hat rotate at the sound, and I ducked behind a whiskered cove of ample girth. This would never do. Sometimes, it's cursed bad luck to be born beautiful.

I was fending off a drunken nob in a top hat and monocle when French stepped into the street and hailed a cab. Damn and blast. I stamped on the nob's instep, flung an apology over my shoulder and threw out my arm for the nearest hansom. I don't know why people complain of the difficulty in finding a cab in this town; the driver of this particular vehicle took one look at me and hauled on the reins. He was off the seat in a flash, opening the door for me and sweeping off his hat in one grand gesture.

"Where to, luv?"

I pointed at French's hansom, fast fading from view down the length of the Strand. "Can you follow that cab?"

The driver clapped his ancient bowler on his head and sprang onto the seat. He slapped the nag's buttocks with the reins, and we lurched away from the curb. I had my head out the window, but it was dashed difficult to see, what with the carriages and hansoms directly in front of us. I hoped the driver had a better prospect from his seat above, and indeed the fellow drove with purpose, whipping his horse through gaps in the traffic and cursing his fellow drivers with a fluency I hadn't heard for some time. We followed the Strand, passing the soaring elevation of Nelson's Column in Trafalgar Square and trundling down the Mall. We turned north, skirting Green Park, and entered the rarified atmosphere of Mayfair, moving steadily into quieter areas where few pedestrians strolled and now and then a cab or carriage creaked slowly down the streets. It was close to eleven o'clock when the hansom halted and the driver's face appeared in the window.

"Tallyho," he whispered. "You'll find him round the corner there, payin' his driver. You'll be alright, miss?"

I handed him the fare and a generous tip. "Yes, I shall be fine. You're a superb driver."

He sketched a salute to me as he jumped up onto the seat and clucked at his horse. I made haste for the corner.

French's hansom was pulling away from the curb, and the man himself was gliding sedately up the steps of a handsome town house of generous proportions. The curtains had been drawn back from the ground-floor windows and lights blazed within. Against a backdrop of glittering candles and emerald watered-silk wallpaper, men in white tie and ladies in pink and mauve gowns chattered animatedly, glasses of champagne in their hands. I had thought French's appointment might be with Dizzy or perhaps an informer; I hadn't anticipated that he would set aside his role as the prime minister's agent long enough to attend a bash. Perhaps he wasn't quite the dedicated spy he'd seemed to be.

This wasn't French's residence; he had rung the bell and was now cooling his heels impatiently, slapping his gloves into his palm. From my vantage point, I had a clear view of the door. I waited impatiently, too. Eventually an ancient geezer with a face like a desiccated pear pulled open the door, bowed precariously and held out an arthritic claw for French's hat.

A rosy-cheeked blonde in a glorious peach satin dress and a diamond choker (well named, that; a monkey would have strangled on that bloody stone) appeared behind the butler, produced a squeal that made me wince and rushed to French, clasping his hands in hers and putting up her cheek to be kissed.

I knew she'd be a vapid little wench.

If you're the romantic type, then you might think this bit of news was shattering and that poor India would be reduced to tears and need a cold compress and a sleeping draught, in which case you haven't been paying sufficient attention and are sadly misinformed about my character. I did feel an uncharacteristic tightness in my throat, which I attributed to a night spent with the anarchist chappies in a smoke-filled room. I will also admit to feeling rather surly for the next couple of days. People are entitled to their secrets, but that rule, in my opinion, does not apply to French, or come to think of it, to men in general. Certainly women are permitted to hold a few cards close to the vest. The last time we admitted to any curiosity or confessed to sampling an apple, we were slapped down pretty hard. Consequently, we've learned to smile and simper and pretend to be agreeable idiots while plotting the best way to winkle a few more quid out of our blokes. Yes, women have always had secrets and always will. I'm afraid men would be very distressed to learn what their sweet darlings were thinking. Frankly, I don't think men are strong enough to bear the shock. But I digress.

The next meeting of the anarchists was looming, and I set aside (temporarily) my musings upon how best to muscle the truth from French about his domestic arrangements and concentrated on contributing some suitably bloodthirsty plan to my radical friends. On the evening of the powwow I armed myself with my Bulldog, summoned a cab and once more made my way to the Bag O' Nails. The fog and mist that had shrouded the city for weeks had lifted, but rain clouds scudded across the sky, visible in the hellish glow from the tanneries and factories along the river. Entering Seven Dials, I almost wished for the obscuring veil to blot out the scenes of destitution and squalor that met my gaze.

Bonnaire and Flerko were waiting for me outside the tavern. Bonnaire held my hand a bit longer than strictly necessary while he gazed into my eyes. I simpered a bit and pulled my hand away like a shy lass, and he lapped it up. After exchanging pleasantries with Flerko, the three of us set off at a rapid pace. On our previous journey the brume had obscured the streets and I'd walked along blindly, propelled by Bonnaire. Tonight visibility was better and I made note of our route, paying close attention to our twistings and turnings and observing any landmarks we passed. We turned right out of the Bag O' Nails and left at a rag and bone shop and skulked along various streets and alleys. Once I thought I heard light footsteps behind us and Flerko swung round and surveyed the street. I was sure our follower was Vincent and sucked in a breath, but the little bugger must have found cover, for Flerko stared for long minutes into the darkness before turning back to us and signaling us to proceed.

When we reached the vacant shop, Bonnaire sent Flerko out for a reconnaissance, and the Frenchman and I groped our way down the passage to the secluded chamber. We were the last to arrive. Schmidt and French had their heads together over a sheaf of ink-smeared papers, Thick Ed was whistling a popular ditty and gauging the thickness of a wire and Harkov was languidly smoking a cigar, his boots propped on a wooden box. Flerko bustled in behind Bonnaire and me and announced that we had arrived at our destination unobserved.

"Let us begin," said Harkov, extinguishing his cigar on the stone floor and sliding the stub into the pocket of his coat. "I shall first report on my visit to the International Congress of Working Men in Geneva that was held two weeks ago. There was not sufficient time at our last meeting to inform you of the events that took place there, nor of the findings of the congress."

I stifled a groan, and I could have sworn I heard Bonnaire do the same. The sound obviously did not reach Harkov, for he polished his monocle and launched into a lengthy monologue of such dullness it would have done credit to a bishop. He told us all about the congress, which apparently was a group of disgruntled workers, socialists, Communards and other revolutionary types committed to the abolition of government and the elimination of the people who employed the workers, all of them gathering at some public hall in Geneva to exchange ideas and plot strategy for the destruction of all governments. My notions of proper anarchical behavior were stretched by Harkov's account, I can tell you. It seems that anarchists are great ones for organization and administration, with a committee for this purpose and a board for that, with a few delegations and councils thrown in for good measure. Frankly, the idea of a bunch of blokes in stiff collars and sober suits saying "A point of order, here," or "May I have the floor?" certainly dented my image of a lone foreigner, grimy and ragged, building bombs by candlelight in a freezing attic.

I don't believe anyone was truly interested in Harkov's account, but that didn't stop him from blathering on until Schmidt finally cleared his throat.

"How very interesting, comrade. It was, I am sure, a worthwhile investment of your time and energy." There was an ironic undertone to his words that made Harkov bristle.

"Indeed, it was," he said. "I had the opportunity to learn what our brothers in arms are doing in Germany and Russia. And there were some Italians there who had some fascinating theories regarding the relationship between trade unions and anarchism. They—"

"I should be very glad to hear their theses," said Schmidt. "Perhaps after the meeting you and I might repair to my lodgings and discuss the matter over a drink. Now, I think, we must plan our next campaign."

Harkov chewed his lip and nodded sullenly. "Of course, comrade. I merely wanted to inform you of the issues we discussed in Geneva."

"I'm sure you enjoyed the intellectual stimulation of the conference," said Bonnaire, "but we were dealing with more practical matters here, namely the destruction of Moreland House."

"What a pity the meeting between the British and the Russians was cancelled," said Schmidt.

I was afraid this line of talk might eventually wander into the territory encompassing the reliability of the intelligence I had passed along, so I thought I'd lead the hounds astray. "Should we select an individual to assassinate, or disrupt a government function?"

"We should choose an action that will have a devastating effect upon public opinion. The newspapers are already critical of the government's inability to stop the attacks," said Harkov.

"We could blow up the Tower of London," Flerko said. "It is emblematic of the power of the British Empire."

Thick Ed snorted. "You got any idea how much dynamite it would take to demolish that thing?"

Bonnaire was stroking his beard. "An individual would be more accessible, though the effect would be less dramatic than destroying the Tower."

"What about Viscount Cross, the home secretary?" I put in.

French's cool gray eyes darted in my direction. "That would certainly stir up Scotland Yard," he said.

"That is why I suggested it. It would be quite a feather in our cap if we could kill the man responsible for policing and national security."

There was a general murmur of approval, and Flerko clapped a hand over mine in his excitement.

"But that would be superb!" he crowed.

Harkov's glistening black eyes were leveled at me. "Have you any clients who could provide information about his movements?"

I hesitated a moment, pretending to think. "I've one or two chaps in mind. I might be able to tease something out of them."

Schmidt had folded his hands over his belly and was contemplating the ceiling. "May I venture to present another proposal?"

Harkov nodded politely.

"It would certainly be a coup if we were to assassinate the Home Secretary. It would indeed have the desired effect of arousing the Yard, but I would suggest that might not be the best thing for us." Schmidt dropped his gaze and surveyed us each in turn. "At the moment, the police are worried about us, but they have not yet brought the full weight of their authority to bear upon us. Should we kill Viscount Cross, every foreigner in this city will be placed on a ship and sent back to his own country. I cannot speak for the rest of you, but I should find the situation in Germany a bit awkward."

Flerko gnawed a fingernail and looked anxious. "The Third Section—"

"Quite," said Harkov quietly. "The Third Section would rejoice at laying hands on me."

"I cannot go back to Russia," said Flerko.

For anarchists, they were a pusillanimous bunch. Of course, I'd never been tortured by the tsar's secret police, so perhaps I should be more forgiving.

"I don't think we should delude ourselves into thinking that the police will be less diligent in hunting us down if we kill a baronet rather than a duke," French said quietly. "Any action we take will prompt a public outcry and increase the pressure on the authorities."

We all sat and contemplated those sobering words. Trust French to put a damper on the party.

"If that is the case," said Flerko, "then we should aim to inflict as much damage as possible with one blow, and plan an escape that will allow us to leave the country and regroup elsewhere."

Damn these radical types. Flerko might be happy floating from country to country, living on scraps and dreams, but I'm fond of England and do not plan to spend the prime of my life scraping a living in some ghetto populated by grubby foreigners who exist on cabbage soup and dumplings. I hadn't signed up to Dizzy's scheme in order to flee the country after a spectacular (and possibly suicidal) gesture. And if we all put up our tails and scattered to the four winds, who'd find the elusive Grigori for Superintendent Stoke? Speaking of Grigori...

"What would Grigori prefer that we do? Assassinate an

important leader or plan a grand stroke that will terrify the public?" I asked.

Harkov squared his shoulders and sat up straight at the mention of our sponsor. He was a self-important bastard, and here was his chance to condescend to the rest of us through his connection with Grigori.

"Have you spoken with him about possible plans?" asked Schmidt.

"Naturally I have consulted with him," Harkov said sulkily.

"And what did he suggest we do?"

"His general view is that we should seek to cause as much confusion and fear as possible. It is all very well to exterminate the odd aristocrat, but that act does not create sufficient apprehension in the public mind. Only when the citizens of the city are themselves at risk will we generate the kind of mass hysteria that undermines the government."

I didn't dare meet French's eye for fear of giving away the game, but I quailed at the prospect of trying to prevent bloodshed at some sort of public gathering. French and I could easily have thwarted a plan aimed at an individual (though it might have been deuced difficult to do so without revealing ourselves as British agents), but a plot on a larger scale would be hard to circumvent.

"We might attack a conference of the Conservative Party," said Bonnaire. "Or a public address by a party leader. Politicians never miss a chance to appear before an audience."

"A football match?" suggested Schmidt.

"Football?" said French. "We want people to join our cause, not hang us from the nearest lamppost because we blew up their favorite sporting club."

Flerko was bouncing in his chair, emitting muted shrieks.

"The memorial! The memorial!"

"What memorial?" asked Harkov.

"On the twelfth of the month the government is holding a public memorial service in Trafalgar Square, marking the twentieth anniversary of the Indian Mutiny. That is this Saturday."

I vaguely recalled seeing the service mentioned in the papers, but it had slipped my mind. Why anyone would want to remember that particular sequence of horrors was beyond me, but we English love to wallow in the darkest moments of our history. Just mention the massacre at Sati Chaura Ghat to any chap on the street and watch his spine straighten and his jaw jut out. It won't be a minute before he'll be looking for a Hindoo to wallop. A commemoration of the poor sods who perished in the mutiny would likely draw a fair crowd, eager to shed a tear at the thought of English innocence and Indian perfidy.

A murmur of interest ran round the table.

"The prime minister will be there," said Flerko, beaming. "And a whole host of cabinet ministers and generals and admirals. What a blow to the state. Boom! Just like that. All gone." He flung up his hands in glee. Lord, but he was an excitable chap. I made a mental note to stand as far as possible from the little Russian at the memorial service. The chap was deuced twitchy.

Harkov rooted in his pocket and found the cigar stub he'd placed there earlier. He popped it in his mouth and sucked it contemplatively.

"A large crowd," he muttered. "Prominent figures. A bloody great explosion." He whipped the cigar from his mouth and pointed it at Thick Ed. "No! Not one explosion. A series of explosions!"

"How many?" asked Thick Ed.

"A dozen," Harkov said firmly.

Thick Ed shook his head. "Impossible. I only have the materials for five."

Harkov sulked. "Well, it shall have to be five, then."

Flerko chortled. "And I shall help you arm the bombs and place them around the square."

"Um," said Thick Ed, "appreciate the offer, comrade, but it might be best if I handled things myself."

Flerko looked downcast at missing the opportunity to plant a device that would eviscerate several dozen innocent bystanders.

"I plan to be in the crowd to observe the effects of our plan," said Bonnaire. "At a safe distance from the bombs, of course. You can join me, Flerko. In fact, we should all attend."

Harkov avoided our eyes. "I shall be in Lyon on the twelfth."

"Another conference?" There was a soupçon of venom in Schmidt's voice.

"A meeting on syndicalism and socialism. Grigori has asked me to attend," said Harkov defensively.

"No matter. We shall manage by ourselves," said Schmidt. He looked around placidly. "Shall I assume responsibility for coordinating our plans?"

I had no difficulty in letting Schmidt take the lead. When the memorial went off without a hitch, it would be easy to point the finger at the man who'd been in charge.

We talked strategy first, agreeing that our objective would be to destroy whatever grandstand or speaker's platform might be erected for the notables in attendance, with secondary explosions to be situated so as to kill and maim the most spectators. Nobody blinked an eye at this proposal; apparently anarchists don't flinch at the prospect of slaughtering innocent bystanders if the end result will be freedom for the survivors.

The slaughtered innocents would no doubt disagree.

After that, we got down to tactics. I volunteered to use my sources to obtain a list of attendees and a schedule (which French acidly pointed out could be found in any newspaper— not the least bit helpful, that). For his part, French agreed to suss out the exact location of stands and bunting and so forth. Thick Ed would have a look at the square and plan the location of the infernal machines. And Flerko and Bonnaire would check train tables and sailing schedules, for those inclined to take to their heels after the big show.

"An event of this magnitude will bring the Yard down on us," said Harkov. "I think Flerko's idea of planning an escape is a wise one. Perhaps we should agree to disperse after the service and fix a time and place to meet again, say in six months' time."

"You'll find me at Lotus House," I said. "I don't care to go abroad. And if everyone keeps quiet about our plans, there'll be no need for anyone to go anywhere."

"You're an inspiration," said Schmidt drily, but he smiled when he said it. "However, I shall pack my bag and be ready to leave London, if necessary."

"As will I," Flerko said.

"And I," said Bonnaire. "You don't understand, India. Most of us have been guests of the authorities before. We do not have faith in your English law. We are not used to having any rights. I'll have a ticket in my pocket, just for peace of mind."

Their pessimism didn't bother me in the slightest. I really didn't care whether all the rats fled the ship, except one, the biggest rat of all. Grigori. But how French and I were to get our hands on him was unclear.

We scheduled the date for our next meeting and then dispersed. Outside the shop, I watched Harkov slink away, head tucked between his shoulders. I trusted Vincent would soon be on his tail. Schmidt's soft footsteps had already faded into the night. Bonnaire insisted that he and Flerko accompany me to the cabstand.

"I am grateful, but that won't be necessary," I said. "Since Mr. French will be going there also, I think I shall be safe enough in his company."

French started. "But I—"

"Thank you, Mr. French. It's most generous of you to offer."

He wasn't best pleased, grudgingly presenting his arm for me to take and stalking off at a rapid pace.

"I was not planning to hire a hansom tonight," said French. "What the devil do you want?"

"Don't be such an irritable bastard," I said. "When you want to talk, we meet. When I need to see you, you act like a feral cat."

"Shh. Someone may be watching us. Keep your voice down. Is there something you want to discuss?"

"Of course there is. Why else would I inflict my company upon you?"

"What is it?"

Now you might think this was the perfect time to bounce French about the pretty blonde in Mayfair, but I had matters of more importance to chat over.

"You do realize we've just spent a few hours planning to kill a lot of innocent people, don't you?"

"Yes."

"You don't sound all that worried by the conversation."

"I'm not. One gets used to these sorts of things. As an agent, you're liable to end up in some strange situations."

Pompous bugger. "I suppose we should alert Superintendent Stoke."

French frowned. "Yes, we must. But I'm afraid he'll jump the mark and arrest our comrades before we have a chance to get our hands on Grigori. We must have more time."

"We surely can't let those bloody idiots explode five bombs in Trafalgar Square," I said.

"Oh, no. That would never do. The plot will fail. But our friends must never suspect that you and I had a hand in that failure."

"Have you any ideas as to how to arrange that?"

"I'm mulling over a few options."

I waited, but French seemed to think that was enough information for the enlisted ranks. Damn him.

"I've a few ideas of my own," I informed him.

"Have you?" He sounded amused.

"I'll let you know when I'm finished mulling them over. Now I have another question for you. Do you know a Charles Goodwood?"

"The Earl of Clantham? Good God. Where did you run across him?"

"I haven't met the man. I've only heard his name mentioned at Lotus House."

"You would have heard it there," French said. "He's a wastrel of the vilest sort. Cheats at cards but has still managed to run through his family's fortune. He's hardly ever sober, and he consorts with a wicked crowd. He keeps a stable of slatternly strumpets and has even lived openly with one or two of them."

French caught himself then. I heard the quick intake of his breath. "I say, India. I didn't mean to—"

"Tell the truth?" I laughed. "I'm not a fragile bloom that has to be sheltered from the harsh wind of reality. I do find it interesting, though, that the first of Goodwood's sins is fleecing his fellow gamblers. The sluts come third."

French cleared his throat. Before he could apologize for his lack of sensitivity, I cut in with a question. "Does Goodwood live in London?"

"He has a home on Eaton Square. Why are you so interested in the man?"

I had an answer prepared. "I thought that if we had to sacrifice some toff to the bloodthirsty anarchists, Goodwood wouldn't be a great loss to society."

French halted in his tracks and turned to face me. He gripped my arm tightly. "Don't get carried away with your role. You're getting deuced enthusiastic about suggesting candidates for assassination."

I shook off his hand. "Why shouldn't I? If we know the target, we can easily protect him. Subverting this memorial plot isn't going to be easy."

"And if our suggestions are followed by failure, our friends in the Dark Legion may put together the pieces of the puzzle and conclude that you and I are in league with the authorities. It's quite common for the police to plant agents provocateurs in anarchist cells for the purpose of suggesting particular attacks, only to have the cell members arrested or killed when they attempt them. It's far better for us to work behind the scenes. Let Flerko suggest the targets. We'll find a way to protect them."

I do so hate being lectured by French on the role of a prime minister's agent. I've never been good at taking instruction, even if it's in my best interest to do so. There's just something about receiving a lecture that grates on my nerves. It's doubly annoying if it's the poncy bastard delivering the sermon.

I felt a childish desire to irritate the man. "I hope you're right, Peregrine."

"Oh, not that blasted idiocy again. Listen, my name is—"

"Don't tell me. I prefer guessing. Is it Aethelstan?"

"No."

"Baldaric?"

"I'm afraid not."

We had reached the cabstand by then, which was just as well, as I know that I was feeling disposed to clout French on the head, and from the tone of his voice, he'd have returned the favor. He handed me up into the cab and closed the door behind me.

"Good night, India. I shall contact you soon."

"Good night, French. Give my regards to the ball and chain." I thumped the roof of the cab, and we sprang away from the curb. It was too dark to see French's face, but I was sure I'd hit the target with my parting shot.

I had much to ponder on the drive back to Lotus House. I had an address for Charles Goodwood, and I planned to pay a call upon the scoundrel. It sounded as if the old boy were susceptible to feminine charms, and I had no doubt I'd wangle some information from him about my mother. His reputation didn't concern me, though French the gentleman clearly had strong opinions about his character. How typical, and quaint, of French. That attitude would never do, not in my line of work. It's the bounders and cads who pay the bills, you see, and I've yet to see a bloke of that type I can't handle.

Of more immediate concern was our jolly band's plan to bomb the Indian Mutiny memorial service. I hoped French had a background in bomb making, and more important, in disarming the bloody things, though I don't know how he would manage to neutralize five of the infernal machines, all timed to explode at the same minute. Unless he was thinking that I might assist him in that endeavor. Dear me, I should have to put some thought into avoiding that situation, as I was averse to leaving bits of myself all over Trafalgar Square.

An inkling of a scheme was bubbling in my brain by the time

we reached Lotus House. Lost in thought, I paid the driver and stood for a moment staring sightlessly into the murky gloom. I should arrange a meeting with French, Dizzy and Superintendent Stoke soon, to get my stratagem on the table before the same ploy occurred to French. To those who would say that it matters not who receives the credit for an idea, I say, "You're a bloody idiot." Icicles will be forming in hell before I let French get a leg up. I permitted myself a smile as I dashed up the steps to the door and inserted my key. I was imagining French's face when someone threw a sack over my head.

12

It was made of hessian cloth and, by the smell of the thing, had once contained turnips. It was not a pleasant sensation, but hessian cloth is loosely woven and I was in no danger of being suffocated. The more frightening aspect of the affair was the fact that a pair of burly arms was wrapped around my torso, squeezing my arms against my body so that I couldn't reach the revolver in my purse. The fellow's grip was so tight, in fact, that my nerveless fingers slipped open and the purse tumbled out of my hand. I confess I was disappointed in myself. I'd been so preoccupied with sharing my ingenious plan with Dizzy and French that I'd neglected to keep a sharp eye out for villains.

I lowered my head and then snapped it back as hard as I could, straight into my attacker's face. He grunted loudly when my skull struck his nose and staggered a step or two, which gave me the time I needed to execute the second part of my plan to escape. I prayed I was still facing the front door of Lotus House, but even if I wasn't, I had a fair chance of catching the rogue off guard. I sagged against the bloke who'd seized me, lifted my feet and extended them. To my utter joy, I planted them against the hard surface of the house. Then I pushed off with all my might. My captor and I reeled backward, teetered precariously at the top of the steps and then tumbled down them to the pavement.

When it comes time for me to write my manual for female agents of the Crown, I shall be sure to include the instructions for this form of escape, along with a proviso that it hurts like billy-o when you hit the ground. The ruffian's arms loosened, and I rolled to one side, eluding his searching hands. A dandy move, that, and it would have succeeded except the fellow who'd bagged me had brought along a second chap, who now fetched me a clip on the ear that prevented me from hopping to my feet. Then the first fellow scrambled to his feet and yanked me upright, enveloping me again in his fierce embrace. Rough hands seized my legs and lifted my feet into the air. I was being hauled away from Lotus House like, well, a sack of turnips. I tried to scream (little good that would have done, anyway, as the local plod was more inclined to arrest me than come to my assistance), but the chap who had clamped his arms around me was as strong as an orangutan and I struggled just to draw breath.

The two brutes who had nicked me were moving at a shocking pace, and I knew if I didn't do something quickly I'd soon feel the sharp end of Mother Edding's pigsticker. I began to wriggle like an eel in a basket, twisting my upper body and trying to bend at the waist to loosen my captors' grip. It worked a treat, and I heard two sharp expletives as I slithered from their grasp.

I had indeed liberated myself, but there was a rather steep price to pay. Being dropped from a height of three feet or so knocked the wind out of me and half-stunned me to boot. I lay in a heap in a puddle of rainwater, wheezing like a retired coal miner, while the blokes stood over me blowing hard and muttering curses.

"Bit o' trouble, ain't she?" said one, in a voice like a barrow load of gravel being emptied onto the ground.

"She tole us she would be, didn't she?" replied his compatriot. Neither sounded as though they were old Wykehamists. "Pick 'er up and let's get on wif it."

"I'd like to finish this one off right 'ere, but she don't want it to be quick. She said to draw it out and make 'er suffer."

My breath rattled in my throat. This did not sound like your average robbery with violence. I had only one card to play and I put it face up on the table. "I've got money," I informed them in a shaky voice. "It's in my purse. I dropped it when you nabbed me. Take me back to Lotus House and you can have it all." What I intended to do, naturally, was recover my Bulldog from my purse and acquaint these two thugs with the business end of Mr. Webley's creation.

I waited while the two geniuses thought this over. After a lengthy pause, Gravel Voice cleared his throat. "Wouldn't 'urt to take the money, 'Enry. *She* don't 'ave to know a fing about it."

I was occupied trying to surreptitiously worm my way out of the hessian bag. The sack had been pulled down to my forearms, but if I squirmed gently along the surface of the road, the bag would ride up and soon my arms would be free to the elbows, at which point I'd be able to reach up and pull the blasted thing off my head.

"'Ere's a plan for you, Tom. Why don't you run back and snaffle the purse and I'll stay 'ere with 'Er 'Ighness. Then we do the rest just like she told us to."

This attracted my attention. I'd be hanged if I let these two louts roll dice for my Bulldog. If they weren't going to cooperate, neither was I. I commenced thrashing like a demented salmon, trying to wriggle out of my hessian shackles and screaming at a volume calculated to raise the ghosts from the nearest cemetery.

"Bloody 'ell!" said Gravel Voice.

"Shut 'er up," urged his friend.

Gravel Voice was trying. He had me in a headlock, with the bag pressed tightly against my face. I informed him that I did not care for this treatment by hammering his body with my fists. I'm embarrassed to admit that this did little more than annoy him, for I distinctly heard him say, "Blasted woman," right before he rapped me sharply on the point of my chin with his clenched fist.

A sour, metallic taste filled my mouth, and a sharp pain, as sharp as the point of Mother Edding's pigsticker, skewered me right between the eyes. My arms and legs flopped limply. Gravel Voice had a hand on my head, pressing me into the ground, but he needn't have bothered. All the fight had gone out of me. I was still conscious, but only just. Sounds came from a long distance away. I heard a window rumble open and a querulous old lady railing against the three of us for disrupting her sleep.

Gravel Voice was still huffing from the exertion of thumping me, but his companion answered. "Nuffink for you to worry about, ma'am. 'Igh spirits among friends, is all."

We were sharply advised to take our high spirits elsewhere or she would set the dogs on us. One of my abductors propped me into a sitting position and pulled up the bag just long enough to stuff a dirty handkerchief into my mouth. Then he yanked the sack down over my head again. I was in no condition to spar with these blokes, but they weren't taking any chances now. I felt a rough cord drawn around my body, entrapping my arms, and a second piece of rope was pulled tight around my ankles. They could have saved themselves some trouble if they'd trussed me up at the start, but I suppose they thought that notwithstanding Mother Edding's warning, they could handle

India Black. Which, if I am truthful, they appeared to have done. I had just enough wit about me to feel a certain amount of satisfaction that the old woman in the window had sent them on their way with such alacrity that they seemed to have forgotten my purse. I wasn't keen on parting with my hard-earned cash, but I'd rather lose a few sous than have my weapon filched.

After binding my arms and legs, the two of them gathered me up and off we went. We hadn't traveled far when Gravel Voice grunted, "'Ere we are," and I was lifted into the air and deposited unceremoniously onto a bed of rough wood. One of the men threw a coarse wool blanket over me. A horse stamped fitfully and nickered, and the cart (for so I presumed it to be) creaked loudly. My resting place tilted precariously, first to one side and then the other, as the two men climbed aboard. Gravel Voice made a clicking noise, and the cart started with a jerk.

Stretched out in the back of the cart, snug and warm and protected from the night chill by a blanket, may sound like a deuced fine way to travel, but it is not. I felt every cobble and brick in the city of London as the contraption jolted along toward its destination. The wheels rattled and the nag clopped along and my head bounced against the crude boards of the cart with every step.

I was floating in and out of consciousness, vaguely aware that we were moving into less sanitary surroundings than my neighborhood. An odor of rot and decay soon penetrated the cloth bag, and the air grew thick and moist. Soon I smelled tar and tallow, spices and coffee, rotting fish, and the stench of human waste being hauled to the dumping grounds east of the city. Even in my half-fuddled state, I felt a prickle of unease. I'd been expecting to be presented to Mother Edding, and at the sight of the ancient trollop I'd regain my strength and give her the walloping she deserved. But we were near the Thames, not Seven Dials. I felt a frisson of fear.

An astonishing variety of items is dumped into the river: kitchen refuse, ashes, broken nails, old boots, oyster shells, Mrs. Drinkwater's muffins and the occasional dead body. This is not a fact that ever gave me pause, until now. There's something about becoming the evening meal for the local fishes that brings one up short. Not that there was anything I could do about it, not strapped down like a lunatic on the way to Bedlam, nor feeling as limp and woozy as I did. Perhaps Gravel Voice and his friend were stopping by the docks for some other reason, to purchase a bale of wool, say, or a bit of ambergris. I felt a jolt of anger at the evil Mother Edding, and then at myself, for underestimating the old horror, and at the fact that I was going to have to engage in some first-rate groveling if I was going to save myself.

The cart rumbled to a halt. It was dead quiet here, save for the lap of waves against the wharf and the sad drone of a ship's horn out in the fogbound reaches of the river. The smell of the foul water was overpowering. I'm a cynical optimist, mostly, or an optimistic cynic, if you like, which means I always expect the worst and I am pleasantly surprised when it doesn't happen. At this moment, though, I wasn't feeling sunny.

Gravel Voice and Company hopped off the seat and walked to the back of the cart, where they seized my ankles and dragged me backward like a rat from a hole. I moaned piteously and mewed like a kitten, trying to extract an ounce of pity, but they were having none of it. I willed myself to struggle, but my limbs were paying me no mind and my head hurt like blazes. The clatter of their boots on the cobbles changed to a hollow thumping noise, which matched the tempo of my heart. Surely those echoing footsteps indicated that my two kidnappers had left dry land and were now carrying me out onto one of the many wharves along the Thames. We straggled onward, and then, to my utter horror, I heard Gravel Voice say "'Eave 'o," and I was falling helplessly through the air. I had the presence of mind to take one last gasping breath before I hit the water.

Shocking cold it was, not to mention greasy and foul. The force of my fall knocked the wind from me and startled me back to full consciousness. Unfortunately, I also expelled the last drops of precious air I'd inhaled in preparation for my dunking. My nose filled with a disgusting liquid. I expelled it with a snort and pondered my situation. At least the hessian bag and the gag would keep the larger detritus from my mouth, but as I needed to breathe, and soon, it hardly mattered that I wouldn't have to contend with spitting out the odd fish head. I lacked oxygen, my hands and feet were tied and I had a gag in my mouth and a sack over my head. Things could hardly get worse, except they could. Even if I were able to loosen my bonds, rip off the bag and float to the surface, I had yet another obstacle to overcome: I cannot swim. Well, I don't know many whores who can.

I need hardly point out that things were looking very bleak. But India Black doesn't give up without a fight. I didn't know if I was upside down, right side up or facing sideways, but damned if I was just going to float there in the current until I died. I pulled up my knees and kicked, fluttering my feet like a fish tail. I sent an abbreviated message to the Venerable Old Chap in the Sky. My lungs were burning, and pinpricks of light appeared behind my eyelids. I heard a roaring in my ears that grew louder and louder. I was starving for air, and the urge to breathe was overwhelming.

Two things happened simultaneously: I burst through the surface of the river blowing like a porpoise, and some object, roughly the size and weight of an elephant, fell out of the sky and landed on me, driving me back under the water. Stunned, I inhaled more of the wretched stuff, shuddered wildly and kicked hard for the surface. I might come face to face with my assailant, but that prospect frightened me less than drowning. My thoughts were not as crisp as usual, but it did occur to me to wonder why one of my abductors had bothered to jump in after me. I didn't concern myself much with the thought, as I still felt the pressing need to breathe.

I broke the waves again and finally got a nose full of pure, blessed air. My God, it was bloody heaven, although I found it hard going, paddling my feet and trying to stay above water while I made up for all those minutes with only river water in my lungs. I choked and spit and gagged, all of which produces a fair amount of noise, but suddenly a sound penetrated the racket. Splashing, and not the gentle paddling of a baby in a tub, but the energetic sloshing of someone headed in my direction.

The bag over my head was becoming quite an inconvenience. I'd have liked to look my attacker in the eye before he held me underwater and ended this affair, but I could only wait, my legs flailing more slowly with each passing moment, while he closed in on me.

A hand touched my shoulder, and I summoned the energy to thrust my feet once more against the weight of the water, shoving the fellow with all the strength I could muster. It must have felt like a gentle head butt from a month-old lamb. I had, however, taken him by surprise, and I heard him grunt when I hit him. I kicked again and succeeded in driving my shoulder into his. He lurched backward and sputtered loudly, cursing faintly. But that was all I had. My hands and arms were numb, my breath came in ragged gasps and the weight of my clothes was dragging me inexorably to the bottom of the Thames. It was small comfort, but I'd be waiting in hell when Mother Edding joined the party, and then we'd see who had the upper hand.

"Stop thrashin' about, India, or you'll kill us bof," said Vincent.

I have to hand it to that little toad. Within minutes of towing me to shore, he'd organized an army of odiferous imps to steal a handcart and haul me home, all the while assuring the urchins that I'd be "'appy to pay up" just as soon as I was feeling better.

I sat in my drawing room, wrapped in a blanket and shivering like a stray dog. Mrs. Drinkwater had provided a glass of hot whisky, with a teaspoon of honey and two cloves floating in it, which I sipped gratefully. Her scones might be inedible, but her toddy was brilliant. Vincent, also wrapped in a blanket (which I would have to burn later) had eschewed the toddy for a tumbler of brandy and a cigar. And French was perched across from me, turning a glass of whisky grimly in his hand and glaring at me as if I'd arranged my own kidnapping.

"Thank you very much for coming to my rescue, Vincent." I smiled sweetly at him. I positively adored the scamp tonight. I allowed myself to indulge the feeling, as I knew it wouldn't last long. "Wherever did you learn to swim like that?"

"Oh, I been playin' in the river since I was a boy," he grinned. That might account for the smell that accompanied the young rapparee.

"You, however, have some explaining to do." This was directed at French. "Why was Vincent following me? He was supposed to be following Harkov."

"Two reasons," said French. "You'd already been attacked by this Edding creature once before, and if you weren't going to take any precautions against another incident, I intended that Vincent would be on hand to assist you."

So Vincent had told him about the disgruntled madam. I would have to settle that score with the whelp at a later time. Actually, I might have another score to settle with him.

"If you saw the whole thing, Vincent, why didn't you intervene sooner? You might have saved me from a Thames baptism."

Vincent looked sheepish. "I was 'angin' back, you see, on account of you always gettin' so fussed about bein' followed and looked after. By the time I got up to Lotus House, those blokes had already wrapped you up and were carryin' you off. I reckoned I'd just follow and take me chance when I got it. I didn't know they was gonna throw you in the river. I figured they'd take you to Mother Edding so she could teach you a lesson, and I'd rescue you then."

"I could have handled Mother Edding, if only the witch had played fair and challenged me directly."

French sighed theatrically. "You're right. It's bloody inconsiderate of your enemy to ambush you."

"And the second reason?"

"I wanted to be sure that no one in the Dark Legion suspected that you are a spy and decided to do something about it."

"I don't know why I would be singled out by that bunch of foreign hooligans. You're just as likely to be thought a spy as I am."

"I'm merely taking precautions."

"Well, then, who's following you? Or don't you need someone to keep an eye on you as well? And don't give me any tosh about my being a woman. I can look after myself." I tugged my blanket tighter around my shoulders and gave French a hard look, daring him to point out that in fact I had been bushwhacked rather easily on my own doorstep. Twice. Best to get on the front foot now. "It's much more important that Vincent stay on Harkov. We need to find Grigori, and following Harkov is the best option we have for locating that Russian devil."

The door to the study opened.

"*Mon dieu,*" Martine gasped when she saw my wan face and bedraggled hair. "I am sorry to disturb you, but Mrs. Drinkwater said you had been attacked by thieves and treated brutally. I was afraid—"

I waved a hand negligently. "It's nothing, Martine. Mrs. Drinkwater was mistaken. It was an accident, nothing more."

Martine's eyes slid across the room to my companions. She gave French the lengthy gaze his dark looks deserved, but did not linger on Vincent.

"Thank you for your concern, Martine. Off to bed now. You need to look fresh for the gentlemen."

The girl nodded and gently closed the door.

"She's a bit of alright," said Vincent.

"She's the girl you hired from Mother Edding? The one who introduced you to Bonnaire?" asked French.

"Yes."

"I wonder if Bonnaire has told her that I'm a member of the group. Do you think she'll tell him that I was here?"

"What does it matter? You'll just be another anarchist who's fallen under my spell."

French shot me a look. "What do you mean, *another* anarchist?"

When I ignored his question, he asked another.

"Do you trust the girl?"

I shrugged. "Who can you trust in this game? She's given me no reason to doubt her, but I wouldn't share any secrets with her. Nor anyone else, for that matter."

"Very wise," said French.

God, the man annoys me with that condescending attitude. "Of course it's wise," I snapped. "You don't have to be the prime minister's agent to appreciate confidentiality. Do you think I'd have Lotus House and a successful business enterprise if I couldn't hold my tongue?"

As he always does at the mention of my profession, French looked embarrassed and quickly changed the subject.

"Why don't you dress, and we'll visit the prime minister and Superintendent Stoke?"

"Now? It's three o'clock in the morning. I don't think Dizzy would appreciate being woken at this hour just to hear about my dip in the Thames."

"We need to discuss the memorial service with him. And I suppose we should summon Stoke. I'm afraid he may want to move against the anarchists immediately. I'd prefer to string them along until we have time to devise a plan to thwart the attack."

"You needn't worry about that," I informed him airily. "I've already thought of a way to prevent the anarchists from detonating any bombs in the square."

I must say that I had anticipated a shade more gratitude than Superintendent Stoke and Dizzy exhibited when I revealed my scheme to them two hours later. The superintendent's black suit was rumpled, and his hair hadn't seen a brush. Dizzy was immaculately turned out in a viridian silk dressing gown and a black velvet fez.

The superintendent sucked his moustache and twittered like an uneasy cockatoo. "Good Lord, that's risky. Sure it will work?"

"I believe it will," said French.

A vote of confidence from this quarter being so unexpected, I nearly choked on my brandy.

"Could send some officers to the next meeting of the cell," mused Superintendent Stoke. "Could arrest 'em all, including you two. Hold you for a few hours. Let you go. No one the wiser. Ship the rest of the chaps back to where they came from."

"And Grigori disappears, only to return to London with a new group of conspirators," I said. "If we do as I suggest, the cell stays together and Grigori remains within our grasp."

Dizzy sipped coffee and looked glum. There's nothing like the prospect of a bomb attack at a public function to put the wind up a politician. If my plan didn't work, the next question-and-answer session at Parliament would be beastly for the old boy. We all knew it was the prime minister's decision to make and it would be his government that fell if things didn't go as planned, so we waited silently while Dizzy turned things over in his mind. He stirred himself eventually and turned to Vincent. French had suggested the young imp come along, as "it was only fair."

"What do you think of Miss Black's idea?" Dizzy asked.

Vincent showed him a gum full of blackened teeth. "It'll be a right doddle."

Superintendent Stoke spit out the ends of his moustache. "Really, my lord, this is most extraordinary. You can't mean to accept this preposterous notion that we should let the anarchists—" The chap had been spurred to utter two complete sentences.

"Plant several bombs in Trafalgar Square?" Dizzy toyed with the silken tassel of his dressing gown. "Put like that, it does sound rather preposterous. However, I am at present inclined to go along with Miss Black's plan, provided that in the days to come we continue to feel comfortable that it will work."

"Not sure *now* that it will work," the superintendent muttered mutinously. "Bloody bad show if things go wrong."

"Don't fret yourself," said Vincent. "I guarantee hit'll work."

The superintendent slurped the ends of his tea strainer into his mouth and sulked.

After the meeting, I pootled off home and had a nap, which was exactly what I needed. Despite having been hauled around the streets of London like a sack of potatoes and imbibing a few lungfuls of the filthiest river in England, I was feeling in fine fettle when I awoke. It was nearly dusk, and I went down to the kitchen to roust Mrs. Drinkwater and see that the whores had dined and were getting ready for the evening's customers. The girls were in a festive mood, for Major Rawlins had sent a note earlier in the day advising that he and his men from the Royal Horse Guards had so enjoyed themselves at Lotus House on their prior visit that they were returning tonight. I felt a little swell of pride that my bints had acquitted themselves so well and that trade was flourishing, for truth to tell, I had been feeling slightly guilty at haring off to chase anarchists. I could rest easy now, knowing that I had done all that a good coach could do and it was up to the girls to play the game once they got on the pitch.

After a dinner that even the prisoners at Dartmoor would have rejected, I gathered my belongings and draped my traveling cloak around my shoulders. When Vincent and I had returned to Lotus House the previous evening, I'd found my purse just where it had fallen when I'd been snatched by Mother Edding's rogues. To my relief not only was my money still in the purse, but so was my Bulldog. I had learned my lesson. From this point on, whenever I traveled alone, I would travel with the Bulldog in my hand, tucked away into the folds of my cloak or in the pocket of my skirt or coat. The next chap who tried to crack my head or deposit me in the river would get some hot lead for his trouble.

As arranged, I met Bonnaire and Flerko at the Bag O' Nails. I would have preferred a more inviting rendezvous, but such establishments were difficult to find in Seven Dials. Flerko was jumping like a flea at the prospect of planning some bloodshed, but Bonnaire was his usual smooth and urbane self, tucking my hand into the crook of his elbow as we made our way through the streets. Flerko chattered aimlessly until Bonnaire sent him to retrace our route, to ensure we were not being followed.

We were the last to arrive. We exchanged pleasantries with the others, remarking on the weather and commenting upon the latest parliamentary debate, behaving much as I imagine Freemasons do before they don their robes and start spouting claptrap. Flerko was itching to get the meeting under way and kept tugging at Harkov's sleeve while Harkov regaled French with tales of the committees he had chaired at the meeting in Geneva. Eventually Schmidt caught Harkov's eye, and the Russian dragged himself reluctantly from his conversation with French and convened the meeting.

I waited until everyone was seated, and then I produced from my purse two sheets of paper delivered to me that day by Superintendent Stoke's messenger. I unfolded them and spread them over the table.

"The list of dignitaries who will be on the grandstand at the memorial, and the schedule for the service."

Six heads bent over the table.

Flerko gave a little squeal. "The lord mayor of London! And General Harmley!"

Schmidt polished his glasses and peered at the paper. "The Earl of Aylesford. Baron Gowe. The Duke of Connaught. But where is the prime minister's name?"

"What?" exclaimed Flerko. "I thought Disraeli would be there."

Well, he'd been planning on attending, until Superintendent Stoke had begged him to stay at home that day, which showed, I thought, a shocking lack of faith in French and me.

"Apparently, he'll be in Paris that day," I said. "Meeting a sheik from some dusty little country who's been flirting with the Russians. The prime minister means to keep him sweet. Or so my sources tell me."

"Blast!" Flerko pounded his fist into his palm.

Bonnaire ran a finger down the list. "Not a bad bag, though. If we assassinate this lot, we'll decapitate the government."

"The service starts at three o'clock on Saturday afternoon," said Harkov, consulting the schedule.

"There's something else," I said, producing yet another sheet of paper. "Here's the duty roster for the Yard. They'll have men in place at the square from six o'clock in the morning on Saturday."

Flerko looked anxious. "We could place the bombs before that, but what about arming them?"

"That won't be a problem," said Thick Ed. "The way those alarm clocks work, I can arm them up to twelve hours in advance. I'll waltz into the square around four in the morning, put the bombs in place and set the clock to go off at a few minutes past three in the afternoon."

Schmidt swept his hand over the papers on the desk. "Where did you get this information, India?"

"I have a friend at one of the dailies. The list of officials and the agenda for the program came from him. As for the duty roster, I obtained that from a young man of recent acquaintance. He's an inspector with the Yard, and the poor lad is rather taken with me. He enjoys showing me his office, late at night." I dropped my eyes modestly. "Occasionally, he falls asleep and I let myself out the door, but not before seeing if there are any morsels of information lying about. I visited him last night, thinking that I might pick up something useful."

I'd rehearsed this speech many times in the last few hours, but damned if the story didn't sound a little thin when I reeled it off. I sneaked a glance round the table, to see how well the tale had gone down. Flerko looked slightly embarrassed at the degradation I'd endured to get my hands on the duty roster. As we were not discussing bombs, Thick Ed looked disinterested. Schmidt was studying the paper, while Bonnaire appeared bored, as did French. Harkov gave me a speculative look, his black eyes glittering in the lamplight. I sucked in a breath and waited for the challenge, but none came.

"Well done," said Schmidt, and replaced the sheet of paper on the table. "So, how do we proceed?"

"I've drawn a map of the square, showing the location of the grandstand," said French, conjuring a page from his pocket. "Yesterday I took a stroll there to verify the location of dustbins and the like, and found that the stand is already under construction. I bought a cup of tea for one of the workmen at a nearby stall, and he was happy to share the details about what he and his fellow workers were building."

Thick Ed studied French's drawing, chewing a meaty thumb. "I'd like to get a bomb right under the grandstand. Maybe two of them. The others I'd place among the crowd. In this area, I think," he said as he tapped the sketch.

"Not there," I objected, leaning over the table. "Why not put the others at the edges of the square? I'd time those to explode slightly later than the bombs under the stand. The crowd will already be panicked and trying to escape. A few explosions along the main streets leading from the square, and we'll create chaos."

I'd scored a goal with that proposal. A thin smile crossed Harkov's lips. Schmidt nodded slowly. Flerko issued a guttural bark, which I assumed was Russian for "jolly good." A fleeting look of horror crossed French's face. I must have a talk with him soon. I feared that he wasn't entering into the spirit of things. In for a penny, in for a pound, I figured. If you're going to infiltrate an anarchist cell, then do so with gusto. I'd only suggested murdering innocent bystanders for effect, you understand. I aimed to boost my standing among my fellow conspirators. I did not think for a minute that our bombs would actually explode on Saturday. As French had backed my plan with Dizzy and Superintendent Stoke, he shouldn't get distracted by my callous proposition that some of Vicky's subjects should be included in our scheme of mass murder.

"I'm going to have a look at the square tomorrow," Thick Ed announced.

"I'm going with you," I said. "If I'm going to be involved in a plot against Her Majesty's government, I want to know all the details. I'm not one to take chances."

Harkov nodded gravely.

Thick Ed, however, did not seem pleased at the prospect of my company. "We can't all go poking around there. We'll draw attention to ourselves."

I concede that fact. A woman with my face and figure rarely goes unnoticed. Nevertheless, I was going to know every last component of the operation or I'd stay home with a cup of cocoa while the rest of this lot skulked about in the early morning hours before the memorial service. I informed Thick Ed, and the rest of them, of my feelings. Anarchists, like most men, collapse as easily as one of Mrs. Drinkwater's imperfectly set blancmanges once an independent-minded female informs them of the way things will be. I could see that French wasn't pleased about my horning my way into Thick Ed's reconnaissance mission. I'm sure French had intended to invite himself along, and was now precluded from joining the party as Thick Ed clearly believed in the old adage of too many cooks, et cetera.

I left the meeting feeling rather pleased with myself. French did not accompany me to the cabstand, disappearing in the opposite direction and leaving Bonnaire and Flerko to supervise my journey. I'd made arrangements with Thick Ed to meet him at Nelson's Column the next morning, and we'd all agreed that as Saturday was just around the corner we would meet again tomorrow night to hear the result of the scouting mission and to refine our plan. One of these nights I needed to stay at Lotus House and keep an eye on the sluts, but there's a lot of work involved in slaying gentry and bringing down the government, exactly how much I hadn't realized. Clara Swansdown was a reliable girl, as far as whores go, and if I passed along a few extra shillings to her, I felt sure she'd do an adequate job of riding herd on the girls. This might be a temporary solution to my present predicament, but I'd have to make other arrangements for the future if I intended to trot off whenever Her Majesty called.

13

The next morning found me sloping around Trafalgar
Square with the less than loquacious Thick Ed. I'll tell you
something you may not know about the square: it's owned by
the Queen, and knowing her propensity for frugality (except
when it comes to her own dinner plate), I expect the British
taxpayer was forking over a fair sum for the rental of the square
for this memorial shindig. The authorities had closed the road
on the north side of the square, and the grandstand, a small
forest of timber beams and joists, was rising there in front of
the National Gallery. All the swells and politicos would have
a grand view to the south, looking down on the masses who
were expected to flock there on Saturday to commemorate those
luckless British folk who'd had the misfortune to be living in
India when the sepoys rebelled. The masses would have to pack
in if they wanted a decent view of Saturday's proceedings. The
fountains to the south had been added to reduce the size of the
square and, consequently, the number of people who could
congregate therein, British politicians having a morbid fear that
any crowd had the potential to become a riotous gang. And

quite rightly, I might add. A London mob can turn dangerous at the drop of a hat.

Thick Ed and I wandered around, closely scrutinizing the dustbins situated around the square and peering up at the statues to see if we could wedge a box containing explosives in between the legs of some admiral or other. We surreptitiously examined the branches of the trees that lined the perimeter of the square and sauntered up the steps to the National Gallery, gazing at the columns and searching for hidden niches. Thick Ed might not be the most engaging of companions, but the fellow was thorough. Long after I'd tired of squinting into nooks and crannies, he was still at it, murmuring to himself as he estimated distance and calculated density and concussive effect. While he was at it, I wandered over to gaze at the grandstand and the gang of workmen engaged in building it. They were an efficient bunch, scuttling about with their sleeves rolled to their elbows. I'd have been knocked flat in ten seconds, as strapping coves darted here and there with boards balanced on their shoulders, but this crew must have done this before, as nobody lost his nut while I watched. The workmen were supervised by a wrinkled, gray-haired gent who looked as though he'd just gotten word that his horse had finished last at Epsom Downs. He stared glumly at the plans in his hand and frowned. The young fellow with him might have been his son, but if so he'd inherited his sunny disposition from the distaff side of the family, for his face was animated and he looked a cheery bloke. I didn't fancy my chances with Papa, but the youngster looked approachable.

"I assume you'd like to get under the grandstand today, to have a look at how it's constructed," I said to Thick Ed. "How were you planning to do that?"

He shrugged. "I thought I'd have a word with one of the

builder boys and see how much he can tell me. If I can't find out anything that way, I'll come back tonight, when everyone has gone home."

"I've got a better idea," I said. "Let's see it in the daylight and save ourselves a trip."

We loitered for the best part of half an hour, waiting to see if the dour fellow and the young chap would part company. I was betting the old fellow would tire of the dust and noise and toddle off to his club for a preprandial snort. I'd gauged the chap correctly, for eventually he handed the building plans to his junior and, judging from the expression on the younger man's face, gave him some unnecessary, or at least unwanted, advice. Then the old fellow climbed into a waiting carriage and left my new friend alone to carry on the work. Thick Ed and I ambled over, as innocent as two pet rabbits.

We must have made an unlikely pair. He appeared to have just finished plowing the south field, and I was dressed with my usual customary elegance. The young man looked up from his plans as we approached. One eyebrow darted upward, but he recovered himself quickly when he got a closer look at me.

"What a marvelous sight!" I exclaimed. I swept a hand in the direction of the stand. "Are you the man responsible for this amazing creation?"

He preened himself a bit at my words. "Yes, I am. I designed the grandstand. I'm an engineer."

"How very exciting. Allow me to introduce myself. I'm Lady Beckinham, and this is my foreman, Edward."

Thick Ed played his part by grunting incomprehensibly and tugging his forelock.

The young man lifted his hat. "David Dawkins. Very pleased to meet you."

"Edward and I are up from Dorset," I chattered on. One of the keys to running a successful bluff is never giving the object of it the opportunity to think about the improbability of what you're saying. It also helps if you're a stunner, like me, which is a further distraction for the average man. "My poor father had undertaken a building project at the Grange, where we live, you know, and then he had the misfortune to suffer a fall from his horse and now he's laid up in bed and I am trying my best to finish out the work for him so that he doesn't fret himself to death and of course Edward here has been a great help. We've come up to London today to look at some materials and we'd read about the memorial service and we thought we'd come down to see the work that's being done and I must say it is impressive and now I find that a young man, just my own age, is actually in charge of this undertaking. It quite takes my breath away!"

It had, actually.

Dawkins blushed. "I'm not quite as young as I appear, you know. And naturally I've the proper degree and training. And I'm not really in charge. My father is."

"Oh, how wonderful! It's lovely, isn't it, to work with your father on such an important project."

Dawkins appeared to doubt the truth of this statement, but he nodded politely.

"I say, do you think Edward and I could have a look at this structure? A close look, I mean. Some of the truss work looks to be just the sort of thing we're thinking of doing at the Grange. Perhaps when the workmen take a break? Would we be imposing on your good nature if we requested a brief tour?"

"You're building something similar to the grandstand?" Dawkins asked dubiously.

"Oh, yes." I said. "And we'd very much like to look at your joinery, if you don't mind."

"What precisely are you constructing?"

"A dovecote," Thick Ed said solemnly. I choked back a laugh. I'd have pegged Thick Ed to have a sense of humor akin to that of the average ox.

"Dovecote?" Dawkins echoed faintly. "How extraordinary. I'd no idea—"

"A very large dovecote," said Thick Ed.

A whistle shrilled and the workmen downed tools.

I batted my eyelids and favored Dawkins with an inviting smile, while my fluttering hand drew attention to my bosom. "What perfect timing," I said. "May we?"

The eyelids, the smile and the breasts had the desired effect, as I knew they would. The poor boy didn't stand a chance. Any objections young Dawkins might have had, had been overruled instantly.

And so I found myself on a work site, dodging pails of screws and stepping over scraps of lumber, all the while prattling on like a debutante after her first glass of champagne so that Dawkins wouldn't notice the intensity with which Thick Ed was scrutinizing the underside of the grandstand. Luckily, Dawkins soon warmed to the task of explaining the technicalities of building the grandstand to such a charming audience. I heard a great deal about proportion and scale, load bearing and massing, and a number of other construction techniques, all of which I immediately consigned to my mental rubbish bin, knowing full well that I should never require any such knowledge in the future. I listened to the building wallah with wide eyes and coos of admiration at some particularly clever bit of structural engineering, while Thick Ed wandered round with one ear cocked in our direction, grunting now and then and asking an occasional question about weight distribution, which young Dawkins was only too happy to answer. I reckon the average construction superintendent doesn't often get a stunning young woman hanging on his every word, for Dawkins rambled on with an enthusiasm I generally reserve for fine whisky and comely fellows. Finally, Thick Ed gave me the briefest of nods, and I interrupted Dawkins's monologue about the proper wood for flooring planks with, "Oh my goodness, is that the time? We must dash, Edward, or we'll miss our train." We left Dawkins gawping after us with his hat raised and the "Pleased to have met you" dying on his lips. I only hoped the fellow hadn't noticed that neither Thick Ed nor I had a watch and that we'd scuttled off in the opposite direction from Victoria Station.

Our cabal convened that night in the damp cellar. Thick Ed had appropriated French's drawing of Trafalgar Square and augmented it with details about the grandstand and the few hideyholes he'd sussed out on our visit that morning. We gathered round the table and stared down at the paper.

Thick Ed tapped the sketch with a massive finger. "Two bombs under the grandstand, to ensure we get all the dignitaries at one go. You lot don't care about the details, but I'll place the machines at the weakest structural points. I'll set the timers so that the explosions are simultaneous and the whole structure will collapse at once." His finger moved to a rubbish bin whose location near the grandstand he'd marked with a penciled circle. "I'll place another bomb here. The other two bombs will go here and here," he said, pointing out the locations on the drawing. "Those three bombs will go off a couple of minutes after the first two devices, just as the crowd is trying to run away."

He'd chosen good hiding places for the last two infernal machines. One would be tucked away beneath the shrubbery growing in a stone planter at one edge of the square, and the second would be hidden inside another rubbish bin at the intersection of Northumberland Street and the Strand, near the southeast corner of the square.

While Thick Ed found it hard to master normal conversational gambits, he clearly knew his stuff when it came to wreaking havoc and was delighted to share his knowledge with the rest of us. The whole scheme sounded bloody efficient, not to mention deadly, and I spared a thought for the poor folk who would otherwise have been turned into mince had Her Majesty's agents not been on the case. Still, there was much to do to avoid an unhappy outcome, including convincing Thick Ed that I had an unrequited love for all things explosive and would be the happiest whore in the world if I could have a tutorial in building bombs.

My request produced a silence so profound that I thought I had erred. Schmidt and Harkov stared at me incredulously. Well, they were the brains of the outfit and despite all that tripe they spouted about equality and such, it was clear they both preferred the intellectual cut and thrust of anarchist theory and not the grubby details. Flerko, predictably, approved of my revolutionary ardor, and I thought Bonnaire might plant a kiss on me then and there.

"Building the devices is a task best left to the experts," said Harkov.

"One cannot become an expert without an education and the opportunity to practice one's skills," I said. "I suppose Thick Ed was born knowing how to make a bomb?"

"Why do you want to learn?" asked Harkov.

"I've already explained to you that if I'm going to trust my fate to you chaps, I plan to know everything there is to know about our operation. And just think of the possibilities! Who would suspect a woman like me of planting bombs? The rest of you might just as well have a placard round your neck that says 'Anarchist Devil' on it."

Harkov sputtered, but Schmidt smiled benignly. "You have a point, Miss Black."

"And I am equally free of suspicion," said French. "I have access to places even Miss Black cannot go. I'd like to learn the art of bomb making myself. Would you have any objection, Thick Ed, if Miss Black and I watched you put together the devices?"

Thick Ed's face was impassive. He glanced at Harkov, who shrugged.

"Alright," said the bomb maker. "But you two aren't to touch a thing, mind. Just watch me. I'll put 'em together on Thursday night before the memorial. Be here at midnight."

I nodded casually, but there was a hard knot in my throat at the prospect of fiddling about with dynamite that no amount of swallowing would remove.

I had a couple of days until Thursday, so I put aside my duties to queen and country and concentrated on the affairs of Lotus House. Major Rawlins and his fellow guardsmen had proved to be loyal customers, returning on a frequent basis and boosting my income enormously. There were the usual bills to pay, including a suspiciously large one to the nearest public house for several bottles of gin I did not remember ordering. I had a think about that and one afternoon while Mrs. Drinkwater was out doing the shopping, I conducted a quick search of her room and found a stash of empty bottles under the bed. Naturally, I had a word with her when she returned, and endured a burned joint for my dinner that evening in retaliation.

Other than the unpleasantness with Mrs. Drinkwater over the gin (an incident the likes of which occurred with such frequency that, frankly, I would have been surprised if it hadn't), things at Lotus House were proceeding on an even keel. Besides the major and his men, our regular customers were returning in droves. Having been kept indoors by inclement weather and forced to endure the company of their charming wives for several weeks, they were a randy bunch and the girls were kept busy. Nothing suits me more than the bustle and hum of a busy brothel. The sluts don't have time for spats, and they're happy counting their shillings. I'm happy toting up the takings and contemplating the seaside bungalow I plan to purchase.

The only event that marred these idyllic days occurred one afternoon while I was having my tea and contentedly reading through my ledgers. I heard a tentative knock at my study door.

"Come," I said, and shoved the books into my desk drawer.

Martine sidled in, lovely as ever but with a subdued and shadowed countenance.

"What is it, Martine? Are you unwell? You are very pale."

"No, mademoiselle. I am not ill." She caught her lower lip between her teeth and looked at me shyly. How I wish I could teach that look to my other sluts; men would go down before it like so many skittles.

"Is something troubling you?"

She hesitated.

"Well?"

She sighed. "Please don't be angry."

In my experience, there's usually a good reason to be when your conversational partner leads with this remark. "Yes, Martine?"

She clasped her hands together and raised them imploringly. "He shouldn't have told me, but he did."

"Who told you what?"

"Julian. Monsieur Bonnaire. He has told me what you plan to do at the memorial service."

I got up from my desk and crossed the room to close the door. "What has Bonnaire told you?"

"That you intend to assassinate many people at the service, and that he will have to flee the country." A sob caught in her throat. I didn't think she was weeping at the thought of the people who might be slaughtered by her boyfriend.

Bugger. I could have kept our plans secret until the last horn sounded, but trust a man to try to impress a girl by baring his bloody soul.

"Nonsense," I said briskly. "There isn't any risk to Bonnaire."

"But he said he would be in danger—"

"Only if we get caught, and if we all keep our mouths shut"— and here I gave her a black look, to let her know I included her in my directive—"no one will know of our involvement."

"You are certain? Julian said—"

I cut her off. "Of course I'm certain. Monsieur Bonnaire exaggerates the peril."

Relief swept her face. "Then he will not die."

"Not unless you tell anyone else that he has told you of our plans."

Puzzlement replaced relief. "I don't understand."

"You know that there are many police informants among the anarchist cells. If any of the others found out that Bonnaire had revealed our objective, they might accuse him of being a spy. They might even kill him."

Martine's pale face grew paler still. "Kill him!"

I seized her arm. "Do not tell anyone else what Bonnaire has told you. His life may depend upon it."

"I will not," she muttered. "Of course I won't."

"Good." I released her and gently patted her shoulder. "Now, wipe away those tears and leave here with a smile on your face. I don't want the other girls asking questions. Can you do that?"

She nodded, and swiped at her eyes with the sleeve of her dress. She gave me a tremulous smile. "I will say nothing, but I still fear for Julian. And for you," she added. "You have been so good to me. I would hate—" She turned abruptly on her heel and scurried out.

"Touching," I muttered to myself. "But unnecessary." Of course there was no danger; not to Bonnaire, nor to me, nor to anyone else who might plan on attending the memorial service. At least, I hoped there wouldn't be.

14

Bonnaire had offered to accompany me from the Bag O' Nails to the cell's meeting place, but I dispensed with his services on Thursday night. I had applied myself to learning the route to the cellar beneath the shop with all the assiduity of a starving Bushman tracking an antelope, and I felt confident I could find my way. I left Lotus House with plenty of time to spare, for I wanted to be sure that I was not followed to my destination. I had my Bulldog for company, and I stalked through the streets of Seven Dials with my hand curled around the revolver's grip, daring anyone to cross my path. I must have looked a right Amazon, for most of the men I encountered, even the drunks, took one look at my face and stepped aside. I wasn't to be trifled with, not tonight, not by that harridan Mother Edding and certainly not by the greasy wraiths who passed for men in this part of London.

French was waiting for me in the doorway of the shop. He lifted his hat politely and bowed his head.

"Good evening," he said.

"Good evening. And before you ask, I was not followed. Were you?"

"I have arrived unaccompanied," he said, a hint of a smile in his voice.

Heavy footsteps echoed down the street, and French ducked his head out of the doorway. "Thick Ed," he said, removing his hand from the pocket of his overcoat. I was not the only one who had come armed.

Thick Ed returned our greetings with a grunt while he fitted the key in the lock. Downstairs we shed our coats and lit the lamps, which did little to penetrate the musky gloom of the place. The bomb maker sat down at his worktable and began to arrange his tools while French and I brought chairs and arranged ourselves on either side.

"Two rules for tonight," said Thick Ed. "The first rule is that neither of you touches a thing on this table unless I tell you to. And the second rule is that neither of you touches a thing on this table unless I tell you to. Understood?"

"Perfectly," said French.

I nodded.

"Right. Let's get started. First we need something to put the bomb in, you understand?"

I did not find this a difficult concept to grasp and averred as much to Thick Ed.

French shot me the "Don't be cheeky" look and said, "What are you using as containers, Ed?"

Thick Ed shoved back his chair and disappeared under the table, emerging like a large disheveled rabbit and dragging a number of wooden boxes with him. He left all but one on the floor and deposited the box he'd selected onto the table with a triumphant thump.

"There," he said. "Ain't that prime?"

I leaned forward. "Consolidated Ironworks," I read aloud.

"Screws. One inch. One thousand. Birmingham."

Thick Ed grinned proudly. I did not see what all the fuss was about, and said so.

"It's from the job site, ain't it? I went back there last night and helped myself to a few boxes and such."

"Splendid work, Ed," said French. "If anyone sees these lying about, they'll think they were left behind by the builders and won't be alarmed."

"That's it. We'll tuck 'em away to one side, of course, but they'll be less likely to attract attention than a biscuit tin or a portmanteau."

I figured our lads in blue might be wary of anything left beneath the grandstand where the lord mayor of the city would be sitting, but if the bombs were found and disarmed by the local plod, then so much the better. The plan would fail, and French and I wouldn't run the slightest chance of being detected. Consequently, I declined to argue with Thick Ed about the logic of his position and made myself comfortable for the lecture. He began to assemble the makings of the infernal device, selecting objects from various containers on the table: a pocket pistol, an alarm clock, a coil of copper wire, a .22-caliber cartridge, some small disc-shaped objects and a knife with a blunt edge.

I picked up one of the discs. "What's this?"

Thick Ed plucked it from my fingers. "A detonator. Didn't I tell you not to touch anything?"

"My apologies, Thick Ed. Now, where's the dynamite?"

"Under the table," he said. "Be careful you don't kick it."

"No worries there," I said, and indeed there were not, as my legs had recoiled under my chair and frozen into position at Thick Ed's words.

He disappeared from view again and came up bearing a

handful of the paraffinned paper packets I'd seen on my first visit to the cellar. Each of the packages was a little over six inches in length and three wide, and a mere half inch thick. I had to squelch the urge to vacate the premises, but Thick Ed was a prudent fellow and handled the packages with all the reverence of an Orthodox priest carrying an icon. He gently deposited the dynamite on the table and exhaled slowly. Despite my misgivings about the deadly stuff, I was curious.

"I've never seen dynamite. What's it look like?"

"Depends," said Thick Ed, "on what's used as the binding agent. Dynamite is nothing more than nitroglycerine and some other material, like dirt or sawdust or charcoal. Some chaps use plaster of Paris. Any of those things will keep the nitroglycerine stable. Otherwise, the stuff is too bloody dangerous to handle."

French had been studying the array of items on the table.

"You figured out what I'm going to do with all this, squire?" asked Thick Ed.

"I've no experience making bombs, but I'm acquainted with firearms. I'm guessing the pistol will fire the cartridge and detonate the dynamite, but I've no idea how the clock comes into it."

"Not bad for an amateur. The trigger of the pistol will be wired to the clock. You notice there's no trigger guard on this gun? That's why I use a pocket pistol. When the alarm runs off, the winding handle of the clock will depress the trigger, firing the cartridge. That will ignite the detonators, and their explosion will set off the dynamite."

"Deuced ingenious," said French. "But you surely can't arm these devices and then carry them about London? If you have the misfortune to trip over a cobblestone, you'll blow yourself to kingdom come."

"Occupational hazard." Thick Ed seemed pleased with this situation. I suppose a bomb maker has a higher tolerance for risk than the average clerk in an insurance office. He picked up the clock and used the knife blade to loosen the screws holding the metal back plate. "But I won't arm the bombs until I've got them in place. Once I've hidden them, I'll cock the triggers of the revolvers and set the time for the alarm to run off, which will be at three fifteen p.m. for the bombs under the grandstands and two minutes later for those around the square."

That was the end of the lesson for the moment as Thick Ed concentrated on the task at hand and French and I leaned over his shoulder and watched him work. I had a particular purpose in learning how to build an infernal machine, but as I observed Thick Ed's beefy fingers moving delicately among the workings of the clock, I permitted myself a little fantasy. It would serve Mother Edding right if her brothel disappeared in a mysterious blast. Now, if I could just find a way to ensure that only the old harridan was in the house and all the girls and customers were safely away. And then there was the problem of the house itself. The buildings in Seven Dials were so rickety that even a small explosion would level a city block. I enjoy revenge as much as the next person, but I draw the line at wanton killing. No, I should have to find a more direct means of removing Mother Edding from the scene. But Mother Edding would have to wait until this sceptered isle was safe from the likes of Harkov and Flerko, and so I settled in to learn how to make a bomb.

Thick Ed's huge hands proved surprisingly dexterous, moving with astonishing ease and grace. He removed the back plate of the clock. Moving cautiously, he packed one side of the wooden box with packets of dynamite, stacking them two deep to the top of the box. Between the packets he gently inserted one of the detonators. Next, he loaded the cartridge into the revolver and wired the weapon to the clock so that the minute hand would make a final turn when the alarm ran off, depressing the trigger and firing the gun directly into the detonator. The hammer would have to be cocked, but once it had been, the slightest pressure against the trigger would be all that was necessary to explode the device.

It was damned fiddly work, and I wouldn't have had the patience to make one bomb, let alone five, but Thick Ed was a man devoted to his work. French and I sat patiently while the fellow fussed with his creations, adjusting a wire here and a string there, and using blocks of wood to hold each clock and pistol steady.

"You'll put these in place early Saturday morning?" asked French as Thick Ed put the finishing touches on the last device.

"I'll be done and gone by the time the police show up at six. Won't take any time to plant 'em, but it will take a few minutes to arm 'em."

"You'll need a lookout," I said. "Why don't we meet you there and keep watch? French could even hide a couple of the bombs for you."

"Of course," French said smoothly, though I could feel the rapier point of his gaze.

Thick Ed peered at us, eyes squinted nearly closed. "Damned if you two aren't more helpful than the rest of this lot put together."

My heart caught in my throat, but I forced a gay laugh. "You mean comrade Harkov hasn't volunteered to carry any dynamite about?"

Thick Ed grinned. "Not him. He's partial to committees and such." We all smiled then, enjoying the bomb maker's little joke, and the moment passed, but it was a useful reminder that French and I were constantly under suspicion, and even our proposals to engage more fully in the anarchists' work was cause for paranoia among our erstwhile allies.

French and I bade good night to Thick Ed, arranging a rendezvous in the early hours of Saturday morning in Trafalgar Square, and then set a sharpish pace toward Lotus House. Gentleman that he is, French wouldn't allow me to travel without an escort for fear that Mother Edding's hired thugs might take another crack at me. Normally, this lack of confidence in my ability to take care of myself would infuriate me, but I had my own reasons for accepting French's overweening solicitude tonight. But before I could raise the subject I wanted to discuss, French spoke.

"Are you confident those devices can be disarmed by an amateur?" he asked in a low voice.

"It seems simple enough."

"Damned dangerous, though. I hope we haven't misjudged the matter. We're endangering a lot of innocent people."

"It's too late to worry about that. We're committed to the plan. Stop fretting. It will all come right, you'll see." I sounded more confident than I was, but I jolly well wasn't going to let French know I had any doubts. Our strategy for foiling the anarchist plot had been, after all, my idea. Best not to exhibit any doubt, for nothing undermines confidence like a general wondering aloud if an escalade was the right tactic just as the ladders go up against the wall.

I, however, would have made an excellent general, for I had considered my strategy for approaching French about his family, and if I do say so myself, it was bally brilliant.

"I say, French. There's something I'd like to discuss with you," I said, making sure to sound rather muted and diffident.

Nothing arouses French's gentlemanly instincts like a female in need of assistance. "I have every confidence that we'll succeed in disrupting the anarchists' plan, but this is a dangerous game we're playing, and I've given a bit of thought to the future. If something should happen to me—"

French swung me round and gripped my shoulders. "Nothing will happen to you, India. I swear it." I could feel his fevered breath on my cheek.

Well, this was deuced gratifying. Since his unexpected appearance at the anarchist meeting, the bloke had been treating me with studied indifference. From the intensity of his voice, he'd obviously been shamming.

"Well, I... I certainly don't think things will go wrong, but... well, one never knows..." I felt curiously light-headed and at a loss for words, a condition with which I was confoundedly unfamiliar.

"I shan't allow... I mean to say, I couldn't bear... Oh, curse it." His arms slid around my waist, and I was crushed to his chest. The Bulldog in my pocket clanked loudly as it encountered his Boxer revolver. Things had taken an unforeseen turn. I'd merely meant to ferret out the truth about his family. My tactical skills and customary composure had deserted me. What to do now?

I kissed him.

I wasn't sure what I expected, but it certainly wasn't that French would recoil from me like a dog whose nose has been bitten by a snake. I've kissed a fair number of gentlemen in my time, and I'm not boasting when I say that most have been more than eager to return the favor.

"Oh, India," said French. "Damnation."

I wrenched myself from his grasp. "I apologize. I obviously misinterpreted the situation," I said coldly. In truth, I was humiliated. Well, who wouldn't be? My first instinct was to pull the Bulldog from my skirt and shoot myself in the head for being such a bloody fool. On second thought, perhaps I'd shoot the poncy bastard. Serve him right for leading me on.

"No, no. You haven't. Misinterpreted the situation, I mean. Oh, hell." French was walking up and down the pavement in front of me, flapping his hands. I'd never seen him this agitated, and I stared, fascinated. He stopped pacing abruptly and stalked toward me. I held up a hand to fend him off.

He drew himself up. It was dark in the street, with only the faintest of light drizzling from the windows of the buildings on either side, but in the pale gleam I saw the anguish on his face.

"I hardly know what to say, India. You must know my regard for you. Surely you know that I would never let any harm come to you."

"You might say the same thing of your aged spaniel," I replied. No one meddles with my feelings.

"I do not have a spaniel," he said in a brittle voice. "Why the devil are you maundering on about dogs at a moment like this?"

"I never maunder," I snapped. "Is this an appropriate moment to discuss a blond wench in Mayfair?"

It was as if I'd slapped him. His head snapped back, and he took a step to steady himself. I had rocked him, but as I was to learn, not in the way I'd planned.

"Good God, India! Have you been following me?" The anguish had melted into a scowl.

"How else would I know about your little woman?"

"You've no right—"

"Don't take that tone with me. I've as much right to traipse around after you as you have to put Vincent on my trail."

"I was worried about you. That Edding woman—"

"Hang Mother Edding," I said. "I can look after myself."

We stared defiantly at one another for a long moment. Then he sighed deeply and removed his hat, turning the brim in his hand and looking up at the sky.

"I haven't the faintest idea how I got myself into this predicament," he said.

"I expect it's because Dizzy—"

"Not the blasted anarchists and their blasted bombs," he said, nearly shouting. My hand shot out and covered his mouth. He reached up and cupped my hand with his, inclining his head. I felt his lips purse beneath my palm, and he planted a gentle kiss there. "You," he said. "India Black."

It was working up to a romantic moment when a rat squealed and shot out of the nearest alley. I heard a muffled oath, and French wheeled like a racing hound and sprinted toward the alley, drawing his Webley revolver as he ran. I ran too, my hand tangled in my skirt, searching for the Bulldog. I confess to feeling rather woozy, and it took me several seconds before I succeeded in pulling my weapon from the voluminous material. One of these days I'm adopting trousers, and to hell with gentle society. French had disappeared into the alley, and I skidded to a halt at the entrance. It was as dark as pitch down there, and I didn't want to risk shooting French. On the other hand, after the evening's events I didn't want anyone else to shoot French. I compromised by whispering his name, softly at first and then louder, until I heard him approaching, swearing savagely.

"He's gone," he announced, emerging from the alley.

"You're certain that someone was there?"

"I heard his footsteps. I chased him for a bit, but I lost him in that godforsaken maze back there." He waved a hand dispiritedly toward the environs beyond the alley. "I wonder if he heard our conversation."

"Would it matter if he did? We wouldn't be the first co-conspirators to..." My voice trailed off.

"Not that," said French. "The part about Dizzy."

"Oh, Lord," I said, crestfallen. "I can't believe I put us at risk by saying that."

"We'll find out at the next meeting. Be sure your Bulldog is loaded. We may have to fight our way out of the room."

"Perhaps it was just a footpad or fingersmith. This *is* Seven Dials, after all, and they're a penny a dozen around here."

"I hope you're right," he said, but he looked grim and he hustled me along.

We walked several blocks without speaking, with French stopping now and then to verify that no one shadowed us. When we reached the brighter lights of Piccadilly, he relaxed his vigilance long enough to hail a cab.

"Where are we going?" I asked, as the hansom pulled to the curb.

"You're going to Lotus House."

"But we—"

He shoved me into the cab and closed the door. "Have much to discuss. I know. And we will. When all this is over." He reached through the window and seized my hand. "Until Saturday," he said, and then he was gone.

15

I reckon most women would have been swept off their feet if a chap like French had declared his interest, but I have never swooned and I wasn't about to start now. For one thing, for a fellow who'd seemed positively love-struck a few moments ago, he'd handed me into the hansom with alacrity and dashed off with scarcely a word. His silence concerning the flaxen-haired maiden in Mayfair had been deafening, and he'd made it clear that I wouldn't be seeing him until Saturday. None of this seemed like the behavior of the smitten, but then French *was* a gentleman, a species mostly foreign to me, and perhaps that's how these coves behaved. I felt a moment of compassion for the bloke (at least I believe that's what it was—I'm so thrifty with that emotion that I may not have accurately identified it), for if he truly had a regard for me, he was no doubt torturing himself about the proper etiquette for dealing with a whore as a lover. I could have assured him on that count, as I had no intention of parading about on his arm and advertising my status as a kept woman, nor did I entertain ridiculous notions of being carted off home to meet Mama. I liked my independence, and I didn't plan to give it up for any man, even a handsome chap with wild black hair and a steely gaze. I was sure French would come around to my way of thinking, after some proper training, of course. In the meantime, he was probably right to shoot off like a startled hare, removing himself from temptation. I can't blame him, really, for I doubt he could resist my charms if he were anywhere in the vicinity. We had a job before us, and it was a damned dicey one at that. We'd need our wits about us if we were to locate Grigori and destroy the anarchist cell. This was no time for dalliances.

The whores at Lotus House had just turned in for the evening when I slipped out to meet French and Thick Ed at Trafalgar Square. It was three thirty on Saturday morning and deuced chilly, with a thick fog hovering over the city and a damp wind blowing off the river. The evening had been hectic. Major Rawlins and his men had descended again on the brothel, this time bringing a group of newly commissioned lieutenants who were ready to quaff champagne and prove their manhood to their brother officers. It made for a raucous night, and I spent a good deal of time pairing the lads and the girls and jollying along those who had to wait their turn. I'm damned good at that sort of thing, but it is exhausting work, especially as I haven't the slightest interest in how Stinky Simons managed to capture the enemy's colors after his braces had been slashed with a *tulwar*. But I soldiered on and did my duty and collected a fair bit of coin for it. By the time I'd counted the takings and seen the last of the chaps out the door, it was time to leave. I gulped a glass of whisky and wolfed down some bread and cheese, then flung a coat about my shoulders and stashed the Bulldog in the pocket.

I must speak to French about a holster for the damned thing, as it's awkward carrying it around this way.

Vincent was waiting for me on the pavement. "'Ow's hit, India?"

"A successful evening. The whores are asleep in their beds, and the gold is locked in the safe."

"'Ow much gold?" Vincent yawned.

"Don't get any ideas."

"I wouldn't thieve from *you*, India. 'Twouldn't be right. But I might 'ave a crack at some other 'ouse."

"Splendid idea. I'd suggest Aunt Maria Taylor. She has a good clientele and charges a handsome fee for her girls." And she was a vicious competitor of mine. I brightened at the prospect of Vincent burgling her establishment.

Even at this hour the streets of the city hummed with a subdued energy. Carts and drays passed by us on their way to the local markets, loaded with fresh flowers, barrels of oysters and crates of vegetables and fruits. The dense fog muffled the sound of creaking wheels and horses' hooves. I heard the measured tread of a bobby on patrol, and we quietly crossed the street to avoid him. You can tell a bobby's footsteps at a hundred steps. Regulations require a standard pace of two and a half miles per hour, and their cadence is as regular as the ticking of a clock.

Vincent peeled off before we reached the square, and I walked the last few blocks on my own. French and Thick Ed were waiting for me in the doorway of a marine insurance company.

"There are a lot of people about," I whispered.

"Step lightly," said Thick Ed. "We don't want to draw attention to ourselves."

Have I mentioned that men are great ones for stating the obvious, especially to the fair sex?

I peered behind Thick Ed's squat frame. "Where are the boxes?"

"I loaded 'em in a wheelbarrow and took 'em to the square this afternoon after the workmen left. They're under the grandstand."

"This afternoon! Wasn't that risky?" I asked. "What if someone had seen you?"

Thick Ed shrugged. "Someone did. There's a guard on the site, but I just told him I was makin' a delivery of nails and such, for some last-minute work we had to do the day of the memorial. Sometimes the best place to hide somethin' is in plain sight."

"We should go," said French. "It'll be dawn soon."

Thick Ed whispered our assignments. I took up a position at the southeast corner of the square, ducking into a nearby doorway that afforded a view of the area where the public would gather that afternoon. French vanished into the misty dark to station himself at the northwest corner of the square, hard by the National Gallery and staring directly at the rear of the grandstand. Should the local plod, or anyone else for that matter, take an interest in Thick Ed's activities, we were to create a distraction and draw off the concerned party. French had decided on the role of an inebriated nob who couldn't find his club despite numerous trips along Pall Mall, and I would be, well, what I was actually, a woman of dubious virtue. I'd rely on charm and if that failed, on a bit of violence. The Bulldog made a highly effective cosh, if handled correctly.

I believe I've mentioned that patience is not a virtue that I value nor, for that matter, possess. I'm much happier running round after spies or traitors, waving my Bulldog or brandishing a rapier, than I am waiting for something to happen. Five minutes after assuming my position I was bored, and after half an hour, I was nodding off. There wasn't much action to speak of in the square, save for a couple of drunks who staggered past Nelson's Column, giggling like schoolgirls, and a steady stream of deliverymen intent on getting their wares to market. It was impossible to see Thick Ed through the gloom, but I trusted that Vincent was as close to the bomb maker as his own shadow.

I yelped when a hand touched my arm.

"Quiet," Thick Ed hissed.

French materialized at his elbow.

"Any difficulties?" I asked.

"No. No one turned up. All the devices are armed and hidden. Unless someone stumbles across them, they'll explode as planned."

On that happy note we separated. Thick Ed walked along the Strand, and French and I waited until he was out of sight before we crossed the square and angled to the northwest, toward Lotus House. Dawn was breaking, though it was a poor sort of dawn, with dirty white clouds scudding across a pearl-gray sky and a fine mist slowly soaking through my woolen coat.

I shivered. "Damn this weather."

"Are you cold?" French reached for me instinctively, but I skipped out of his reach.

"Vincent," I murmured.

French put his hands in his pockets and contrived to look innocent. For the prime minister's agent, he can be damned unconvincing sometimes.

He cleared his throat and said, "The weather may work in our favor. If it's raining, the crowd will be smaller."

I needed only to mention Vincent and the filthy scamp appeared, inserting himself between us and grinning cheerfully. I wondered what he had seen.

"This 'ere job is beneath me," he announced. "Hit's no challenge."

"There are several pounds of dynamite in those bombs," I said warningly. "Don't get cocky."

"Pish," scoffed Vincent.

"Is everything arranged?" asked French.

"Count on it, guv."

"Cheeky sod," I said. "You'd better be right or there won't be enough left of any of us to make a good meal for the pigeons."

"Stop bickering," said French. "We still have much to do today."

We hurried back to Lotus House to do it.

There's nothing like a bit of bunting to bring out the patriot in an Englishman. Despite the clinging mist, thousands of loyal men, women and children had thronged Trafalgar Square to pay homage to the poor souls who had died in the Indian Mutiny of 1857. The occasion might be melancholy, but the crowd was festive, with vendors hawking chestnuts, pies and muffins. Some enterprising folk had erected stalls around the edge of the park and were ladling up tea and mulled cider for customers. Newsboys darted through the horde hawking the latest broadsheets. Nobs in top hats and working men in flat caps jostled for space while children scampered underfoot and women chattered gaily.

I had no idea where my fellow conspirators were, except for Harkov, who was no doubt just now having a natter with a group of foreigners in Lyon about conditions in English factories. At a previous meeting we'd agreed to observe the impending carnage separately. Flerko had expressed a fear of our intrepid band being discovered and easily captured if we attended as a group, and no amount of discussion would convince him that the odds of being identified as the perpetrators of the chaos were virtually nonexistent. I'd have liked French at my side, but we'd agreed that we should abide by the group's decision and not risk being seen together. That is how I came to be standing alone on the steps surrounding Nelson's Column, with a fine view of the grandstand. Of course, I wasn't alone, for the steps were thronged with people, and I had to employ a sharp elbow and the occasional shove to maintain my view. I wouldn't have waded into the middle of this seething mass except that I knew where the infernal machines were located, and I planned to be as far away as possible if our plans went awry and the bombs exploded. Not that I expected them to, you understand, but a good agent always has a contingency plan. In this instance, mine included attaching myself like a limpet to the admiral's column in the event there actually were any explosions today and the crowd turned into a surging, panicked mob.

A file of elderly blokes dressed in uniform and sporting a variety of medals and ribbons began to totter onto the grandstand. I presumed these were the military wallahs who'd been responsible for the mutiny in the first place, turning a blind eye and a deaf ear to the grumblings and discontents of the Indian troops. Dealing with the issues would have required foregoing port at lunch and an afternoon nap. Ironic, isn't it, that the blokes who sat behind desks issuing orders gét the medals and the invitations to the celebrations, while the poor devils who risked their lives on the field of battle have to make do with half pay and a hand-whittled crutch? But I digress.

The generals and colonels and what have you were followed onto the grandstand by a line of dignitaries, who'd clearly dined well at lunch and now looked plump, pink and slightly boozy, sporting ceremonial robes representing the Society of Squint-Eyed Jewelers, the Worshipful Company of Drunken Brewers and other notable London guilds. It was quite a sight, those rows of fellows looking stiff and very stately in their glittering uniforms and scarlet robes. A few of the chaps were kitted out in dark suits and respectable headgear, and among them I spotted Stoke, looking as though he'd swallowed a cup of hemlock before ascending the grandstand. A thin, stooped figure in a top hat and pince-nez stepped forward and lifted his hands. The crowd strained forward as one, ears cocked. It takes a prodigious voice to address a crowd in Trafalgar Square, and this chap wasn't up to the task. He gave it all he had, but no one past the first few rows could hear a word. This being a London crowd, the fragile old coot soon learned of their displeasure. From the back of the crowd, where the tough boys and louts had gathered looking for a chance to pick a pocket or steal a purse, came a rising chorus of catcalls and hooting. The old fellow's face grew red, and he appeared fussed as he struggled to project over the shouts of "Speak up, there," and "Can't 'ear you, Granddad."

And then came an interruption of a different sort. I couldn't see from my vantage point, but the crowd shifted and muttered, and I heard the whoops and cries of a youthful and undisciplined mob surging toward the square. Some of the fossilized gentlemen on the grandstand stood up and looked about anxiously, no doubt reminded of the war cries of the sepoy regiments who'd turned on them during the mutiny and wondering how to find immediate transport to the rear. The guild members and the other dignitaries craned their necks and looked annoyed. Things were not going as planned. The thin bloke in the top hat stuttered to a halt, looking, I thought, rather relieved at the disruption. Behind him a few of the dignitaries, including the lord mayor of the city, held a hurried confab, and one of them gestured peremptorily to Stoke, who'd been sitting quietly in his seat feigning complete ignorance of the developing situation. The last thing I saw before all hell broke loose was Stoke getting a flea in his ear from the lord mayor.

Then the crowd shuddered around me and from the edge of the square came hoarse shouts and the sound of women screaming. Over the noise of the crowd I heard the eldritch cry of what appeared to be an Apache war party.

"'Ere, wot's that?" exclaimed the fellow next to me. He turned to his friend. "Boost me up, Dick, so I can see wot's goin' on."

Dick steadied himself with one hand on the base of the column and crooked a leg for his friend to stand upon. His friend clambered up, clinging precariously to the base of the column.

"See anything, Ned?" the lifter called.

"Oi, there's a mob o' street Arabs up by the church, runnin' through the crowd like a pack o' ruddy wolves."

I knew he referred to the venerable St. Martin-in-the-Fields, which stands at the northeast corner of the square.

"Oh, what's happening?" I cried, doing my damnedest to imitate the type of hysterical female I despise. I had no idea where the other anarchists might be in this crowd, but if any of them happened to catch sight of me, I'd be looking just as shocked as everyone else.

The people around me had grown uneasy, and at Ned's words there was an apprehensive ripple through the audience.

"What are they doing?" a voice shouted.

Ned stared keenly in the direction of the tumult. "They're liftin' up the ladies' skirts, the miserable little sods. And they're pushin' and shovin' the men. Crikey! They're 'eaded this way!"

Indeed they were. The crowd around the church had fallen

back among much confusion. It was as though the infantry had been routed by a cavalry charge. Men, women and children were surging toward me, intent on fleeing the pesky lads who had appeared from nowhere and seemed intent on creating havoc. A woman charged past me, dragging a small boy by the arm. His feet hardly touched the ground as they flew by. Pretty young girls, their bonnets askew and curls bobbing, pelted past, shrieking deliriously. Two portly gentlemen careened through the crowd, clutching their hats and walking sticks and using the latter to good effect to clear a path. The panic of their flight infected the multitude around the column. Ned clambered down, and he and Dick departed posthaste, shoving an elderly woman to the ground to expedite their escape. I hung on grimly, trying to avoid being swept away in the flood.

I saw my first urchin then, darting through the law-abiding citizens with a maniacal grin plastered on his face and a kidskin wallet in his hand. More members of the dirty, ragged gang whisked by, yelling like banshees and pursued by a determined group of constables, to little effect. I watched one policeman swing his baton at a boy's head, but the object of the attack danced away and disappeared into the crowd. The lads were everywhere, taunting the constables and terrorizing the crowd, overturning rubbish bins and pelting the constables with rotten oranges and apples. The noise was deafening, what with the war cries of the youngsters, the squeals of frightened women and children, the angry shouts of the men in the crowd and the roaring curses of the police. I clung to my post and pasted an anxious frown on my face.

A group of nippers peeled off from the general melee and pushed through the crowd toward the rubbish bin containing one of our bombs. I thought I spotted Vincent but couldn't be sure, really, as those bloody tykes all looked the same to me. But it *was* Vincent, for as the boys approached the bin they formed a phalanx round it, creating a barrier, and I saw my young friend deftly remove the lid and plunge his head into the interior. Crumpled newspapers, orange peels and other trash spurted from the bin as Vincent burrowed deeper. Then the deluge of garbage halted for a time, and finally he emerged with a wooden box in his hand, which he handed off to a pinched-face, grimy lad who sported a fine gray bowler (recently acquired, I venture to say). The lad sprinted off, headed southwest for Cockspur Street. Then Vincent rallied his ragged warriors, and the pack loped off in the direction of the shrubbery where another infernal machine waited. They made short work of the decorative plantings, ripping up the shrubs by the roots while Vincent huddled behind them, deftly handling the container housing the bomb. He was as cool and efficient as an army sapper, and I felt rather proud of the little scab, though I'd no intention of telling him that. He's insufferable enough as it is.

The chimes of St. Martin-in-the-Fields struck the quarter hour, and I held my breath as the last remnants of the crowd scattered to the four winds and the wild boys pursued them, hooting and jeering, while the constables raced after the lads in a futile attempt to lay hands on them. The square was growing quieter as the mob disappeared into the streets around it. Figures milled about on the grandstand. There was a great deal of gesticulating and shouting, and I knew Stoke was bound to catch hell. The press would have a field day as well. Confoundedly unlucky for the superintendent, but he'd have to bear it until French and I could capture Grigori, and then Stoke could take all the credit and wallow in the public's adulation while French and I disappeared into the shadows, eschewing the thanks of a grateful nation in favor of anonymity.

I climbed down from my perch then and picked my way through the litter left behind by the fleeing throng. There were some jolly nice purses lying about and one silk bonnet that was rather fetching, but I regretfully passed up the chance to rifle through the handbags. Lucre is always welcome, as is a free addition to the wardrobe, but I didn't want to attract attention to myself. I hurried west along Cockspur Street, turning into a mews a few blocks from the square. I opened the second door on the right and found Vincent and French counting packets of dynamite.

"Well done, Vincent. Your boys were brilliant."

"Aye," said Vincent, distractedly chewing a nail. "But we got a problem. We only got four of the bombs."

"Four!" Indeed, there were four boxes sitting on the floor of the mews. The three of us stared at them with apprehension.

"I got the two unner the grandstand and the one in them bushes and one in that rubbish bin. But there weren't no bomb in that bin at the southeast corner."

"There were five," I insisted.

"You sure about that?"

"Absolutely. Thick Ed made five bombs. The fifth was supposed to be in the bin near the southeast corner of the square."

"And I just tole you, I looked there and there weren't no bomb in that bin."

"Could one of your friends have taken it? After all, you could sell the dynamite for a goodly sum," I said. "Those boys—"

"They're me mates," said Vincent flatly.

It is sometimes better to retreat than advance. "And that's good enough for me," I said. "So what happened?"

Vincent went to work on the fingernail again. "Could that Thick Ed chap 'ave changed 'is mind? Maybe put one of them bombs someplace else?"

French and I stared at each other. If Thick Ed had moved one of the bombs... We turned and raced for the square.

16

Trafalgar was crawling with bobbies and a passel of grim-looking coves in street clothes surveying the scattered programs, hats, purses and other detritus left by the departing crowd. Superintendent Stoke was huddled with a group of dignitaries at the bottom of the grandstand, nursing his moustache.

"We can't be seen with him," I said. "Any member of the cell could be hanging about, watching. In fact, we shouldn't be seen with Vincent, either."

French pulled a notebook and pencil from his pocket and scribbled a message. "Vincent, you'll have to get this to Stoke. Mind those bobbies. They're liable to collar you and cart you off to gaol."

French watched Vincent slip away. "Let's go back to the mews. I asked Stoke to meet us there."

We hurried back up Cockspur Street to relative safety. French pulled the door to, but left a half-inch crack through which he scrutinized the cobblestoned yard. "No sign of any of the anarchists, but that doesn't mean one of them didn't see us in the square with Vincent and follow us here."

"What do you think happened? To the fifth bomb, I mean?"

"Damned if I know. It should have been there. The only explanation that I can think of is that Thick Ed came back after he planted the bombs and moved that one. But why move that one and not the rest? It doesn't make sense. And if Thick Ed did move the bomb, why hasn't it exploded? Could he have removed it entirely? Why would he do that?" French peered through the crack in the door. "Here come Vincent and Stoke."

The superintendent shoved open the door and stumped inside, followed by his ragged guide. A drop of spittle hung from one end of Stoke's moustache, and he was breathing hard from the rapid walk. He had the irritable, distracted and slightly panicked air of a colonel who's just been told his battalion has been demolished by an inferior race.

"I'm needed at the square," he barked. "What's this about?"

It would be an understatement to say that Stoke was not best pleased to hear that we couldn't account for the fifth bomb. Stoke's face flushed the color of old bricks, and his jowls quivered like a turkey's wattle. His moustache lay in two lank strands around his mouth, which hadn't closed since French and I had delivered the news. The old copper stood gaping at us so long that I was mentally composing the anonymous letter to the home secretary that would advise him of Stoke's demise from apoplexy when, at long last, the superintendent rallied. His mouth snapped shut, and he shot me a malevolent stare, as hard and sharp as forged steel.

"This is what happens when an amateur is permitted to play at spying. I was against using you from the beginning, Miss Black. I see that my worst fears have been confirmed. This was your plan, and it's gone disastrously wrong. I hope the prime minister is satisfied. For my part, I shall have nothing further to do with you. And now I must find that device. If one of my fellows is killed when he stumbles upon the blasted thing, I shall have your head." Vincent opened the door for him, but Stoke gave him a half-hearted cuff on the ear and stalked out.

Vincent uttered an oath and took a step after the superintendent, but French grabbed his collar and held him back.

"Don't bother," he said. "I have something for you to do now."

"But the bastard hit me," said Vincent, rubbing his already reddening earlobe. "I won't stand for that, guv."

"Neither will I, Vincent. But we'll deal with Stoke later. I need you to get back to the square and see if Stoke's men turn up the fifth bomb. Someone in that cell has a plan of his own. If he's moved the device, he may be watching the square, waiting for it to explode." He patted Vincent on the back. "Bring us a report at Lotus House. I'll be waiting there with India."

The happy news that French would be spending a few hours at my establishment might have been expected to cheer me, but it was confoundedly difficult to muster any romantic feelings under the circumstances. Stoke's indictment of me was understandable; after all, he'd be the poor bugger raked over the coals in the papers for the chaos that had overwhelmed the memorial. It would be bloody unfair, of course, as the newspaper johnnies wouldn't know the bit about the four bombs that had been disarmed by the unruly gang of urchins, and the brilliant mind behind the plan (that is to say, mine), instead focusing only on the public relations disaster that had occurred. The lord mayor would be blaming the Home Office, the Home Office would point an accusing finger at Scotland Yard, the editorials would call for a thorough investigation of the matter, and Stoke would be blamed by everybody. Things would drag on until the next anarchist attack, and then the whole cycle would start again.

I didn't permit the superintendent's words to trouble me unduly. I was more concerned with unraveling the mystery of the fifth bomb. So was French. We retreated to Lotus House, closeted ourselves in the study with a good fire and a bottle to hand and applied ourselves to working out what had happened. French thought Thick Ed the most likely candidate for removing the device, but I pointed out that we'd openly discussed the location of the bombs and the timetable for planting and arming them and therefore any one of our small cell could have been the culprit.

"Could someone else in the group be working as an informant?" I asked.

"That's a possibility, although Schmidt and Flerko seem dedicated to anarchist ideals. Thick Ed doesn't strike me as the ideological type, but he seems happy enough to be building bombs. He probably sells his expertise to the highest bidder. I'm not as sure of Bonnaire's views. He says and does all the right things but doesn't appear particularly enraged by the system, the way Flerko is." French's eyes met mine briefly. "Perhaps you know him better."

"Mmm," I murmured. "I'd agree with your assessment of his commitment to the cause," I said neutrally.

"And then there's Harkov."

"It couldn't be him. He's eating snails and decrying the working conditions of the poor at the moment."

"I wonder if that's true," mused French. "I'll have Stoke verify that he left England and arrived in Lyon."

"I'm sure the superintendent will be happy to do that for you, seeing as how he thinks this whole affair has been a cock-up of the first order. I wonder what he'll tell Dizzy?"

"Perhaps I should wander round and have a chat with the

prime minister before Stoke pays a call. The superintendent will be tied up for a few hours looking for that bomb."

"I'll come with you," I said, rising.

"I think it would be best if you waited here for Vincent," French said smoothly. "I shouldn't be long."

"It wasn't the plan that went awry," I said stubbornly. "How could I have known that someone was going to play silly buggers with that fifth bomb?"

"There was nothing wrong with the plan, and I shall tell that to the prime minister. Someone in the group has a different agenda than the others, and that makes it more important than ever that we remain with the anarchists and get to the bottom of this. Superintendent Stoke won't like it, but he can go hang for all I care." French clapped his hat on his head and stalked out. Ah, there's nothing more arousing than a resolute chap defending his damsel's honor.

I sat for an hour or more, nursing my drink and feeling chuffed at the idea of French stating my case to the prime minister. Then, as I was topping off my glass, I caught a glimpse of myself in the mirror over the mantel, grinning foolishly. The sight brought me up short. Bloody hell. What was I thinking? A week ago French's chivalry would have sent me into a rage, as India Black did not need a bloke riding to her rescue. I'd have pushed my way into that meeting with Dizzy and informed him that Stoke was a whinging old woman who couldn't stand the heat and if he wanted to the leave the kitchen, he should do so with speed. I'd have thumped French on the head for presuming that I needed his protection. And I'd have chewed up Stoke and spit him in the gutter. Damnation, I was going soft. Well, it was time to pull up my boots and fight my own battles. I was collecting a cloak and tying on a bonnet when Vincent walked into the foyer, gobbling a piece of cold ham. He shoved the last of the meat in his mouth.

"Where did French go?"

And that's another thing that needed putting to rights: French wasn't my superior anymore. I'd been called in by Dizzy, and by God, I had as much right as French to direct operations and Vincent could bloody well answer to me once in a while. Whether I had the experience to handle matters was a completely different matter, but I'm not one to concern myself with trifles.

"He's with the prime minister," I said curtly. "What have you learned?"

"Where were you goin'?"

"To see Dizzy."

Vincent strolled into the study, wiping his greasy fingers on the seat of his pants and selecting one of my upholstered chairs. He plopped down in it and stretched his feet toward the fire.

"Well, unless you got somethin' to say to him that French didn't, I'd save myself a trip."

"Why?"

"'Cause I seen French comin' up the street. 'E'll be 'ere any minute."

The front door opened and French came in, removing his hat and shrugging out of his overcoat.

"Ah, Vincent. What's happening at the square?"

"Nuffink, guv. The plods are all over the place, pokin' at anything bigger than a muffin and everyone of 'em as nervous as a cat around a rocker. Ole Stoke was stormin' round the place, frothin' at the mouth and shoutin' orders, but they didn't find a fing. They finished a while ago and gone 'ome. Wot did ole Dizzy have to say?"

French poured himself a whisky and sank into a chair. "He congratulated us and observed that the plan would have been

240

wholly successful but for this unforeseen intervention. We are to stay on the case until we identify Grigori and the whole lot can be arrested. The prime minister will have a word with Stoke, and we are not to take the superintendent's words to heart, as the poor fellow is under a great deal of stress and may have overreacted." French looked quizzically at me. "Why are you wearing that bonnet and cloak? Were you going out?"

"I had thought to join your meeting."

"Didn't trust me to fight our corner?"

"Something like that."

He grinned, fondly I believe, and I granted him a meager smile. Vincent was watching with interest. Too much interest. He's a shrewd little bugger, but he noticed me staring at him and his expression faded to one of studied indifference.

"Wot do we do now?" he asked.

"We find Grigori," I said briskly, "and put an end to this."

The morning brought a message from Bonnaire, requesting my presence at a meeting of the cell that night. I'd been expecting our little band would be all aflutter, and everyone would be anxious to discuss the failure of our plan. It was a glum group of anarchists who gathered in the cellar later that evening. To my surprise Harkov was there, presiding over the table with an expression of extreme displeasure on his saturnine features. He must have made a hasty trip from Lyon when he heard the news. Schmidt idly polished his glasses, puffing a pipe and staring sightlessly across the room. Bonnaire and Thick Ed appeared calm, the Frenchman lounging in his chair with his hands laced over his stomach and our bomb maker busying himself at his worktable. Flerko was a bundle of nerves, twitching like a rat in a trap when I walked in. I suppose he had expected a representative of the Third Section. French had arrived before me and sat leaning with his elbows on the table, looking severe.

Harkov screwed his monocle into his eye and let his gaze sweep the table. "I return from Lyon, expecting to read in the papers of our great achievement and the fall of the British government. Instead, I am greeted with the news that a gang of boys disrupted the memorial service. What's more, not a single bomb exploded. Grigori—" He stopped to correct himself. "*I* demand an explanation. Thick Ed?"

Thick Ed looked up from his examination of a detonator. "Don't know, comrade. I planted the devices just like we talked about. I armed each one. I don't know what happened, but I can guess." He looked meaningfully around the room, without really making eye contact with anyone, before returning to his study of the items on the table.

Flerko jumped. Harkov's eyes were moist and dangerous. Most of the air went out of the room, leaving it dank and still.

"If you are accusing one of us of sabotaging the operation, then it would serve you well to remember that most of us do not have the expertise to build a bomb, much less dismantle one," said Bonnaire calmly. "Your words accuse only yourself, comrade." The last word dripped sarcasm. Bonnaire glanced obliquely at French, then at me. "And, I might add, those who helped you assemble the devices."

Flerko had just caught up with the rest of us. "Wait one minute," he said. "Are you accusing Thick Ed and French and Miss Black of being spies?"

Schmidt stirred. "We cannot ignore the facts, Flerko. It would appear that we have indeed been infiltrated by one or more agents," he said around the pipe stem in his mouth. "However, I would venture to say that our spy works for someone other than the British."

The color drained from Flerko's face. "The Third Section," he whispered.

"Why do you say that it is not the British?" asked Harkov.

"Look at the disruption of the service. A group of what, a hundred boys, put a crowd to flight, and in the chaos our bombs are conveniently disarmed and vanish. Had the informant been working for Scotland Yard, they would simply have rendered the bombs ineffective and removed them before the service. Certainly they would not hire a mob of guttersnipes to create a distraction while they collected the bombs. What would be the point? No, I think our friend must be working for another government, and our spy was forced to devise an informal means of thwarting our scheme." He sucked on his pipe, discovered it had gone out, and frowned at it. "We know how frequently the Sûreté, the Third Section and the *Landespolizei* forces of the German states attempt to infiltrate our combat units. I fear they may have been successful in our case."

There was silence as we all contemplated Schmidt's words. My heart was thundering in my chest. I hoped my compatriots couldn't hear it. I was finding it hard to swallow as well. I'm a dab hand at appearing innocent, having practiced my craft over many years (it's surprising how many blokes like the virginal type), and I prayed my skill would continue for the duration of the meeting.

Schmidt had found a piece of straw and was cleaning his pipe. "Quite frequently the spy will urge the group to act. He has no value to his employers if the unit he penetrates does nothing."

Flerko's already pale face blanched. "If you are implying that

I am the spy just because I suggested the memorial service as a target, I must protest."

Schmidt lit his pipe and stared thoughtfully at Flerko through the smoke.

Flerko licked his lips and put a shaking hand to his mouth. "You might as well accuse Harkov. Everyone knows that the government agents who join our groups always seem to go missing whenever a dangerous deed is committed."

The situation was becoming intolerably tense. At this rate, the group would disintegrate before we found Grigori.

"You're all being ridiculous," I snapped. Harkov opened his mouth. "And don't tell me that I don't know what I'm talking about because I haven't had a cigarette extinguished on my arm by the brutes in the Third Section. If we have been infiltrated, then you can bet we wouldn't be sitting here now accusing one another of treachery. We'd either be dead or in gaol or on our way out of the country in the hold of a ship. You're seeing ghosts, comrades."

"How do you explain the fact that not one bomb exploded?" Schmidt asked.

"The police might have searched the park again before the service." I turned to Thick Ed. "You said that our bombs would have less chance of being discovered if they were placed in those boxes from the construction site, but it's certainly feasible that *any* container would have been considered suspicious. I think the constables found them. That sounds more likely to me than some fantastical story about one of us hiring a small army of street Arabs to break up the memorial."

Put like that, it did sound absurd.

"Why did we not hear of this great triumph of the British police? Surely they would have trumpeted their superior work in the press," Harkov said.

"Do you think so? What politician in his right mind wants the public to know that anarchists had succeeded in hiding bombs in Trafalgar Square? I think they'd keep it quiet so as not to alarm people."

"There is truth in what you say." Bonnaire's forehead was wrinkled in thought, his brows knitted. "It could have easily happened that way."

"I remain unconvinced," said Schmidt.

Harkov nodded in agreement. "Perhaps we should disband."

"Certainly we should remain alert to the possibility that someone is here under false pretenses." Bonnaire unlaced his fingers and stretched out his hands on the table. "But all we have are suspicions, and those can dissolve our group. I have been involved with cells before where infiltration was suspected. The fear, the paranoia, destroyed those units. I suggest that we continue to operate as usual. If we have been penetrated"—he gave a Gallic shrug—"then we will either catch the villain or bear the consequences. We cannot go running into the hills every time we get the wind up. It is the nature of our cause that we will encounter duplicity and danger." He looked straight at Harkov as he said this. The Russian met his eyes for a moment, and there was hatred there, but Bonnaire continued to gaze mildly at Harkov until the latter looked away. I was waiting for Harkov to pull a revolver from his belt and demand the right to avenge this slur upon his courage, but apparently our brave leader was anything but.

"You are suggesting that we select another target? Even though we may have a backstabber in our midst?" asked Schmidt.

"I am," said Bonnaire.

"But if we have a traitor—" Harkov protested.

"Yes," Schmidt interrupted. "I believe you are right, Bonnaire."

"But—" Harkov said,

"I also agree with Bonnaire," French spoke for the first time. He'd been deuced quiet over there. I'd been hoping he'd speak up, afraid that his silence might be interpreted by the others as guilt.

Schmidt lifted a hand. "Let us proceed with a plan. If we do nothing or disband, our turncoat will live to penetrate another cell. If we do have a traitor in our midst, we owe it to our anarchist comrades to deal with him before he infects more combat units." He challenged us with a look. "What shall be our next objective? Our next prey?"

There was dead silence around the room, as you might expect when the suggestion of a proposed target had just been mooted as proof of treason. We all sat on our hands, metaphorically speaking, shifting in our seats and finding great interest in the bare stone walls of the cellar.

"Come, come," Schmidt said impatiently.

"I have a plan," said Flerko hesitantly.

"Your last proposal failed miserably," said Harkov. "We should hear what the others have to say."

"It is a brilliant plan. I insist we discuss it." Flerko jumped to his feet. "It is a plan that will shock the European heads of state and send Britain into chaos. The people shall lose all faith in government and flock to our cause."

You can always count on Flerko to produce a grand scheme. His mind must be stuffed with plans for exterminating the cream of society.

Harkov looked at Schmidt. The latter shrugged.

"Very well, Flerko," Harkov said.

The little Russian leaned forward. "I propose that we kidnap the prime minister. We shall try him for his crimes and execute him. We shall cut off his head and place it on a pike on London Bridge." Flerko's eyes were luminous and his smile beatific. "It is a beautiful plan, is it not? In one stroke we will demonstrate our ability to reach anywhere into the halls of government. No minister or politician will feel safe. The people will see that their government is feeble and ineffective, and will rise up against their leaders. The Dark Legion will be a legend." He looked eagerly at each of us, like a pup who's done a trick and now expects a bone.

I hoped my face did not register my thoughts at the moment, for what I was thinking was that Flerko was cracked. Smoke dribbled from Schmidt's nostrils. Bonnaire evaluated the silkiness of his beard. Thick Ed absently scratched an armpit. Harkov looked pained, and French's right eyebrow was twitching.

I was the first to speak. "It's... audacious," I said lamely.

"Perhaps too audacious," Bonnaire said, frowning. "How would we get access to the prime minister?"

"I've done a reconnaissance," said Flerko excitedly. "He lives on the first floor of the Langham Hotel, and in the evening there are only two men on guard, one at the bottom of the stairs and one at the door of the prime minister's room. Two men! They pose no challenge to us. We can dispense with them easily enough and force the door to Disraeli's room."

I was not best pleased to hear that Flerko had been prowling around the Langham. French and I had visited Dizzy on numerous occasions, and I hoped the pint-sized anarchist hadn't seen us sauntering in to chat with Dizzy and Superintendent Stoke. But as Flerko was as excitable as your spinster aunt, I felt sure that if he had caught sight of us he would have confronted us then and there.

"Why not just blow him up and be done with it?" asked Thick Ed. "It would be much easier to do that than grab the bloke and whack off his head. And where we gonna find a pike?"

"Your bombs have proved ineffective," said Flerko, though not without some trepidation as he looked at Thick Ed's massive hands. "Besides, the boldness of the plan will shock the world. I'm afraid the press is getting blasé about infernal machines."

"What day were you planning to conduct the operation?" Harkov asked.

"Perhaps three or four days from now. As soon as we are ready."

"Ah." Harkov shrugged. "Unfortunately, I shall be—"

"At a conference," Bonnaire concluded his sentence. "How many damned conventions can a man attend?"

Harkov stiffened. "Grigori requests that I go. I am an important contact between him and other leaders of the movement. He is aware that I may not always be here when operations are conducted."

"I find it hard to believe that the prime minister's security is so light," Schmidt said, prodding the bowl of his pipe where the fire had gone out again. "Are you sure you didn't miss anything, Flerko?"

"I am certain of the details. I have spent many days and nights watching the prime minister's movements. He shares the arrogance of so many other British politicians. They seem to think that no anarchist would dare attack them."

"Have you followed the prime minister since the memorial service?" I asked. "I would have thought the police would have insisted on increasing the number of his bodyguards after we came so close to blowing up half of Her Majesty's government."

"We would surely have to disband after an operation of this

magnitude," Harkov said. "The police would not rest until they brought the perpetrators of such a deed to justice."

"Yes, we should all have to leave the country immediately, but what a coup! The Dark Legion would serve as an inspiration to combat units all over the world. What does it matter if we have to flee England and regroup somewhere else?" Flerko had his tail up, all right, bouncing on the balls of his feet with suppressed excitement. I was about to object on the grounds that I was not about to leave Lotus House when it occurred to me that Flerko's hare-brained scheme just might be the easiest way to round up the members of the Dark Legion. Provided we could convince Grigori to be present at the scene of the crime, that is, so as to join the others in the clink.

"There is one other thing," said Flerko. What next, roust Queen Vicky out of bed and force her to parade through the city in her bloomers? I'd draw the line at imposing that sight on the poor citizens of London. "If there *is* a traitor among us, as Schmidt believes, then this will surely expose him. Or her," he added hastily, glancing at me and turning pink. "No agent could possibly allow such an important figure to be kidnapped. He, or she, will have to reveal the plan to the authorities."

"But how will we know which one of us is the snitch?" Thick Ed asked.

"Perhaps," Bonnaire ventured, "we should meet again tomorrow night and discuss Flerko's proposal in more detail, along with the matter of the turncoat in our midst. It is difficult to concentrate tonight."

"The threat of an enemy agent among your rank should focus the mind," a voice said drily.

Schmidt rose. "Grigori! Welcome, brother."

Flerko sprang to his feet; Bonnaire stood up gracefully and

bowed his head briefly. The legs of Schmidt's chair screeched along the stone floor, and even Thick Ed deigned to rise. French and I sat frozen to our chairs, for I had recognized that voice and so had he. His hand had disappeared beneath the table and was no doubt resting, at this very minute, on the handle of the revolver he wore tucked into his boot.

17

Into the room strolled Major Vasily Kristoforovich Bloody Ivanov, last seen by yours truly off the coast of Calais, floating facedown, arms outstretched, his body bobbing on the waves. There could be no doubt about that lean, wolfish face with the predatory smile and the glass green eyes, hard as emeralds. During the period of our previous acquaintance, he'd been serving as an agent in the military intelligence department of the Russian army, not in the least concerned with domestic security issues. What the devil was he doing here? Well, explanations would have to wait, or indeed might never be given, as Ivanov had a hand in his pocket and I doubted that it was because his fingers were cold. He spared me a glance and his mouth quirked, but his eyes returned immediately to French, who had risen to his feet. If there was going to be a battle, then I was going to contribute my shilling's worth. I moved my hand cautiously to my Bulldog. Ivanov saw the movement and a frown creased his forehead. He shook his head, an almost imperceptible motion. Very slowly, eyes flitting between French and me, the Russian agent's hand emerged from his pocket, and he turned to Harkov and extended it to his minion. Harkov grasped it quickly, babbling like a bloody serf caught pilfering the vodka. Ivanov grimaced at the flow of words, cut Harkov off midstream and acknowledged Schmidt with a quick nod.

Ivanov's arm swept the room. "Introduce me, Harkov. I have not yet been fortunate enough to make the acquaintance of our friends here."

It was all deuced polite as Harkov led the treacherous bastard around the room, introducing each of us with a brief description of our reasons for joining the cause. I waited for my turn, fear turning my bowels to ice as Ivanov worked his way down the line. I wasn't sure what the man was up to, but I reckoned "no good" covered most of the options. Then his eyes were inches from mine and he was smiling cool as, damn it, as if we'd just been introduced by a mutual friend on a Sunday afternoon in Hyde Park. Hard to believe that mere months ago he and French had shot it out aboard a wretched, leaky boat and I'd been prepared to exterminate Ivanov if I'd gotten the chance. Now we were smiling at one another, though my smile was as rigid as a corpse's. Ivanov was more relaxed. Indeed, he looked as though he were enjoying himself. I'm sure he said something, but I'll be hanged if I can remember what it was. I was too preoccupied wondering whether French would be able to shake hands with a man who'd once put a bullet in his chest. As much as I loathed the green-eyed spy, French hated him more, and who can blame him, really? Of course, French had returned the favor by plugging Ivanov with a bullet from a Remington .41 rimfire derringer, which had knocked the Russian rogue overboard and left him bobbing on the ocean swell where I'd last seen him. But by the time I'd tended to French's wound and dispatched some of the thugs Ivanov had hired and gone chasing after Ivanov's female accomplice (with no luck, confound it), Ivanov had disappeared. I had hoped he had purchased a one-way ticket to Davey Jones's locker, but here he was in the flesh and clearly planning some fresh mischief.

Ivanov stepped up to French and met his eyes squarely. I fancy no one else in the room could see the smoldering rage behind French's bland smile. I had to applaud the chap, for he seemed positively cordial as he shook hands with the fellow who'd shot him.

"So this is Mr. French, our patrician convert? Pleased to meet you, sir." Smooth as silk, our Ivanov.

"The pleasure is all mine," French purred. The two old adversaries shook hands, smiling grimly. A look of wary understanding passed between them. I hoped that if the others had noticed, they'd chalk it up to that unspoken camaraderie that exists between gentlemen of a certain class. Well, it appeared we had a truce on our hands, but for my part it would be an uneasy one. That Russian bugger was about as trustworthy as a crocodile, and I had no intention of lolling about on the sandbank while he was in the water.

Neither, it transpired, did French. We'd endured a hellish half hour, sitting across from that wicked devil Ivanov while Harkov fluttered about like a crazed moth, trying to impress the boss with a load of codswallop about our future plans and the heroic deeds we'd commit in the name of international anarchy. It had all been a bit awkward, really, and I even felt a little sorry for that stick Harkov, for though I didn't like the fellow, it was rather humiliating to see him boasting like a schoolboy with an overactive imagination. Ivanov had sat silently most of the time, inscrutable as a Buddha, breaking in only to question Harkov, which flustered him so that he tied himself in knots trying to answer. Eventually Schmidt would interject a calm observation, which Ivanov listened to with interest, and each of us contributed a comment or two, so as to demonstrate our commitment to the anarchist cause. We talked mostly of our next campaign, which proved a lively discussion as everyone wanted to weigh in with a suggestion since our sponsor was present. But lurking in the room was that rather sizable elephant, Schmidt's assertion that we had been infiltrated. I don't think I could have stood it if we'd embarked on that conversation while Ivanov was present. I'd kept a cool head until now, but it was going to be jolly difficult playing the dedicated radical while Ivanov lurked nearby. To my great relief, the meeting had broken up without anyone raising the subject of betrayal, and I'd hightailed it back to Lotus House where I had a restorative glass of whisky while I waited for French.

As I expected, he soon appeared with Vincent (who'd been following me, ready to prevent an attack from Mother Edding's hooligans) in tow.

"Blimey!" Vincent exclaimed. "Hivanov's back."

We huddled down before the fire with whisky in hand to talk over the Russian agent's appearance.

"I'd like to get me 'ands on 'im," growled Vincent. "I almost froze to death chasin' 'im to... to—"

"France," I offered helpfully.

"Right. France. Knew it was one of them foreign places where they talk queer. Wot's 'e doin' 'ere?"

"God knows," I said. "But I don't want to. He's bound to be trouble. I say we wait for him before the next meeting and grab him. I'd enjoy visiting him in one of Her Majesty's prisons."

French stared moodily into his glass. He shook his head morosely. "Who knows if he'll be at the next meeting? If we've seen the last of him, I'll regret it. I want to know what he's playing at. Has he transferred from military intelligence to the Third Section? Is he trying to sabotage the group, or does he want it to succeed?"

"Don't the British and Russian governments cooperate when it comes to hunting down anarchists?" I asked.

French took a deep draught from his glass and grimaced at the strong spirits. "Theoretically, they do share information. But agents from every nation are working to infiltrate these combat units and they don't always bother to inform the British government when they're operating on British soil. I wouldn't be surprised if the anarchist community isn't riddled with government agents. I admit to being shocked when Ivanov walked in the room, though."

"Christ, so was I. I thought I'd keel over and pass out when that bugger came through the door. He's a cool one. He must have known we were there."

"Of course he did. Confound the man, he took a huge risk in popping up like that. We could have given away the game, and then the three of us would have been in a hell of a tight spot."

Vincent scratched an ear in bewilderment. "I still don't understand, guv. You said Ivanov might want to 'elp them anarchists? Why would 'e do that?"

"The Russians are no friends of ours, Vincent. A British government distracted by domestic problems is much less likely to interfere with Russian plans for the Ottoman Empire or India. I wouldn't be surprised if the Russians aren't behind the whole affair."

"But if this is a Russian scheme to destabilize our government, why would Ivanov show his hand?" I asked. "Surely he'd hide in the shadows. And if he wanted to create some deviltry, all he has to do is throw us to the wolves. Dizzy would be horrified to lose two agents."

"You are charmingly naïve, India. Our places would be filled quickly. Governments do not mourn their dead."

"Oh." I must say, I found that attitude rather appalling. I must take a moment someday soon and think about why I'm risking my neck for such an ungrateful bunch. "If that's the case, then the tsar probably doesn't care a fig about Ivanov. I say we just kill the brute and be done with it."

French frowned censoriously at me. "Really, India. You're becoming as bloodthirsty as Vincent. There's more to Ivanov's actions than meet the eye, and I intend to find out what the fellow is doing. It could be of vital interest to the prime minister."

"So we just go to the meeting tomorrow and if Ivanov shows, we have a friendly game of whist and forget all about the gunshots we've exchanged? This espionage game has strange rules, French. I don't like playing about in the shadows, trading polite nothings with a cove who tried to kill us and wondering if he'll try it again. It's not natural."

French seemed hurt at my depiction of his chosen profession, but I soothed him with more whisky and then we nattered on about Ivanov and his intentions. An hour later, we were none the wiser. Vincent had nodded off on the floor, and French yawned and stared at the dying embers of the fire. I nudged Vincent with the poker.

"Let the boy sleep," said French.

"He's not sleeping in my study. Do you have any idea how long it takes to clear the stench if he's here for more than an hour?" I bestowed upon French my most bewitching smile, which usually scythes down men like ripened oats. "I could do with some rest myself. I don't suppose—"

French blushed. "Regretfully, no. Not with Vincent around. And not when I'm exhausted from all this late night palaver. And not when I've been mucking about in Seven Dials. I'm filthy. I need a bath and my bed."

I must have looked petulant (and who wouldn't—what kind of a man turns down an offer like that?) for French tilted his head and gave me a rueful smile.

"You know how I feel, India. It's just that... just that—"

"Don't stutter, French. And don't stew over it."

He brushed a dark curl from his forehead. "This isn't a good time, for a number of reasons. But I promise you, when this affair is finished—"

"Right," I said brusquely. "When we round up these radicals, we'll—"

What would we do? French and I exchanged a glance. Confound that blond lass in Mayfair. She was going to prove a difficult hurdle for French to jump.

"It's late. I'll see you tomorrow night at the meeting." I prodded Vincent with my toe. "And take this one with you when you go."

French nodded, looking uncharacteristically downcast, and for a moment I thought of taking his hand and assuring the poor fellow that I wasn't a succubus and not to fret. But I steeled myself and watched from the front door as he and Vincent trudged away, until they were lost in the darkness. In truth, I was just as grimy and exhausted as French, and it would be a relief to fall into my bed. I lit a candle, extinguished the lamps in my study, picked up my revolver and staggered up the stairs to my bedroom. It felt grand to shut the door behind me, sealing off the world of rabid radicals, double-crossing agents and explosions for a bit. I put the candle and my Bulldog on the bedside table and opened the door to the wardrobe.

I don't know about you, but there are certain times of day when I prefer to be attacked. Midmorning is capital, as I've had my breakfast and some coffee and I'm full of vim and vigor then. Just past teatime is also prime. And in a pinch, I can hold my own after dinner, though I'd rather settle before the fire and count my earnings. But I definitely dislike being ambushed at the end of a long night, when I'm wrung out and haven't had a bite to eat and have imbibed rather too much whisky. It's a damned shame that louts don't bother to consult you on your preferred time for a contretemps, but they're inconsiderate creatures and generally have the manners of ill-tempered ruminants. Goats, for example.

This fellow even smelled like one. When I opened the wardrobe door, a hand shot out and encircled my wrist. Then the chap was on me, his weight taking me to the ground (though the smell might have laid me out flat eventually) as he wrenched my arm and covered my mouth with a horny hand. We fell on the carpet with a thud that shook the house and should have woken anyone within the building, provided the occupants did not include a group of bints sleeping off the evening's work and a drunken housekeeper. I concluded that I could not rely on any immediate assistance.

My attacker was sprawled over me, his dirty palm shoved into my mouth. I gnawed at the thing like a crazed rat, but he was pressing it so firmly against my face I couldn't close my jaws and get a grip. All I succeeded in doing was dislodging a fair amount of filth into my mouth. I must have inflicted some damage, though, for he swore quietly and vehemently, and removed his hand long enough to punch me in the jaw with his fist.

"You shut up," he hissed, and reared back to deliver another blow. He still grasped my right wrist, but my left hand was free and I brought it up forcefully, leading with the heel of my palm and catching him under the nose with as much force as I could muster, which, on account of my being right-handed, was not as strong as I had hoped. I'd wanted to break his nose, you see, and I don't think I succeeded because I didn't hear the satisfying snap of cartilage. But any blow to the nose hurts like the devil and so this one did. My assailant's head snapped back and he swore again, more loudly this time. He scrambled to his feet, still holding my arm, and yanked me up after him. Most men seem to think that sheer strength is all they need when dealing with a woman, but despite being such strong brutes, men have some curiously vulnerable parts and one well-aimed blow can leave them gasping on the ground, staring up at you in astonishment, as if to say, "That ain't fair." No it ain't, my lad, and don't you forget it. The way I see it, those tender bits are the Big Bearded Bloke's way of making up to us ladies for that serpent-and-apple business. But I digress.

As the chap hauled me up by the wrist, I stiffened the fingers of my other hand and jabbed him viciously in the eye. Mother Edding's messenger let out a muted howl, but he hung on to my wrist. He pulled back his arm and prepared to deliver a roundhouse that would have knocked me in to next week. Silly man. As long as he persisted in hanging on to me with one hand and trying to strike me with the other, I had free run of his defenseless appendages. I balled my hand into a fist, crouched to avoid his own swinging fist and caught him with an uppercut in the tallywags. I'm a great fan of rattling a chap's bollocks when he gets feisty. You don't have to be an Amazon to lay a bloke out flat, just be sure you catch him square. He won't have much appetite for shenanigans after that.

Some fellows are more resilient than others, however, and my assailant proved to be made of sterner stuff than most. True, he did fall over as if he'd been poleaxed, but as I brushed past to fetch the Bulldog, he managed to kick out a leg and sweep my feet from under me. I crashed to the floor, and he grabbed a handful of my hair, pulling hard. He was wicked strong, and I yelped. My hair felt as if it was being torn from the roots, and my scalp burned. Now the bugger had done it. I've beautiful black hair, you see, soft and thick as sable, and if the bastard had pulled a single strand of my crowning glory from my head, he'd bloody well pay for it. Not to mention that hair pulling is a woman's trick and any thug who resorted to it deserved the punishment that I was about to mete out.

The blow to his testicles had weakened him, but he staggered to his feet, dragging me upright with him. Instead of trying to wrench myself from his grasp, I took a half step to the right and drove my fist into his unprotected ribs. It wasn't a hard punch, but it was strong enough to make him flinch and curse, and loosen his grip on my locks. Then I lifted a foot and kicked him hard in the kneecap. He uttered a feeble cry and collapsed, but the bugger still wouldn't let go of my hair, dragging me down with him. Enough was enough. I used my knee to pound him sharply in the ribs, and finally the ruffian called it a night. He lay on his side with his legs drawn up, moaning piteously. I fetched the Bulldog and drove the butt of the revolver down onto my attacker's skull. The moaning ceased, and it was a damned good thing it did, for the fellow was beginning to get on my nerves by this time and I had been tempted just to dispatch all five rounds from my gun into his head.

Mrs. Drinkwater opened the door, yawning belligerently.

"When you wants your tea, all you have to do is ask. No need to throw a barney."

When my visitor regained consciousness, I served him tea and buttered toast and attempted to have a civil chat with him regarding his employer. You'd think that after these courtesies he'd have been forthcoming about her identity, but the fellow proved to be either excessively loyal or exceedingly stupid, claiming he had picked up the job at a pub in Seven Dials from a stranger and knew nothing more than that the bounty on my head was five guineas. That news only increased my anger. For a woman like me, five guineas was an insultingly paltry sum, although to a man from the rookery of Seven Dials it must have seemed like a fortune. I dismissed the fellow from my presence with a warning that if I saw him again, I'd part his hair with a bullet.

It was time to put an end to Mother Edding's clumsy attempts to introduce me to the grim reaper. Frankly, I didn't understand the old trout. In our business it's only natural to lose a girl now and then. Of course, if your bint flounces down the road and joins a competitor's nunnery, you'll demand some recompense from the other abbess and if she isn't forthcoming with the ready, you'll do your best to steal her customers and besmirch her name. Just like any other business, really. What you don't do is hire some dirty thugs to abduct the madam who stole your girl and toss her in the Thames like a dead cat. That's beyond the pale. Consequently, I thought it best to reacquaint Mother Edding with the unwritten code of conduct for our profession.

I didn't bother to knock when I reached the house on Endell Street. I gave the front door a prodigious shove that sent it flying into the wall, and the resulting crash made the whole building tremble.

Two wretched creatures gaped at me from the shabby parlor. Their dresses, poor maids, were little more than rags. One was barefoot. Neither had seen a bar of soap in donkey's years. Evidently, Mother Edding's customers were not particular, but then the customers themselves were probably not out of the top drawer.

"Find Mother Edding and tell her India Black wants to see her. Now!" I barked.

My voice brooked no disobedience. The girls scampered from the room, looking relieved at having escaped from the well-dressed lunatic who had appeared in the parlor at eight o'clock in the morning, before decent people were up and about.

I heard the gabble of voices overhead and then the ponderous tread of Mother Edding on the stairs.

Her stumpy form appeared in the doorway. "Wot the 'ell do you want?" she rumbled in that basso profundo voice of hers. God, she was a frightening sight: a prizefighter's jaw thrust forward pugnaciously, quivering red jowls, and the mean little eyes of an angry shoat.

"I'm here to settle our differences, once and for all," I said. "I'm getting bloody tired of brawling with your hired ruffians."

"Wot the 'ell are you gabblin' about?"

The venerable matriarch must be going deaf. I raised my voice. "I said, I'm through sparring with those chaps you're sending round. If one more of your boys tries to bash me over the head or dump me in the river, I'll send him back to you in a coffin. Then I'll be by to put you in one, too. Is that clear?"

The madam's face was screwed into a puzzled frown. "Don't know wot you're on about. I ain't sent anyone to do you 'arm."

"You threatened me."

Mother Edding snorted. "'Course I did. Wot'd you expect

me to do? Let you walk off wif Martine wifout liftin' a finger to stop you? I had me reputation to fink about. But I never made good on the threat. It was all for show, so's you'd fink twice about comin' 'ere when you need a new girl."

I wouldn't have even thought once about raiding Mother Edding's establishment, but for Superintendent Stoke's directive to do so. It wouldn't do to disparage the abbess's establishment, however, not when she was standing between me and the door.

"So wot's all this about me tryin' to 'ave you killed? And mind you," she added, "if I wanted you dead, you would be. I'd 'ave done it meself. Do I look like I got the money to pay someone to 'ammer you?"

A sensible question, that. I studied the old abbess, who looked truly befuddled by my accusation.

"You're not trying to murder me?"

Mother Edding scowled. "Over Martine? Why, girls like her are thick as fleas in Seven Dials. I 'ad a new one in 'ere 'fore Martine's bed got cold." She gave me a shrewd look. "So someone's after you, eh? You been stealin' girls from other 'ouses?"

I was beginning to feel that the botched attempts on my life might have nothing at all to do with Mother Edding. It was not a pleasant thought. Had someone in the anarchist cell targeted me? Had I done something to tip my hand? And if I had earned the mistrust of the group's members, why not confront me directly rather than lumbering around in the dark, making clumsy efforts to do me in?

As you can see, I had a fair bit of thinking to do, and my efforts were not assisted by the sight of Mother Edding's wicked grin and triumphant air. I ignored her question and fixed her with a basilisk glare.

"My apologies for accusing you," I said coldly. "But you

would do well to remember that I am not to be trifled with."

"Coo," Mother Edding breathed, cocking her head mockingly. "Get 'er! Not to be trifled wif!"

I like to have the last word in most exchanges (who doesn't?), but it wasn't worth the effort of formulating a reply to Mother Edding. I had some cogitating to do, and quickly. I brushed past the madam without a word and stalked out the door. I'd reached the street when she called after me. "Don't go slanderin' me, India Black, and tellin' people I backed away from a fight wif you. It won't do my reputation a bit o' good. You spread any lies about me gettin' old and soft, and I *will* 'ave to kill you. You 'ear me?"

18

I walked until I found a hansom to hail, and then I rode the rest of the way to Lotus House. I scarcely noticed the journey, not even the hike through the hellish streets of Seven Dials, as I was preoccupied with the disturbing news that Mother Edding was not trying to murder me. That meant that someone else was. There were plenty of candidates in our radical group, but why were they so deuced slow about cutting me down? Had the intention been to frighten me rather than to kill me? Well, it was hard to argue that my dunking in the Thames had been meant as a warning, not with my hands and feet bound and a bag over my head. Under those circumstances, the odds favored death by drowning. Was Ivanov behind the assaults? Of course he could be, as he was a treacherous Russian bastard who hadn't hesitated to shoot French and wouldn't scruple at eliminating India Black. But I'd be damned if I could fathom why Ivanov might do such a thing. French had been right: we must get our hands on the devious bugger and find out what he was doing masquerading as an anarchist.

Mrs. Drinkwater had been watching out the window for me,

and she flung open the door before I'd finished climbing the steps.

"Ma'am, I'm sorry, ma'am, but them gentlemen insisted, ma'am, and they wouldn't take no for an answer." The cook's bosom heaved in agitation. She smelled strongly of rum.

"You reek of rum," I said.

"Making a pudding," she mumbled. "Must have spilt some on my apron."

I sighed. Now the wretched woman would feel compelled to produce one of her inedible concoctions as proof. I'd have to send her to the chemist's for some bismuth.

"What men?" I asked.

"Strange men," Mrs. Drinkwater said, clutching her apron and raising it to her mouth. "They look like Fenians." Everyone looked like an Irish terrorist to Mrs. Drinkwater. She'd once chased a baronet from Lotus House, brandishing a broom and accusing him of advocating Home Rule for Ireland. "They're in your study. I told them you weren't at home, but they ignored me and came in anyway. I tried to keep them out, but they weren't to be denied."

I patted the cook's arm. "Everything is fine, Mrs. Drinkwater. I shall see what the gentlemen want."

I wasn't unduly concerned. Strange men often turn up at Lotus House. I'm proud to say that my establishment has garnered a favorable reputation and its fame is spreading. These fellows had likely just arrived from the colonies, where they'd heard of the glories of Lotus House from some officers or colonial administrators. The prospect of new customers always lifts my spirits, and I breezed into my study with a spring in my step and my most alluring smile on my lips, only to be greeted by the sight of Harkov and Schmidt sitting stiffly in my Queen Anne chairs.

No good could come of this development, I thought, but there seemed no way to avoid having a natter with the two of them, so I greeted them politely and draped my coat over a chair. The Bulldog was in the pocket, and I wanted it close to hand. My visitors looked severe, if not downright menacing. Harkov's black eyes glimmered in his saturnine face, and his mouth was stretched in a bitter grimace, as though he'd just discovered a weevil in his porridge. I'd never cared for that face, and I cared less for it now. If the fellow had turned up at Lotus House as a customer and offered to pay ten times the going rate, I'd have turned him away. He looked more like Old Nick than ever, and I hoped my spoon was long enough to sup with the fellow today.

Schmidt's presence was reassuring, though I couldn't tell you why. After all, he'd been the one to suggest that our cell harbored a traitor. I just hoped he hadn't concluded that the traitor was me. But he resembled a kindly grandfather with the sunlight reflecting off his spectacles and his bald pate gleaming, and I found it hard to credit the notion that he was about to judge, condemn and execute yours truly.

I offered them refreshments, but they declined. Harkov glanced at Schmidt, who nodded gravely, granting permission for the Russian to speak.

Harkov cleared his throat. He sat stiffly, with his hands on his knees. "Schmidt and I are here to discuss the issue raised at last night's meeting, namely the possibility that our cell has been penetrated by a government agent."

I began to wish that the Bulldog was not close to hand, but actually in my hand. My mouth felt dry. "I'd have to defer to you gentlemen on that subject. You've had more experience at that sort of thing. Rooting out spies, I mean. I wouldn't recognize a spy if I met one. Not that I've ever met a spy. That I know of, anyway." Confound it, I was babbling. I clamped my mouth shut.

Harkov and Schmidt looked at one another. I wished they would stop doing that. It must signify something, but what?

Harkov leaned forward, staring intently at me. "You have impressed us, Miss Black, with your commitment to our cause."

"Not just your commitment, but your skills as well," said Schmidt.

When a bloke starts the conversation with a compliment, you can bet you're not going to like what follows.

"Thank you," I said cautiously. "But it appears that others in the group may doubt my dedication to the cause. Last night, Bonnaire was pointing out how likely it was that I was an agent provocateur."

Schmidt's smile was humorless. "Bonnaire does not speak for the group."

"He does not," added Harkov ominously, "speak for Grigori."

"Are you insinuating that Bonnaire is a government agent?" I asked cautiously, for if they suspected the debonair Frenchman they might also suspect his recruits, whom, I need scarcely mention, included me.

"What do you know of Mr. French?" Harkov asked abruptly.

I was caught off guard. A muscle at the corner of my eye twitched. Had Harkov and Schmidt noticed? "French? Well, nothing really, beyond what he told us the night he joined the group."

"He has accompanied you from the meeting to the cabstand on one or two occasions. What did you discuss on the walk?"

I assumed an air of serious study. This was not difficult, as my mind was racing. Clearly they were suspicious of the poncy bastard. Tread carefully, India, I thought. "He's a quiet chap, and we didn't talk a great deal. We mostly talked about the meeting and what we had discussed there, and our plans for the memorial service."

"Aha!" Harkov looked significantly at Schmidt. "You see?" Dear God, they *did* suspect French.

"See what?" I did not have to feign perplexity.

Harkov leaned across the table and fixed those serpent's eyes on mine. "We have reason to believe that French is an agent of the British government."

My mouth felt as parched as the bloody Sahara. My eyes flickered over to Schmidt. "Why do you think French works for the British government, and if you do think that, why did you let him walk out of the meeting last night?"

Schmidt was filling his pipe, pushing the tobacco into the bowl with intense concentration. "You see why we prize you, India? For a woman, you think quite logically." I could see that I'd have my work cut out for me in the worker's Utopia. These anarchists weren't half as egalitarian as their propaganda would lead you to believe.

"As for your first question," said Harkov, "the answer is that French has been seen with men who are known to work for Her Majesty's government."

If he had, that was a startling lack of judgment on his part and I'd have to have a word with him. In the meantime, I wasn't sure what tack I should take. Defend the bloke, or scream for his blood? I'd try protecting French first and if that proved dangerous, I'd have to switch to the outraged radical mode. Just for the moment, you understand. I certainly didn't want French being targeted as a spy, but he was free, roaming about outside, while I was closeted with two anarchists who were not in a convivial mood. I needed to ensure my own safety first.

"French could be gathering information from them. He *is* a

member of the establishment. He's quite likely to use his contacts in government to try to find out information that would be useful to us. Perhaps he's deflecting attention away from our group."

"Grigori is satisfied that French is an agent," said Harkov. "Grigori does not make mistakes." I could see the truth of that, as Grigori was dead right about French. Now to the second question.

"Then why did you allow French to leave alive?"

"That is quite simple. Grigori has only told me of French's treachery this morning. I went right to Schmidt, and we came here."

Damn and blast. Ivanov had put the cat among the pigeons. It was clear that he had waited to tell Harkov until after the meeting. You did not have to have a degree to understand why. If the wily Russian had accused French at the meeting, either French or I might have revealed Ivanov's identity to the others. But why had Ivanov betrayed French at all? And why were Harkov and Schmidt telling me?

"Why are you telling me this?" I've never much cared for flank attacks. You might as well draw your saber and charge.

"Grigori instructed us to discuss the matter with you. He would like to know your views on the subject."

Bloody hell. That Slavic brute was a cruel bastard. He was playing with French and me, like a cat toying with a mouse before he kills it. I could just picture Ivanov's green eyes glowing with sadistic pleasure as he formulated this fiendish plan.

"Are you confident that Grigori is correct about French?"

Harkov reared back in his seat. "Naturally." He sounded deuced offended that I had dared to doubt Ivanov. This was probably not the best time to tell these two chaps that their beloved leader Grigori had another life as a Russian military agent.

"What do we do now?" I had a sinking feeling that I already knew the answer to this question.

"We must kill French," said Harkov.

I took no pleasure in learning that I was correct in my assumption.

"When?"

"We shall ask for a volunteer at tonight's meeting." Harkov leered at me. "Nothing exhibits loyalty like executing a Judas."

I had to bite my tongue from asking Harkov if he'd offer to scrag French, or would he be busy at a committee meeting somewhere?

The two anarchists were studying me intently. There was no point in protesting or in trying to deflect suspicion from French. I'd only turn it on myself. In situations like this, a bold approach is required.

"I shall shoot him myself." I sounded calm, despite the inferno raging in my internal organs. Now don't go rupturing yourself over what I said. I fully intended to tell French that I'd signed up for the firing squad, but the first order of business was for me to emerge from this encounter without meeting the fate planned for French. My mind had been racing since Harkov and Schmidt had announced their suspicions of French, and I'd come up with an absolutely wizard idea while chatting calmly with Harkov and Schmidt about putting a bullet in French. My talents had clearly been wasted as a madam; I was a natural at this espionage game and I'd have to speak to French and Dizzy about a promotion.

After my visitors left, I sent an urgent message to French and spent the next hour knocking about Lotus House, pacing feverishly up and down the hallways and snapping orders at any slut who wandered into my path. I'd put the first phase of my plan into place before Harkov and Schmidt left the house, and now I sent Mrs. Drinkwater to the butcher and the grocer, to lay in supplies for that evening. The next meeting of the Dark Legion, you see, was to be held at Lotus House.

French returned a message saying he was occupied at the moment but would be with me at one o'clock. Confound it, that was three hours away. I should have to find a way to busy myself until the meeting. So I walked the halls and chivvied the whores, examining complexions and looking for contraband in their rooms (haul: one empty bottle of gin, a pouch of tobacco and three novels of romance among the upper classes). When I'd completed that task, I conducted an inventory of the pantry and the liquor cabinet. There wasn't a bottle of sherry, brandy or Madeira in the house, though I distinctly remembered paying for several bottles just last week. Damn Mrs. Drinkwater. I was prepared to look the other way if she wanted a nip now and then, but at this rate I'd soon be running Lotus House just to pay her bill at the bottle shop. I resolved to have a word with her after killing French, and went upstairs to have a kip before he turned up at one o'clock.

But I couldn't settle, and is it any wonder? I had a few things on my mind. On three occasions someone had attempted to kill me, and though I had weathered two of the attacks, being tossed into the Thames would certainly have been my death warrant had not Vincent possessed such surprising aquatic abilities. If Mother Edding wasn't the culprit, then the villain was still at large and I could expect to be fending off knives and clubs and assorted other weapons for the foreseeable future. It wasn't a pleasant prospect, and it was doubly unsettling because I was busy masquerading as an anarchist. Not to mention that Ivanov and his intentions needed sorting out, and something needed to be done about French's proposed demise. Trying to sleep was a waste of time, with all that whirling around in my head. I needed action.

I left a note for Mrs. Drinkwater, informing her that I would be out until one, that Mr. French was expected then, and could she please have a cold luncheon prepared for us? Even Mrs. Drinkwater could slice and butter bread and put a cold joint on the table. I hoped. Then I donned a sober but well-cut dress and my finest bonnet. I had to look my best; I was on my way to one of London's wealthiest districts.

I secured a hansom and directed the driver to drop me at Eaton Square. It's a fine park, as parks go, which is to say that if you like grass and pigeons, you'll like this one. It's the second most fashionable square in Belgravia, after Belgrave Square, and is chock-full of earls and duchesses with the odd merchant banker and shipping magnate thrown in just to prove the inhabitants aren't complete snobs. The park is surrounded by a row of terraced houses faced with white stucco, in that classical style that the toffs think demonstrates their good breeding and superior education. The whole affair might look dazzling in the sunshine, but on this rainy morning the stucco was streaked with water and the white walls reflected the dull gray of the clouds overhead, looking dismal and foreboding.

You might think a girl of my humble beginnings would be impressed by a show of wealth, but I've prowled the halls at Balmoral and attended a ball at the Russian embassy. I've even met the Queen and dodged the attentions of her randy son Prince Bertie. They're an odd lot, and if they were your family, you'd be deuced ashamed and pretend to be Italian or Polish or something. Frankly, I'd rather take tea with my good friend Rowena Adderly. She may be a whore, but she's class. But I digress.

As you will have surmised from my destination, I'd come to have a natter with Charles Goodwood, Earl of Clantham. I ambled along the perimeter of the square looking at the numbers of the houses and seeing if the local plod was lying in wait for visiting whores, but it was quiet in the square. The light drizzle that glazed the pavement and streaked the stucco had discouraged most visitors to the park, and the social hour was not yet in full swing. Toward lunch, I expected the streets would be thronged with carriages and landaus delivering the wealthy ladies of the neighborhood to their engagements.

The earl lived in one of the terraced homes near the northeast corner of the square, near to St. Peter's Church. A memory of playing among its massive columns came unbidden to my mind. Then a flood of memories engulfed me: strolling with my mother in the square on a sunny afternoon, cadging a book from the shelves of an enormous library, drinking a cup of warm milk in an attic bedroom. A final, unbidden recollection of a scrawny old man calling my mother's name. It was dashed unsettling. For a moment I felt as ill as if I'd eaten one of Mrs. Drinkwater's meat pies.

An old battle-axe was bearing down on me, followed by a maid in uniform tugging a decrepit Maltese on a leash. The battle-axe and the Maltese both glared at me through bulbous dark eyes. The old lady looked pointedly at the earl's house, sniffed loudly, thrust her nose imperiously in the air and studiously ignored me as she passed. If I'd needed confirmation that the earl was still a bit of a bounder, the woman had provided it.

The Maltese snapped at me as it sauntered past. The maid gave the leash a sharp jerk and me an apologetic smile. The dog yelped.

The battle-axe wheeled with surprising dexterity. "Rose, did you pull poor Maximus's leash? He despises being hauled about." She rested a glove on the mutt's head and scratched an ear. "Poor Maxie," she crooned. "She didn't hurt you, did she? If she did, you shall have permission to bite her."

The maid looked resigned. The trio marched away. I summoned my courage and mounted the steps.

When the butler opened the door to me, I had to stifle a gasp. I'd never seen such an ugly cove. His brow and jaw would have attracted most female apes. A hank of unruly white hair tumbled over his forehead. His skin was pocked and sallow. One eye was missing, the socket puckered closed. The remaining eye was as cold as a shark's.

"Yes?"

"I'd like to speak to His Lordship, please. I am India Black."

The single eye gave me a swift appraisal. "Did His Lordship send for you?"

I'm not one to waste a good opening, even if it does involve telling a lie. "Yes, he did."

"Ah." The cove didn't move. "Are you from Mrs. Snapely's house?"

"Yes."

The butler shuffled to one side and allowed me entrance. He shut the door behind me and then motioned for me to follow him. "Wait in here," he said, and ushered me into a parlor that had once been grand. The air smelled musty in here, with an overtone of stale cigar smoke and whisky fumes. The velvet curtains at the windows were shabby and coated with dust. A layer of dust covered the marble mantle. The cushions in the chairs had last been plumped in King William's day (William III, that is). I wandered over to the window and stared out at the rain, now beating down on the grass of the square. Lights had appeared in the house windows. Like many London mornings, this one was as bright as twilight in more temperate climes. I hoped the battle-axe had been caught in the deluge.

"India Black. The name is familiar." The voice was high-pitched, imperious and faintly mocking.

I took a deep breath and turned to face my father. Or more accurately, the man who might be my father.

I took one look and knew immediately that he was not. There was no way a gorgeous apple like myself had fallen from this blighted shrub. The Earl of Clantham was an unprepossessing twit, struggling to top out at five feet, with a hooked nose, a crabbed expression and the crazed eyes of a fighting cock. I exhaled a sigh of relief that whoever the man was, he certainly wasn't any relation of mine.

"Come away from that window," he said. "I can't see you against the light."

I walked forward until I was a few feet from him. He gave me a head-to-toe survey that was anything but fatherly. I might have been a slightly superior chop, for he gave me an approving, and avaricious, smile as I drew closer.

"Well, well. Mrs. Snapely has done herself proud."

Time to get on the front foot. "Mrs. Snapely didn't send me."

His forehead wrinkled. "Not from Mrs. Snapely? I confess I am confused. I hardly do business with anyone else." Comprehension dawned and he snapped his fingers. "Of course. Dear old Featherstone. I believe he mentioned you at the club the other day." He chuckled. "I must say, his description of your charms was entirely inadequate. What did you say your name was, m'dear?"

"India Black."

Again his forehead wrinkled. "That name. Have we met?"

"Many years ago, I believe."

"Surely I would remember the occasion." My God, the little ferret was simpering. "Although I must say, you look dashed familiar."

"I was a child," I said coldly.

He recoiled slightly, and the smirk died on his lips. "A child? Then I daresay we have not met. I do not trifle with children." The last was said stiffly, with an air of self-satisfaction.

"I believe you trifled with my mother. Her name was Isobel Black."

A fond and foolish smile cracked the earl's face. "Isobel. It's been years since I've heard that name. You say you are her daughter?"

"Yes."

He rubbed his chin thoughtfully. "I do believe I remember a little girl."

"That was me."

"Ah. I see. I didn't recognize you. You spent most of your time upstairs or stealing books from my library. You were a wee sprat with a vicious temper, as I recall." He gave me a frankly appreciative look. "You've grown into a fine woman."

"Yes, I have. But I didn't come here to listen to compliments."

"Why are you here?" he asked. The demented eyes were suddenly cunning, and suspicious. "Is it money? Do you want money? I'll tell you now—"

"I didn't come for money. I've plenty of my own, thank you."

"What then?"

"I want to know more about my mother. What she was like. Where she came from. How long we stayed here and why we left."

"I see. A genealogical quest."

"Yes."

He put his hands behind his back and rocked on his heels. "Hmph. Well. I don't know if I can be of much assistance."

"I'd be grateful for anything you can tell me."

"And you are not expecting cash remuneration?"

"I am not."

He sighed. "Oh, very well." He crossed to the door, opened it and bellowed, "Clump, come here."

The grotesque butler appeared.

"Bring tea for us," snapped the earl.

Clump regarded his master balefully through his single eye, nodded briefly and shuffled away toward the rear of the house, feet scraping audibly over the marble floor.

The earl indicated that I should sit and I did so. He remained on his feet, choosing to stand by the mantelpiece. I suppose it gave him some confidence to be able to look down at me, for I had towered over the poor sod.

We waited silently until Clump returned with a tea tray. It was deuced poor fare for an earl. The tea leaves had been used before, the cake was crumbling from age and the bread was green with mildew at the edges. Perhaps I should introduce Clump to Mrs. Drinkwater. They could exchange ideas about how to poison their employers. I accepted a cup of tea and waited while the earl cut a large portion of the cake and tucked in. I suppose cutting corners at the tea table enabled him to spend more money for whores. Normally, I'd applaud such careful planning, but I felt a twinge of horror at the idea of the earl as a faithful customer.

The earl slurped his tea. "Go on, m'dear. Ask your questions."

"How did my mother come to live here?"

"I asked her, of course. She was a handsome filly, full of life and utterly beautiful. You favor her greatly." His leer made me wince.

"How did you meet her?"

He leaned his head back on the cushions and stared at the ceiling. "Well, now. That's difficult to remember. She might have come from Mrs. Armfield's, or Mother Farrell's. I had arrangements with both of them at the time. It's possible she was recommended to me by one of my friends. You know how these things work, m'dear, unless I'm very much mistaken."

"You are not mistaken, and I do know how things work." That's fact, but it still pained me to speak of my mother as though she were a cough remedy, the efficacy of which was debated by acquaintances.

"Can you remember when she came here?"

"The mind isn't what it used to be, but let me think." He pulled his lip and rumpled his hair with the effort. "I remember it was summer. It was very warm that year, and the roses in the square were luscious. Just like your mother. It might have been '52. Or perhaps '53. I don't know how old you were then. I know nothing of children." He glared at me resentfully. "I wasn't keen. No, I wasn't keen at all on having a little nipper about the place, but your mother was damned persuasive. I told her to farm you out to one of those women who care for bastard children, but she wouldn't have it. Told me that if I wanted her to stay, you were part of the arrangement. So I gave you a room on the servants' floor and let your mother come up to see you now and then."

"I remember the room," I said through gritted teeth. "It was freezing in the winter, and too hot to sleep in the summer."

"Was it?" He didn't seem disturbed by this piece of news. "Frankly, I thought it was the best place for you, up there with the maids. Thought you'd learn a useful skill if you lived with the servants." He frowned. "Your mother had other ideas, of course. She taught you to read, which I believed a great waste of time. Naturally, I was shocked that *she* knew how to read, but she could. Her tastes were catholic, m'dear, as were yours."

"How long did we live here?"

"A good many years. Your mother was a rare beauty, and every man I knew envied me. Pleasant times, they were."

I'm sure they had been for the randy old goat.

"Why did we leave?"

He gave me a sidelong glance, and I reckoned he was figuring out how much to tell me.

"Your mother became ill," he said carefully. He'd weighed that answer a long time. I remembered what Edina Watkins had told me. This bantam cock had tossed my mother out after she sickened and ceased to adorn his scrawny arm. There was no point in aggravating the gent at the moment, as there was still plenty I wanted to know, but I added Charles Goodwood, Earl of Clantham, to the list of rascals who deserved a good cudgeling.

"Did she ever tell you about her past? Did she mention her home or her family?"

"She rarely talked about the past. It made her... uncomfortable." The earl looked rather uneasy himself.

"You will not offend me, no matter what you tell me. As you have discerned, I make my living as my mother did. There is nothing you can say that will shock me." Brave words, indeed, but an icy chill had crept into my bones and I dreaded hearing what the earl might say next.

He sipped his tea to buy a few seconds' grace, studying my face. My gaze never wavered, though that cold, hollow feeling had enveloped me. His cup tinkled as he placed it on the saucer. The earl had resolved to tell me. I could see it in his face. He leaned back against the cushions, steepling his fingers and staring over them at me.

"As I said, she did not discuss her past as a rule. However, on one or two occasions she did condescend to inform me of the reason she had entered pros... er, the profession of... er—"

I threw the fellow a rope. "How she came to be a whore."

"Ah. Yes. Quite. Apparently, your mother became attracted to her father's groom. A fellow named Black. The two of them were resolved to run away together, but before they did so, your grandfather discovered the plan. He dismissed the groom and sent your mother to live with his sister. This Black fellow found out where your mother was staying and traveled there. They resumed their relationship, and your mother soon discovered that she had become pregnant."

"With me?"

"Yes, you were the child. Your mother's aunt contrived to keep the news from reaching your grandfather, but he learned of her condition somehow and forbade her to return to her home. Your mother said her aunt would have allowed her to stay and have the child, but Black insisted he would care for your mother. They came to London. Sadly, Black caught typhus and died, and your mother was forced to fend for herself."

I hadn't taken my eyes from the earl, but I was finding it dashed difficult to follow what he was saying. I felt as though I had plunged my head underwater, for there was a roaring in my ears like a stream in torrent.

The earl had abruptly shut his mouth. He was watching me carefully. At length he rose and fetched a decanter of brandy from a table near the window. He splashed some into my cup. I raised it to my mouth, hands trembling, and drank it all in one swift motion. I can't say it cleared my head, but it did dispel some of the frigidity that gripped my body. The earl extended the decanter, offering to fill my cup again, but I shook my head.

"Is there more?"

"Are you certain—"

"Yes. Tell me everything."

"There's not much left to say. Your mother had been working for a couple of years when we met. She was a beauty and had no shortage of regular customers. Gentlemen," he hastened to add, as if that made a difference, and in a way, I suppose it did. At least she'd been appreciated and had perhaps escaped the rougher sort of life endured by many fallen women.

"We exchanged services, your mother and I. I offered her security, a steady income, a handsome property, and I took in her bast—" The earl remembered he was speaking to the bastard child. "That is to say, I took you in with her. The arrangement suited us both."

Until she'd lost her bloom, and then he'd turned us out. But it was ever thus. Under the circumstances, it had been damned sporting of the fellow to keep me around at all. He must have been fond of my mother, in his way, and up to a point. When she failed to arouse the envy of his friends, he'd found another woman who would. There's no use getting angry; it's just the way things are.

"Did my mother ever tell you where she had lived before she came to London?"

The earl poured a tot of brandy into his own teacup. "Somewhere in Scotland, I believe she said. Tullimore? Tullicairn?"

"Tullibardine," I said flatly.

The earl cocked his head. "Yes, I think that might be the name of the place."

19

I returned to Lotus House just in time to meet French and Vincent for a council of war. Of course I'd fretted about the information the earl had given me. The Dowager Marchioness of Tullibardine figured into this somehow, and I was jolly well going to find out how, just as soon as I'd saved French from death at the hands of the anarchists, put Ivanov in a British gaol and closed down the Dark Legion. The old crone was going to deliver the goods about my mother's past or else. What comprised "else," I did not yet know, but I'd find something suitably wicked for the marchioness.

French and Vincent were reclining in the study, having a lively discussion about nitroglycerine and detonators. I'd have to have a word with French. It was too much to expect that Vincent would not make use of this information in some criminal way. After wrapping up the present assignment, I wouldn't be surprised to learn in the weeks to come that someone had blown the doors off the nearest bank and absconded with all the money.

"'Allo, India. Where's the clobber? I'm famished."

"You'd have to be to eat Mrs. Drinkwater's cooking," I

muttered. "Oh, hello, Mrs. Drinkwater. Yes, we'll have lunch in the study." Damned woman was getting as adept as Vincent at slipping around without any noise.

Lunch was a joint of beef, the cold white fat flaking onto the platter as French sawed gamely. Even for an expert swordsman, he found it rough going. I chose a slice of bread and butter. Much easier on the teeth, and the digestion. Vincent and French made rough sandwiches. Vincent attacked his like a terrier going after a rat. French took a dainty bite.

"Are you ever going to get a decent cook?" he asked, delicately extracting a piece of gristle from his molars.

"Wot's wrong with ole Drinkwater?" Vincent was working away heroically on his sandwich. "Nuffink wrong wif this. I've eaten worse. One time, I et a—"

"Not now, Vincent. We've got a crisis on our hands." I recounted my conversation with Harkov and Schmidt.

"Blimey," said Vincent. "That bugger Ivanov is somethin,' ain't 'e? Puttin' the 'ounds onto French like that."

"What the devil is the man doing?" French scowled.

"I should think that was obvious. He's planning to kill you. Or," I corrected myself, "planning to have you killed. It amounts to the same thing. We should have snatched him after the meeting."

"Perhaps," mused French. "I just wish I knew what Ivanov is thinking."

"Wot's it matter, guv? Don't matter wot 'e's finkin'. We got to find a way to keep you from gettin' your throat slit. Or takin' a bullet. Or gettin' your 'ead cracked, or—"

"Yes, yes. We all understand the situation," I said.

"Maybe you should just stay 'ome tonight," Vincent suggested to French.

"I can't do that. Harkov and Schmidt will suspect that India has told me of their suspicions. They'll turn on her if I don't attend the meeting."

Vincent mulled this over. If it came down to sacrificing either his hero or me, the odds were not in my favor.

"I wonder why Ivanov is throwing me to the wolves and leaving you out of it?" French asked me.

"You know Ivanov. He's probably enjoying the dilemma he's presented to me. Save you, or reveal myself as a British agent. He's got a nerve, that one. That's what comes of letting those bloody Russian aristocrats own serfs. They start to relish cruelty."

"You might be next," said French, turning an anxious face to me. "Do you have your Bulldog?"

"I'm never without it," I hastened to assure him.

"You may need it tonight. If Ivanov comes to the meeting, I see no alternative but to kill him and arrest the others."

I liked the sound of that plan and said so. It may be shocking to contemplate cutting down a man in cold blood, but Ivanov wouldn't scruple at pulling the trigger. He was a cold one and deserved to be treated the same way he would treat us.

"So wot do we do if Ivanov doesn't show, and that Harkov bloke tells someone to kill French?" asked Vincent.

I smiled. Smugly, I might add. "I have a plan. Hand over that Remington pocket pistol of yours, French, and listen."

An essential part of this plan was to hold tonight's meeting of the Dark Legion here at Lotus House. It had been dashed easy to convince Harkov and Schmidt that the delights of a warm fire, gaslight and a full bottle of whisky outweighed the charms of a dank, musty cellar that smelled of sewage.

"Men are in and out of here all the time," I said. "No one

will bat an eye." That was true to a point, though Thick Ed and Flerko might raise a whore's eyebrow, not being the class of men we usually serviced here. Still, it shouldn't be difficult for them to slip into the house in the early hours of the morning. The brothel's inhabitants would be winding down for the evening and Mrs. Drinkwater safely in bed by the time my fellow anarchists would come in through the back door. I instructed Mrs. Drinkwater to make some sandwiches and brew some coffee, for I was meeting tonight with some prospective clients and given the hour, I knew they'd be peckish. Mrs. Drinkwater responded as she always responds: a sniff, a nod and a boozy retreat to the kitchen.

I had many hours to kill before my guests arrived and French bit the dust, so I occupied myself by writing a number of letters to the marchioness, trying to strike just the right tone. I finally settled on the following:

> *Dear Lady Aberkill,*
> *You bloody woman. You've known all along that my mother came from Tullibardine.*
>
> *Tell me what you know, or I swear you'll not live to breed another collie.*
>
> *Sincerely,*
> *India Black*

A bit ungrammatical, that, but it gets the point across. Of course I meant that the marchioness would not live to breed her collie bitches to her collie studs, but I felt that a lengthy explanation of the point would detract from the overall effect. The old trout would know what I intended.

In truth, I doubted that my words would roust the marchioness. Likely, she would inhale a quantity of snuff upon reading it, then sneeze uncontrollably and spew the nasty stuff all over the page. Come summer, I'd probably find myself on a train to Tullibardine to beard the lioness in her den, but I didn't hold out much hope of being successful. The marchioness was a wily vixen and had bested better than India Black in her time. I sent one of the girls to the postbox and spent the remainder of the day resting in preparation for the evening's festivities.

Being a Wednesday, it was a quiet night at Lotus House. We always have a midweek slump, and tonight was no different. The girls nattered among themselves, the few customers who appeared were hastily assigned to their designated bints, and all went off like clockwork. I spent a restful few hours in my study, loading, unloading and reloading the rimfire Remington pocket pistol in .41 caliber that French had loaned to me. It's a beautiful little thing, squat and thick but absolutely deadly at close range. Ideally, your target would be sitting across from you at the poker table at one of those Wild West saloons, and you'd pull the trigger and send him to play five-card stud with the Prince of Darkness. It was the perfect weapon for tonight's activities.

I was nodding by the fire, close on to two o'clock in the morning, when someone rapped lightly at the back door. Harkov was the first to arrive, and he scuttled in like a startled crab, peering suspiciously into the open doors leading into the parlor and my study.

"You're sure we will be undisturbed? What about the girls?"

"They're in bed asleep. They won't come into the study without my permission, and what if they did? They've seen men before."

"I wish we were meeting at the cellar," he said. "There is too much risk in meeting here. I passed several constables on my journey, and I'm sure they suspected me."

And quite rightly, I thought. I escorted Harkov into the study and put a glass in his hand. Nothing special, you understand, just garden-variety brandy from the local wine shop. I certainly wasn't going to waste the good stuff on the likes of Harkov and Flerko.

The others stole in shortly after, arriving separately and every one of them as nervous as a grouse on the Glorious Twelfth. Their trepidation proved short-lived, however, when they saw a fire burning in the grate and the brandy in Harkov's glass. Who wouldn't prefer this over a damp, moldy cellar and broken wooden chairs? French arrived last, bustling in with an air of purpose. I watched him carefully, but I could detect no sign of nervousness in his actions. He greeted the others, poured himself a drink and took a seat calmly. I was the one who was nervous. My palms were damp, and my hands trembled slightly as I sipped my brandy.

"May we smoke, Miss Black?" Harkov asked. I gave my assent and heartily wished I enjoyed tobacco. Its consolation would have been welcome tonight.

French lit a cheroot and puffed away placidly, hand draped casually across his waist. I knew his Boxer revolver was in a holster under his coat, and he could reach it with lightning speed if necessary. I was on edge and kept bustling about, refilling drinks and fetching ashtrays, which shows you just how nervous I was, as normally I wouldn't stoop to such behavior. Under other circumstances, the gents could fetch and carry for themselves (unless they were prospective customers, of course; I can always rouse myself to deliver a glass of whisky if there's money in it for me). I watched the hands on the clock move slowly, ticking away the minutes while I listened anxiously for a knock at the door. If Ivanov visited us tonight, it would be the last call he paid in his life, and though I cared not whether the wily devil lived or died, it was difficult not to contemplate the potential destruction to my study in the event a gunfight broke out. Bullet holes are costly to repair. Too late I remembered that I had planned to move the lovely little French table out into the hall and take down that rather nice oil painting of the ballerina that Lord Deveraux had given me so many years ago.

The minutes passed. Harkov looked at the clock and frowned. "I had hoped that Grigori would join us tonight, but we cannot wait any longer. Let us begin."

I hadn't expected the Russian wolf to attend this meeting. He had no way of anticipating whether French would be accused and murdered, or I'd show my hand as a British agent, or Ivanov himself might be killed or captured. Best to stay home with a bottle and a good book and see what developed.

"I took the liberty of drawing up a preliminary list of duties for each of us," said Flerko.

"Pardon me, Flerko," said Bonnaire, "but before we talk about the abduction, I should like to discuss the informant in our cell. We must root him out. The success of our plan depends upon it."

"There is no need to concern yourself with identifying the spy in our midst," said Harkov. His monocle glittered in the moonlight. "Grigori has already informed me of the traitor's name, and I have told Schmidt."

My stomach plummeted to the floor and stayed there. French still reposed languidly in his chair, but as I watched him, he reached over casually and tossed his cheroot in the fire. Bonnaire shot a startled glance at Harkov. Thick Ed cracked a knuckle and looked grave. I felt a chill wind pass through the room, as though someone had opened the window.

"What!" Flerko's mouth gaped open. He looked wildly about the study. "Who is it? Who is the traitor?"

"Tell us, Harkov." Bonnaire's voice was scarcely louder than a whisper.

"Mr. French, you remain silent. Don't you want to know the name of the man who has betrayed us to the British government?"

We'd discussed this moment, French and Vincent and I, and had debated whether French should deny the accusation. In the end, we'd concluded that a palaver over his guilt or innocence by a group of paranoid anarchists wouldn't accomplish much other than rousing them into a hot fury and making our plan that much more difficult to execute. Now French shrugged, directing a hostile stare at Harkov.

Harkov smiled, a triumphant smirk that would have been right at home on Beelzebub's visage. He waved a genial hand in French's direction. "I regret to tell you that Mr. French joined our band under false pretenses. He is not the son of a wealthy manufacturer. He comes of rather more ancient stock. Permit me to introduce Mister Lachlan Nathraichean Alasdair French."

Bloody hell. I'd only been joking when I'd asked French if his name was Aethelstan or Baldaric. I reckoned he'd be James or William or even Percival, but his true appellation exceeded anything I could have imagined.

Harkov continued, oblivious to my astonishment. "His father is Major-General Anthony French, and his mother is the daughter of a wealthy Scottish aristocrat. Mr. French is a product of Eton and Balliol College, with a first-class degree in classics. He is engaged to Lady Daphne Kenilworth, daughter of the Duke of Allingham."

Engaged? The poncy bastard had kept that quiet, and no wonder. I sent him a look that would have melted iron. French's face had been immobile, but he shifted uncomfortably at Harkov's words. His gaze flickered to me.

Harkov continued with his recitation of French's resume. "He is also Major French of the Forty-second Regiment of Foot and has spent time teaching Queen Victoria's colonial subjects proper respect for their British masters. French is quite a brave fellow, actually. He's received several medals for his courage in combat. I suppose that is what drew him to the attention of the prime minister. In any case, Mr. French now works for Disraeli in whatever capacity the prime minister requires. Mr. French's latest assignment was to penetrate the Dark Legion."

Flerko snatched the poker from the hearth and brandished it over his head. "I'll kill him," he shouted.

Bonnaire vaulted from his chair and closed a hand over the poker. "Wait, Flerko," he said soothingly. "He will not escape."

"Have you nothing to say for yourself?" asked Harkov.

"There'll be another after me," French drawled. "You lot are about as hard to deceive as a forty-year-old virgin."

"Traitor," Flerko screamed and drew back the poker.

"Traitor," I echoed. French's Remington pocket pistol had appeared in my hand. I pointed the barrel at him, and his eyes widened. There was fear in them, and the sight was so unexpected I almost lowered the gun. French's hands came up, and he took two steps back. I advanced on him. The pistol trembled in my grasp, but I steadied my grip and sighted down the stubby barrel. I had a perfect view of the buttons on his weskit. Engaged? To that vapid blond wench? I pulled the trigger and shot him.

20

The bullet struck him in the chest, yanking him backward with the force of the blow. Blood spurted from the wound, a bright red stream that soaked his weskit and flowed down his ribs onto my Turkey carpet. Damnation. I hadn't thought of that before I pulled the trigger. I never would get that blood out. I bent over him and listened to the ragged sound of his breathing. He stared up at me, a puzzled expression on his face. One hand groped for his chest and feebly batted his bloodstained clothes. He looked at the crimson smear on his palm, whispered something unintelligible and then took one long breath that rattled in his chest. His eyes fluttered closed.

"Good God," exclaimed Bonnaire.

"You've killed him," said Harkov, ashen-faced.

"You wanted him dead, didn't you?" I snapped. "Quick, now. All of you, out the back door. That shot will have the police here any minute."

"But what about the body?" asked Harkov.

"Flerko and I can take it," said Bonnaire.

Thick Ed grunted. "Let me. I can carry him by myself."

I was already at work, folding the carpet over French's inert body. "Don't worry. French isn't the first to die at Lotus House. I've had half a dozen geezers with dicky hearts board the train for paradise in my time. French will just be another. I have a friend I trust who'll help me get rid of the body without any questions." I finished wrapping French in the rug and gave the package a swift kick. "There. In a little while, he'll be swimming in the river." I quickly surveyed the group, who looked as though they'd just seen a war party of Iroquois in the distance and weren't quite sure which direction to flee. For a group of hardened radicals prepared to commit mass murder a few days ago, they seemed unduly shocked by tonight's events.

"Leave now," I said, "while you still have the chance to slip away unseen."

"Oh," Flerko exclaimed. "Oh!"

These sorts of ejaculations usually preceded one of Flerko's imbecilic notions.

"Why don't we cut off French's head and put it on London Bridge? We could post up a sign, saying this is what happens to those who betray our cause." To be fair, it wasn't a *new* imbecilic notion, as earlier he'd proposed the same treatment for the prime minister. Still, I couldn't permit this to happen.

"It would be nice to make an example of our late colleague, but that would be foolish," I said briskly. "If the prime minister knows we've found their agent, he'll do everything in his power to run us to ground. It will be better if French just disappears. Let the prime minister worry about why they haven't heard from him. By the time his body is found, we'll have dispatched Disraeli and vanished."

Thick Ed was kneeling beside the rug, testing the weight by

lifting French's legs. He looked up in consternation. "Christ! He's still breathing."

"Is he?" I opened my desk drawer and took out a sharp, silver-handled letter opener. "He won't be in a few minutes."

Thick Ed swallowed. "Are you sure—"

"Oh, yes. I've had to deal with some unpleasant situations in my time. I'll finish him off and then fetch my friend. He's a big brute. It'll be dead easy to dispose of the body. Now please leave. We won't be able to strike a blow for liberty if we're all in gaol for murder."

They gathered their hats and coats and milled around, and I had to direct them down the hallway to the kitchen, where they could slip out into the garden and exit through the gate in the wall. I waited until they were out of sight, and then I waited a little longer. It was drizzling again, and the night was as dark as Dizzy's complexion. After a good long while, I heard a low whistle and whistled back, and Vincent appeared beside me, shaking the rain from his cap.

"All clear," he whispered. "They ran like rabbits. Couldn't get away fast enough. I followed 'em back to Seven Dials, and then I come back 'ere and 'ung about to make sure none of 'em come back to see wot we were doin'. I reckon we're safe now."

I'd extinguished the lights in the study as I'd ushered my fellow radicals out the door. Now I slipped to the mantelpiece and groped for the matches, lighting a single candle. I hastened to the window and peeked through the curtains, but detected no movement on the pavement outside Lotus House.

"Did you check St. Alban's Street?"

"'Course I did," said Vincent. "Quiet as a cathedral at evensong."

"You've been to evensong?" I was quite incredulous at the

thought of Vincent attending a service.

"One of them charities got 'old of me once. 'Orrible, hit was. Them ole ladies ran me ragged, takin' me to church and teachin' me my letters."

"Meddling cows." I sympathized, having been the all-too-frequent object of some do-gooder's grand plan.

"Could the two of you debate the merits of charitable efforts some other time?" French asked in a muffled voice. "I'm cold, this blood has congealed, and it stinks."

Vincent and I unfolded the Turkey rug, and French sat up gingerly, probing his chest where the wadding from the blank charge had struck him. The front of his shirt was scorched and pocked with powder. The bladder of pig's blood I'd obtained from a theatrical company and that he'd concealed beneath his shirt had contained a copious amount of blood, indeed much more than I had expected, a fact that may be useful to know, but I doubt it.

French was correct: the pig's blood was highly odiferous. I sent him to the kitchen to wash. I hoped he'd brought a clean shirt, as I tossed the one he'd been wearing, along with the weskit, onto the fire.

"Worked like a charm," said Vincent.

"Except that I failed to take into account the effect a pint of blood would have on my Turkey carpet."

"Can't you wash it?"

I was not surprised at Vincent's lack of knowledge about the limits of soap and water.

"I'll send it out to be laundered, but I'd be very surprised if it comes back clean. Oh, well. I'll just have to purchase a new one and send the bill to Superintendent Stoke."

French returned, scrubbing the last traces of blood from

his torso with a towel. That would have to go in the fire as well. As this was the first time I had seen French *en déshabillé*, I took the opportunity to evaluate his masculine attributes. To my satisfaction, he possessed a nice chest with some noticeable muscles, strong arms and a lean, flat stomach. That would do nicely. He caught my frank appraisal and blushed. Fancy, a grown man turning pink like that. Most blokes would stick out their chest and flex their biceps, but not French. Sometimes I despair of ever corrupting the fellow.

He draped his coat over his shoulders and huddled before the fire.

"Do you think they fell for our scheme?" he asked.

Our scheme? As I recall, I'd been the sole author of this particular plan. I may have developed, shall we say, an affection for French, but that didn't mean he was free to steal my thunder.

"Aye, I fink they did. They couldn't get out of 'ere fast enough," said Vincent.

French smote his forehead with his hand and swore softly. "I'm a bloody fool. I should have had Vincent stay on Harkov. He's bound to report back to Ivanov, and we might have been able to capture the villain."

"It couldn't be helped," I said. "We had to be sure that the group believed I had killed you and that they weren't suspicious enough to wait around here to see your body carried out the door."

"The others might have fallen for our ploy, but I think it unlikely that Ivanov will believe that you shot me, India."

"He probably won't believe it. But I've thought of a way around that problem."

"Oh?"

"It's quite simple, really. I shall send a private message to Ivanov informing him that I regret my previous work for the

British government, that I was shabbily treated during the whole affair over the War Department memo, and as a consequence I am committed to the anarchist cause and have pledged my undying allegiance to the Dark Legion. When you appeared at our meeting, I suspected immediately that you were working for Dizzy, and I planned to use you to plant disinformation with the government about the anarchists' plans. Before I could put this scheme into action, Harkov and Schmidt unmasked you. There was nothing to be done at that point but kill you. Which I have done. Thus, my anarchist credentials are impeccable, but his, meaning Ivanov's, are not. I suggest that he demonstrate his own fidelity to the enterprise by participating in Dizzy's kidnapping, or I shall be forced to denounce him to the others. That should draw him out."

French was brooding over the fire, eyebrows knitted in a frown. "Exactly how do you propose to find Ivanov to deliver your message?"

I confessed, with some irritation, that I had not given that aspect of the project much thought.

"Send it to 'Arkov. Tell 'im hit's for Ivanov's eyes only."

"That might work," said French. "Although Harkov might be angered at not being trusted with the message and suspect that you are positioning yourself to become the next leader of the Dark Legion."

The thought made me hoot with laughter.

"And even if you are successful in getting a note to Ivanov, do you think he'll fall for your story? Frankly, I'd find it hard to swallow. If you were disenchanted with the way you've been treated, I can see you marching into Dizzy's office and haranguing the poor man, but I can't envision you joining forces with a bunch of anarchists. Ivanov has met you; he'll surely see through the pretense."

"For God's sake, French. We can't get wobbly at the knees just thinking of Ivanov. If you've got a better idea for getting that worm out of the woodwork, then by all means, let us hear it. Otherwise, let's quit flapping about like frightened geese and figure out how we're going to wind up this assignment. I'm tired of worrying about what Ivanov is thinking or doing or planning. To hell with Ivanov."

French glared at me. "What if he decides the best thing to do with you is to put a bullet in you. Your note might result in him appearing on your doorstep with a revolver in his pocket."

"Even better. We shoot the Slav bastard and round up our anarchist friends. I'd be jolly pleased if Ivanov tried to kill me."

"You're proposing yourself as bait," French sputtered. "You can't do that. I won't stand for it."

"You won't stand for it? Who appointed you as my guardian? I'm perfectly capable of taking care of myself. I have managed to toddle along without you for twenty-seven years, and I venture to say I can make the next several decades without a nursemaid."

"I am not implying that you need a nursemaid. God knows you're tough enough to take down Ivanov without my help. If he'd seen the look in your eye when you shot me, he'd head for Moscow tonight."

"You're lucky I didn't pull out my Bulldog and do the job properly. You deserve a bullet in the heart for withholding information from me. Harkov knows more about you than I do. What kind of moniker is Lachlan Nebuchadnezzar whatever? And you're engaged?"

French reached for my hand, which made his coat fall off his shoulder and exposed one side of that handsome torso. *Quite* a virile body. Just the right amount of dark, curling hair on his chest, contrasting nicely with the olive skin. I forced myself to look away. I don't mind saying that it was jolly difficult to do so.

"Clothe yourself, French. It's deuced hard to concentrate when you're strutting around half-naked."

He thrust his arms through the sleeves of the coat. "I am not half-naked."

"You were."

"Well, now I am dressed. You were spouting a load of drivel. Please continue."

I had forgotten that Vincent was present.

"Oi, can you two stop flirtin' wif each uvver until we get our claws on Ivanov?"

French and I rounded on Vincent. "We're not flirting," we said simultaneously.

Vincent shrugged. "Well, I don't mind wot you call it, s'long as we grab Ivanov and put the rest of them blokes in gaol. And listen, you two don't need to put on that act for me. You've been makin' calf eyes at each uvver since you met."

"I have never made *calf eyes* at anyone," I said coldly. "Especially not at French."

"Neither have I." French stood with his arms crossed.

"You could bof do worse," Vincent announced. "Listen, guv, no duke's daughter can stand the strain of bein' married to a secret agent. And India ain't 'ad no luck wif men, unless you count that gentleman thief. 'E was the best of the bunch, which ain't sayin' much. What was 'is name, India?"

The Turkey rug was already soaked with blood, so I didn't think Vincent's would be all that noticeable. If I'd had my rapier handy, I'd have run it right through the cheeky little sod. I was sure French shared my views, but when I snuck a glance at him, I noticed a grin hovering on his lips.

"A gentleman thief, eh? Sounds interesting, Vincent. When this is over, we'll repair to the nearest pub and you can tell me all about the man."

That didn't worry me any. Vincent can always be bought. The thought of how much that might cost in this instance, however, did arouse some anxiety.

French and Vincent were grinning like ventriloquists' dummies. Men are so infantile.

"We'll discuss this later," I said, tight-lipped. "Right now we've got a Russian agent to snare."

At the mention of Ivanov French's smirk disappeared, to be replaced by a scowl. "I know you don't care to hear this, India, but I disapprove of you trying to lure Ivanov out into the open. It's bloody dangerous, and I'd hate to think of anything happening to you."

"How very sweet of you, but I've got my Bulldog and you can't hang around Lotus House. You'll have to lie low. You can't be seen gadding about London when you're supposed to be at the bottom of the Thames. Between the three of us, we should be able to trap that Russian wolf. And this time, please refrain from exhibiting any honorable behavior. If we can't take him alive, just shoot the fellow."

That afternoon I retired to my room for a nap. I was just dozing off when someone knocked softly at the door. I was fully awake in an instant, searching under the pillow for my Bulldog. I found the revolver and tucked it under the bedclothes and then bade my caller enter.

Martine put her head round the door. "I'm sorry to disturb you, mademoiselle. May I come in?"

I usually don't allow the bints in my bedroom. It's the only room in the house that's off-limits and where I can enjoy some well-deserved privacy. I wasn't best pleased to see Martine, but I needed to keep her sweet until I'd rounded up Ivanov and the others.

"Yes, of course. Is something the matter?"

Martine looked haggard. Her olive complexion was muddy and her eyes dull. She must be ill. I'd have to summon the doctor immediately and send the girl to her room. I just hoped she hadn't infected any of the other trollops. I had my hands full, and caring for a brothel of sick whores would strain even my capacity for juggling multiple tasks.

Martine came in hesitantly, dragging the door shut behind her. "What is it, Martine?"

"I have not heard from Julian in several days. I am worried."

So that was it. The girl wasn't truly sick, only lovesick.

"You needn't worry. I saw him just last night, and he is fine. We're very busy right now, and I expect he just hasn't had time to be in touch."

"You saw him last night?"

I do dislike repeating myself. "Yes," I said curtly. Any sympathy I'd had for the girl had evaporated. I'll go to great lengths to keep my fillies in racing form, but when a girl lets herself go because she's fallen for a bloke, my patience (never very pronounced) disappears altogether.

"You see more of Julian than I do. Much more." Martine took a few paces toward the bed. "I begin to suspect that your interest in him is personal rather than political."

"Don't be ridiculous." I flung back the covers and swung out of bed. No employee of mine was going to stand over me and accuse me of pinching her boyfriend. It was time to assert my authority, though the diaphanous nightgown I was wearing and my bare feet did not exactly scream "power."

I was still rising to my feet when Martine slapped me.

"Julian is mine," she hissed.

"You should inform him of that fact. I don't believe he's aware of your ownership."

Perhaps it would have been wiser not to have provoked Martine, but I will not tolerate being slapped by a woman, especially when that woman works for me. The apathetic creature who had walked through my door minutes ago was gone, replaced by a savage. Martine vibrated with energy. Her eyes were no longer dull but blazed with a manic fury, and the veins in her neck stood out in sharp relief. Bloody hell. I faced a berserker. All that was lacking was a wolf's pelt slung over her shoulders and a sharp spear.

"Julian loves me," she spat. "He does not care for you. But you refuse to see that. You must be taught a lesson. Every man I have hired to kill you has failed me. Now I will kill you myself."

She swung a fist at my face, and I ducked instinctively under her arms, enveloping her in a bear hug. I'd meant to drive her back and force her off her feet, but when I'd dodged her blow, I had lost my momentum. We stood upright and wrestled, panting breathlessly, each of us trying to gain the advantage. I felt her hand twist in my hair and then a searing pain as she yanked my tresses. I shoved my foot between her legs and tried to hook an ankle, but she danced away from my maneuver with my hair still grasped in her hand. That was a mistake on her part, as the separation allowed me to take two steps and shove hard against her. We toppled over, Martine grunting loudly as my weight drove the air from her lungs. Her fingers clawed at my eyes. I got a forearm under her chin and shoved, and her hands moved to dislodge my grip. She pushed away my arm and brought her head up sharply, catching me on the bridge of the nose. Lights flared at the center of my vision and tears sprang to my eyes. We thrashed about like two cod in a basket for what seemed hours, both seeking the advantage and neither of us finding it.

I was wondering how much longer I could parry Martine's probing fingers and swinging uppercuts when the cavalry arrived. I was yanked upward at astonishing speed, and Martine came with me, still grasping me with deadly intent. My rescuer was French. I am sure he saw the look of astonishment on my face as he thrust an arm between Martine and me. He put a hand in Martine's face and pushed. He swore as her teeth clamped down on his palm. He cuffed her hard with his other hand, delivering a stiff blow to her temple that sent the girl staggering.

"Are you hurt?" French asked. Martine wobbled into his line of vision, and he gave her a shove that sent her to the floor. She collapsed in a heap, breathing shallowly. At last the bloody girl was down for the count.

"No major wounds, except to my pride. I knew Martine fancied Bonnaire, but I never suspected she was so jealous that she was mentally unstable. She always seemed so... so... bland."

"Appearances can be deceiving," French intoned.

"Yes, they can. For example, I wouldn't have taken you for a gent who uses clichés. Or, if you do, I'd expect you to spout them in Latin. By the way, French, what the devil are you doing here?"

"Keeping an eye on you, of course. Vincent and I have been camped out in the vicinity in case Ivanov has you in his sights. I just happened to be in the kitchen when I heard the commotion up here."

"In the kitchen?"

"Drinking tea with Mrs. Drinkwater. And attempting to eat a fairy cake. Hard going, that. I'm thinking of putting in for hazard pay."

"I thought I made it clear to you and Vincent that I could look after myself."

"You did. We chose to ignore your statements of independence."

I glanced at Martine, who was snoring gently. "I suppose I'll have to forgive you, just this once. But don't make a habit of ignoring me in the future."

"I wouldn't dream of it." French nudged Martine with the toe of his boot. "What shall we do with her?"

"I can hardly keep her locked up in the attic. Even Mrs. Drinkwater might become suspicious. Let's hand her over to Superintendent Stoke. He can keep her under wraps until we've corralled the anarchists."

I was becoming quite adept at removing bodies from Lotus House. French bound and gagged the dangerous minx while I sent a message to the superintendent informing him of the situation and requesting his assistance.

The whores flocked to the door at the sound of an ambulance drawing up before Lotus House. Two stocky attendants in the uniform of the Royal Free Hospital clattered up the stairs bearing a stretcher and returned in a few moments with a swaddled figure strapped to the litter. They loaded their burden into the ambulance and drove away. I informed the girls that Martine had become deathly ill and I had sent her to the hospital. There was the usual panic (really, it can't be avoided when working with whores; they're always finding some pretext for hysteria), and I wasted a good deal of time soothing the girls and assuring them that Martine did not have the plague or typhus or any other contagious diseases. I summoned Mrs. Drinkwater and requested tea, and after endless cups of that vile brew, the chatter finally subsided, the whores' fear abated, and I returned to my bed. I needed my rest, after all, for tonight I would be kidnapping Great Britain's prime minister.

21

The anarchists, still shaken by French's death, had developed a new level of respect for me. At our next meeting Harkov was positively deferential, and the others, save for Flerko, treated me with a wary esteem. Flerko had decided that I was a bloody enthusiast, just like him, and greeted me as though we'd served in the wars together. I assured my confederates that French's body was even now floating in the Thames and that I had not received a visit from the local constable, enquiring about gunshots and such. The anarchists were relieved at the news, and we settled down to sketching in the last details of our plot to kidnap Dizzy.

As usual, I was the tethered goat. Thick Ed had recounted my triumph with Dawkins, the young engineer at the construction site for the memorial service, and the rest of the anarchists had been suitably impressed. Men being the unimaginative creatures that they are, it was immediately proposed and seconded that the only proper job for me during the abduction would be to sashay past the guards and dazzle them with my undeniable attractions. Under other circumstances, I would have been reluctant to attempt to work my magic on Dizzy's guards. I'd seen them many times, and they were just the sort of chaps you'd expect to be protecting the head of state of the greatest nation in the world: lean, hard and flinty-eyed. They weren't barrack room soldiers. They were professionals. If a half-naked nautch girl had glided up to them and proposed a rendezvous in the alley, they'd have dropped her with a single shot to the head.

I'd have been up against it, except that the men on duty tonight had been specially selected by French and instructed not to open fire when I came slinking up to them. Still, I was nervous as Thick Ed, Flerko and I made our way to the Langham. The three of us had been deputed to seize Dizzy, while Schmidt waited in a carriage down the street. I had been rather surprised to see Schmidt on the box handling the horses. He seemed too much the intellectual to have any practical skills, and he guided the nags with a deft hand. I'd have preferred that job, as waltzing into the prime minister's hotel with Thick Ed and Flerko seemed fraught with all sorts of danger, especially with Flerko's propensity for over-enthusiasm.

A block from the hotel we slipped down a street and into an alley, approaching the building from the rear. With a bit of luck, I might have been able to wheedle my way past the desk clerk, but Thick Ed and Flerko would never have passed muster in the Langham's lobby, not with Thick Ed being a lumbering brute who might have been there to clear the drains, and Flerko smelling faintly of herrings. The odor had provided the cover for Flerko, as he'd visited the Langham on numerous occasions, trying to flog his wares and managing to penetrate the upper corridor where Dizzy's room was located. He'd been tossed out on his ear each time and warned never to come back, but the little fellow had wormed his way past the watchful eye of the employees in several instances. When Flerko wants to murder someone, he lets nothing stand in his way.

Soundlessly, we picked our way through the detritus in the alley. Flerko stumbled over a cat and an anguished yowl echoed off brick walls. Despite being in one of the better sections of London, the alley reeked of rancid fruit and stale water. A central gutter was filled with viscous black liquid. I plucked up my skirts and winced as I splashed through the puddles.

We reached the Langham and stood in the shadows watching. We'd chosen an hour when almost everyone inside the hotel would be snoring in their beds, bar a bleary-eyed doorman at the front entrance and an equally sleepy-eyed clerk who would be dozing at the desk. But we waited a good few minutes anyway, just to be sure that no one was moving about the service entrance. It had begun to rain lightly, an icy mizzle that reduced visibility and seeped slowly through my cloak. I studied the alley intently, as I knew Superintendent Stoke had stationed men there, but I saw no signs of the watchers. We might as well have been alone in that dreary place.

Then Thick Ed put his lips to my ear. "We go now." His hobnailed boots grated against the cobblestones as he crept away. I touched Flerko's sleeve and we followed, gliding swiftly through the darkness to a thick wooden door. But Flerko's prior visits had already informed us that this entrance was locked and barred from the inside, and so we bypassed it to stop at a low frame window just beyond. I heard the snick of a blade as Thick Ed opened his pocketknife and set to work on the latch. Moments later metal creaked and the bomb maker grunted in satisfaction. He prized open the window slowly, but the Langham's owners did not neglect any details of housekeeping and the window slid smoothly upward in the oiled frame without a sound.

Flerko scuttled through the opening first while Thick Ed and I cooled our heels outside. The little Russian was gone for a few minutes, then thrust his head out the window and whispered, "The hall to the stairs is clear." I accepted his hand and clambered over the sash and into a darkness more profound than that of the alley. I stepped to one side as Thick Ed heaved himself through the window. We were in a storeroom, where the excess luggage and trunks of the hotel guests were kept.

"Take my arm," Flerko murmured, and I clutched the sleeve of his coat. Thick Ed grasped a handful of my cloak, and we inched forward. My eyes had adjusted to the gloom by then, and I discerned a faint line of light along the floor, indicating the existence of a door and a lamp beyond it.

"When we reach the hall, we turn right," Flerko whispered. "We walk ten paces, and then we reach a second turn to the right. Just as you turn the corner, you will be at the stairs. The guard is sitting in a chair at the foot of the stairs. He will see you immediately when you come around the second corner."

"We've gone over this before, Flerko." Anxiety made me curt.

"Don't hurt to go over it again," Thick Ed said.

"If you two keep gassing, the guard is going to hear us. I'm going now. Try to be quiet when you follow me."

I marched away with confidence, opening the door of the storeroom to find myself in a long hallway whose gloom was only partially dispelled by a few gas lamps, burning feebly. With all the guests in bed the lamps had been turned down low, but there was enough light to see the shadowed aperture that marked the next turning. I strode along, not bothering to muffle my footsteps. Thick Ed and Flerko crept along behind me as silently as mice. One step away from the corner, I drew a deep breath, hesitated momentarily, then plunged on. There was no going back now.

"Oh!" I drew up sharply, with a hand at my mouth. "You frightened me."

Dizzy's first guard had been sprawling at ease in a straight-backed chair he had tipped up against the wall. He was a good-looking fellow, with a square jaw, the thick neck of a circus strongman and eyes that sparked with intelligence. He was on his feet in an instant, doffing his hat, challenging me with a look that was both shrewd and appreciative.

"Good evening, ma'am. You're out late tonight." A lady would have bridled at such a bald statement, but as I am no lady, I did not.

I unleashed a coquettish smile in his direction. "Indeed I am. As are you. But I believe my time shall be more gainfully employed than yours."

He returned my smile with interest and shrugged. "I wouldn't doubt it."

I placed a foot on the first riser, and the fellow half-turned to watch me walk up the stairs. I rested a hand on the banister. "What time do you get off duty?"

Thick Ed burst around the corner. My interlocutor caught the movement from the corner of his eye, and he flung his coat open with one hand, reaching for a revolver tucked in a holster at his waist. The man's mouth opened to raise the alarm, and Thick Ed smashed a fist into it. Blood spurted in a wild arc, spattering the anarchist's face. The guard staggered back, swiping at the fountain of red spurting from his nose and lips and looking dazed. Thick Ed cocked a fist and swung again, catching the guard squarely on the chin. The poor fellow's head jerked backward, and Thick Ed caught him as he was falling to the floor.

"Hsst!" Thick Ed summoned Flerko, who darted around the corner and seized the guard's ankles. Thick Ed stuck his hands under the man's armpits and lifted his shoulders. The guard's head lolled limply. The two radicals shuffled hurriedly down the hall to the storeroom with their burden. Once there, they were to gag and bind the man, removing any weapons they found and return to me to remove the second guard, who waited outside Dizzy's room. I had a few moments to reflect, which is not conducive to one's confidence when one is in the midst of knocking out chaps and nicking the prime minister. You start to doubt the wisdom of your plan (dicey, at best) and whether you're placing the most important man in Europe, if not the world, in danger (you are) and if you'll be able to protect him from that danger (God, I hope so, as I'm very fond of Dizzy, and while his views on the franchise are questionable and he writes dreadful novels, I'd hate to see the old boy with an axe buried in his neck). You also have time to mull over the fact that the anarchist chappies have one plan and you (and French) have another and while the two plans are meant to coincide for the moment, very soon they'll diverge sharply and it will be up to yours truly to see that that happens without the radicals sussing out the trap you've laid for them. A lesser woman might quail at the prospect of such responsibility, but I merely girded my proverbial loins and waited for the return of my co-conspirators, who were taking a deuced long time to wrap a rope around a bloke's hands and feet.

Finally they appeared. Flerko was bubbling with excitement, but Thick Ed was grimly professional. "He'll sleep a good long while," he whispered, referring to the guard. "Let's collect his friend."

The second guard sat outside the door to Dizzy's room, which was a few steps down the hall and to the left of the staircase. I sauntered up the steps and into the corridor. The guard's head swiveled in my direction. He was a twin of the fellow we'd dispatched below, only his jaw was more pronounced and his expression craftier. As instructed, he hadn't heard a sound when we'd attacked his compatriot at the bottom of the stairs.

"Oh, I say. I wonder if I have the correct floor," I stammered. "I'm looking for room number twelve."

"Bit late for room service, isn't it?"

I edged past him, craning my neck at the numbered plates attached to the door frames.

"Hold on, miss. Where do you think you're going?" He'd taken three steps to catch up with me, and now his fingers twitched on my sleeve. "You shouldn't be up here."

All his attention was focused on me, and Thick Ed chose that moment to strike. He bounded up the stairs and charged down the hall, running on the balls of his feet. The second guard whipped round and shoved me into the wall just as Thick Ed delivered a haymaker to the bloke's cheek. The man's knees buckled. He was out before his head bounced off the floorboards.

Thick Ed was already at work with a picklock, twisting a thin metal blade in the lock of Dizzy's room with an air of purposeful concentration. Flerko stood next to him, whispering unnecessary instructions.

"Watch the stairs," I told him, and the little Russian scuttled off. It was all for show, of course, but I had to maintain the illusion that we could be caught at any moment. Then the lock rattled and Thick Ed muttered. He turned the doorknob, and the two of us peered into the room.

Dizzy lay on the sofa before the fire, feigning sleep. A sheaf of papers was scattered over his stomach, as though he'd been reading state papers and dozed off. French and I had wanted the prime minister to be sawing wood in his bed, but Dizzy had refused to be kidnapped in his nightshirt and without his boots. I can't say that I blame him. The wind up a nightshirt was bound to be chilly, and Dizzy was prone to chest complaints. At least he was snoring, though rather unconvincingly, inhaling vigorously through his nose (and you'd have thought that a prime instrument for such use) and blowing out air like a whale breaching the surface of the ocean. We'd have to roust him soon, before the old dear opened one eye to see if his act was going over with the crowd. I pulled out my Bulldog.

Thick Ed strode to the sofa, grasped Dizzy's shoulder and simultaneously put a thick hand over the prime minister's mouth. Dizzy's eyes flew open and flooded with alarm at the sight of the burly chap towering over him. Dizzy wasn't shamming now; there was real worry on his face. I hoped this affair wouldn't prove too much for the old boy.

Thick Ed gave him a friendly grin. "Now then, squire. You just keep quiet and everything will be right as rain. And don't think about calling your guards. We've taken care of them. You see that lady over there?" He indicated me with a jerk of his head. "She's a wizard with that revolver of hers. You open your mouth just a crack and you'll be joining the big parliament in the sky. Is that clear?" It was the longest speech I'd ever heard from Thick Ed and it was deuced effective.

Dizzy nodded, and Thick Ed removed his hand. Dizzy cleared his throat, but somehow found the strength to remain silent, which for him was quite an accomplishment. All politicians love the sound of their own voices, but Dizzy positively worshiped his. Thick Ed yanked a rag from his pocket and thrust it between the prime minister's lips. Then he extracted a cord from the same pocket and, stepping round Dizzy, tied his hands.

Thick Ed returned briefly to the second guard and trussed him tightly, pushing a square of cloth into his mouth and wrapping a second length of cloth around his head to hold in the gag. By now Flerko had joined us and was staring at Dizzy with an expression of utter revulsion. I doubt Dizzy had seen such a look of repugnance since he'd last encountered his old enemy Gladstone in the halls of Westminster.

"You are vermin," Flerko informed Dizzy. "I spit on you." He pursed his lips to make good on this statement.

"Don't taunt the prisoner," I said. "You'll have plenty of time to sneer at him later."

A blade appeared in Flerko's hand. Dizzy cast a frantic look at me. Confound it, this wasn't in the script.

"Save that for the guards," I said crisply. "Iv—, I mean, Grigori will be furious if you stab the prime minister before we get a chance to try him for his crimes."

The mention of Grigori did the trick. Flerko ran a thumb along the knife's edge while he mumbled a few threats at Dizzy, and then reluctantly sheathed the weapon. The prime minister's face was as pale as a tallow candle, and a bead of sweat trembled on his upper lip. I tipped him a quick wink as Flerko retreated to join Thick Ed.

I believe I mentioned previously that the time was approaching when our scheme would have to trump that of the anarchists. Our radical friends, being the bloodthirsty buggers that they were, had intended to knife the guards and leave behind their dead bodies. Well, it wouldn't do to let them live, as they could easily identify Flerko, Thick Ed and me. Naturally, Dizzy had baulked at this aspect of the plot, and it had been left to French and me to devise a way to circumvent this heartless deed without alerting the members of the cell. I was to judge the proper moment when we must intervene to stop the guards' death, and then things must go as clockwork if we were not to wind up with two dead blokes on our hands. Judging by the look of killing rage on Flerko's face as he bent over the second guard, the time had come.

I stepped to the window and pushed aside the curtain. "I see someone in the alley, Thick Ed."

Thick Ed had been arranging the guard's body to permit more expeditious throat slitting. He sprang up and joined me at the window.

"Where?"

But there was no need to point out the nonexistent interloper. On the floor below us, a ruckus had erupted. Several men were shouting unintelligibly, and the stamp of feet could be heard on the marble floor of the lobby.

"Flerko! Quick! Run down and see what's happening." Thick Ed yanked Dizzy to his feet, and Flerko hared away to return in a few minutes, blowing hard and with his hair standing on end.

"There are men in the lobby," he huffed, "and they're shouting at the desk clerk."

"Police?" I asked.

Flerko shook his head. "I didn't see any uniforms."

"Can we reach the storeroom?" Thick Ed asked.

"If we hurry."

Thick Ed pushed Dizzy toward the door. "Not a sound, remember? If you make a noise, we'll kill you."

Flerko led the way, sprinting down the corridor to the stairs and darting down them to ascertain the lay of the land. He motioned to us from the first landing, and we careered after him with Thick Ed dragging Dizzy and me bringing up the rear. We gained the ground floor and peered cautiously down the hall toward the lobby. We saw nothing, but heard voices barking questions, followed by the drowsy reply of the night clerk.

"If anyone tries to stop us, keep going," said Thick Ed. "All we have to do is get to the storeroom and lock the door behind us. Move now."

We moved. Thick Ed hustled Dizzy along with me at his heels and Flerko dogging my footsteps. We reached the storeroom and bolted inside. Flerko eased the door closed and turned the lock.

"Out the window," ordered Thick Ed, which turned out to be confoundedly difficult for Dizzy as he's about as spry as an iron post. But we managed somehow, lifting the prime minister bodily through the opening and hurling ourselves into the alley. We jogged along at a rapid clip, or attempted to, for Dizzy, besides being an inflexible old coot, was also slow. Thick Ed kept dragging the prime minister and swearing under his breath, while Dizzy staggered and bumbled about making an enormous racket as he tripped over boxes and collided with empty barrels. At this rate half of London would hear us and come to investigate. Thick Ed realized the same thing at the same instant, and letting out an exasperated curse, he swept up Dizzy in his arms and flung him over his shoulder. Dizzy issued a stifled grunt, and I stifled a smile. I reckon I'm the only whore in history who's ever seen the British prime minister carried about London like a side of beef.

We made good time after Thick Ed hoisted Dizzy to his shoulder. The prime minister constituted a light burden, and Thick Ed carried him as easily as he would a child. He even had breath to speak.

"Where's that bloke you saw?" he asked.

"What bloke?"

"You said you saw a man in the alley. Why haven't we run into him?"

"It must have been a vagrant, looking for a place to doss

down. Perhaps the noise frightened him away. Do you see anyone, Flerko?"

"Not a soul."

We reached the street where Schmidt waited with the carriage, and Thick Ed whistled softly. Schmidt had been enjoying a pipe. He knocked out the ashes on his boot and stowed the pipe in his pocket. He wrenched open the door of the carriage.

Thick Ed tipped Dizzy onto the seat, which elicited a groan from our aging statesman. Poor fellow. He was as game as they come, but this escapade was proving a bit much.

"Were there difficulties? Did anyone see you?" asked Schmidt.

"There was a flap in the lobby as we were leaving." Thick Ed shoved Dizzy's legs inside and offered me his hand.

Schmidt made a noise in his throat. "The police?"

"We didn't stay to find out. And I'd bloody well suggest we do the same thing now."

I pulled Dizzy upright and straightened his legs for him, which earned me a grateful look. I hoped no one else had noticed. Flerko sprang up on the box with Schmidt to keep watch, and Thick Ed tumbled into the carriage as Schmidt whipped the horses and the carriage shot away from the curb.

Our destination was an abandoned warehouse on the river, selected by Flerko and approved by Harkov and Schmidt as the perfect place to hold a mock trial and an actual execution. Our journey there was made in silence, but for the creaking and rumble of the wheels and the clatter of hooves on brick and stone. Dizzy and I occupied one seat, and Thick Ed sat across from us, staring impassively out the window, though there was nothing to see, and occasionally stealing a glance at the prime minister. I kept my eyes on the floor. I daren't look at Dizzy for fear that our acquaintance might reveal itself by some gesture or gaze. That left me with nothing to do but think about what was to come, and hope that by dawn my anarchist comrades would be spooning up gruel at Scotland Yard and Ivanov would be contemplating the irony of life as a British prisoner. It was a jolly long carriage ride and one I wouldn't care to repeat.

Our progress slowed as we neared the water. Dank walls closed in around us, and the only sounds were the rush of water down the streets and the constant patter of rainfall on the cobbles. The air was rank with the smell of human waste and the bitter smoke of thousands of coal fires. I pushed aside the curtain and rubbed a circle in the clouded window glass. Decrepit buildings towered overhead, their windows shattered or boarded shut and the lintels sagging with age. Their exteriors, whether brick or stone or wood, were fouled with soot. It was a fitting place to bring the anarchists' ill-starred plans to conclusion.

The carriage slowed and then rolled to a stop before our destination. Flerko tugged open the door and made a derisory bow toward Dizzy. "Welcome. Your destiny awaits you here."

If this portentous twaddle was an example of Flerko's epistolary style, it's a jolly good thing he gave up novel writing for anarchy.

Thick Ed helped Dizzy down from the carriage, and Schmidt drove the carriage down an alley and out of view. He returned shortly, bringing the key to the heavy padlock on the massive wooden door. We crowded inside, and Schmidt lit a candle for himself and one for me.

"Harkov, Bonnaire and Grigori are waiting for us upstairs, on the second floor."

My heart leapt at the news. Ivanov had snapped up the fly like a starving salmon. Of course I realized that Ivanov might have come only to silence me, but I felt a rush of exultation at how close we were to destroying the Dark Legion and capturing one of the tsar's most trusted agents.

We navigated through a series of chill and clammy rooms and up a warped staircase that groaned alarmingly under our feet until we reached a cavernous room, bare but for a few empty packing cases and tea chests, a few oil lamps and the dim figures of our fellow conspirators. Harkov had been pacing the room but swung to an eager stop as we entered. Ivanov had made himself comfortable on an empty crate and was enjoying a cigar. He did not rise at our entrance. A look of amusement crossed his face at the sight of Dizzy. I had to control the urge to draw my Bulldog and inform the Russian he'd be laughing out the other side of his face soon. It's all well and good for me to mock my leaders, but I draw the line at any damned display of Russian arrogance. My anger must have been palpable, as Ivanov's eyes slid in my direction and I saw a fleeting smile before he smoothed his face into impassivity.

Harkov advanced on us anxiously. "You are late."

"We're not late." Thick Ed sucked his battered knuckles.

"And all went according to plan?" Harkov asked.

"Not exactly," said Thick Ed. "We didn't have time to kill the guards. A bunch of blokes were shouting down in the lobby. We had to get out of there."

"The guards saw you?" Harkov's cheeks paled. "They'll recognize you. They've surely been found by now, and the authorities will be after you." Bloody observant of Harkov, if only he'd known it, except the police had arrived at the warehouse hours ago. He flitted to the window and prized open a shutter. "They might be out there at this minute, watching." He whirled round. "Perhaps we should abandon our objective and leave now. We can be on a mail boat this morning."

Flerko was pushing a great wooden box into the center of the room, panting loudly with the effort. "I shall not leave here until I have cut off the head of this louse and raised it high on London Bridge." He scurried into a dark corner of the room and emerged with an axe in his hand. Up to that minute, I'd always considered Flerko an emotional but not particularly dangerous chap. Seeing him there with that maul in his grip, the blade honed so that the edge gleamed dangerously in the candlelight, I revised my opinion.

"We were going to try him for his crimes," protested Harkov.

"There is no reason to do so. We all know he is guilty. And if the police are following us, then we must kill him now."

"You," he said to Dizzy, "kneel down and put your head on that crate." Dizzy cast a terrified glance in my direction. I expect Louis XVI had looked much the same on his way to the guillotine. The Bulldog was halfway out of its holster. Flerko's mouth was stretched in a rictus of hate, eyes gleaming maniacally. He looked round frantically as if daring anyone to interfere with his plan.

Someone did.

"I'm sorry, my friend. I can't let you do that." Bonnaire took a casual step forward. In his hand he held a Chamelot-Delvigne revolver, of the type issued to the French military and police. It was not what I would have chosen to carry, as the bullet lacked significant velocity, but for a small chap like Flerko at this range it should be just the ticket. The unexpected sight of his comrade aiming a revolver at him checked Flerko's movements.

"Bonnaire?" The little Russian's face was anguished. "What are you doing? We have waited for this moment for such a long time."

"Inspector Bonnaire," the Frenchman corrected him. "Of the Sûreté." His gaze swept the room. "All of you, move over by

Flerko. Lord Beaconsfield, come this way, please."

Poor Dizzy. I don't believe he'd ever been as flummoxed as he was now. I could see he was already calculating the odds that the story of his kidnapping by anarchists and rescue by an agent (and a *Frog* agent, no less) would make the morning papers. I felt rather perturbed myself. This was supposed to be a British operation. What the devil was Bonnaire doing interfering in our business? My temper was not improved by the realization that Bonnaire had successfully deceived me for an extended period of time. Me. India Black, who prides herself on seeing through men like so many gauze curtains.

"I was wondering how long you'd wait before you announced yourself," I said coolly. "I was afraid I'd have to step in before you had the chance to do so. That wouldn't have gone down well with your colleagues at the Sûreté, would it? By the way, I'm with the British government. If you'll remove the prime minister's gag, he'll confirm it." I hadn't produced the Bulldog yet, but my fingers were firmly gripped around the handle.

Dizzy nodded frantically.

Bonnaire grimaced. "Very well, Miss Black. You may remove the prime minister's gag and let him speak."

Schmidt lifted a hand apologetically. "Pardon me, Bonnaire, if that is indeed your name. I shall take it on faith that you are with the Sûreté, but I shall request that you grant me the same indulgence until we may compare documents. I am Gerhard Hoffman of the Berlin *Landespolizei*."

"No," screamed Flerko. "It can't be true."

I had removed Dizzy's gag and untied his hands. Being muzzled is unpleasant for anyone (and I speak from experience), but for a man of Dizzy's loquaciousness the last hour must have been sheer bloody torture.

He rubbed his mouth painfully and coughed. "Miss Black speaks the truth. She is employed by the British government." He cast a baleful eye at Bonnaire and Schmidt. "And I shall demand an explanation from your ambassadors as to your presence in England. As for you," he said, turning to Ivanov, "you shall accompany Miss Black and me to Scotland Yard, where we shall discuss your employment as an agent of the tsar."

Harkov clasped a hand to his chest. "Grigori! What does this mean? And you, Bonnaire, and you, Schmidt, you are all traitors? I cannot believe it." His knees sagged, and he sank slowly until he was sitting slumped on one of the packing cases.

"His name isn't Grigori. It's Ivanov, and when I last saw him, he was gathering intelligence for the Russian Army," I said.

"My allegiance is to the tsar." Ivanov glanced dismissively at Harkov. "Had these other fools not intervened, you and Flerko would be accompanying me to St. Petersburg. As it is, the two of you may wind up back in Russia anyway when Scotland Yard is finished with you."

"You certainly won't be escorting them." The Bulldog was in my hand now, covering Ivanov. "You'll be staying here. We have some unfinished business."

Ivanov laughed, a guttural bark that echoed around the room. "You're still angry about French, aren't you? I shall never forget the pleasure I derived from manipulating the two of you. And you call yourselves agents? I maneuvered you both like chess pieces. But, tell me, pray, where is Mr. French?"

"Why, he's dead, of course. Miss Black shot him," Harkov bleated.

"Of course she didn't kill him, you idiot. Those two performed an entire drama for you all, and you believed it was real. Miss Black would never harm French. She's in lo—"

"That's quite enough," I cut in. Dizzy's face was a study; he looked like a young vicar hearing confession for the first time.

"We'll have many interesting discussions, Major Ivanov." French strode into the room, trailed by Superintendent Stoke and four men with drawn revolvers and grim countenances. We made an interesting tableau, this group of various representatives of law and order in our respective countries squaring off like a group of boys in the schoolyard on the first day of term. Schmidt and Bonnaire looked uneasy, and I couldn't blame them. They'd clearly stumbled into something more than a den of anarchists. The tension between Ivanov, French and me was positively glutinous.

French waved his Boxer at Ivanov. "Were you planning to stand by while this idiot Flerko decapitated the British prime minister?"

"Of course not," Ivanov said scornfully. "I had intended to rescue the man, the rescue unfortunately being preceded by a gun battle in which everyone but the prime minister and I had been killed."

"So you were going to shoot me, you bastard." I cocked the hammer of my revolver.

Ivanov grinned wickedly. "Just imagine what the papers would say when it was revealed that an agent of the tsar had saved the life of Benjamin Disraeli. Heads would roll, would they not? Your intelligence services would be decimated, and your ministers would be occupied with domestic political issues, leaving Russia with a free hand in the Ottoman Empire."

Thick Ed shoved a thumb inside his vest and scratched vigorously. "It's all up, ain't it?" He was taking it like a philosopher. Harkov was a picture of despair, sitting with his head clasped in his hands.

When it comes time to write down "India Black's Rules for

Government Agents," I shall be sure to include the following: "Never forget about the lunatic with the axe." Flerko had been following the sequence of disclosures with horror. Now he flung back his head and an enraged howl filled the room. He swung the axe over his head and charged, not at Dizzy as I had feared, but at Ivanov.

Several guns, my own included, fired at once, unleashing a hail of bullets that struck Flerko and sent him spinning, arms flailing, until he collapsed to the floor. He jerked once, eyes wide and staring as he glimpsed Utopia. His outstretched hands closed into fists. He took a juddering breath, and it was finished.

The noise had been earsplitting. The silence that followed was even more deafening. Smoke eddied in drifts and billows toward the ceiling. We stared at the crumpled figure of the little Russian. I thought I caught the subtle hint of herring beneath the corrosive odor of gunpowder. I had hated to fire on the little fellow, but one could hardly stand by and watch as he chopped Ivanov into pieces, a decision I was sure I would regret.

Ivanov made his move then, while the rest of us were frozen into immobility. He turned his revolver on us and fired at point blank range. A bullet slapped into one of Stoke's men and he staggered, gripped his shoulder and collapsed to his knees.

I threw myself at Dizzy, who'd been staring open-mouthed at Ivanov. I caught the prime minister at the knees, and we tumbled to the floor. Chaos erupted. Bonnaire, French, Stoke and the Scotland Yard men scrambled for cover in the nearly bare room, emptying their guns as they dived behind empty crates.

Ivanov fired as he ran, but he was angling away from the door and toward the back wall of the warehouse, which overlooked the river. He crashed headlong through a window, shattering the few panes of glass that remained in the frame.

"Cease fire," shouted French as he clambered to his feet and rushed after the Russian. He dived gracefully through the window, like an acrobat in full flight, and the last I saw of him was the soles of his boots disappearing into a black void.

22

You'll be wondering what happened after Ivanov and French did swan dives out the window of that abandoned warehouse. Stoke's man had been potted in the shoulder and while the wound was painful, the fellow was in no immediate danger. Stoke and his men rocketed off to find a boat to scour the river for the Russian and our man. I helped Dizzy to his feet. He looked surprisingly fresh, and he bucked up awfully well after the uproar died down. I suppose if you've survived dozens of scurrilous political attacks and nasty comments about being a Jew, a gun battle is mild in comparison.

Bonnaire and Schmidt (or Hoffman, as he preferred, but I'll stay with Schmidt so as not to confuse things any further) introduced themselves more formally to each other, and Harkov began to cry. Though he looked the very archetype of a Slavic villain, I don't believe his heart was ever in this anarchy business. He's just the sort of bloke who likes to spout ideological nonsense without getting his hands dirty. Once he gets out of prison, he'll likely gravitate to a missionary society. Thick Ed went meekly. I don't think he was committed to assassinating politicos and such; I think he just liked to tinker with dynamite and blow up things. With his mechanical skills, I had no doubt he would be out of gaol before summer arrived.

I was about to load Dizzy into Schmidt's carriage and enlist the German policeman to drive us back to the Langham when we heard footsteps and shouts on the stairs, and French marched in with a hand on Ivanov's collar, Vincent trailing in his wake, while Stoke and his chaps brought up the rear with guns drawn. Ivanov, French and Vincent were soaked, their clothes dripping water. They smelled like the river mud at low tide.

French gave Ivanov a brisk shake. "We've got him this time, India."

Vincent's buttons were about to pop off his coat, his chest had swelled to such an extent. "French tole me this Russian devil might make for the river, and I was waitin' for 'im in a rowboat down there. When he popped 'is 'ead up out o' the water, I belted 'im 'ard. All French 'ad to do was grab 'im by the scruff of the neck."

"Quite true," said French, grinning with pride at the little sod.

"Why didn't you shoot him?" I asked. "It would have been much more convenient just to kill him and throw his body in the river."

Ivanov's eyes widened in mock surprise. "You shock me, India. Where is your compassion?"

"I believe I lost it at sea, on a trip I made once to Calais." It had been an involuntary journey, courtesy of Ivanov, and it had been a nightmare.

There wasn't much to say after that, and the superintendent and his lads ushered Ivanov away, along with Schmidt and Bonnaire, who agreed that it would be best if they cooperated with their British counterparts and pooled their knowledge about anarchist activities. French manned the driver's seat of Schmidt's carriage, and we ferried the injured policeman to the hospital and then repaired to Dizzy's room for a medicinal dose of spirits. Stoke meandered in a couple of hours later, and we rehashed the whole affair from beginning to end. He'd had a brief conversation with Schmidt and Bonnaire and had solved the mystery of the missing bomb.

"Schmidt, I mean Hoffman, confessed to taking the fifth bomb, not half an hour after Thick Ed planted the infernal device. He planned to disarm and remove the rest, but then he got nervous about thwarting the plan and decided not to risk it. He wanted Grigori, er, Ivanov, as much as we did, and was afraid to spook him. Bonnaire also chose to let the plan proceed so as to keep the group intact until *he* could lay hands on Grigori, er Ivanov. It's all rather confusing, and I've instructed those two that we don't take kindly to government agents from other countries operating here without our consent. They'll be out of England by the end of the week."

"And their desire to catch Grigori meant they were willing to stand by while I shot French?" I was beginning to loathe French and German agents as much as Russians.

French shrugged. "Obviously, they didn't want to reveal their identities as government agents. It's a wretched business, but things like that do happen. The Third Section has even been known to sacrifice one of its own informants in a cell to protect another."

"Extraordinary," Dizzy muttered, "that so many members of the group were government agents."

"Not uncommon these days." Superintendent Stoke sucked his moustache thoughtfully. "Almost as many men on government payrolls in Europe as there are anarchists."

Dizzy took a fortifying swallow of brandy. "Still, it is remarkable. Why, if I had read of this situation in a piece of fiction, I should have found it unconvincing. Even a novelist would have a difficult time conjuring up such a convoluted plot."

"Dashed odd," agreed the superintendent.

"Beggars belief," said Dizzy.

I remained silent, but I resolved then and there to commit the story to paper someday. I'd have to wait a bit, for the British public isn't quite ready to grapple with the nefarious doings of these combat cells and the machinations of the men who seek to stop them. They're a simple folk, the British, and don't take kindly to stories of double-crossing and treason, even if done in the name of all that's good and true in the world. They prefer their heroes and heroines to be virtuous types who confront evil directly, with a firm resolve and the cross of St. George under one arm. They're likely to sniff disapprovingly at brothel owners skulking about Seven Dials and playing blind man's bluff with a bunch of nasty foreigners. I'd record the affair in my notebooks and keep it hidden until the appropriate time came along.

Such was my intention. Then one day in 1908, when I was advanced in years and had enjoyed some success with earlier tales of my adventures, I was shocked to discover a book in my local bookseller's by a portly, wild-haired fellow with a moustache that would have done credit to a Corsican bandit. Chesterton was the chap's name. The title was clever: *The Man Who Was Thursday.* Intrigued, I picked it up and began to page through it, with growing outrage. The man had stolen my story! Only in his version, *everyone* in the anarchist cell was a government agent. That bloody Stoke must have spouted off the details about the Dark Legion, probably while he was in his cups at his club and reveling in past successes. The destruction of the anarchist cell had been kept from the newspapers at the time so as not to frighten the public, and because Dizzy (and who can blame him, really) didn't want anyone to know that he'd participated in his own kidnapping. Somehow this chap Chesterton had got hold of the story and thought it would make a dandy thriller. I bought the book and took it home, and I have to tell you, I thought it a second-rate effort and still do. But I digress.

It was dawn when the party broke up, but French and I were still too excited to sleep. We walked back to Lotus House and popped the cork from a bottle of champagne. French assumed his favorite position, sprawled in a chair with his boots propped on the fireplace fender. He leered at me over his glass.

"I don't think we've quite finished celebrating."

"Oh? What did you have in mind?" Was that a twinkle in the man's eye?

"We haven't had a bout in some time. Are you game?"

"Do you mean fencing, or are you speaking euphemistically?"

It *was* a twinkle in his eye. There might be hope for French after all.

Mrs. Drinkwater knocked on the door. "Ooh. Sorry, dears," she said, taking in the champagne bottle and French's flushed countenance. "Letter for you, miss."

The envelope was dusty with snuff.

Dear Miss Black,

If you want to know about your mother, ask French.

Sincerely yours,
Lady Margaret Aberkill
Dowager Marchioness of Tullibardine

Ask French? Oh, I certainly would.

"You wanted a bout?" I enquired coldly. "Let me get my rapier."

ABOUT THE AUTHOR

Carol K. Carr is the national bestselling author of the *India Black* series of mystery novels. A lawyer and corporate executive in a previous life, Carr now spends her time writing novels and indulging her interests in British Imperial history, Elgar, shooting handguns and watching rugby. She lives in the Missouri Ozarks with her husband.

INDIA BLACK
CAROL K. CARR

A new mystery series about a strong-willed Victorian madam, who becomes swept up in the world of British espionage after a civil servant dies in her establishment. Working with Agent French, an exasperating but handsome British spy, the beautiful India Black battles Russian agents, saves Queen Victoria, and prevents revolutions—while not busy keeping her girls in line.

India Black
India Black and the Widow of Windsor
India Black and the Rajah's Ruby (eNovella)
India Black and the Shadows of Anarchy
India Black in the City of Light (eNovella, July 2014)
India Black and the Gentleman Thief (August 2014)

PRAISE FOR THE INDIA BLACK NOVELS

[A] breezy, fast-paced debut."
Publishers Weekly

"Readers will enjoy this impressive debut novel, which
provides a colorful portrait of Victorian society as seen
through the eyes of a strong, intelligent woman."
Booklist

"This saucy debut is a satisfying amusement, with the
happy promise of more to come."
Kirkus Reviews

"Expect to stay up late reading this fascinating and at
times hilarious novel of espionage and intrigue; you won't
want to put it down."
RT Book Reviews

THE MORIARTY NOVELS
MICHAEL KURLAND

A sweeping and eloquent detective series featuring
Sherlock Holmes's nemesis, Professor James Moriarty.
Aided by an American journalist Benjamin Barnett,
and his infamous network of informers, criminals and
'specialists', Moriarty reveals himself to be far more than
just "The Napoleon of Crime", working for both sides of
the law, but always for his own ends.

The Infernal Device
Death By Gaslight
The Great Game
(July 2014)

The Empress of India
(September 2014)
Who Thinks Evil

"Michael Kurland has made Moriarty more interesting
than Doyle ever made Holmes."
Isaac Asimov

"As successful as its predecessors at bringing fin de siecle
Europe to brilliant life… the action veers and twists like
that in a contemporary spy thriller."
Booklist